MW00892682

CHRONICLES
OF THE
WEIGHT BREAKERS

A NOVEL

BY

T.T. MCGIL

CHRONICLES OF THE WEIGHT BREAKERS

Editor: Zane

Original Text Reviewer: James Derryl Hockett

Cover Creator: Justin Green

MEDICAL DISCLAIMER

PRAISE
FOR
CHRONICLES OF THE WEIGHT BREAKERS

"T.T. McGil's Chronicles of the Weight Breakers is a
must-read book for all women who want to reevaluate, reimagine,
and recharge their lives.
Through memorable characters, empowering and uplifting
nuggets of wisdom, and a creative imagination,
readers will be reluctant to put the book down until the final page."
--Zane, New York Times Best Seller

"T.T. McGil takes you everywhere, through a myriad of
characters and all their life's realities of situations.
How she breaks down familiarities and concludes solutions is
not only entertaining but inspiring. A glorious beautiful outlook on self-
care and self-love.
A must read!"
--Dianna Rochelle, Writer, Producer and Comedian

"Chronicles of The Weight Breakers is a study guide and book all in one!
I can relate to every character. Take notes, this book is relatable!"
--Tiesha Robinson, Motivational Influencer

Spin off of the Sparrow Mystery Suspense Thriller Series

T.T. McGil

CHRONICLES OF THE WEIGHT BREAKERS

A Novel

Also by T.T. McGil

Sparrow: The Water's Edge

Sparrow: The Night Ends

A MESSAGE FROM THE AUTHOR

Dear Weight Breaker—

Have you ever felt weighed down by life-wondering if there was a different way to approach it? Pondered how to handle the proverbial and physical weights of life, in a productive way to navigate your unique life's journey? Because we know that life is not, one size fits all—you have to have a plan to walk this thing out.

I've always been intrigued by individual's coping mechanisms of weight. In addition, how various people handle the proverbial and physical weights are embedded in this book, *Chronicles of The Weight Breakers.* This redundant question you will be asked is, can you think like a weight breaker, not like a weight taker? The premise is to disrupt the way weight taking enters our space. In addition, together we will walk through if there is a secret to being a Weight Breaker? Also, we will entertain from the perspective of looking at our life from the balcony—how God sees us. How does God see how we are handling weight from his perspective? That requires us to work on our vision, faith, along with our resilience intelligence.

I hope you enjoy your voyage through these pages, don't let the page count intimidate you. What should intimidate you more is the wiles, along with the cumbersome task of being a weight taker.

Moreover, my prayer is that you refuse to leave the book the same as when you opened the first page—implementing a new declaration over bulky destructive weights that attempt to easily beset you. You are a weight breaker! So be mindful of what you declare over your life, your declarations start with how you see yourself, followed by words that spill out of your mouth.

Most of all, I want you to be intrigued with *Weight-Breaker-ology?* The practice of walking this concept out as you are faced with weights. Your unique expedition has been filled with sacrifices; you've exuded heroism; furthermore you are filled with excellence. You are a reflection of God's masterpiece—you're a designer original! Consider that your sacrifices, heroism and excellence are tied together like knots on the rope of the thread of your life. Remember, sisterhood comes in many different ways—moreover you need sisters, not a project.

Say it out loud: I Can! I Matter! I Rock! And I Will! Let's go into your powerful new declarations over your life—we can all transform the positive impactful trajectory over our lives! Bring to mind, if nothing changes—nothing changes.

Your fellow Weight Breaker & *Your Author,* T.T. McGil

TO WEIGHT BREAKER_____ ,

WHY T.T. MCGIL'S LATEST BOOK, CHRONICLES OF THE WEIGHT BREAKERS, IS THE CHICK LIT BOOK YOU NEED TO READ!

Midwest-based author T.T. McGil tells us about her latest book – *Chronicles of The Weight Breakers*—which is a fascinating take on when smart women from different backgrounds world's go awry, until a chance encounter brings them together to facelift the weights of life! If you love chick lit woven throughout women's truth and beauty, you should check it out!

When you come across the term chick lit, one's mind tends to gravitate fun filled book full of shopping, spa days, with relationship trouble, however this book deviates from cheesy duplicative settings with fairytale endings, as the new age fire age of chick lit is here through the eyes of acclaimed author T.T. McGil, in *Chronicles of The Weight Breakers*.

Her goal is to craft tales that readers are eager to show up for, anticipating the next word, chapter, and book. Each of the themes of her novels raises the stakes of the characters, to resist their past failures, in hopes of defining a new future for themselves.

A new age type author, T.T. McGil has been penned with the highly sought-after mystery suspense thriller novels with the arrival of *Sparrow: The Water's Edge (2018)*; *Sparrow: The Night Ends (2020)*; now Chronicles of the Weight Breakers.

The Declare Chick Lit Genre is finally here to stay, thanks to new-age writers like **T.T. McGil.**

PROLOGUE

"GIRL, BREAK THAT WEIGHT. DON'T TAKE IT!"

[BEING A WEIGHT TAKER IS <u>SO</u> LAST SEASON...]

"Zachary, not tonight—back up off me. I have this brief to finish. I have so much that's weighing me down," she snapped, as she took a sip of wine, swallowing hard, biting her lip. Her fingers hammering her laptop nestled atop of her thighs. He rolled over, assuming his *natural position* of sleep.

"Get those spring rolls ready!"

"I'd like to spring roll your *fat donkey!*"

"What did you say?"

"Nothing!" she snickered, feeling the weights of her conflicted worlds—joy in life's journey versus legacy, bound from heritage.

"When I look into your eyes, I see forever."

That statement startled her as he did not fit into her world. However, nor did she.

"I know I can. I think I can. There must be a better way to live my life, than in *the shadows* of someone else—*right?*"

"My baby and I will be fine without that sorry shell of a man. I'm not going to cry. No, I'm not going to cry!"

"Hello, yes—I need your services to find out information regarding my husband. I will pay in cash only. Meet me at 75th & Ambassador…"

"Man, you are going to have to sit down for this news. I got you a contract for ten million dollars, with a signing bonus. Chiefs, here we come. I told you that I would hook you up."

"You did it, Sis. You're one of the *baddest* boss brokers in the male dominated sports/entertainment game. You're *rockin' on the cover* of *Forbes*—damn, girl, do your thing," she smiled, but her jubilee shortened as she received a text.

"Hey, thought you'd want to know—Luke has awakened. I know, I can hardly believe it, I'm still by his bedside, trying to put pieces of our fragile worlds together. Nonetheless, I am in hopes that Mack and I can survive this next phase of our lives—my husband is my start to finish. Please keep me in your prayers. Life has a tendency to keep weighing us down. Believe that!"

"I'm so sorry to inform you that your fibroids have returned with a vengeance. There is no way you will be able to carry a baby to term. We've done all we can, your next best management of your condition is a hysterectomy. Don't be sad, you can always adopt or utilize a surrogate…"

In various worlds, whimsical thoughts of weights of life swirled without hesitation.

Should I stay or go?

Should I follow my dreams, or halt?

Continuing down their current paths meant three things: to accept insurmountable weights of this world; succumb to unhappiness; moreover to live under the chronicles of weights…

Sunset skyline was embarking in the dark night mist. Whirlwinds of unbalanced souls felt like piranhas encroached upon them in their prospective bath tubs.

Ouch—that hurts!

Their weighted demeanor gave an aura of *don't mess with me resonating* through their pores.

Their quick-witted sharp tongues—*muscles of a woman's gotta do what a woman's got to do*—uncertainty is a grain of salt in their world. They embraced towards forgetting the hurts of their pasts. Forging onward with upward mobility, at the end of the rainbow, of obtaining a new *momentum* for their lives.

Wouldn't that be nice?

Each *momentum* had revenge fantasies of what could have been their weighted lives. Sincere in wanting some type of recognition of what they felt that life *owed them*; ultimately creating an abyss of distractions of truth.

Uncertainty lurked around every corner like a stalker, causing them to want to declare something new over their lives, but how?

Who the hell knows?

How do you break addiction to being overwhelmed, loneliness, self-doubt, as well as the need to fit in? When what seems to be your favorite hobby is to be a wallflower of the life that you wished you were bold enough to have...

Can you risk it all, to finally break weights?

Only you know answers to that perplexing question.

Is a weightless life a fantasy or a muse?

Is it possible to create a weight-free life, or is that a figment of our imagination?

Get a good education—we are programmed.

Get that money, girl—we are programmed.

Get that squad body—we are programmed.

Then, you will reach that pinnacle of success. Like Cinderella, you are whisked away, swept off of your feet, to live in a bliss full of *rainbows adorned with lucky charms*—we are programmed.

What if all of that glitz glamor has weights that we are thrust into like quicksand, not programmed to handle without proper tools?

What is a Weight Breaker?

Maybe it is a choice. Maybe it is a way for us to rise, choke holding every bit of self-doubt that inches its way into our souls, telling us that we are nothing more than weight takers.

Or is there a *Weight Taker Bus* that we have a free pass to get on—we choose to ride on to navigate our life?

You pray that you will make it through this thing called life. We all feel vulnerable, confused, desperate with uncertainty ringing through your cerebrum—all of this echoing into your core. Whether she admits it, every woman has *swum* through that season in her journey.

My matriarch, my grandmother—whose wisdom diffused from her pores, commonly proclaimed in a sweet southern drawl,

"Be kind to everyone. You never know what someone else is going through, so you better not be too *judgy* girl!"

I still hear echoes of her speaking those prolific words of wisdom in my mind. Yet, it's difficult not to judge since we are all human. If we are downright honest with ourselves, we are all a little *judgy* from time to time. Even more so as women, we can be so hard on each other. We often don't offer each other grace that we would a lonely ant walking towards its anthill on a sidewalk. We would generously *step over it*, with decency—that's what we should do as sisters. We must learn to offer one another some form of *grace*. We must stop attempting to trample out each other's vulnerability.

We grow from cute little girls in frilly dresses playing hopscotch on a chalky sidewalk, to executive boardrooms in our finely pressed suits, designer briefcases, stilettos *that hurt like hell*—perfectly glossed lips, *going gangster* to stake our claim. Furthermore, to this very day, the pressures that we place on ourselves weigh us down, depleting our souls:

Am I pretty enough?

Am I smart enough?

Do I deserve a seat at the table?

Did I ruffle feathers or rock the boat?

Did I let them see me sweat?

Suck it up!

Don't you dare cry—you'll look weak!

Clawing out from attics of our thoughts, all we want is to be bold, *bad-ass chicks* that are fulfilling our purpose, while burning midnight oil, kicking self-care all the way to the curb, adding arches in our back, stiffening our jawlines, while standing calm to secure our places in this world.

Immense pressure can weigh us down like cement bricks on our feet, all while *talking shop*, maintaining our femininity, attempting to remain true to who we are.

It's common knowledge that pressure creates diamonds. Consider those diamonds that are crushed to smithereens during this process, rendering invaluable dust. Although in a million little pieces, they are still fragmented pieces of a diamond; still valuable. Regardless of the fact that the nuances of our journeys can be tattered and torn, broken into a million little tiny pieces—we have that same value, as those diamond rhombus fragments.

Each of us has so many weights that we carry on our backs. Coming together to shed *the proverbial weights* along with *the physical weights* of life would create more love, sisterly kindness, changes in our vantage points, while yielding unity—resulting in a *Weight Breaker Sisterhood*. This kinship encourages us to cultivate accountability.

The Chronicles Of The Weight Breakers Podcast sparks a sisterhood that helps to banish negative connotations that we hold about ourselves, purge insecurities, self-doubts, and unnecessary comparisons. Many of us deal with unique situations along with similar circumstances throughout our journey's, compounded with various perspectives that we have based on our life experiences.

What generally makes us question ourselves about unique things that make us stand out, I generalize that as our momentum type. Simply put, momentum can be defined as speed or rhythm that you navigate through something. In a bigger scope, how one can move through life. A woman has her momentum to unleash her power when she declares her life's trajectory. SHE, through her sacrifices, heroism, and excellence will become a Weight Breaker, if only she declares.

This book is dedicated to you. You are destined to be a WEIGHT BREAKER, not a weight taker!

I proclaim bountiful blessings over each reader, their own personal chronicles that they're living towards while being Weight Breakers in their own lives.

When you realize who you are, *whose you are*—that you are one of God's gifts to the universe, you will fully understand deep down in your soul that:

You Can!

You Matter!

You Rock!

You Will!

You Got This—Let's Go!

So girl, Think Like A Weight Breaker. Not Like A Weight Taker!

Or better yet…

She Can!

She Matters!

She Rock's!

She Will!

She's Got This—she forges into life as a Weight Breaker!

6

Regardless of everything that she was going to accomplish, from this point forward, if she failed—she'd declare to cause herself to *fall forward* into being a weight breaker.

She fully acknowledges that weight taking stops when she declares it so.

So sisters, let's take a galactical approach to our new thought process. We all know there is: Pluto, Neptune, Uranus, Saturn, Jupiter, Mars, Earth, Venus, and Mercury. Henceforth, right next to the sun is the phenomenal—*The Weight Breaker Planet*. On *this planet* we will walk in our purpose, glean from good soil in which we were birthed out of, where our destinies exude from our pores. Moreover self-love, not a conceited love, however a pure love that God instills in us is radiated from our impressive sun. Once we declare it so, nothing is impossible in the galaxy of God.

Moreover, don't be surprised if you get crumbs before the cake. Buckle up, full speed ahead to break that weight!

"The heavens declare the glory of God; the skies proclaim the work of his hands. Day after day they pour forth speech; night after night they reveal knowledge."—Psalms 19:1-2

1

URGENT!

"WITH SYMPATHY!"

[CHRONICLES OF THE WEIGHT BREAKERS PODCAST]

Hi, Weight Breakers!

It's your girl, Dr. T.

To be completely transparent with you; my heart is very heavy today. I feel weighted to share some unfortunate news. Thank you in advance for bearing with me while I muster up enough courage to get through this podcast. Usually, this space is centered around empowering women. However, today is going to be different.

She couldn't believe that she had to let these next five words flow from her lips.

The Abigail Lancaster is dead.

Tears welled up into her eyes.

Most knew Abigail as a literary critic megastar, but she was one of my dearest friends. She was frequently a guest on this podcast, a *lit* panelist at THE CHRONICLES OF THE WEIGHT BREAKERS CONFERENCE—our followers are still raving about it.

Abigail made it an even more beautiful experience for all in attendance. Furthermore, she supported the launch of my new book: *Think Like a Weight Breaker. Not Like a Weight Taker.*

The pod-cast host took a deep breath to muster up enough courage to carry on, with the startling announcement.

What we learned at the conference can be summed up in six powerful words: I will be a Weight Breaker! Now come on ladies, continue walking into your truth—breaking out of that shell like Abigail Lancaster did. It took her some time, but I know that deep down she was a true weight breaker. We can all learn something from her death. Abigail was *The Vault.* You would never know if something was bothering her. Some people judged her on her hard exterior that was embellished with accolades; red carpets, private jets covered with a top-shelf lifestyle. As I got to know her, I called her Abby, not *"The Abigail Lancaster."* She went from *"The Vault"* to wide open—surrendered her life, goals, along with her mission. She exuded sacrifices, heroism, and excellence in everything she did.

A tear relished from her sorrowful eyes.

As tributes are pouring in for Abigail, I ask that you keep her children in your prayers. My Lord, just thinking of those poor kids losing their mother rips my heart to shreds. Please enjoy this presentation of our last interview with Abigail, along with *Wind Beneath My Wings*, the Bette Midler version. Nobody can sing this like Bette. Abby, this one's for you. You will be missed.

Love,

Dr. T.

As tears flowed, she played the song while empathetic sincere messages populated:

:I'm completely devastated. Abigail Lancaster is gone! I'm in tears, but I am also so grateful for her friendship. I recalled recently that we were at The Meadows Country Club where we spent precious time together. Furthermore, she arranged a book signing for me.—Dr. Sparrow Mack

:Abigail, rest in peace. We loved hanging out with you at THE CHRONICLES OF THE WEIGHT BREAKERS CONFERENCE. You stood by my family during the injustice—your support during that time was priceless. I cannot believe this, that you are not with us any longer. As a mom myself, this is heart wrenching. She loved her kids to the end of time. We will take care of your kids—as well as Gadsden. Love you, Abby—Judge Regi Hinson

:What are we going to do without her quick wit, snap-back wisdom? I'm so saddened by this. You're the glue to our crew.—Penelope K.

:My sister, you made me realize my true beauty.—Anjali N.

:Tell me this is not true! I refuse to believe this.—Chaka B.

:Not our sister. Words cannot express how much pain I'm feeling right now. She got me through some of my worst days. No, Abigail, no!—Fawn P.

:Prayers for your family. Abigail, you have always constantly told it like it was... —Dr. Sophia Clark

:I just saw this horrific news. This cannot be! Thank you for always brightening my day. Constantly saying things that most of us think, but don't have the *balls* to say. R.I.H. — A Loyal Fan

___ declares

"I can do all things through Christ who strengthens me."

Philippians 4:13

2

THE PODCAST

"IT ALL STARTS WITH YOUR MINDSET"

[ONE MONTH AGO, BEFORE DECLARE–]

Sparrow sat up in bed breathing heavily, another one of her night hauntings abound her R.E.M. sleep. Mack left for the day early, probably for his morning jog before taking little Weston to school.

PING!

:Sparrow you up?—Luke A.

:Barely. Luke, make sure the respiratory therapist changes your tracheostomy shield today, no time for any infection.—Sparrow M.

:I'm good. I have some business to take care of.—Luke A.

Sparrow wiped her eyes, perplexed and deeply overwhelmed.

Can I handle all of this—Luke's constant drama?

:Business? The only business you need to have right now is with your physical therapy. I will try to swing by later, after The Chronicles Of The Weight Breakers Podcast. Can Grandma Liz go by the grocery store for you?—Sparrow M.

:Yes, but she won't pick up my *Black & Milds*—she said I need to quit. Take care of your brother, hook me up!—Luke A.

:She's right! What the hell are you still smoking with a tracheostomy tube in your neck? Are you serious?—Sparrow M.

:Yep, I might blow up some shit in here with my shenanigans. Let me put this last KOOL I *coped* from the janitor. I had one of those damn nightmares again.—Luke A.

Sparrow's heart skipped a beat. *Oh shit, not him, too. Not again*, she thought while looking at the time, scurrying to the shower—as she got dressed in between texting with her literal *ride or die* best friend.

:Which night terror this time?—Sparrow M.

:Blood dripping down the wall. There was no "Jack" around here to help me deal, so I had to get a smoke.—Luke A.

:You will never know how much your friendship means to me. I'm sorry, I got you caught up in all that mess, however we got through it, right?—Sparrow M.

:Barely, if you call making it without having any *game* left in me to even get the attention of one of these *IG thots*.—Luke A.

:Boy, you are a mess. The only *thought* you need to be having is how to get stronger, so we can get you up out of there. I just pulled up at the studio. I'll hit you back when the interview is over. When you get done with rehabilitation in three months, I was thinking about booking us a flight back to the islands. Now that all of this drama has died down, it'd be nice to sit at The water's Edge like old times, right?—Sparrow M.

:Sounds good. If I haven't told you enough already, I don't know where I would be without y'all.—Luke A.

:All the way up shit's creek without a damn paddle. That's where you'd be for sure!—Sparrow M.

:You are cold-blooded, *Ro*. Much love. You're going to kill that interview.—Luke A.

Sparrow smiled after pressing the final SEND. She threw her phone in her purse, parked in the V.I.P. guest parking space.

She was greeted by Dr. T., the podcast host, holding the door open for her, "Girl, get on in here. Dr. Sparrow Mack, you are a breath of fresh air."

"It's always good to see you," Sparrow replied while she wrinkled her nose to take a whiff of the familiar aroma while leaning into a sisterly hug. "Chai tea? Come on, girl. You're always trying to butter me up—hook me up with a cup. How's your family?" Sparrow asked, wanting to get *the word in the streets* on everything surrounding a woman she admired.

It's so good when women can celebrate each other's successes, not see each other as competition, Dr. T. thought as she crafted her response; as she envisioned the highlights of all that was going on in the conundrum of Dr. T. 's world.

The ladies walked towards the sound booth, with their mason stoneware Pottery Barn mugs filled to the brim with smooth, rich cinnamon, clove, allspice, star anise, white pepper—cardamom goodness.

Sparrow took a sip from the billowing piping hot mug, " Sis, this is fire. A shot of *Jack*—we can get this party started."

"Hold on. Wait for *the big dog*..." Dr. T. summoned her assistant from the back. In walked her intern holding a tray of *ooey-gooey* goodness.

"Girl, you better stop—just looking at these pumpkin bars, I can feel fifteen pounds trickling down from the clouds wrapping around my cellulite, thick thighs while cradling my *pufa*. How did you know these were my favorite?"

Dr. T. smirked while carving the perfect square with the stainless-steel spatula, "*Voila!* Go ahead; lick your fingers. I know you want to. Besides, in your novel *Friction Ridges* you talk about these goodies at the Big Gulp. I did my best to make you feel at home, with some of the highlights of what they're known for."

"I really needed this, with all that's going on," Sparrow took a bite in pure out loud thought.

"You've been through a lot. Hell, you've been through some *Ozark*-type shit, Sis... living to tell the story," Dr. T. replied.

Sparrow chewed, then took another sip, "You damn skippy. We never thought *that night would end*. I don't know how we made it through."

The ladies looked at each other, their faith on the tips of their tongues.

"By the grace of God," they said in unison.

"How is Luke?" Dr. T. concerned knowing the history all too well of Sparrow and her best friend.

"Same old Luke, *running amuck* at the rehabilitation center. Putting a dent in my savings account. Girl, he's on the floor playing dice everyday taking everybody's money while smoking through his tracheostomy tube in his neck. Just a plain hot mess, however he is physically getting stronger every day—which is nothing but God's grace."

"Y'all have always been oil and water. Speaking of that, I hate to even ask, but how's your marriage going—you know since all that has happened?"

"Transparently it's been really rough, I think we are on the mend—only time will tell. We've been asked to help out with some type of *investigations;* like some *Hart to Hart*-type stuff. We're still pondering—we need to see if we're going to bypass divorce court first," Sparrow gingerly replied.

Dr. T. 's eyebrows raised, "Mack is your rock, you all will be fine. You've made it through so much. Plus, God's got you, your marriage—your family. Henceforth, don't give up. Black love is so beautiful. Come on now *Barak & Michelle,* hang in there."

"Roger that!"

"Sparrow you okay?" Dr. T. asked.

Sparrow saw her lips move with propelled back onto the trail of retribution the duo had embarked up many moons ago...

The lingering in my spirit of the trail that Luke and I'd forged down, damaged me to the core.

Concerned, Dr. T. inquired, "Sparrow, you need a minute, or are we good to get started?"

SNAP!

Sparrow came back to herself, from a journey like no other in her horrific attic.

"Girl, you had me concerned. Maybe you need to see someone. I have a sister friend-Dr. Sophia Clark, I'll give you her card when we finish today." She stated as she washed her hands from the sugary contradictory delights of what she preached on The CHRONICLES OF THE WEIGHT BREAKERS PODCAST.

She attempted to lift Sparrow's spirits, she knew all that she had be going through lately,

"From the depths of my soul, I pray that one day I will not have to ask, *God, are these ten pounds stored in the cloud?* The proverbial weights and the physical weights of life we deal with, so they don't constantly trickle down into our lives to damper our joy, steal our happiness—trampling out all that is awaiting us on the other side of the weight. When you're a willing participant to drive meaningful change by walking out the exercises that we talk about, you're exercising a new love language towards yourself, Sparrow."

"Dr. T. Weight Breaker my ass when you speak of the physical weight, you know I can walk by a bakery—feeling the pounds magnetically pounce onto my body. Besides, I'm going to put you on blast, trying to sabotage me. So yes, the pumpkin bar is gone, winding down on my tea, so I'm good. As you say *Mrs. Weight Breaker, WE CAN!*" Sparrow winked at Dr. T.

"You ready girl?" Dr. T. asked her podcast guest.

Sparrow nodded.

Dr. T. pressed the GO LIVE button...

CHRONICLES OF THE WEIGHT BREAKERS PODCAST

Hi Weight Breakers!

Welcome to The Chronicles Of The Weight Breakers Podcast, thank you for sharing a portion of your day with me! I'm Dr. T. your biggest ally, your girl, your podcast bestie. Along with this empowering podcast, I have a newly released book, *Think Like A Weight Breaker. Not Like A Weight Taker,* that gets into the attic of your brain to unleash the powerful woman that you are within. We have to start with our mindset, ladies. If anyone tells you differently, they're not really your friend. I developed this tool because of the conversations I've had with each of you, when you call into the radio station, during my book tours, and from the posts on social media. We can all agree that being a Weight Breaker starts with your mindset. My book gives you tactics to deal with your mindset. We are going to talk about those blossoming tactics that will cause your momentum to move. In the building today is a dynamic weight breaker in her own right, Dr. Sparrow Mack! She's a woman of God, a wife, mother, physician, motivational speaker, author—to top it all off the screenwriter of the box office hit, *Friction Ridges*. Show some love through your emojis for my guest this morning. We are going to talk about defining what a weight breaker is, creating your *weight breaker space,* establishing your tactic hit list—taking this journey together as weight breakers within the momentum types.

The ladies settled into their seats inside the radio booth in front of their respective microphones with warm cups of chai tea in hand.

"Dr. T., thank you for having me, I see all of the love The Chronicles Of The Weight Breakers Podcast is giving me. The preview copy of *Think Like A Weight Breaker. Not Like A Weight Taker;* is fire sis—filled to the brim with nuggets that I'm sure each listener and reader should resonate with. Let's dive in, talk about those tactics, I define tactics as a strategy. I'm looking it up on my phone. The thesaurus describes a tactic as an approach, course, ploy, policy or, to put it simply, a way of doing things. I love that by implementing some of these exercises in your book, I'm able to comprehend that I have been a weight taker—I did not even realize it."

Really—do tell what you've done about it?

Dr. T. prompted Dr. Mack, hoping the author would share more of her experience with the exercises in the book.

"Well, Dr. T., I'm making some changes by starting to do the work. As you know, I have been through so much, with the presumed death of my best friend Luke. Intertwined with all of the drama surrounding that, coupled with being a wife in a strained marriage, mother, demanding career, seemingly caregiver resource to all. I took your advice in the book—creating a space in my life so I can heal. I believe you call it *Weight Breakers Space,"* Sparrow exhaled.

Sis—Let's all exhale. I love your full transparency. To all the potential weight breakers out there, we're going to become very familiar with approach, course, ploy, policy, way, device—maneuvering as we learn how to handle the proverbial and physical weights of life. The first challenge I have for you is to establish a specific space for you to do the work. I realize a lot of you are listening in on The Weight Breaker App, you may be driving. However, I encourage you to create your very own WEIGHT BREAKER SPACE.

I want to encourage you to think of your Weight Breaker space in terms of this:

Block out the outside noise!

Reset your schedule to make time for you!

Examine the tactics!

Answer your calling!

Keep yourself committed to yourself!

Expect the greatness in you!

Rejoice in where you have come from in addition to where you are going!

In your weight breaker space, you've established that you understand Philippians 4: 13, *I can do all things through Christ who strengthens me!*

"Ladies, as the book states, having this space is not just a space to retreat to, it is to do the work. Dr. T., that is one of my favorite verses. It gives me a new declaration that I can call into my life."

Indeed. In order to declare a new thing in our life, we must do the work. So in your weight breaker space, the first thing we need to do the work is your equipment. The equipment is the following: *Think Like A Weight Breaker. Not Like A Weight Taker* book; *Think Like A Weight Breaker. Not Like A Weight Taker* journal or your favorite type of essay book/notebook; a writing utensil; a highlighter; a timer (or dedicated ten minutes per day); earplugs & Your WEIGHT BREAKER SPACE!

"Next, you need to create your Weight Breaker Tactic Hit List. I'm going to encourage you to write down all of the things that cause you to go astray when dealing with the proverbial weight and the physical weight of your life. What are some of the triggers that slap you off course? That is what makes up your ***Tactic Hit List!*** Make that list, that's your target to overcome. What are the feelings that overwhelm you? What are the feelings that cause you to lose focus—question God's purpose for you? That is what you put on your tactic hit list!"

Let's get to work! When you observe those emotions—navigate those situations, you will learn about new ways of thinking that can favorably shape your response. I see the comments in the chat. Keep them coming.

17

Dr. T. stated as she took a sip of her chai tea. The women nodded at each other, enthused by the comments.

:What do we do with our Tactic Hit List, Dr. T.?— A Loyal Fan.

I see you *A Loyal Fan*—we'll talk more about that as we address dealing with our mindset. We all know what triggers lead us down an unproductive path. We have to acknowledge some behaviors we have that cause us to linger in the proverbial weights of life, that can lead to packing on the physical weight of life.

"Interesting. I want to know more," Sparrow replied while she nibbled on the remainder of the pumpkin bar, feeling the calories surrounding her space. She can't help but think,

Here we are talking about being Weight Breakers— my sister sabotages me with all of this deliciousness.

Damn, would it be bad if I got another bar?

Okay, ladies, you know about your weight breaker space, so now let's talk about the mindset. I'm going to get really personal with you all.

"Oh, boy, here it comes," Dr. Sparrow Mack responded as she grabbed a *handy dandy* Kleenex nearby.

Dr. T. winked at her podcast guest, letting her know everything was going to be okay.

My epiphany about WEIGHT starts right here. It was not easy getting to this point, but I only did it with God's guidance. It was hard for me to think of myself as a weight breaker because I had constantly been a weight taker. I humbly admit that I'm still a work in progress. We're all in this together. Therefore, let's encourage each other, relish in our truth. If we are not constantly evolving, then we are simply going through the motions of life. We are merely facing yet another birthday without making progress towards our goals or addressing the stress of the proverbial/physical weights of life.

She turned towards Dr. Mack. They smiled at each other, nudging to look at all the comments that were popping up.

These words are swirling in my gut, like I drank some out-of-date milk. Despite all of what appears to be glam on the outside, currently my life appears stagnant, Sparrow thinks as she dabbed a transparent tear that lingered in the apex of her eye.

"Sista's, I see you commenting. Furthermore, Dr. T., you are so right. I'm so set in my ways. Can I make any changes that are meaningful? I asked myself that question often. I'm glad I'm not the only one."

No, you are not alone. Let's entertain this thought. Think of yourself as a grape.

"A grape? Sis, are you serious?" Sparrow turned her head, wanting to hear more about the analogy.

Dr. T. chuckled, she rendered on.

Walk with me, weight breakers. Yes, a grape. Your greatest desire is to become part of a fine bottle of wine.

Sparrow's lips turned upward as she snapped her fingers, "I love my wine, Sis! This analogy has my name written all over it." Sparrow got comfy in her swivel chair, doing a happy dance at the thought of a chilled glass of Riesling.

Dr. T. excitedly shared,

Each of you is *a grape* in its most natural—pristine organic form. There is an evolution that you must go through to transform into wine—this evolution must take what?

"Time."

Yes, time. No matter where you are in the maturation process, it's not too late to develop. This is how I know that you have the capability to become a weight breaker! Time to modify your mindset is where it all starts.

"I love that analogy. I'm going to add in my clap backs that *I am as fine as wine*. You put it so nicely in this workbook. Each of us has the ability to determine how we're going to cope, respond, and handle life. Weight Breaker, in reading this book, it's so apparent that we're all connected in this thing called life. We must consider a new mindset!"

The podcast crew smiled in agreement.

I've been calling you Sparrow; I should be calling you Dr. Mack.

"Before I was ever Dr. Sparrow Mack, I was little Sparrow. Girl, I don't get caught up in titles. Plus, with all that we've been through together, we are more like family—"

You've got that right, we are sisters—hell sis, we have the scars to prove it. Well, Sparrow, I beta-tested this process of challenging myself to establish a new mindset! Going back to our productive innate natures, we're built to be both proactive along with being reactive. However, many times regarding the way we think about ourselves, we are reactive. We've got to put sweat equity into how we can be proactive about how we address the weights of our life. We have to implore *Weight Breaker-ology...*

"Weight Breaker-ology, what is that?"

19

Weight Breaker-ology is a phrase that I coined, however in any standard dictionary "ol-o-gy" is a noun—meaning the subject of study; a branch of knowledge. Within the book *Think Like A Weight Breaker. Not Like A Weight Taker,* that provides T.I.P.s for approaching what life throws at us, which are the weights of life, thus those thought processes are what I call *Weight Breaker-ology.*

"I'm going to start using Weight Breaker-ology, you can take that to the bank and cash it."

Sparrow, I love it. Let's dig a little deeper. *Weight Breaker-ology* lends to a new perspective. For example, that philosophy is to equip you with looking at a distraught valley moment, and being able to speak mountain top proclamation's over cumbersome situations.

For example, "I'm overweight, and I will never be healthy and well," which is the Weight Taker perspective. The Weight Breaker-ology perspective is to take out the negative connotations of the verbiage surrounding situations, like the word *never.*

A Weight Breaker perspective approach utilizing that same factual data. For example, "I realize I am overweight. In order to be healthy and well, I will make small changes in my diet to accomplish my health and wellness goals, to be the best person God has called me to be."

You see the difference in the tone, perspective? You have to speak and write positive affirmations over your life, in order to walk into the promises of God.

"Dr. T., I challenge everyone to be proactive with handling *the weights*. Let's get this *Weight Breaker-ology* verbiage in our life!" Sparrow looked into the camera directly, getting a lot of positive feedback.

Let me tell you about the *meat* of this book. Within each of the chapters act as if you're having an intimate sit-down with yourself in a meeting or town hall. Ultimately, it's *a vessel* towards accomplishment of personal goals. Moreover, speaking of mountain's, be very aware of who is by your side in the valley, as well as the mountain top.

Dr. T. shared as she continued to scroll through the comments. She added,

So, my friends, no more *outsourcing* handling of the weights of life to others. You are responsible for how you respond. We now take ownership! You are responsible for being aware of who you surround yourself with. Make sure you are aligned with loyal allies. You are the Chief Executive Officer of your life!

The ladies high-fived.

"*Damn Skippy*! I am my very own C.E.O.—yes!" Sparrow added loudly, causing her headphones to reverb.

"Speaking of being the C.E.O. of my life, I've had to fuel myself up with motivation."

I feel you, sis.

"My library is filled with motivational books. To be honest, your book is a little unique. It stands out from the others that I've read. Here, look at this pic," Sparrow showed a picture of her personal library to Dr. T.

Now I know why they call you *the literary gangster*. Damn, sis, how many books do you have in your library? *A gazillion?*

"Over five thousand. I love to read all genres. However, of the non-fiction, self-help motivational-type, about one-thousand," Sparrow smiled in deep reflection of how reading those books; writing in her library caused her hectic life to *even-out*.

She zoned out somewhat as flashes of visions of blood dripping down the white walls of the woodshop, along with horrifically looking down into the dungeon in the backwoods of the country pierced her clouded soul.

Dr. T. noticed her pause, touched her elbow—mouthed to her,

Sis, you okay?

The touch, accompanied by the question, brought Sparrow out of her stupor. She nodded, "Yes."

Like I was saying, I've been asked why a book like this has not been developed before? I searched high and low for something like this. I realized no one had addressed these topics or combined the proverbial and physical weights of life. Therefore, I decided to be the problem-solver of this plight.

Sparrow finished off her cup of chai tea. "Dr. T., that's wonderful! I love how you tailored *The Inspirational Pathway* in the workbook or, as you like to call it, *T.I.P.s!* They motivate me daily, those T.I.P.s are what I carry with me always—like my favorite carry-on luggage."

Girl, you and your carry-on luggage. Listener's, this is the only woman I know that can travel all across the globe with only a carry-on piece of luggage.

"And I am not ashamed about it."

How can you do that? I always have a purse, carry-on, and check two large pieces of luggage?

"Girl, you know how I roll? You never know when you just may have to pivot quickly, slipping off to do some detective work!"

Sis, I know how you roll.

"Don't hate. I call my packing technique *The Sparrow Hack.*"

The ladies chuckled.

21

Sparrow, speaking of hack—you would faint if you found out how I *landed* on those T.I.P.s.

"Really? Do tell..."

I did not want this book to simply be about *whooping and hollering* about how to *walk in your purpose*. There had to be more substance that I was going to contribute to the world. So, I orchestrated TACTICS TO TRANSFORM, surrounding The Inspirational Pathway.

Ultimately, we're striving to get to the bottom of what we're dealing with; these weights that we're handed daily. To put it simply, we must find a way to manage carrying so much weight on our backs!

I wish it was as easy as going to the store looking for a bottle of *Weight Breaker Juice* stocked on the shelves. Or better yet, imagine if we could go to a restaurant to order, *"I would like to have the piping hot Weight Breaker entree, with a side of T.I.P.s.—tell me how those Tactics taste? I think I'll try those. BOOM!"*—there you have it!

The remarks were rolling in, in agreement, while the women chuckled as they were handed bottled waters by Dr. T. 's assistant. They both took *a swig.*

"Girl, you are too funny. I guess we can look at this book as *our menu.* It's got all the necessary ingredients—gives us the strategy, playbook, whatever you want to call it, to succeed! This will not be your first pass through this type of book. I can see how this book is meant to be read multiple times. It's asking to be dog-eared, post-it-noted—highlighted to the point that it glows in the dark—just like I've done,"

Sparrow said as she held up a preview copy of the book that looked like it had been *to war and back.*

Dr. T. grabbed Sparrow's *Think Like A Weight Breaker. Not Like A Weight Taker* book, thumbed through it, smiled at all of the notes she held it to the video monitor.

You see, this is what I'm talking about—Dr. Sparrow Mack, bad-ass physician and *literary gangster*, you got it! Through your first pass, *foster* the concepts and ideas. The second pass, practice *adoption* of the principles. Over time with each read, this book will become a part of *the family* of books that you lean on through your journey. The *R.O.I.* is worth the effort you put into it!

Become your own champion! Subsequently you'll be able to champion others with *Chariots of Fire* playing as your background music.

"Can you clarify the weights of life for the newbies?"

Great segue. There is proverbial weight; the weight that occurs within the natural process of life. It manifests from the stressors we endure, such as being an adult, having to support a household, our careers, life obligations, alongside all of the other hats we wear in life. More tangibly present is the physical weight we acquire by making bad eating habits, mismanaging our dietary consumption—not incorporating physical activity into our lives on a regular basis.

"I love how transparent you are when sharing what drives the different weight in our life."

Ladies, trust me when I tell you, I was *living purposefully unaware*. In *bold neon lights. I'm too busy* to handle the weights of life; that was my excuse. However, I wanted to feel better, look svelte in my clothes, and manage stress on a higher level.

"You are preaching to the choir. Can I get an Amen?"

Amen! So, what's a girl to do? I wasn't a true representation of wellness, even when I was in the business of taking care of my patients as their physician. I was weighted down by my lack of self-care. Instead of making changes, I was hanging my stethoscope over a bigger lab coat I had to buy each year.

I embarked upon multiple journeys to address both weights, but there was no momentum. I didn't realize what tools I needed to achieve the results I so badly wanted.

"Sis, you are all up in my headspace. I feel you. I have yo-yoed in weight-stress all of my life," Sparrow took another sip of her tea, as she thumbed through the book. "Most people judge you based on seeing the end result, not knowing the cumbersome journey you've been on to get there. That is why I am so *anti-hater*."

Ditto.

"Dr. T., what do you do when you try everything, yet everything stays the same? I believe that is called an unhealthy continuum?"

You are right! It is an unhealthy continuum of life. Let me share with you my personal experience. I was a motivational speaker about weight, however not living it out. Therefore, there was an amalgam of physical circumstantial evidence every time I looked in the mirror. I was conflicted about what I was preaching since it wasn't how I was living. I was obese—obese with both weights.

"You're right. One of the biggest drivers of weight is to pretend it is not there. If you don't identify it, you can't address it. I call that *living unaware.* Life is tough, we're all used to going through the motions, but before we know it, it's another unaware day, another unaware month, another unaware year! That has been the story of my life as well," Dr. Sparrow Mack identified.

Listeners, hear me well. Even in the midst of my conflicted spirit, as I was unaware, living out epic fails in my life. I traveled the world, gave motivational talks to women. I still found the drive to encourage people of all walks of life to be their best selves.

"I see the conflict there."

23

It was a massive state of conflict. I have shared wisdom through radio, keynote speaking engagements, mentoring, books, articles, along with stage performances. All the while being a present mother, devoted wife—the icing on the *weight cake*, dueling with a very demanding career. My candle was burned at both ends—was almost out of wick. Not effectively balancing it all, led me to not wholeheartedly walk in my purpose.

I have had many doors shut right in my face due to me being a woman. Specifically, an African American woman coming from meager beginnings—attempting to debunk naysayers when I professed my aspirational goals. That pressure was enough to snuff out any person's ability to manifest their dreams.

"Agreed, the weights of the world can make you feel many emotions. Weight can make you cry, feel unworthy, and make you doubt your true capabilities. To add to that, you feel unappreciated, unloved, uncomfortable, overlooked, weak, empty, invisible, abandoned, ostracized or wanting to give up."

Ladies, you may have personally felt the way Dr. Mack expressed she felt, but what adds to that layer of weight is when you're constantly depleted before you've tapped into a source for replenishing.

The ladies looked at the comments. One caught their eyes...

:Curious, what caused your thought process to change? Needing to know, I have a lot I need to break in my life right now!—Fawn P.

Fawn, one day my husband, who is one of the most generous and motivating people that I have ever met—I'm still baffled at how God placed this person in my life, told me something very profound, *"Babe, you go around the world motivating all of these women, and you are constantly reading motivational-spiritual books, so you've got to start walking it out for yourself! The same faith that you're sharing with others, you have to work on that for you!"* He said that with nothing but love in his heart, but it stung my soul because he was so right!

"Dr. T., I bet those words hit you like Mike Tyson!"

Yep, I was lights out before the eight-count when he told me that. The bottom line was that I had some serious work to do. But how did I get started? I decided to start small, knowing I had to work on how I allowed myself to think. I grabbed some post-it notes, accompanied with tears streaming down my face, I started to think about the things that I wanted to change in my life. I also needed to address the weight of my insecurities—decided to start by writing down positive things I felt about who I am. I peeled off post-it-notes, I wrote: I'm a mother; I'm a wife; I'm a creative person; I'm a visionary; also I'm thoughtful. I pulled another post-it note, I jotted down some goals that I wanted for myself: I will exercise three times per week; I want fifty pounds off my body; as I lose my weight I will give away the clothes that I can no longer fit; I will get organized; I will incorporate meditation; I will be more present with my family; I will have balance in my life; I will be grateful for the small things; and last but definitely not least I will keep God first.

"I love this—I'm a post-it note girl, too!"

Girl, I thought I was one of the last ones to be obsessed with those.

Sparrow smiled as the woman fist-bumped.

So, on the last post-it-note, I wrote down a self-inscribed quote that I made up on the spot that resonated with the journey, "I'm *not perfect, but I'm a damn good person!"*

"You are a damn good person, sis." Sparrow said, giving a sisterly side hug.

Awe, thank you. As women, we don't tell ourselves that enough, right? It was like those post-it notes had *magical powers* or they were the catalyst for epic change. I was bound and determined to create a new view of myself.

Dr. T. said as she took another sip of her water, she saw the cue card from her assistant, indicating some of the topics that were not yet covered in detail.

T.I.P.s, I got it! she thought to herself.

Written words are profound. It's one thing to say something. However, to write the declaration over your life is another. Soon, I started compiling those notes into a folder in hopes that the words *leaped off the pages,* which caused a stirring in my spirit. I wanted those words to catalyze my being; to be the very best version of myself that I could be.

"I get it. We all truly want to be able to be what God would have us to be, a vessel to do His will."

Sis, you totally get it. I prayed to discover what pathway I could place myself on to keep the inspiration in my spirit going. It was revealed to me that there are things that I must do daily, I've started to refer to them as The Inspirational Pathway (T.I.P.s).

"Yes, girl. I live by those T.I.P.s! I *walk them out* every day!" Sparrow snapped in the air.

The T.I.P.s were causing me to download *novel* information into my spirit collaterally, modifying my mindset. By no way or any means am I a psychologist, however orchestrating positive deposits into my space, spirit, moreover my mind— affording me an enhanced vision, faith, and resilience.

"Girl, ditto. This book caused me to morph the way I was living my life. I became more aware, started storing positive affirmations in my mental cloud. Now, I take life one decision at a time, like the decisions not to eat another one of those pumpkin bars."

The ladies laughed. Sparrow had visual of herself once again not capable of buttoning her favorite YSL jumpsuit that she waxed and waned in fitting due to her questionable dietary choices.

No, I will not have another pumpkin bar, she committed to herself.

"I'm a fiction writer, so pardon the verbiage I am going to use. The weight of life can be paralleled as *a desperate stalker that is waiting to attack*. It imposes desperation, unhealthy comparisons, *FOMO,* low self-esteem, lack of self-worth, topped off by a dwindling confidence that leads to an overall poor self-image—"

Dr. T. craned her neck back.

Damn, Sparrow, that is deep. However, you are so right. All of which can be the weight that affects our overall perspective on life. Henceforth, you will put you as the first priority on your to-do list.

She leaned into her sister while they channeled their struggles with encouragement over the airwaves.

Sparrow gazed deep into the camera.

"You hear that, ladies? We all must make ourselves the first item on our priority list! Creating a new love language towards myself, I love that."

The ladies high-fived.

Weight Breakers, for the duration of this podcast, let's journey together to make some meaningful change towards healthier living. By no means will you have lost all the weight you want implementing the tactics or feel like you can handle all the stresses of life like *a cakewalk*, however these tools will help you get there.

Sparrow adjusted her pants while she sat at the microphone, chuckling— feeling on her muffin top that she'd been working on by utilizing the *3W's* The Weight Breaker talked to her about, in the past.

I sure did because we need to treat ourselves from time to time as well. Okay, ladies, if you haven't gotten the book yet, it's called *Think Like A Weight Breaker. Not Like A Weight Taker*, by yours truly. They are on pre-order now. So, order yours today to get your signed copy. One of the first challenges that we have to address is to truly understand the difference between a Weight Breaker vs. What is a Weight Taker?

Sparrow interrupted.

"May I take a stab at the definitions?"

Yes, *monarch butterfly,* you may.

26

"Well, a WEIGHT BREAKER has a strategy to make meaningful changes in life. A WEIGHT BREAKER does not allow their daily decisions to be swayed by negative thinking or operate from a clouded judgment. A WEIGHT TAKER is a person who is easily swayed by the fluctuations of life without a plan—it is hard for them to remain true to their vision, faith, and resilient intelligence. In addition, they don't lean on tactics to inspire themselves. Thus, taking on unnecessary pressures. By no means am I a butterfly yet, I'm still at the caterpillar stage—"

Girl, that was so good, yes you are definitely out of the cocoon. Your illustration of that was so well done, the listeners are going to think that you were my ghostwriter.

"Please don't bring up a ghostwriter or, rather, ghost-stalker..."

Dr. T. used that phrase, forgetting the actual experience that Sparrow had with an individual as such, mouthing,

Sorry.

"No worries."

Dr. T. went on to share,

I want everyone to put in the chat, also say it out loud ten times, wherever you are: Think Like a Weight Breaker. Not Like a Weight Taker!

If you have your book, or if not, within your journal or even on a post-it-note, what would be the benefits of being a weight breaker? You may ask yourself, what if I just want to be *weight breaker-like?* Well, to put a positive spin on this, that means that you are no longer a weight taker. However, we are on the verge of being fully committed to being a weight breaker, which is a new *momentum* to have!

Production gave the signal to Dr. T. to start wrapping up the conversation. Dr. T. nodded with acknowledgement.

Sparrow opened her book to the section that they were referencing.

"Okay, I have it right here. I'm going to leave you with some nuggets that I got from the book. I'll try not to be *a spoiler*, but the top priorities in this book are: objectives of dealing with the weights of life are clearly defined; obstacles identified addressing the obstacles the weights of life; and deliberate tactics needed to be sustained to make meaningful change. I cannot tell you exactly what outcomes you will have when you dive into this book, everyone reading it will glean different nuggets. However, I do know that with positive intention, you will have an open attitude to project the willingness to take on the challenges that will help you in becoming a Weight Breaker."

Sparrow smiled as she placed her thumb to hold the book open.

Well said, Dr. Sparrow Mack. The bottom line is that, as a collective, we have to support each other—we can make changes to live our best life! Ladies, *Friction Ridges* is in a theater near you! This sister right here is doing big things—I want each of you to support her!

Dr. T. nudged Sparrow.

"You are so kind, but we are here to focus on the Weight Breakers that are listening in! Everyone under the sound of my voice, go out, pre-order the book of *Think Like A Weight Breaker. Not Like A Weight Taker.* It's worth the investment. Your biggest investment has to be you! Oh, one last thing. One of the biggest takeaways from the book was identifying *your momentum type*. Dr. T., can you share about that briefly?"

She turned towards Dr. T. with eager anticipation.

Absolutely! I orchestrated momentum types, regarding how one navigates through life. This is not based on data or science, but on pure personal experience. Just humor yourselves on finding out which momentum type you are. Okay, let's run through each type. I have livened up the descriptions of the momentum types because I truly believe that what you speak from your lips or *declare* has a profound effect on what you think about yourself! I wanted to keep it sassy; make it a little spicy. So, for a bit of extra fun, I have suggested the perfect little lip lacquer for each momentum type. I'm working on a little something with Dean Baby—

"Girl, stop! Dean Baby is my boy. He did my makeup for the New Authors Symposium; my face was *beat to the gods*—I've been using him ever since. I love him. He sent me this coral stain on my lips—melon infused."

Sparrow grabbed her never full L.V. bag, grabbing her compact to lather another layer of the color.

I see you, girl—that color is fire, so you get it, right? Let's tag team these momentum types. Okay, so the first type is: *The Juggler*—sheer lipstick—a little shine, spark. This person is that go-to person for all of their family, friends and loved ones. They have difficulty saying *"No"*, so their plate is full at all times with no reprieve. That is a weight that they bear. They must juggle everything, keeping everybody happy – meeting the needs of all that depend on them.

"Damn, that sounds just like me," Regi thought.

The second type is *The Mirage*—balm tint with a dash of color. Even though they're depleted, they want it to appear that everything is all good. They put so much energy into making sure that the facade is *on point* to hide their true reality, which is a weight.

The third is *The Chameleon*—creamy/crème lipstick with a combo of texture and gloss—we all know what that is. It is someone attempting to blend in. What I'm referencing is more of a self-hatred that will cause you to deny or neglect your heritage, culture, or true value in order to be accepted by the mass index of people by any means necessary unhealthy, which is a weight.

Sparrow chimed in, " Okay, the fourth is *The Aspirational*—stain or lip tints with more color, less shine. This individuals' consciousness is in the clouds, neglecting the realities of life. They have monstrous dreams, however they're not practical on how to achieve them, which is a weight."

Sparrow, I'm impressed with how engaged you are with the book. The fifth is *The Shadow*—liquid matte lipstick with a moisturizer. This individual is the wind beneath the wings of so many people, nonetheless not in the forefront at all. They have talents that they don't share, remaining in the background. They're weighted down by constantly having to dim their light so others can shine, which is a weight.

"The sixth is *The Vault*—matte lipstick with a sophisticated velvet finish. This is the individual that you never know what they're feeling or what their opinion is. They're a danger to themselves because they keep so much bottled up inside that they're not able to let their true feelings show. They associate their own vulnerability with being weak. Without that release, their soul is toxic. At their core, they're good, but you would never know because their true feelings are hidden deep down in their soul—that is their weight," Sparrow added.

The seventh is *The Reasoner*—matte balm with a matte finish. This is the individual who has to make sense of everything. They often miss out on a lot of blessings due to that fact. They're so practical that everything must add up. They do not leave room in their space for the possibilities of miracles—that is their weight.

"The extra-momentum type that can similarly be considered the eighth, is *The Emulate*—glossy lipstick with glamorous luster. This is the person who exemplifies newness by taking on a whole other persona, as if to blindly want to put their own life into a dungeon."

I have seen these eight momentum types live their best life, as well as some may have more than one momentum type. Regardless of the type, if one addresses how they think about themselves, they can declare a new trajectory over their life.

"We must break the yokes that bind us! Once we do, we will handle varying circumstances with gracious optimism. Understanding that God has given us the acumen to *BE* weight breakers."

Also, there may be certain people who feel as if they exemplify a particular momentum type in certain circumstances, however in another aspect of their life, they embody another form of momentum. It's very normal. All of this is a way to illustrate how weight can manifest in your life based on your momentum. Regardless, together we proclaim you to *Think Like A Weight Breaker, Not Like A Weight Taker.*

Sparrow applauded all of the comments, as they scrolled.

29

"Dr. T., this is so *Dope!* I love it! However, for right now I'm going to keep my momentum to myself."

The women tittered.

Please stay tuned for a fabulous weight breaker event upcoming soon. Remember, time is the only thing that all of us have, that levels the playing field.

Therefore, what are you going to do with your time? I vote for enhancing your thought process, so let's welcome the tactics into our life. By going through these exercises, you are going to manage your risk for being a weight taker...

Sparrow interrupted Dr. T.

"Can I share the Weights of Life Poem with the ladies that have tuned in?"

Sure.

"There is a part in this book called, *The Last Dance."*

Sparrow opened up the book, reading the poem to the LIVE audience,

Sparrow, you read this so well, I might have you do the audio for the audiobook. I love your voice.

"Count me in."

As we conclude, ladies, what are some of the weights in your life that you are going to put on notice? Which weights are you going to inform that this is *the last dance*? Ladies, it's *the last dance* for everything that is holding us back or keeping us down.

YOU CAN! Don't you ever forget it! Blessings to each of you. Stay tuned to The Weight Breaker website for more information. On The Chronicles Of The Weight Breakers Podcast, we will be having some phenomenal guests, along with giveaways.

Sparrow, I know you have the weight of the world on your shoulders, moreover I want you with all of the listeners to know that—*you can!* Also, don't forget to cling to Philippians 4:13, *I can do all things through Christ that strengthens me. Amen!*

Love, Dr. T.

Dr. T. blew a kiss to the podcast audience, pressed END to the podcast. The women took a deep breath as they embraced, like they were a relay team that had just crossed the line with a victory in one hand, with the baton in another.

Sparrow, that was really good; I know we impacted a large number of women. Thank you for gracing my listeners with your presence today. We didn't speak enough about your book, as well as your movie, *Friction Ridges, or* the interview you had with Abigail. Girl, I heard that interview—I told you she could be on a stone-cold *trip.* However, you handled yourself well—like I knew you would.

30

"Girl, barely. I felt like I was a body double for that actress that played the assistant in *The Devil Wears Prada*—she's ice cold," the women laughed.

Sparrow added, "You have to have me as a speaker at THE CHRONICLES OF THE WEIGHT BREAKERS CONFERENCE you were talking about?"

Dr. T. smirked while pulling out the white paper that housed the draft copy of the roster of speakers.

I'm already all over it, sis! See, I've got your name right here.

Dr. T. said as she pointed to the list of platinum presenters.

That warmed Sparrow's heart, which was much needed those days with all that she'd gone through lately.

The women embraced jovially like they were getting ready to walk to the music of show *Girlfriends*, minus two.

Before I forget, here is Dr. Clark's business card. She's good.

Sparrow, turned her lips up, took the card, "I'll consider it."

It's a dynamic space in the universe when women lament in each other's victories, they surely had to conquer being weight takers to overcome the wiles of life. The Chronicles Of The Weight Breakers Podcast is not just one woman's story of struggle, decorated with overcoming, it is the blueprint to trust and follow the unique path that each of us was called to follow by God. We just have to take our Q-tip cleaned ears along with an unclutter spirit to hear his voice.

"Cocktails? We headed to the bar—right?"

Sparrow—It's only noon, girl.

They both looked at each other, simultaneously saying,

"It's five o'clock somewhere!"

They laughed hysterically.

3

JUDGE REGINA "REGI" HINSON

"THE JUGGLER"

[SHEER LIPSTICK-A LITTLE SHINE AND SPARK]

The bright illumination of the Brookstone digital alarm clock broke through the silent darkness at 5:00 a.m. in the Hinson's master bedroom suite. There two souls lay still behind the room's gilded solid oak double doors in an opulent four-poster California King. The sounds of Sirius The Chronicles of The Weight Breakers Podcast quickly began to ascend from the alarm clock penetrating Regi's tired ear canals. The room was dark, but a hint of orange sun caused the curtains to glow as the cascading rays welcomed the morning of the Hollywood Hills. The rays kissed the peaks as they brightened the depths of the valley where *stars* were made.

The tired judge was fast asleep with her stressed jaw clearly clenched; lips slightly puckered with sheer lipstick still in place. Nestled in the corner of her mouth was a mix between Crest toothpaste along with the Napa Valley Merlot she drank before bed. The irony of what Regi was unconsciously listening to was a stark contrast to her practical self; that *motivational, feel-good, hokey pokey B.S.* that was a total waste of time and money, in her view. Publicly, she was not at all a fan of *self-help, feel good gibberish*. Nonetheless covertly, those motivational resources were becoming vital, to cope with all of the sacrifices that her life was filled with. She recently began to lean into those resources more heavily after being notified by Chief Judge Reynolds that she was a candidate for Associate Chief Judge of her *George Washington-Faced courthouse*, minus the wigs—of course. Soon after word got around that Regi was next in line, people started throwing *darts* from the left, the right, above, and below. The stress was blasting from every freaking direction, trying to hinder, intimidate, and cause her to question herself.

"What gave Regi Hinson the audacity to throw her hat into the ring to become Associate Chief Judge?" were *the darts* Regi heard daily. It was apparent to her that people were uncomfortable with a woman, let alone a woman of color, being even a candidate for such a spot. The daily murmurings around the courthouse caused bouts of self-doubt. Consequently, she welcomed as many encouraging resources as she could find. Regi became a self-professed, self-help-obsessed, book-buying, *podcast-engaged snob* that needed the constant reminder to not shut down and to stay focused on getting the job done.

She was the wife to a husband that was even busier than her. He loved every atom of her, but finding time for each other was always difficult. Also, being the mother of two boys with a healthy interest in signing up for new projects or sports added to her workload. The icing on her *life-cake* was having to deal with the *mother-in-law from hell* that she had inherited in the union.

So, due to her schedule, the fact that a blaring podcast shattering the silence of her room didn't pull her out of R.E.M. sleep wasn't startling at all. Most people could relate to being so exhausted that their souls felt tired. That was Regi; weighed down to the point that if her bed frame had disappeared, her mattress would've been forced down like cement bricks to the bottom of the ocean. Long workdays had gotten the best of Judge Regina Hinson. With her heroism on her sleeve, she'd been up all night preparing for a briefing she had to present to Chief Judge Reynolds in an early litigation preview. There she laid in bed next to her husband, with her MacBook settled on top of the thousand-thread Egyptian cotton sheets that she was elated to get at Saks Fifth Avenue during their annual white sale for fifty percent off. Her bronze hands affixed perfectly posed in a typing manner on the keyboard—fixed on the delete button. Unbeknownst to her, she erased the brief she had spent the entire night hammering away at that was due the next morning, while a bottle of Merlot sat empty on her nightstand.

Adjacent to her, a man rested motionless with slow, methodical breaths. His tortoise shell-rimmed glasses were fixed on his strong European nose; his ivory skin soft against the sheets that engulfed him in his birthday suit—he liked to sleep that way. While in slumberland, he leaned into his wife; body arched in her direction. He adored this woman, but life with kids, family stress—pressures from work often got in the way of their closeness.

They met as study partners in law school—then coined *The Ebony and Ivory Litigation Tsunami*, because they'd argue cases until *the paint fell off the wall.* Law school opponents shuddered when they would blindly draw their names out of *the basket,* to debate in mock trials.

Regi chose to take her talents to the corporate arena, taking on Big Pharma Fortune 500 corporations as the lead attorney on closing big deals for the betterment of the underserved, until she got an opportunity as a judge in the city circuit courts. Little Regi had come a long way from the alleyways that she would walk down to get to school in Compton, but never forgot where she came from.

Zachary Hinson grew up with a silver spoon in his mouth on the periphery of Beverly Hills, as he was the nephew of Julia Madeline Chandler Ernesto and Dr. Enrique Ernesto, who tragically died in a single engine plane crash. The Chandlers came from *long green,* the Hinson's descended from that dynasty lineage. Despite his equestrian lessons, water polo championship trophies, overall elite upbringing, he was drawn to *chocolate.* Although he originally paraded his Barbie doll-type girlfriends around his mother at their socialite events, while growing up, Zachary spent hours in Compton's nightlife, hanging out— *straight kicking it* with people of a bronze hue. He was truly *a brother* on the inside. When he met Regi, he knew she was the one the moment they locked eyes. He was drawn into her beautiful goodness, moreover captivated by her intellectualism, way with words, and beautiful full lips that puckered when she spoke her mind, letting everybody know that she was not going to allow her people to be forgotten.

Coincidently, he started working for the local defense fund, which was not what his parents had in mind. Together, they marched for political equalization of access to healthcare along with food disparities of the underserved—that quickly caused them to connect. Two people from polar-opposite ends of the spectrum of life, with one thing in common that bonded them: equal justice for all. It took some time for Zachary's parents to come to terms with their grandsons that were ever-so-sun kissed bronze.

To top it all off, Regi was taking full financial support for her mother who still chose to remain in the thick of her relatives. Her mom worked as a certified nurse assistant that suffered from a minor injury that incurred while transferring a patient. Though her mother was approaching retirement, a couple of weeks off from work turned into a failed attempt at disability, resulting in her becoming yet another person on Regi's payroll.

Over time, these instances encouraged disconnection between Regina and her family. She would catch wind of conversations between her mom and sister about Regi having the audacity to think that she was better than her sister, who had multiple children by different men. Regi was the one that *made it*, that separation in social class seemed to weave a lot of tension with her family. Regi had become so used to being the *A.R.M.* of the family—*Automatically Regi's Money*. Her family members continued to drain from her, but she knew they needed her to stay afloat—she was thrust under survivor's remorse. She juggled everything, often feeling like she should be the brand owner of the world's worst wife and mother. She was successful at fighting for justice in the world, but when it came to managing her children's academics compounded with the robust extracurricular activities calendar, she was an epic failure in her own eyes.

She laid next to her husband appearing to wince in pain-infused wonderment, with tight eyelids along with tension and an apparent clenched jaw. Still deep in sleep, she heard the misty echo of serene yet eerie music playing as she took in the crystal-clear skies surrounding her. Quickly, her dream swirled into nightmare territory,

Tempered blue skies filled the panoramic view, suddenly were scratched out with a conundrum of heavy black clouds. A cold wind swept across the land. With a shudder motion, Regi's vision burst—she found her younger self tucked in the corner of a basement. The cavity began to churn in disarray around her, as if she were in the center of an F5 tornado. The winds ripped through the windows. Her eyes darted towards the ceiling as the roof was ripped off—all the air was funneled out of the room. She tried to catch her breath—the vacuum felt as if her lungs were being extracted from her chest. The catastrophic vision filled her view as the room shook—mangled bodies flew from every angle…

Screaming, Regi sat up abruptly in bed—with cold beads of sweat rolling down her forehead into her robust cleavage. She had completely soaked her Yves Saint Laurent one-piece nightly.

"Damn," she said, breathing heavily as she ripped off her "Fly Diva" sleeping mask to come into her current reality—hoping not to yield to the mental hoarding of the terror she experienced long ago. She reached for her two-piece carafe on the nightstand to grab a gulp of water, her hand shook—*the scar* apparent.

"Baby, what's wrong?" Zachary sleepily asked as he leaned into his wife.

She adjusted her eyes to look at her laptop—her pinky finger affixed to the delete button.

"Oh, shit—my brief. It's gone!"

"What? What do you mean, sweetheart? Why are you yelling?" Zachary wiped his eyelids with slits of his baby blue eyes peeking through.

"What did you do to it?" Regi asked in an accusatory tone.

"Me? Baby, when I went to sleep last night, you were still working on it. I watched the nightly news—then I was out. Here, let me see," he reached for Regi's computer.

"Shit, this is the last thing I need," Regi said in disappointment. "Chief Judge Reynolds is already down my neck. It's just my luck that I would have to appear before him today. If I'm not able to pull this off, I'm for sure going to look like I can't handle being Associate Chief Judge."

Unable to take the anxiety, Regi jumped out of bed, popped a Xanax on an empty stomach, chasing it with the extra water in her glass. She paced the floor as her husband—still in his *birthday suit*, worked his magic on the computer. Fully aware that expectations control disappointments, usually of a sound mind—Regi's heart raced, all of her practical thinking thrown out the window with her aspirations of becoming Associate Chief Judge.

"Regina—you see, here is your document—it's right here. I turned on autosave on your PC last week when we did the upgrades. You're all set, baby."

Regi grabbed the computer. "Thanks—but wait. This is only half of the document I prepped."

"I don't know what else to say, babe. This is all that popped up. I've got to get up to get the boys ready. I have a briefing this morning as well. Can you take them to school?"

"Are you freaking kidding me?" She sneered, still hammering away at her computer. She picked up the empty bottle of Merlot, threw it across the room into the trash can.

"I told you; you didn't have to top that bottle off last night. But no, you said you could *hang*, but I see you can't," Zachary taunted lovingly.

Regi picked up a pillow, tossing it across the room to hit her now standing husband, who was picking out his clothes for the day stark naked. He grabbed the pillow, walked over to her, planting a gentle kiss on the forehead of his frantic wife.

"I got the boys. I'll get them dressed and ready for school. Are you still good at dropping them off?"

"Yep, I'm cool," Regi barked back as she organized a respectable document that would hopefully suffice for the stern Chief Judge.

Regi grabbed her robe, packed her briefcase, while Zachary got the boys up—corralled their sleepy bodies towards their morning routine. In the air, she smelled the aroma of pancakes and bacon coming from the kitchen. She hung up her robe outside the shower, as she welcomed the waterfall of warm beads of hydration beating against her shoulder-length curly hair. She rubbed the soapy foam brush against her thick body, held her head down to let gravity pull the water from the nape of her neck to the small of her back—down to her toes. She stepped fully into the water, attempting to wash "*it*" away. Whatever "*it*" was.

The "*it*" in Regi's life stood firmly on the back of her tense neck. The pressures of work, the stress of being a mother that didn't have it all together, the pain of being a wife that loved her husband, but understanding that he would never fully know all that came with being a person of color. Moreover, the intense gravity of having to be conscious about not inviting "intimidating" energy into her relationship with her *mother-in-law-from-hell*—who made it apparent that she thought her son could have married better.

Topping it all off was the weight of being the one that *made it out*. That guilt ate at her every day. She could not get away from that need to be the rescuer of her mother, the legal plus financial support to her family, also the one to give whatever else they needed in order to keep her brittle self-worth afloat. The water beat on Regi's tired mind as she soothed the weights on her life. At least she could drown them out with their exorbitant wine cellar or the exotic rain shower that Zachary had installed last year. It wasn't enough, but it would have to do.

Nothing is ever going to change for me!

I've become used to the weight!

It's so hard juggling all of this shit!

"Regi, I got your coffee ready," Zachary said as he peeked in, disrupting her conflicting *Calgon Take Me Away* moment.

"I'm coming," she shouted as she shut off the shower, dried off, and looked at herself in the mirror. "Girl, quit tripping. You've got this! You're Judge Regina Hinson, *dammit!*"

She reached over to her phone to press PLAY on her "Self-Love" play-list, with Beyoncé's "Brown Skin Girl" beginning to boom from her Bluetooth speaker while she readied herself for her morning routine. Applying her skin with a Vitamin C-enriched moisturizing foundation, she also applied her bronze eyeshadow, sun kissed rouge to accent her strong Nubian chestnut eyes, stroking her full luscious lashes. She stared at herself in the mirror, her spirit resonated:

Come on Regi, you're a boss chic. I'm going to get this money plus handle my business. All my haters haven't gotten the memo that they're really just fans! Things might look perfect on the outside, but this is no easy job. Being everybody's everything stresses me out, but I get it done. It's so hard to juggle. I've come so far.

My mother raised Ryan, Rain, and I all by herself— that keeps me grounded in who I am. I would do anything for her, even if I don't know how she is going to show up for me. Will she be quoting Bible verses or hiding a bottle of Old E in her purse? She always tells me that I will understand everything, by and by—I cling to that. On the other hand, are my extended family, well that is a whole other story…

People don't know how challenging it is with my in-laws not accepting me. I'm a mother attempting to raise black boys in a harsh world, with a husband that does not completely understand. That's just at home! While I'm quick with my clap-backs, that is not always perceived in the best way professionally.

I'm honest, in addition unapologetically–me. I often question my ability to align my business acumen and my ability to represent myself as the best judge possible. While my male colleagues are known as go-getters, I'm known as the Angry Black Woman. Still, I will "check" a person really quickly, it's not because of my race—it's due to my expertise. I'm a lawyer, I graduated top of my class. I know how to shine above the rest. I'll show them how it's done when I become Associate Chief Judge of the circuit courts.

Regi gawked at herself in the mirror, basked in her finished work.

"Girl, you got this!"

Her self-admiration was seized by an echoing voice from the next room. "Regi, it's getting late. The boys have eaten breakfast."

Zachary knocked on the master bedroom door. Regi grabbed her briefcase, and she arrived in the kitchen.

"Where are my little kings?" the loving mother beckoned as she rubbed her oldest son's natural curls—kissed her son's on their foreheads.

"I'm your King Mansa Musa," Isaiah said to his mother.

"Oh really?" Regi smiled as she realized that he had been reading his African history books that she had given him for Christmas.

"Yes, Momma. He was the emperor I read about in the books you gave me," he took a big bite of toast. With his mouth full—eager to share, "He was known to be the richest person who ever lived—"

Regi, all about manners, however intrigued by his enriched liking regarding his heritage, cut him off. "Don't talk with your mouth full sweetie. Yes, you're right—when you get some of that money, you're going to take care of your momma, right?" She lovingly ran her hands through his curly fro.

"Always, mom," his dimples flexed as he chewed his breakfast.

"How are you Isaac—what are you looking at on your phone? You know we don't allow that at the table—"

"Mom, it's El Corazón."

"*El*—what?"

"You know babe, it's the WWE wrestler—the boys just love watching him battle."

"No watching WWE right now, especially not before school. Put your phone away so you can finish your breakfast, or we are going to battle young man—" Regi lovingly kissed the top of her son's head, he was surprised by his mother's constant shying away from WWE.

Regi took a bite of a piece of buttery toast.

"Mom, can I get a tattoo?"

"What? You know better than that—"

"But mom, El Corazón has one on his back, it's a bible verse Psalms 19: 1-2. That would be so cool…"

"No, and no! Don't even ask again," Regi scolded as she finished her breakfast.

"That's all you're going to eat, babe? I can make the *Zach Special*; an egg with some bacon between that toast. You know how I do?"

Regi touched her stomach. "I need to cut back on calories. *Zach Special* or not, I've got to get this weight off," Regi said as she caressed the lateral aspect of her thick thighs in her tailor-made suit.

"I like you, *thickums,*" Zachary said, kissing Regi on her cheek, then reached around her waist.

Their kids appeared to be grossed out by their parent's display of affection.

The Hinson family is a pure reflection of joy in their welcoming kitchen, with scrabble letter large tiles that all spelled out their names over the breakfast table—in the center, *The Hinson's.*

PING!

"Who's texting you this early?" Zachary leaned into his wife, glaring over her shoulder.

Regi let out a huge sigh,

:Hey cousin, I'm in a bind, I have a court appearance, can you help your favorite cousin out!—Roscoe

"It's Roscoe," Regi shook her head, "I don't have time for his shenanigans. He needs to quit *riding dirty,* then he won't have these types of problems—"

"Just ignore him, you can't help people who don't want to help themselves—always in a mess. I'll handle *it* for you, you need to focus on your hearing today. Let me see what I can do. Besides, whatever he is involved in now, is hindered by his rap sheet that is as long as a grocery receipt," Zachary joked as he scooted his family towards the garage.

"Thanks babe, come on boys, let's get going," she beckoned to the boys as she pecked Zach's cheek *goodbye.*

The boys piled into the car, her eldest son jumped into the front seat and reached for the radio knob. Regi was startled by the *Gangsta Rap* blasting through her speakers. She looked over at *D.J. Isaac*—he sat in the passenger seat, not missing a beat. Shock spread across her face, realizing that her young son knew every lyric.

"Oh, no, Isaac, you're way too young for this," she said as she started to flip the station.

The boys pleaded for her to turn it back, but she found a classic Hip Hop station playing the legendary Sugar Hill Gang. She began to spit the rhymes—her boys stared in awe of their mother pretending to be in a self-proclaimed rap battle, while they nodded their heads.

Regi looked back, putting the car in REVERSE and started to pull out of the driveway, "Momma, stop!" shrieked Isaac—she slammed on the brakes.

"Boy, you scared me. What is it?" Regi exclaimed, grasping her heart at the alarm in his voice.

"There's a puppy," he said softly.

Regi shifted the car back into PARK, turned off the engine, put the emergency brake on. She jumped out of the car, her eyes widened as she looked down, inspecting the back of the vehicle.

"Isaac, I don't see anything. Where is he? You said you saw a dog?"

Whimpering drew her attention underneath the car, behind the tire.

"Hey, little fella—"

Regi put out her hand so he could smell her palm. The dog slowly crept up to her. He was a purse pup with a bountiful fur coat. He walked right into Regi's hands; she held him close—he licked her chin.

"Well, well, well. Where is your collar? You must belong to somebody, with your cute self," she said as she got back into the car with the puppy in hand.

Her boys totally geeked out. "Momma, can we keep him? Can I hold him?"

The dog jumped from her hands—pranced around the car as if he was totally at home.

"Yes, Mom. I think he likes us. He's peeing on the floor mat," Isaiah rendered.

"No way, not in my Benz S-series—you little stinker. Pick him up, boys. Here are some wipes, let's clean up this mess!"

"Too late! He let it all out, Mom."

The boys let out a phantom laugh that enveloped the car. Though she wanted to be pissed, Regi could not help but join into the contagion of pure childhood joy.

They arrived at the school drop-off line waiting for their turn to depart, however before leaving the car, the boys pleaded in unison, "Mom, can we keep him?"

"No, he belongs to someone. No one that I know of on our block has this kind of dog. I'll check with the HOA guy. He knows about all the pets in the entire neighborhood—he'll know. If there's no news there, I'll take him by the vet up the street and see if he has a microchip. That'll tell us who the owner is. Don't worry; we'll find out who he belongs to."

"But, Mom, we want to keep him—"

"Boys, he's going to be fine. Grab your backpacks, get to class before the bell rings. Besides, I'm sure his owners are missing him. If he was your dog, and you'd lost him you'd want him back—right? So that's what I'm going to do today; make sure he gets back home. That is the right thing to do."

41

"Maybe we can get a reward?" Isaiah asked, his eyes saw dollar signs.

"Reward or not, we're getting him back to his family. You both sticking your lips out will not make us keep him."

The boys got out of the car, but not before petting the troublemaking pup one last time.

"Get on up here in the front seat, *Troublemaker*."

The puppy followed commands as if he'd been a part of the family a long time.

Regi began to make phone calls and send text messages at stoplights.

The phone rang; it was Zachary.

"Hey, baby. Did your brief work out?"

"I haven't been gone long enough to get to the office. Besides, I have a stop to make."

BARK! BARK!

"What the hell is that?"

"Well, I have a passenger accompanying me today."

"A dog? Are you serious?"

"It's the cutest pup. You can tell he's been well taken care of. After my meetings, I'll take him to that vet near the house. I'm sure he has a microchip or dog tracker or something—"

"Regi, you have court today. You don't have time for a dog!"

"He's small, he'll fit in my work bag. What can go wrong? I grew up around dogs, I know how to handle them."

Regi arrived at her first appointment of the day. The building was tall and wide. She made it up to the 12th floor, however not before she made sure the *Little Troublemaker* was stroked all the way up the elevator in her eel-skin Birkin bag. Regi stood outside the door that always seemed a little too big—as it represented something that she despised, nevertheless it was something she had to do. The nameplate of the door read: Dr. Sophia Clark, M.D—PhD. Inside, Dr. Sophia Clark, psychiatrist psychologist, seated in an opulent Queen Anne armchair, holding her Tiffany & Co. ballpoint pen, twirling it in her apple red-dipped fingernails with lip lacquer to match. The office was sleek and upscale.

In no time, Regi was laid out on the chaise lounge in her Yves Saint Laurent suit, staring at the ceiling, all glammed up and looking totally out of place.

"Regina, your lip color is beautiful. Just the right amount of sheer lipstick with a little shine. It adds a spark to you," Dr. Clark attempted to connect with her client.

"Why, thank you, Doc," Regi responded *with attitude* as she defiantly folded her arms in an upright position on the couch.

Dr. Clark professionally left a pregnant pause, giving Regi time to decompress—to get a little more comfortable.

"So, you're continuing to have the same dream for the past several months? What do you think your dreams mean?"

Hesitantly, as it was clear Regi was not willing participant in the exercise, she was prompted to answer for fear of the consequences. Judge Reynolds was already down her back—she was skating on thin ice with him.

Namaste Regi, relax…

She bit her long-stay lacquered Ombre coral lip, realizing that her defiance could get reported back to the court system, if she handled these intervention sessions incorrectly.

"First, I still don't know why I'm here. However, since you're all up in my business, my dreams could be caused by the simple fact that I'm doing way too much these days—"

"I see. Go on—"

BARK! BARK!

Dr. Clark stood up, pulled her glasses down over her nose, seemingly irritated by the surprise guest. "You brought a dog in here?"

"He's a stray. I'm taking him to the vet to see about a microchip after my hearing today."

With a shaking hand, Regi reached into her purse to calm the pup, she brought him out of her purse, laying him on her chest. Surprisingly the counselor suddenly appeared to be at ease from witnessing the pup nestled into her trunk.

The scene was endearing to Dr. Clark, she made a note on her legal pad. "Regina, continue please, you better be glad I love dogs. I have a pup of my own, but I don't allow clients to bring dogs' in here. Employees only can bring pups here on *Bring Your Dog to Work Day."*

"Gotcha!"

Dr. Clark leaned in to listen more. "Tell me more about your dreams."

"Well, I've been pulled in so many directions recently, all of that swirling motion seems to seep into my dreams nightly, making me feel like my life is *a tornado*," Regi shared with a sigh, looking down at her right hand where *the scar* was, she attempted to hide the aged horrific marking on her hand, paranoia set in as usual as she felt wherever she was this marking on her drew attention, she reflected,

I heard a pastor say one day, that our scars are what make us unique, that God knows us by our scars. Well this scar is one that haunts me to infinity, it reflects the biggest weight I've juggle all my life, no Mederma, cocoa butter, airbrush makeup or laser treatment could erase the symbol of pure terror that was branded on me years ago.

Dr. Clark shifted gears in her questioning, repositioned her body in her seat, she sensed Regi's discomfort. "First, calm down. Tornados in this part of the country are extremely rare, so you don't have anything to worry about. Do you feel like the issues with your mother-in-law recently are playing more of a role in these dreams?"

Regi glanced over to the bookshelf where two pictures of baby ultrasounds were encased in a frame tucked behind some medical and psychological books.

I didn't know that Dr. Clark had kids? Regi redirected attention from her bewildered self,

"Dr. Clark, you have children?"

An emptiness came over Dr. Clark, she snapped her fingers at Regi,

"Regi, you care to answer my question? Do you feel like the issues with your mother-in-law recently are playing more of a role in these dreams, lately?"

"Definitely, I'm sure. This is the story of my life. Everybody keeps adding more and more weight on me. To the point where sometimes my head swirls, moreover I feel like I can't breathe. I don't know what to do; I can't keep blaming everything on my mother-in-law. Last week I cussed out another Associate Judge again. To top it all off, I almost got ejected from my oldest son's soccer tournament because of a *whack* call that the ref made—Zachary is about to take my keys away due to a recent road rage incident. Look, Doc, I'm way out of control—"

Regi stated with panic in her voice, she held the pup tight.

Dr. Clark went into her curio, grabbed a small bag of doggie treats—handed Regi a couple.

Regi smiled as she fed the *Little Troublemaker.*

"What's his name?"

"Not sure; no tag. Since he pissed in my Benz, *Troublemaker* is what I've called him today."

"Oh, how cute. However, surely you can think of a more positive name than that. A name is who you will become—"

Regi smirked, clapped back quickly. "Look, Dr. Clark, don't try to psychoanalyze me about a dog that's not even mine."

"Regi, when you're in here, all you ever do is talk about work. There's clearly an imbalance—what about your spiritual life?"

Regi clenched her jaw, "Trust me, you don't want to go there with me—"

Dr. Clark put her hand on her temple, she wanted Regi to become transparent feeling that this may be the culprit of Regi's behavior. There was a pregnant pause that lingered in the room,

"Dr. Clark, I guess I had faith long ago—you know when I was a little kid in Sunday school. However, that same God that died on the cross for our sins, somehow let my brother get ripped from my hands. I just don't know—"

Dr. Clark struggled with her capability with all of her training to come up with an appropriate logical response for the judge,

"You know, God is a good God. He is a God of love—"

Regi interrupted, "When I returned home after the traumatic event that happened with my brother, it appeared that the whole town looked at me with judgmental eyes, especially the church folk. I did not expect pity, but I expected more of Christians—"

Regi wept, while she stroked the pup.

Dr. Clark, handed Regi more Kleenex, stroked her arm as she thought,

We are finally having a breakthrough here—thank God!

"Dr. Clark, let's change the subject please. Because as soon as I started to have faith again as an adult, I overheard some pastors negotiating how they were going to split *the pot* 80:20, for one of the pastors being a guest speaker. How can I have faith in that?"

"Regi, first let me tell you that I hear you. Second, that I empathize with everything that you have gone through. However, what you have shared with me, has everything to do with people, how they have treated you or mishandled you. These are not the actions of God! Trust me, God loved you so much that he died on the cross for your sin's—"

Regi sat up on the chaise lounge, "I have not been to church in a long time—"

I know God is not pleased with me for that.

Dr. Clark angelically smiled, "God will meet you where you are. You don't need to go to church to have an encounter with God—"

"Dr. Clark, I'm not going to ask you again, switch the subject or I'm leaving right now!"

Dr. Clarks chest flustered in angst that she crossed the psychological spiritual line. Not wanting Regi to leave, she obliged,

"Regi in the last session, we talked about you being isolated— lacking socially. Do you ever get out? Have a little fun outside of work and your home life?"

Regi shrugged. "No time."

"What about any good girlfriends? Girls night out needs to be on your calendar. They are a must, second to date night. What university did you say you went to again?"

Regi pulls her head up from the sofa, with authority and professes proudly, "H.U."

"You know!" Dr. Clark smirked back at her junior alumni.

"Our Howard bond is true to the bone; I know you have some girlfriends that you keep in touch with—"

Regi interrupted,

"There was a group of us HBCU grads that gathered frequently. It's been a while since we met up; you know how it is?" Regi said in a reminiscent way while aimlessly stroking the dog as he nibbled on the treats.

Dr. Clark pulled open a desk drawer and grabbed a book: *Think Like a Weight Breaker, Not Like a Weight Taker*.

"I have some homework for you to do. It's all about doing the work. If you did not prepare for a litigation, you would have no shot at winning a case, right? This is so with life. We must prepare to do the work. This workbook has assisted me. I have used it to assess myself, to learn about my momentum type. It has helped me tremendously—I'm a *Reasoner*. Simply put, this book helped me make changes in my life towards my goals. I've had double fold losses in my life; therefore I needed a way to have self-enrichment. By doing the exercises in this book, I'm making strides. The daily downloads have been very impactful."

Dr. Clark handed Regi the book, which she hesitantly accepted in her manicured hand.

"Regi, I have a sense that we haven't even scratched the surface with you. Moreover, I believe that you're *The Juggler*, which is described in the book."

Regi stood up, holding the book and looking at the cover, without even thumbing through the book, declined the offer.

:Judge Regi, get your ass to the courthouse now—the deliberation is due!—Maxine S.

Regi fumbled with her phone to read an urgent text in one hand, with *The Troublemaker* in the other. "I have to get to court!"

Dr. Clark attempted to continue the session as Regi frantically gathered her Birkin bag with Troublemaker nestled inside, responding to the urgency of the text.

"Well, if you won't read this, how do you think we can solve your issues, Regi?"

"We don't solve *this*. This is my life, that's just what it is! There's no book that can solve *this*. Weight Breaker, my ass! This is a bunch of *bull!*"

Regi's eyes zeroing in on Dr. Clark's apparent expanding waistline, her stomach bulging more than usual through her black St. John knit pant suit,

Regi slammed the book down on the table,

47

"Weight Breaker, for real sis. We both look like we need to break some weight!" Infuriated, Regi slammed the door.

Dr. Clark's shocked hand rubbed her abdomen, her brow winced. She sat in her chair, as she watched the back of Regina's presence leave her office. She picked up her Tiffany teal blue pen, pondered for a few seconds about the crude disposition of the judge.

How dare she make a mockery of me, when I tried to do each session to encourage her?

Does she not realize that the weights of her past, can haunt her future?

How can I make a breakthrough with her?

I have to tread lightly, because I don't want to undo all of the progress that we've made.

Despite not making much headway, I'm optimistic that we can make improvement in the weights that are in her life.

Moreover, how she approaches them...

PROGRESS NOTE:

Anger Management Session for Judge Regina Hinson:

No improvement! Progress is stagnant.

Recommendations to Judge Reynolds:

Additional sessions for Judge Regina Hinson—*ASAP!*

COMMENTS/RECOMMENDATIONS:

At the next meeting, check and see if Regi is willing to work on her faith intelligence.

THE COURTHOUSE

Regi arrived at the courthouse, walked up the cobblestone steps.

"Regi, where have you been? Chief Judge Reynolds allowed you some grace by pushing our case back on the docket. I told him you had a family emergency," Maxine replied nervously.

"Family emergency? Really? Why did you say that? I'm not late. I'm already skating on thin ice with him—"

"When I didn't hear from you, I didn't know what to do," her assistant said as she recessed into her skin like a turtle in a tortoise shell.

"I was at a court-mandated appointment. I'm a little late but not *push the motherfucking docket back* late. You're tripping," Regi said, blowing off steam.

Her assistant, Maxine, could tell that Regi was internally wanting to *knock her block off*, but she couldn't hold back the words trying to escape from her mouth,

"Well, get your head right—there have been some *doozies*— two overturns. So, I believe that our odds have gone from eighty-twenty to possibly forty-sixty—not in our favor. You have the brief?"

"Yes, here it is," Regi pulled out the brief.

BARK!

"Regi, what the hell? When did you get a dog?" Maxine timidly reached down towards the purse, almost getting nipped. "I should take *the water rat* or whatever *it* is. You can't take *it* into court!"

"I got this. Help me with the door."

The courtroom was cold—full of Regi's peers: judges. At the bench was Judge Reynolds, one of Regi's arch nemesis. The assistant recognized Regi's concern once she met eyes with a judge that she was not expecting,

"Don't choke, Judge Regi, you've got this!" Maxine attempted to encourage.

"Oh shit," Regi said under her breath as her eye's locked with the stern judge who held her fate in his hands—clearly she was mortified.

"Judge Regina Hinson, please approach the bench," Chief Judge Reynolds commanded her, she tiptoed forward.

"Yes, your honor," Regi started with a slight quiver in her voice.

"Where is the brief?"

Regi handed the bench memorandum to the bailiff attempting to temper her shaking hand, who handed it over to Judge Reynolds.

He looked over his glasses. "This doesn't look complete. Judge Hinson, I expected more of you!"

Regi's body language told it all as she shrunk, slightly hung over from the night before, still contemplating the night terrors, coupled with an anxious aura that spilled from her pores. To top the disaster all off, she'd self-declared that she did not need anger management—her blood boiled with defeat along with embarrassment that her brief was inadvertently partially deleted.

I'm up shit's creek now! She choked, yielding any response.

"I will give you forty-eight hours to get this brief completed, then we can pursue the next steps—"

Judge Reynolds picked up his gavel and pounded it down several times loudly—*doing way too much*, when one pound of the gavel would have done the job.

This startled *Troublemake*r. Before Regi noticed, the pup sprang out of her bag scurried onto the litigation room floor. He slid under tables, pounced up onto seats, through the pews as the aged Bailiff flailed around trying to catch the quick pup. *Troublemaker* leapt onto a desk, up onto the Chief judge's platform, where he looked Judge Reynolds square in the eye.

"Don't you do it, you little damn dog," Judge Reynolds yelled as Troublemaker began to circle clockwise, round-and-a-round, until he sniffed the perfect location and then he squatted.

There was Troublemaker at the edge of Judge Reynolds bench, taking a *Bonafede shit*. When he was done, he wagged his tail, met eyes with Regi, as she bent down he jumped back into her arms, as if nothing happened. Mortified of what just occurred, sure that she would be disbarred, kissing that Associate Chief Judgeship goodbye, she stood frozen.

The litigation room was in absolute disarray—papers everywhere, chairs toppled over, with a pile of shit on top of the bench of Judge Reynolds.

"Judge Hinson, to my chambers now!" Judge Reynolds yelled out as fumes of fury spewed from his now bloodshot eyes.

With the courthouse in her rearview mirror, Regi said, "Troublemaker, you really did it. I barely escaped being in contempt of court. I had to pay a small fine and I still have to take you to the vet. I need to get you back to your home because you've totally tilted my world even more off its axis today." Regi moaned. "I still have to tell Zachary that I almost got disbarred and lost my opportunity of being appointed as associate chief judge. And my brief, did not exude the excellence that I'm known for—"

The pup's eyes looked up at Regi as if it knew exactly what she was talking about, that calmed Regi's spirit, to have a non-judgmental listening ear.

She pulled into the parking lot of the veterinarian.

"Hello, my name is Regina Hinson. May I speak with the veterinarian, please?"

"I'm the veterinarian. We're a little short-staffed today. How may I help you?"

"We found this dog this morning."

"This morning? Where?"

"A couple of blocks from here. At my home. Not sure where this little guy belongs, I wanted to make sure that he made it back to his owner. I figured with how well-kept he looked; he should have a microchip." Regi picked the pup up, snuggled him. "Besides, this little fella almost cost me my law license today—didn't you, Troublemaker?"

"Come here, little fella," the dog went quickly into the veterinarian's arms, the assessment began.

"I have some good news. We found the owner. Here is their name. Do you know this person?"

Regi's eyes enlarged when she read the name on the contact information. "Wait, do you mean *The Abigail Lancaster?* Why would her dog be in my neighborhood? I would think that she lived in some type of mansion on a hill somewhere—she's famous."

"Here is the contact information, how would you like to proceed? We can keep the pup here or you can make outreach. In the system, we have the consent form signed to share the contact information with the person that finds the puppy in case it was lost."

"I'll take the info along with the pup," said Regi.

Troublemaker jumped back into Regi's purse, wagging his fluffy tail, nestled himself next to her Louis Vuitton makeup bag. She smiled into his precious mischievous eyes. As crazy as today was, he was an absolute slice of joy in her day. Besides, how could it get worse? Almost losing her brief, going to Dr. Clark—who clearly thought she had anger-management issues—amid the *shit-ca-pade* with Judge Reynolds.

I know Judge Reynolds is going to make sure I am not appointed as Chief Judge—I can't take it…

Regi felt unbridled, but deep down in her core, that was her natural state. She started to walk back to her car, but suddenly started to feel like she was forgetting something. Out of nowhere, she was reminded when she received a text from her mother-in-law.

:Regi, this is Suzanne. I'm sure you forgot about the bake sale for the boys' school. I can take care of it; I know you don't have the cooking gene.—The Queen

Oh no she didn't! If she was not Zachary's mom, she would make me catch a case.

:Thanks, but I got it, Mrs. Suzanne!—Regi H.

She better back the hell up. With the day I've had, I'm not in the mood.

:No store-bought goodies for my grand-babies, Regi! From scratch. Just for clarity, please no Pop-Tarts. Remember that foolishness you presented two years ago for their bake sale? You would think you had no common sense, girl. —The Queen

:Suzanne, I said I got it!!!—Regi H.

Regi could feel her blood boiling. Her *monster-in-law* really knew how to get under her skin.

Just for the record, the Pop-Tart idea for the bake sale a couple of years ago was a complete hit. Each pack sold for a dollar, making a killing for the Parent Teacher Association, so go straight back to hell where you came from! Regi thought to herself, *popping* her collar.

Troublemaker sat quietly in the front seat, as if he had belonged to the Hinson family forever. Regi got a little misty eyed as she dialed the number for Abigail Lancaster.

"Hello, this is Judge Regina Hinson, I've found your puppy."

Just then the clouds came rushing in.

"My puppy? That damn girl!" Abigail echoed through the phone.

"No, the puppy isn't a girl."

"I know what kind of puppy I have, missy!" Abigail snapped back.

Well, damn. I had heard Abigail Lancaster was an outright trip, but with the day I've had, I have cuss words on deck, ready and

CHRONICLES OF THE WEIGHT BREAKERS

waiting, so she better calm down. I'm trying to be a good Samaritan here.

"Well, ma'am, what I was trying to say is that I found your puppy this morning. Our neighborhood veterinarian obtained the chip information. I'm out and about, I can meet you to give you your pup—"

"What side of town are you on?" Abigail judgmentally whipped.

"Midtown," Regi replied, as if her tail was tucked between her legs.

"Perfect. Do you know Gadsden's Grocery?" Abigail questioned.

"Yes, I know it well. I have some shopping to do for a bake sale for our son's school—"

"Yeah, yeah, yeah, meet me there at seven. Don't be late!"

Regina buckled up Troublemaker—took a deep breath.

"Well, that was interesting, but I bet you're used to her— little cute pup?" she asked Troublemaker, whose eyes twinkled at her. She turned up the radio, scrolled through a few stations, landing on something intriguing,

THE CHRONICLES OF THE WEIGHT BREAKERS PODCAST

Hi, Weight Breakers!

We're going to get really deep, so buckle up. You may be a little startled that I don't have any guests today, but we have a lot of work to do. So, let's get to it! As you already know, this is an interactive podcast, where I need to know what my weight breakers are thinking. Start commenting, and we will get started. Wow, you all are already online; that's amazing, I see you...

"Oh, no. Not this crap again. This is the lady who wrote the book Dr. Clark wanted me to read. I don't have time for that. Actually, silence is better. I need to soothe my nerves from this crazy day," Regi said as she turned the radio off.

She took a deep breath, looked over at Troublemaker, who was all too content in the passenger seat.

4

THE PODCAST

"THE THREE INTELLIGENCES"

[LIVE WITH *"CASSIDY GENTRY"?]*

Dr. T. was in her home office, as the morning sunrise blazoned bright with brilliancy atop the hills. She set up her tripod—she could do that blindfolded; this was her niche.

"I need more lighting. Yes, that's it," she pivoted the angle of the circle light.

Still a little groggy from her late night, she ventured towards the kitchen to make herself a cup of *joe* to start her day. Her eyes twinkled as she unpeeled the note off that was taped to the Keurig:

```
Mom,

I'm headed to basketball practice. I'll text you
             when I get there.

                  —Your Son.
```

She smiled, her heart filled with endearment as she peered out the kitchen window, spotting her son backing down the angled driveway.

"Lord, protect my baby," was her prayer.

She had always been protective, more than a helicopter mom...She called herself a *TANK MOM*-beyond being a momma bear—someone who would blow you to smithereens behind her baby.

In the kitchen, scanning her pantry, she wondered what she should eat. She glanced over her shoulder at the cinnamon rolls with white icing adorned with glistening caramelized walnuts in the glass cake top.

The devil is a lie. No, I shouldn't, she thought, grabbing the column container with the man on the front that looked like George Washington.

Moments later, she was stirring a bowl of steel-cut oatmeal topped with blueberries.

"I need more fiber in my diet. This should be a great start. Fasting labs are in a couple of weeks; I'm trying to get ahead of the game," she chuckled to herself, after completing her hot cereal.

What should I talk about today on the podcast?

Sparrow and I covered the mindset along with the definitions of proverbial versus physical weights of life.

That session was on fire.

The Weight Breaker followers are still raving about that one, they especially loved the momentum types. It would be nice if I could drop some more nuggets about THE CHRONICLES OF THE WEIGHT BREAKERS CONFERENCE that is upcoming.

The Intelligences would be good, to fit in there as well.

Dr. T. looked at her notes, went to the section to talk about the Intelligences.

Yep, the Intelligences; that's it.

Let me enlighten the Weight Breaker Posse on the Intelligences.

Let's get this party started.

"Oh no, blueberries all up in my teeth," she looked at her reflection in her monitor," she grabbed her toothbrush, *going to town* to remove every evidence of the *monster breakfast* she had devoured, before freshening up her face. She closed her eyes, to say the prayer that she always did prior to starting her podcast...

"Lord, thank you for taking me on the steadfast journey of being a Weight Breaker, no longer a weight taker. Because of your grace, I know that each day, I'm standing under the promises that you God have given me. You have provided me with ALL the tactics I need to break the weights of life. Thank you for strengthening me to approach each issue: boldly, resiliently, encouraged, abundant, kind; elevated and restored! Thank you for allowing my intelligence's to shine bright, so I will be your servant and draw weight takers to me—to encourage them to break the weights in their lives. It is not by accident that you called me from your magnificent existence, to be here on earth, so I can impact the world. In Jesus' mighty matchless name, Amen."

She went LIVE.

Hi, Weight Breakers!

We're going to get really deep, so buckle up. You may be a little startled that I don't have any guests today, but we have a lot of work to do. So, let's get to it! As you already know, this is an interactive podcast, where I need to know what my weight breakers are thinking. Start commenting, and we will get started.

Wow, you all are already online; that's amazing, I see you.

:We are ready, Dr. T. Let's get to work.—Fawn P.

:Got my journal, I'm ready to take notes!—A Loyal Fan.

Okay, ladies, I see you! Let's get to it. When we're born, we are graciously allotted a certain number of days for our earthly assignment, that is such a blessing. Whether you think so or not, you have innate intelligence. We are all born with several intelligences. There are natural instincts installed in your being from birth, with time they mature in unique ways. To effectively walk out your earthly assignment, it is important to recognize, hone in on, appreciate, moreover nurture those intelligences. Today, we will talk about the four categories of intelligence that are needed to navigate through the beautiful nuances of this life: Vision Intelligence, Faith Intelligence, Resilience Intelligence—as an added bonus, Spiritual Intelligence. Each category needs to be worked on for a person to be their very best to walk into their purpose.

Let's break down the various Intelligences, learning how we implement them in our lives. When disappointments start to outweigh the positive aspects of our lives, Vision Intelligence acts as our compass. It will highlight what you will and won't allow to infiltrate your space—taking up your mental bandwidth. Once you're aware of your own Vision Intelligence, you will be able to put those unacceptable energies into their place—eliminating them. That way you can focus on what's important. When we actively work on Vision Intelligence we are more easily able to heal from past disappointments, releasing them—especially if they don't align with the vision God has for our lives. Knowing this will equip you with the tools to recognize what should remain in your space versus what you need to remove.

:Dr. T. what is the benefit of Vision Intelligence?—Penelope K.

Penelope, I'm so glad you asked that question. It's like shooting an arrow at a specific target. You know your purpose is to hit the bullseye, so you'll always know what is the most important to you as opposed to what's not. So you have to have a vision of hitting the bullseye, even before you pull the bow back on the arrow.

Overall, if you haven't figured out your purpose, you'll be somewhat scattered as you spend your energy on a thousand different things; none of which will bring truly outstanding results. Let's think about Vision Intelligence as this exercise: Imagine your consciousness is standing at the peak of a towering mountain, shoulder-to-shoulder with the Almighty. You look down onto all the land below you, moreover your life. A profound question is that, would God be pleased with what you are putting your energy into? And what you put your energy into is directly related to your vision for your life or lack thereof.

Furthermore, your very own consciousness is able to see the real Y-O-U by the paths you choose and the choices you make. Vision Intelligence is that skillset where you're able to yield optimal understanding because you see the path before you, even before you get there. It allows you to prepare for your destiny. However, you must also do the work—you can't say you want to make it to the N.F.L. without ever picking up a football.

:Touchdown. I got it!—Penelope K.

One of my favorite Bible verses to illustrate Vision Intelligence is, *"Write the vision and make it plain,"* Habakkuk 2:2.

:Me too.—Penelope K.

:This is an interesting spin on how we view our vision. But what is the real benefit? Rachel R.

Rachel, the real benefit is training your mind to spot pitfalls before you have to figure out a way out of them. Your ability to use Vision Intelligence can be the difference between life and death.

:My targets in life are different from what my family has for me.—Chaka B.

Chaka, hang in there. Pray about your vision. Create a vision board. Also include action steps to help you focus on what you want for you. This is your life along with your vision. That may not always align with what your family sees for you, nonetheless that's okay.

Next is Faith Intelligence. We've all heard, *faith is the substance of things hoped for and the evidence of things not seen*—that's in the Bible.

:Yep, I learned that in Sunday School years ago.—Aretha W.

:Good idea. I will make a vision board.—Chaka B.

Great, Chaka. I make a vision board yearly. It helps me keep my aspirations and visions for my life at the forefront of my mind. Ms. Aretha, my roots are also in the church, one thing Minister Brown would say that stuck with me is, *Work out that faith muscle!* Ladies, I have a question for you, what happens when you don't exercise a muscle?

:It gets flabby as hell. Jiggling everywhere.—Chaka B.

:Your muscles can shrink.—Aretha W.

You're both right—muscles that are not used can begin to atrophy, rendering themselves useless. We must exercise our faith daily because we need to be healthy to allow us to step into new realms, embracing our full potential.

:This is good stuff.—Brenda P.

:I like this analogy. I have faith, but many times when things get tough, I freak out. I want to know more about Faith Intelligence. Please share.—Charlotte I.

Weight Breakers, when we think about the real definition of Faith Intelligence, it is the capacity to be aware of, control, and express one's faith. People have different meanings of faith. However, to me, it means trusting in God for all things.

:Yes, the verse that comes to mind is: *The Lord is my rock.* Luke 1:37.—Dwan H.

Dwan, that verse speaks to me. We have heard time and time again that faith is the substance of things hoped for and the evidence of things not seen. Which, simply put, is that you have to have hope that you're able to handle the proverbial/physical weights of life. In addition, I can just about guarantee that you've had to step out on faith to attain every accomplishment in your life. Whether it's getting a new job, or being the first in your family to go to college, making it through the ranks to get something accomplished requires faith.

:I need to work out my faith. Who am I kidding? My body too, lol.—Kasia C.

Kasia, you're right on target. Each day when we awaken, we must celebrate the opportunity of exercising our faith, while stepping into our greatness. It is by our faith that we are able to create a plan to complete the goals that we are destined for.

So let's think about the benefit of Faith Intelligence. If you don't have clear Faith Intelligence, it's easier to fall off and stay derailed. You go about building your faith intelligence muscle by praying, meditating—serving the higher power. In my view, when you build up that faith muscle, you're able to have a closer relationship with God, help serve, minister to people in a greater way. A strong *F.I.* will rid your life of worry from the many weights of the world because God already has it under control.

:I appreciate that we are not alone in this, thank you. What is the 3rd Intelligence? I believe you said there are 3?—Stephanie H.

Stephanie, you're correct, there are three intelligences—you're absolutely not alone in this. We have God's grace; we must have faith to seek His guidance to get us through! We must have the Vision, the Faith, and the third Intelligence is Resilience.

:Resilience, I need some more of that! Just getting ready to start my bike ride. I love listening in while I ride my bike through the park.—Fawn P.

Sis, break that weight! I love that you're getting in physical activity while listening to the podcast. Fawn, you are not alone. We could all use a little more resilience. The proper definition of resilience is the capacity to quickly recover from difficulties. I define Resilience Intelligence as the ability to be prepared to bounce back before something occurs that is not planned.

:Wow, I was just talking about how all my life I have had to bounce back. Situation after situation...—A Loyal Listener

Loyal Listener we love you, we are here for you. I urge you to cling to Romans 8:18, *For I reckon, the sufferings of this present time, shall not be compared to the glory that will be revealed in us.* Your Resilience Intelligence may already be at a great level!

:Thank you for that encouragement.—A Loyal Listener

Weight Breakers, I will eternally refer to you in this manner, I speak this into existence for each of you. What life has taught me is that there are two types of people in this world: those that are presented with a mountain in their life—when they see the mountain, they're discouraged, afraid and filled with despair. They see the mountain as too challenging to overcome, they doubt their abilities, succumbing to fear. I equate that kind of person with being a weight taker.

There is another type of person that sees the mountain as a doorway to their success. Sure, they will have to climb the mountain, they may lose their footing sometimes, maybe even slipping all the way back down to the bottom of the mountain, nonetheless they get back up again! That is a weight breaker mentality, equated to Resilience Intelligence.

:Preach, sista. This is so true.—Amber S.

Amber, even though the path over the mountain is not smooth, a resilient person will overcome it. No matter how many ups and downs are thrown at them, they will prevail.

:Dr. T., this is good. I'm going to speak to those mountains in my life!—Xena R.

Xena, yes! Speak to those mountains. So, you may ask, are there benefits to Resilience Intelligence? You may be asking: *How do I go about developing a resilient soul?* Resilience is being able to find other ways of entry when *the doors of life* seem to have changed *the locks* on you. You may feel lost, but a resilient soul will look around for the open window, continuing to enter into their purpose. Always look for the open window. Being resilient allows you to continue to push forward—to quickly bounce back from setbacks. Your resiliency will be a witness, moreover a light for others as an inspiration of how to handle the weight of life.

:I love that perspective.—Cheryl M.

Cheryl, I do too. As you mature, you will understand the pure pricelessness of resilience. If you have not figured it out yet, I hope that you will by the close of this book. I want these resources to act as tools in *your arsenal* to level your perception, enhance your vision, to strengthen your faith. These are the foundations of human existence. Resilience is the *fuel* that you need to make the wheels of your life turn. More than anything else in life, you will have to be resilient.

:To be honest, this is really heavy. I was not brought up to change the way I think about life based on a book. I'm not sure if I'm a believer. I don't think that I can make a change like this; this may be a bit much. I'm not sure about all of this.—Raven U.

Raven, I hear you wholeheartedly. I'm not a psychologist or psychiatrist. However, I have seen these tactics change lives. I want to share these tips I've curated over the years to help women be at their best. When talking about Intelligences, I am simply highlighting what's already in you. These tactics can assist you through troubling circumstances that will occur in this life.

At the core of it all, we have to know that there are things that we will not have control over, yet what we can control is how we respond. That is where the Intelligences come into play. Enhancing these Intelligences that I've shared in *Think Like A Weight Breaker. Not Like A Weight Taker*, they will hopefully allow for deeper change within yourself.

New ways of thinking can be very difficult, cumbersome, and overwhelmingly hard. I often equate that type of change to grieving. You are letting go of an old mindset—it's okay to say goodbye to it. Not to disrespect anyone who has ever lost a loved one, but Kubler-Ross orchestrated The Five Stages of the Grief Cycle in the 1969 book, *On Death and Dying*. "Those are: denial, anger, bargaining, depression, and acceptance." In some instances, when a new thought process or change presents itself, each one of us can deal with it in a similar way.

I don't have a problem in this area of my life. (Denial)

How dare you think I have a problem in this area of my life? (Anger)

If I make some changes in this area in my life, then maybe things will get better. (Bargaining)

This is too overwhelming; I cannot make all of these changes in my life. (Depression)

Yes, I do need a new mindset to possibly make some meaningful change in my life. (Acceptance)

Many times, our thought processes are generational: *This is how my grandparents thought about this. This is how my parents thought about that. Therefore, this is how I think about that.* Technically, if the generational thought processes contribute positively to society, then there is nothing wrong with it. Nonetheless, there are some *weighted* thought processes that are passed down that are not kind. Still, I believe that we are placed on this earth to evolve—building upon the legacy of our ancestors to enrich our contribution to history.

:I have never thought about it like this. Wow, letting go of an old mindset can ignite grief. I never realized I could grieve old ways of thinking. Also, I do think I harbor some negative thoughts that have been passed down.—Mai C.

Mai, we have to let old baggage go. WEIGHT BREAKER, dig into your mind, body, and your spirit. Even if you do not have a *millionth* degrees, you have a skillset that is designed only for you! I'm so excited that you all were engaged in talking about these intelligent thought processes today. All of the information we talked about is in my new book, *Think Like a Weight Breaker. Not Like A Weight Taker*.

Just a quick recap, we got a good overview on each of the three Intelligences. We learned the benefits of the Intelligence types, provided an Intelligence exercise spot check, furthermore contemplated about how each Intelligence is implemented into our lives. I encourage you to look at the proverbial and physical weights of your lives through the lens of each Intelligence we discussed today. Lastly, drum roll please! It is now time for the drawing for the signed preview copy of my book, *Think Like A Weight Breaker. Not Like A Weight Taker.* The winner is, drum roll please—Fawn Paige!

Fawn, I hope you enjoy this resource, furthermore that you will use this book as a tool to help you to position yourself to do the work to Think Like a Weight Breaker. Not Like a Weight taker.

To all of you fabulous Weight Breakers out there, thank you for joining us today. We have some wonderful news coming down the pipeline soon! Until next time.

Love,

Dr. T.—The Weight Breaker

Dr. T. concluded the podcast, taking her bowl to the sink, washing it.

PING!!

She looked at her phone,

:Mom, I made it to practice.—Your Son.

:Praise God!—Dr. T.

:Mom, you worry too much. God's got me. I heard your podcast while driving to practice; you did *your thing!* Proud of you.—Your Son.

:Love you son, be careful. Text me when you leave the gym. Work on those *jumpers,* nail them free throws. I'm proud of you, baby.—Dr. T.

61

:Yes, ma'am. But mom, you've got to stop calling me baby, I'm a teenager now. Got to go, love you.—Your Son.

"God, please protect our children from dangers seen and unseen. Help them use all of their intelligences to navigate through this beautiful, but rough world that they are living in. I know they can! Amen," is every mother's prayer.

Little do they know, no matter how grown they become, they will always be our babies, Dr. T. thought to herself.

5

FAWN PAIGE

"THE MIRAGE"

[BALM TINT, WITH A DASH OF COLOR]

"Oh wow! I can't believe I won the autographed preview copy of *Think Like A Weight Breaker, Not Like A Weight Taker*, by listening in today. The Chronicles Of The Weight Breakers Podcast always gets me hyped to get ready to cycle through the park—the words of inspiration gets me focused. Watch out world—Fawn is here to break the weight!" she said, laughing to herself, as she placed her foot on her pedals as she left her home.

Fawn got a later than usual start to her morning because of some *late-night cyber stalking* that got carried away.

"I can't believe I was on *IG* all night watching my so-called *Boo* out in these streets. He told me that he was with his physical trainer for *extra* kinesiology therapy, but *lo and behold*, my DM's got flooded with photographic evidence that he was at the strip club. I swear, I couldn't spot a good man if Jesus came down from heaven putting a bow on His head. Along with an arrow pointing down to him that indicated—*hey Fawn, he's the one!*"

Fawn approached the park, only a few blocks away from her condo.

Maybe Dr. T. is right, I really ought to work on my Vision Intelligence.

Things have been rocky—I need to be the best version of myself for my daughter.

"Okay, Fawn, you can do it. Take this hill," she professed.

People scurried out of the way as Fawn went into overdrive to get up the hill in front of her. She was letting out all of her frustrations of being a woman scorned, on the pedals pounding the pavement below. Her neon athletic shoes moved methodically, thrusting in circles that would make any onlooker dizzy. Fawn's furrowed brow was all anyone needed to see to get out of her way. She was determined to make it up the hill. As she reached the top, she spotted an overweight lady jogging at a slow pace.

"Hang in there. I was where you are a while back. I know it's hard—"

The lady stopped, wiped her brow—smiled. "Yes, I'm trying one last time to get some weight off. If not, it's the lap band for me."

"Surgical options are good for those who need them. However, I was your exact build when I started. I know you can do it. Don't give up."

Fawn reached into the fanny pack that she carried when she rode, pulled out a flier for her spin cycle class, handing it to the determined woman. The lady thanked her, Fawn faded into the dust as she raced over the top of the hill, letting the morning breeze flow through her hair as she glided down.

The mention of her own weight loss journey caused a bit of anxiety to bubble to the surface. Fawn could remember how hard it was for her to navigate her own personal issues with her figure. As the cold breeze grazed her face, she couldn't help but to remember herself as a pudgy teen with a mountain of low self-esteem. She recalled as an outcast teenager, she drowned herself in the love of her Peruvian heritage by consuming all of the home cooked authentic delights such as Pollo a la Brasa, topping it off with drizzled Picarones. Then one day the dare came—

"Here comes Pudgy Donut Fawn, I bet you can't even turn a cartwheel," rang in her head just like yesterday from the popular cheerleaders who made her life a living hell during her teenage years.

What started out as a dare to try out for cheerleading, turned into my saving grace. With hard work, the weight began to fall off. To everyone's surprise, I made the varsity cheer squad. That "cartwheel dare" led me into the world of cheerleading, which caused me to earn a cheer scholarship to a D-1 school. Everyone wanted to know how I morphed from high school "Donut Fawn" into college cheerleader, then one of the leads on an NBA dance squad, but I chose to keep it a secret. It was not the healthiest way, but it kept me the size I needed to be to get what I needed to get. I needed an opportunity to better my life— I got it by any means necessary.

As her wheels spun faster, Fawn started to think of her time on the NBA cheer squad.

I miss the way the lights would halo over my body as I would look to the sky of the Superdome in my spandex leotard with my shoulder out. I looked good.

I'll never forget that moment when I caught the eye of soon-to-be NBA Hall of Fame inductee, Beckett Trent "B.T." Blaze, the number one NBA draft pick for the Kings. During their timeouts, he would watch my every move on the sidelines. Beckett would wander from city to city with the team, but I was the only one that got caught up in his whirlwind. I really thought he would "wife me"—simply, that was not the case. Even when my body was at its best, I was still disposable, just like a grocery paper bag.

Why did I sacrifice my own career for what I thought was love?

She pedaled faster through the park, almost hitting some joggers that were jogging way too slow, she was like an arrow that was shot towards the bullseye.

"My bad! Excuse me," she spat at the walkers behind her.

Taking on the hills and valleys of the community park— paralleling her own life. Her mind wandered back to the day she took the pregnancy test.

I wasn't thinking that I would get a ring when I called him to meet me on the beach to tell him that we were expecting. In my mind, I merely hoped for a modicum of respect— nothing more. What I got was something appalling, "It can't be mine!" How dare he? He was the only one I had been with. My blood boiled. I didn't know whether to scream, to cry, or to try my hardest to make him accept that he was indeed the father of my baby.

The denial destroyed me. Alyssa's father refused to claim her, even after the hundred percent confirmation of the paternity test and the court dates for child support. The ultimate humiliation was from the bloggers classifying me as a "gold digger." Worst of all, he had me removed from the one thing that I loved the most at the time—The Kings NBA cheer squad.

However, by God's grace, the league agreed to pay for my medical insurance for the delivery of the baby, up to one year after the delivery. After that, it was all on me. My family was in no way able to help me. Furthermore, they thought I was completely nuts for wanting to follow my dreams of being on a professional NBA dance squad.

To add insult to injury, when I told my family who the father of my baby was, instead of coming to my defense, they took every opportunity to brag about Beckett Trent "B.T." Blaze being my baby daddy. The weight of it all was unbearable.

As soon as I had my child. I got back on my feet, I walked into a fitness club noticing a help wanted sign—they needed a spin coach. This type of class wasn't something I was very familiar with, however with my athleticism they gave me a chance—a trial first class to teach.

After instructing the very first class, while they watched me from the back with a critical eye, they hired me on the spot. God is so good. At that point, I had it all mapped out. If it was going to be just Alyssa and I, I was going to make it work by any means necessary. My journey to self-love was a long winding road that eventually blossomed out of the collateral damage of that rattling ordeal.

Fawn returned to her block, she was floored looking at her watch,

Wow, that's my best time yet! Self-gratification exuded out of her pores.

She got up to her neighbor's door—knocked. The blue door swung open; a sleeping Alyssa was handed to Fawn.

"Every time I see her beautiful cherub face, I fall in love all over again. She makes it all worth it," she said to the helpful neighbor.

With Alyssa's little body cradled in hers, she walked a short distance home with Alyssa in one arm, her bike in the other.

"Hey sweet girl, when I get back home today mama's going to make you some Cajun shrimp pasta. I think I'll try those low carbohydrate noodles I picked up the other day. How does that sound?" Alyssa smiled while resting her head on her mother's chest, Fawn gently kissed her ringlets.

Trying to cut back on carbohydrates is a beast. Especially with my Louisianan mixed with my Peruvian culture. I love to eat—YOLO, with all that I am going through, I need to enjoy life to the fullest. I'll work the food off with my morning rides along with teaching spin.

After bathing, dressing her daughter, then feeding her baby girl, she dropped her off at Mrs. Mary's—Alyssa's babysitter.

Dressed in her spandex with the sheer netting on the sides, a blinged out halter top, with her hair in a messy bun, she peeled her banana to make sure she got potassium back in her system as she drove. Next to Fawn in the passenger seat was her preview signed copy of *Think Like A Weight Breaker. Not Like A Weight Taker.* The book nestled in her backpack. She was still geeked that she'd won it by listening to the podcast.

Off to teach my spin class I go! I'm on fire today!

Fawn entered the fitness studio, which was adorned with hardwood floors, mirrored walls, with mounted spin cycles in five rows of five. All twenty-five seats were set upon by women with different expressions on their faces. Some ready to *kick butt*, versus some so damn scared of what they were about to encounter that they were ready to run for the nearest exit. However, all eager fully committed Fawn Paige followers. She approached each of her classes as if it were her first day of school—with an unwavering youthful excitement.

They love my classes because, despite their sizes, I make sure they all feel at home. I work them out at their own fitness levels.

"Hello, everyone. I see a lot of familiar faces. It's also wonderful to see many new sister-friends in the room. Let's get fit, ladies! For the newbies in the building, I'm Fawn Paige, your fitness accountability partner. In this building, you are not a mother, not a wife, not a doctor, not a lawyer, not a teacher, not a stay-at-home wife, but you are a sister weight breaker! We are going to do this! There are no titles in this room; just sisterhood! You got that?"

The room went into pandemonium, with women jumping up and down eager to get on their stationary bicycles to start their spin class.

Fawn pressed PLAY to get the music system blasting.

"I'm a personal trainer, mostly everyone would describe me as upbeat, free-spirited, furthermore completely optimistic. Some recent events have rocked my world, nonetheless the only books that I read are fitness and health and wellness. However, my life coach recommended that I read this new book: *Think Like A Weight Breaker. Not Like A Weight Taker.* I just won a copy the other day by listening to the podcast. I'm so eager to read it. However, I'm an avid listener of The Chronicles Of The Weight Breakers Podcast, there was an epiphany. Knowing this, we all have a choice to either be weight breakers or weight takers. Now repeat after me, I'm a weight breaker!"

The ladies yelled in unison, "We are weight breakers!"

"That was cute, however I asked you to shout it out. Now let's take it up a notch, ladies. Let's go; let's ride. Before I came this morning, I rode five miles through the park. You can do this! Your mind space needs to be pure, sound, and uplifting. I've become conscious that I had been gaining *weight* for far too long—I needed to shed some of the proverbial weight of life. I had been allowing myself to be *The Mirage*, not being my true self. So, after I comprehended, I started taking inventory and taking action. I checked my connectivity and storage programming. Ladies, we are going to change the way we think, moreover, what we allow in our space!"

Fawn was pedaling in the spin class; her students were eagerly attempting to keep up with her dizzy feet. You could see the intensity in her eyes—she looked as perfect as could be. However, she was a single mother, whom the father of her child was not taking responsibility for. Moreover, she didn't have the support she needed from her family, which all weighed her down immensely. Despite that, she was an upbeat, free spirit and an optimistic, loving mother who strived to impart heroism in the women who dared to put themselves first by taking time out of their busy days to just *spin*.

When the class was over, she encouraged the women who were eager. However, they were now exhausted participants post workout.

"Ladies, I'm so proud of each of you! I will see you next week. Remember to make smart choices in your eating habits. Remember to get your water in. You can do this!"

Fawn wiped her brow, gathering her belongings as she communicated with the janitor who was sterilizing the equipment. She went to the central music monitor so she could turn it off.

One of the new patrons approached her, "Fawn, is it?"

"Yes, hello. How are you?" Fawn gave a welcoming smile, while she sipped her water.

"I'm good. I enjoyed the class," the woman replied as she held a Louis Vuitton oversized bag that looked all too familiar; a bag for travel—not for the gym.

"How did you enjoy the class?" Fawn asked, her towel now draped around her neck.

"I loved it. I'm trying to get fit for my upcoming wedding." The lady had svelte arms; pure cut biceps and triceps that she flexed as she extended her ring finger. That had to be the biggest rock Fawn had ever seen in her life.

"Well, congratulations. That's wonderful," Fawn shared in an eager sisterly tone.

"Yes, it is. Trying to keep these *thirsty ass bitches* away from my man is a little tough."

Her tone caught Fawn a little off kilter as she stood back, inadvertently startled.

The lady stepped to her a little aggressively, stating, "My name is Miranda Snyder, soon-to-be Mrs. Beckett Trent "B.T." Blaze. Here is your shit. Now, stay the hell away from my man. You hear me?"

The vixen dropped the Louis Vuitton travel bag at Fawn's feet. The stunned Fawn remained still—mortified of what she'd experienced. *Switching to the fullest*, the beautiful brick-house woman walked away, twirling her thick beautiful locks.

Fawn unzipped the bag, all of her belongings that she had left months ago at Beckett's house were contained within. Memories flooded her cerebrum of when she was six months pregnant, spending the last night at Beckett's six-million-dollar mansion. After that encounter, she was flooded with DM's along with an unsavory social media alert with Beckett being videoed in compromising positions with many women. At that moment, Fawn decided she was fed up with being disrespected. For once and for all, she left not looking back, figuring it would be better to deliver and raise their child alone, unbeknownst to her leaving some of her belongings that she was now reunited with. She was baffled because she had never asked for anything from the low-life NBA player, other than acknowledgement of the baby—for him to fully claim his daughter. She did not even ask for any child support, which her parents thought she was absolutely insane not to.

Fawn found herself pathetically in the corner of the spin studio. She slid down onto the cold floor with huge tears pouring out of her eyes, meanwhile scrolling through pictures of her with Beckett not too long ago. Any onlooker, who saw those pics would swear that they looked like they were a blissful couple anticipating the birth of their daughter. She was urgently pulled out of the rushed images in her faded memories, topped by a true definition of a pity party when she got a text.

:Fawn, this is Mrs. Mary. I just put your daughter's last pull up on. Also, she is going to need some more snacks.—Mrs. Mary

:Got it. Thank you, Mrs. Mary. I will head by the store before I pick her up. Give her a kiss from me. I'll be on my way soon.—Fawn P.

This text snapped Fawn out of her pity party. However, with tears still lingering in her eyes, she picked up *the bag of shame* with her belongings nestled inside. Off to the store she went.

"Just like the podcast said, I need to work on my Vision Intelligence. I've only identified myself with being on the arm of Beckett. Deep down, I believe I deserve more. I will struggle, but I will seek a new vision for myself and my daughter. I'm committed to working on my Vision Intelligence. I need to exude self-excellence.

6

THE LIVE PODCAST

"YOU ARE A MAGNIFICENT EXISTENCE (M.E.)!"

[One Month Ago]

BEEP!

BEEP!

BEEP!

Dr. T.'s hand slammed down on the alarm clock. She sat straight up in bed, feeling as if she'd forgotten to do or say something.

She jumped into the shower. The water was soothing; awaking her remembrance,

Oh, no! I forgot to share with the Weight Breakers about how they are a Magnificent Existence.

She wrapped her hair in a towel, grabbed her robe, got a cup of hot tea, then pressed LIVE.

Hi Weight Breakers!

Good morning my Gorgeous Weight Breakers. It's your girl, I know it's early, however we are LIVE! No judgment zone here; your eyes are not deceiving you. I'm sipping tea in my bathrobe with my hair wrapped in a towel. I felt it in my spirit that I had to do this with some sense of urgency. Look at me, in a very vulnerable state, because I have failed you in a sense. Yes, I do have tears in my eyes. I've been talking about the Intelligences yet, in my haste, I did not lay the foundation for that.

Dr. T. took a sip of her tea.

It woke me up out of my sleep early this morning. I got up at three a.m., went for a run on the treadmill, read my devotion, cried my eyes out, took a shower—grabbed

71

some tea. I decided to go LIVE with my Weight Breaker Podcast off the cuff, sharing with you something that can be life-changing. I want each of you to change your reference of *me* that you refer to yourself to equate it to a whole new meaning. I call this the *me* narrative. God made you a Magnificent Existence (M.E). In my book, *Think Like A Weight Breaker. Not Like A Weight Taker,* I call this portion of the book changing the narrative.

She adjusted her monitor on her camera.

You have connected with your Vision, Faith, and Resilience Intelligence—now you truly understand that they're all floating around your magnificent existence to make yourself flow through life. God made you to be in His image—you are a magnificent being, or rather a magnificent existence. This is not to say that you are God, by any means. It is to say that just like God made the magnificent air, the rain, the sun, the moon, and the stars—he made a magnificent you!

If we all thought of ourselves as a *magnificent vessel*, we would take better care of it. Most of our grandparents, or even parents, growing up had China cabinets. In those China cabinets were thought to be where the nice dishes were housed. You took so much care of those dishes when you washed them after utilizing them for a special occasion. Not like you rough-handled the dishes that you used on a day-to-day basis.

She smiled in reflection as she pulled up a diagram she orchestrated in the *Think Like A Weight Breaker. Not Like A Weight Taker* book.

Think of yourself as fine China. You are valuable. Take extra care of yourself, understand that God made you—you are a magnificent existence. I like to think of myself as a magnificent existence because that is what God said about each of us; that He made us in His image.

I'm excited about the purpose of our lives because Jeremiah 1:5 says, *Before I formed you in the womb, I knew you.*

Circling around us, or *me,* daily are the Intelligences that we have to be consciously aware of. When one of them is out of balance, the proverbial weight of life and physical weight of life can be a little challenging to handle, causing you to be a weight taker.

This is the model that is floating around you. God, your higher power, is the stratosphere circling all around you, connecting your vision, your faith, and your resilience.

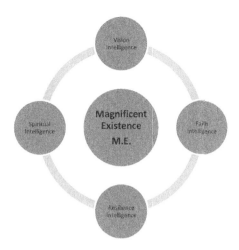

In life there are mountains along with valleys, that is to be expected, but it is so important to take pauses in your busy life to evaluate those mountains, as well as those valleys. We will explore them more later. The Inspirational Pathways (T.I.P.s) that I will encourage you to partake in are designed to help you level set; to deal with the mountains (good times) as well as valleys (low times) that you may face. Use this as a freestyle whiteboard to write some mountaintop experiences that you have had and some valleys that you have experienced.

She used the analogy in her own life, in the ups and downs that she dealt with throughout her own journey.

It is good to give titles to those mountains and valleys. Both the mountain and the valley need to be celebrated, call them both by name! Because if it were not for the valleys, you would not recognize the mountains. This will give you a balcony view of your journey. Let's change our perspective—looking from God's perspective of who he designed us to be, fully capable of handling the valley's and the mountains. By acknowledging both of them, you are a weight breaker. Knowing that you had to exercise the muscles of your vision, faith, and resilience to get to the mountain experiences—to pull up out of the valley experiences. Regardless of the valley or the mountain, you were designed to shine through the valley of adversity to be the glimpse of hope for others when you get to the mountain. Journal on how you take the different vantage point of who you are. Not only your momentum type, but the magnificent existence of who you are called to be.

Dr. T. looked at her watch.

Hey, Weight Breakers, I have to go. However, before I do, I want you to evaluate what can happen if we are not assessing the risk of not changing your thought process and remaining in the valley. In looking at your mountain and valley experiences, we need to closely evaluate the latitude and longitude of life. Technically, by default, you are not built to abandon hope. Simply by being placed in this life, you represent the epitome of hope—kick the old hats of weight breaker thoughts to the curb. I'm showing you something right now—that is a diagram that I made up to show how there are so many things intertwined in the weights that come our way. Look at the diagram; absorb it. This exemplifies the stakeholders in the execution of you becoming a weight breaker, it's not just about you. Yet, your responses to the proverbial/physical weights of life affect so many individuals around you.

She smiled as she thought about how her viewers would perceive the diagram.

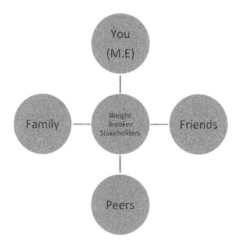

Journal on how others have been affected by the weights that affect you. Henceforth, you will put you as the first priority on your to-do list!

Weight Breakers, you have to choose to make yourself a priority to address the proverbial and the physical weights of your life. If you don't, no one else will.

Weight Breakers, we have to put at the forefront of our minds the epiphany of weight! Don't settle; you got this! Let only *weight breaker words* drip off your lips. Weight Breakers, this next song is for you.

Love, Dr. T. "The Weight Breaker"

Dr. T. played, *Good Morning Gorgeous*, by one of her legendary favorites Mary J. dancing LIVE with her hair wrapped in a towel. Swaying in her bathrobe, grabbing her brush—singing into it.

A full-fledged un-airbrushed concert with her arms swaying, strutting in the mirror.

The comments were rolling in from the impromptu LIVE social media video. They appeared to be enjoying seeing Dr. T. cut loose, letting her hair down—*giving life* to her listening audience.

7

ANJALI "A.J." NADKARNI

"THE CHAMELEON"

[CREAMY/CRÈME LIPSTICK: TEXTURE & GLOSS]

A.J. put her earbuds in her ears, started listening to Lizzo's "Good as Hell" as she was exiting a cab. She walked up to the twenty-five-story high-rise. She was the VP of Marketing—the only woman, moreover the only person of color in the C-suite.

"Yes, this is my *jam*," A.J. said as she looked in her compact, refreshing her hair as she entered the building.

I got this? A.J. thought, she attempted to muster up enough faith with her ivy league background, summa cum laude from Harvard Business School, along with her business acumen. She confidently landed a C-suite job as business marketing lead for this Fortune 500 company right out of *B-School*. She approached the door, catching a glimpse at herself. In the reflection was a beautiful, full-bodied Indian woman, but what she saw was that she wished she had worn another body shaper.

Not that another would work. I already almost passed out putting on this one.

She wished that she would have used a lighter foundation, the next time she would ask her hairstylist to lift her hair color—dare to rock blonde tresses. A.J.'s weight was all in her head. Her lack of faith in the beautiful being that God had gifted her—made her anxious. Her stomach churned daily.

A.J.'s trip down *"What-if Lane"* was interrupted by Scott, her colleague, who appeared as if he was waiting for her arrival. Opening the door, he did not hesitate to go right in with his entitled *in-your-face antics.*

"A.J., Winston can't wait to hear your pitch. I *warmed the bench* for you."

"For me, Scott? No need for *bench warming*. I've got *it* in the bag—"

"This one could be good for *your people*," Scott replied, wincing.

A.J.'s eyes told it all.

"What do you mean? My people? The American people?"

"Well, you know—" Scott attempted to clean up his outright microaggression.

Hell yeah, Scott, you put your foot in your mouth again.

A couple steps ahead while walking up to the second floor, A.J. paused, turned to face Scott. "I'm listening, but still not understanding."

"You know—*the Mexicans, your people*, " Scott said in an entitled manner.

"Scott, you asshole, my heritage is from India. My grandparents were one of the wealthiest families from Mumbai. We came to this country because my father was a sought-after astrophysicist. So, don't get it twisted because of my skin color. Please ask before you speak—"

"For the love of God, *you people* always get your panties all in a bunch, A.J., I was just saying that you should be proud of your work. You laid out a nice foundation for the Bollinger account. I saw your rough draft in the recycling bin—"

I should have shredded my rough drafts! Damn!

"So, you're *recycling bin stalking* me now?" A.J. stated while she walked away, fuming, although she'd done her best to subtly represent her culture and diversity in an informational manner. It was unfortunate; however she was used to microaggressions out the *wazoo*. She was attempting her hardest to be Americanized, an overwhelming weight for her. She experienced a lot of microaggressions of people simply not knowing *what she was*—Indian, Mexican, or Arabic, correspondingly an added weight. She attempted to temper her culture that was very present when she entered the room. Her culture was deep.

A.J. grabbed her mouth—headed to the ladies room.

"Excuse me." She entered the stall—*letting it rip*. This time it did not involve her putting her finger down her throat. She was absolutely sick of it. She'd been on pins and needles to get the pitch organized, somehow Scott had gotten her notes. Then had the audacity to approve her work.

As if I need that motherfucker's approval!

There she was, seated on the periphery of the long boardroom table, popping a breath mint to get herself collected after *letting it loose* in the restroom. She was the only person of color in the executive suite, which was a weight in itself. Scott was seated at the table, the C.E.O. Winston Chase sat at the head of the table. Chase was totally not impressed with any of the projections that he had heard to align with the forecast of the projects that were upcoming.

"Come on, people. You're going to make the clip from my aneurysm burst. I'm so not ready to meet *My Maker*. I told you that what I needed was a game changer—what I'm hearing so far definitely is not it!"

A.J. cleared her throat. She really wanted to chime in, she realized the perspectives that she orchestrated for the Bollinger account would be *the game changer* that the C.E.O. was looking for.

A.J., still fuming from the interaction with Scott in the hall that morning, felt the building of courage in her stomach, "Well, Mr. Chase, I have been working—"

"Who is speaking?" Mr. Chase responded cluelessly, curiously looking around the room.

You could feel the real embarrassment come over A.J. because she had been with the company for several years, yet her C.E.O. had no clue of her identity. With quivering legs, she stood to make the eye contact that she needed to speak directly with the C.E.O.

"Mr. Chase, I'm Anjali Nadkarni, a VP of Marketing for the Project Scope Opportunities."

"I don't know any Anjali." He butchered the pronunciation of her name.

The CFO whispered in his ear. "They call her A.J. You know, the diversity hire—"

"Ah, yes. You were *the one* that brought the sweet dish for the potluck?" Winston asked, diminishing her importance from *mega-million-dolla closer* to the *Potluck Queen*.

"Yes, Sir, the Puran Poli," A.J. spoke with hesitancy, attempting to temper her accent even more.

"Well, what do you have to say?"

All at once, A.J. was paralyzed by a flashback to grade school, when she was initially learning the English language with the room full of children laughing at her. Paralyzed from speaking, she had all of the documents on her PC—even had the printouts. However, she froze in fear of not being accepted, as she attempted to hide her pride in her culture—Jaipur festival of colors. Frozen in her stance, in her mind she sees *herself* on a stage, with a sash draped across her body, that was not a sari, however read, *Miss Corporate America*. In her vision, the announcer beckoned her to the stage,

"Welcome to the stage, Miss Corporate America. Give it up for A.J. Nadkarni, who has totally denied her heritage to fit in. She denounces her native accent, lightens her melanin infused skin, along with high-lighting her hair so others will not see her unique self, however sees herself as one of them."

The crowd goes into pandemonium as she is catapulted to the stage, taking her place she begins her stroll waving, while the crown is placed on her head. The announcer stated how she sacrificed her beautiful culture to win the title.

"A.J. is proud that she changed her hair color, tempered her accent, and tossed out her native cuisine at lunch each day to buy bologna and cheese at the corner store, to be invited to sit with the cool kids at lunch. Give it up for the woman who feels awkward in her own skin, A.J., don't call her Anjali Nadkarni."

A.J. is brought out of her stupor, as Scott pulled at her arm for her to sit down—bringing her out of her imagery of taunted grandeur. However, she remained tongue tied not able to muster up a response.

"We don't have all day," Mr. Chase belted out, losing patience.

All at once, the room felt so big as the soul inside of her shrunk.

Scott stood and took the floor, ambitiously stated, "Bollinger is a new tech company—they're hungry. They need our marketing expertise to take them into the next dimension of their platform…"

A.J. sat back down as she realized that, word-for-word from her presentation deck, Scott was reciting as if he was an actor. He surely would have won an Oscar for reciting all of her work even better than her.

"We have an inside track to make this happen, Winston. They have the capital we're looking for, if we can get Bollinger, they recently acquired Aberdeen Inc. We could capitalize on all of their subsidiaries."

The C.E.O. looked around the room, there was a pregnant pause. You could hear a pin drop.

CLAP!

CLAP!

CLAP!

Mr. Chase stood up, as he proclaimed, "You see, that's the kind of leadership we need in this marketing division. Scott, I'm making you the lead on the Bollinger account. This is brilliant. Close that deal, you'll be considered for partner."

A.J. sat there, her eyes wide as a deer in headlights, Scott was the Mack truck that had run her completely over.

The meeting was over, A.J. *hightailed-it* back to the restroom. She performed *her routine* all over again. To cope with her identity issues, she was bulimic. Weight was the one thing she could control.

She emerged from the stall, took her small toothbrush, brushing her teeth, to erase her weight.

A.J. get yourself together, she beckoned of herself.

She examined her skin covered in a lighter foundation, saying to herself in disgust,

I'm sick of microaggressions. I've tried so hard to fit in and become Americanized, which is a lot of weight. Why do I have to continue to profess who and what I am? Are you Mexican? Indian? Arabic? Am I only good at being the mouthpiece for my people and only good for bringing the delicious, sweet delectable to the work pot-luck lunch? There is no heroism in self-denial.

I cannot take it anymore. I have allowed these bastards to get me so choked up, I literally was paralyzed with fear. Damn, I couldn't even present the deal I've worked months to secure. I've even tempered my skin foundation, attempting to temper my culture=weight.

I can hear my beloved mother in my head telling me,

"Anjali, you need to be proud—you have a rich heritage."

A.J. did not want to linger in the low moments she apparently had the address to, visiting frequently. This flop that she'd experienced today was just another notch on her *I'm not good enough belt,* that she wore ever since she was the taunted girl by the cool kids in school.

Despite graduating Summa Cum Laude with bachelors in finance; graduating top of her business school from Harvard, working for the top Marchitecture firms in the United States, *the I'm not good enough weight* hampered her shine. In between slightly social media stalking the girls in high school that made her feel less than, who for whatever reason she gave them the power to be her yardstick, their airbrushed images, along with pouty lip photos, constantly made A.J. felt that she was missing out. In reality, those girls, many of whom had gotten strung out on drugs along with other misfortunes, but they used social media to allude that their lives were a fraction of what A.J. 's had actually become.

She then thought about Sean, an African American beautiful king she had met who was now her beau. He worked as an emergency room physician, as well as being a barber on the weekends to serve his community. The duo met out and about. However, the romance had secretly sped up after hours as he was introduced to her culture; her Naan, Malai Kofta, Chicken Tikka Masala, alongside Samosas. In the same token, she was introduced to his; oxtails, collard greens, macaroni and cheese, with decadent red velvet cake.

He had attempted to get her to speak up and build her up to break out of the restrictions that she had placed on her immense talent. He recognized early in her that she tried so hard to blend in that she struggled to truly be herself. He had some concern about the *self-harm* that he witnessed when she was stressed; her bulimia. She claimed she had *it* under control, but he was not convinced.

I don't want to tell Sean or my mom how I flopped my presentation today. A.J., get it together girl!

She thought to herself while she touched up her foundation in the places where streaks from her tears traced her cheeks during her retching in the bathroom mirror.

She received a text:

:Anjali, on your way home, would you mind stopping by the store to get some basmati rice, also turmeric. Swing by the family home, on your way to your condo, if it's not too much trouble.—Mom

:Sure.—A.J.

:Oh, Anjali Jagruti Nadkarni, remember that you are magnificent! You have to have faith that God made you perfect just the way you are, don't you forget that.—Mom

How does Mom know that I'm having a bad day?

When she addresses me by my first and middle name, I can tell she's all up in my head.

She did not even ask about the presentation, but innately, I can tell she knows it did not go well.

:I'm good, Mom. I'll get the groceries. Then stop by to drop them off before dinner.—A.J.

:Remember that Anjali means divine offering. Your middle name Jagruti which means awareness. You are a divine offering of awareness. Please my love, don't ever forget that.—Mom

:Thanks, Mom. See you soon.—A.J.

A. J. got herself unruffled, touching up her lips stain. Then Rachel came out of a stall, A.J. glanced over to her colleague, embarrassed *as shit*, while Rachel glared at her.

"I heard it was rough in there," Rachel said as she leaned into A.J. with a shoulder bump while she washed her hands.

"I know—I choked," A.J. said shrouded with pure shame.

"You're overthinking it. Embrace who you are. They're not just hiring *us* to hire *us*—people of color. We're talented girl—do you! You're speaking for all of us. The African Americans, the Mexicans, and Indians. When one rises, we all rise. Now, you get back out there, get a mentor. You are smart as hell; you graduated top of your class. But you have to realize that *the Scott's of the world* are perpetually waiting to catch us *slipping*—"

"Thank you, Rachel. I needed that pep talk—"

"Don't thank me now because I *will* be on your ass! When one of us chokes, it makes it hard for the rest of us. Get it together—you need to work on your faith intelligence. Your faith is a muscle and you have to build it up. Stop trying to be *them,* when they hired you for your uniqueness."

That startled A.J. because she did not expect it from Rachel. She assumed she was supposed to mentor Rachel. Yet, A.J. understood that she was now *the grasshopper*=mentee.

Damn, I need to get myself collected. What is this faith intelligence that Rachel is talking about? I'm so tired of this B.S., I can't ever fit in, Anjali pondered as she put one earbud in, walked out of the restroom defeated.

A random selection, as if on cue, started to play The Chronicles of The Weight Breakers Podcast. Her eyes zeroed in on the traitor, Scott. He was spotted down the hall. He cut his eyes quickly to not face the person that he had *stabbed in the back* in the all-hands executive meeting only moments before.

A.J. stepped right in front of him.

"You stole my shit, man!" A.J. blazoned as her temples bulged in fury, heat arose in her chest.

"Stole? Are you kidding me? I saved your work, you ingrate" Scott stood firm in cockiness. "You couldn't even articulate the pitch. You do know what articulate means, don't you?"

Anjali stepped into Scott's space to make her point heard. "Let me tell you something, you low-down dirty bastard. You will not get away with this. I own the relationship with Bollinger and Aberdeen, don't you forget it!"

"Yeah, yeah, yeah," Scott spat back as he emulated playing a violin. He went on to say, "You want to play with the big boys, you can't risk choking, A.J. You had your chance."

He walked past A.J., nudged her shoulder as he brushed past her, full of himself.

Just in that moment, she rendered, *I have sold my soul to the devil. I've done everything to change myself to fit in. Even with all that work, I am still an outcast.*

The push and pull that she constantly felt in this office was her life-sucking normal—most days, this aura hung over her head like an impending columnar cloud holding hail ready to pounce on the pavement of her soul. Not even the strongest umbrella could prevent her from the hail that Scott was always on deck ready to shower her with. She was startled out of her funk by an alert on her phone.

:How was the meeting today, sweetie?—Sean

:It was a disaster, but I'll be fine.—A.J.

:That backstabber, Scott, did you wrong again. Right?—Sean

:I wish you would *wax his ass. Just kidding...—A.J.

:I will if you want me to. I'll have a few choice words for him—then commence to bust his ass on eighteen holes at the country club. Not cool.—Sean

:No, I'm good.—A.J.

:No, seriously. Take a deep breath, sweetie. Come on home. I'll make Italian tonight. Will that cheer you up?—Sean

:Sounds delicious. I have to stop by the store. You want me to get anything?—A.J.

:French sourdough bread and fresh garlic cloves. I have everything else.—Sean

:I'll stop by my mom's house before heading home. Just use your key to get the meal started. You cook, I'll do the dishes. Deal?—A.J.

:Yes, I'll kick Scott's ass, cook, then we will clean the kitchen together. Even better deal.—Sean

:*Word?* Got to go. Love you, *Boo.*—A.J.

A.J. put her earbuds in her briefcase, put her phone away, got *the hell out of dodge,* attempting to get her blood-boiling down to a simmer.

I'll listen in the car on the way to the store, A.J. thought as she gathered all of her belongings. She saw a book that caught her eye at one of the open cubicles outside of the boardrooms.

Wow, this is the book that they are talking about on this podcast. In the midst of this pure chaos, I should pick it up.

A.J. quickly grabbed the book, *Think Like A Weight Breaker. Not Like A Weight Taker*. Her eyes dove right into the section of the momentum types. Her eyes widened when she reached The Chameleon momentum type.

Wow, I've been making daily decisions to attempt to change my appearance, moreover my demeanor to fit in. I've failed to accept the beauty in who I am—who God called me to be, a magnificent existence, A.J. thought to herself as she began to tear up a little, wiping a single tear that rolled out of her left eye, down her perfectly blushed cheek.

I need to start to download deep soul activities so I also can be a weight breaker, not a weight taker.

She looked down the hall, got distracted from the book when she overheard Scott and Winston Chase at the end of the hallway talking about golf. Scott was showing off his self-proclaimed pristine swing, pretending he was holding a nine-iron. Internally, she felt more defeated than she had ever felt before. The air left her body as the weight sat on her chest. A.J. was not a white male; she was not a native of this land. She had a thick accent that practicing at home in the mirror could not release itself from her being. She magically imagined that she could release it, miraculously awakened with blonde hair, pale skin, blue eyes—most of all, be taken seriously. That would be a dream, right?

But not my dream. I love the melanin in my brown skin. I love my full lips, most of all, I love my heritage—where my people come from, deep in India. Our rich culture, our food, our dress and, most of all, that culture produced my parents. My mother, who is my backbone, my father— who would have shuddered at what I have become, a person changing their colors to fit in; The Chameleon, which is not the true definition of excellence.

8

THE PODCAST

"T.I.P.S & THE INTELLIGENCES"

[DON'T IMITATE LIFE, LIVE IT!]

"Dr. T., your hair is on fire. Mika came over this morning right to bump them curls?" Dean Baby applauded as he put primer on her lids, accenting her hazel eyes.

"You just missed her; I'm surprised you didn't see her exit out the back. I want to look fierce today. I'm going to be on LIVE TV. To be honest, I'm a little nervous…"

She took a deep breath, ruffling the cape draped around her not to allow the makeup powder to stain her fine threads.

Dean Baby snapped in her face,

"You have nothing to be nervous about; you got this. Don't forget who you are. You're *The Melanin Poppin Goodness Bomb Girl*, but you have to believe that in your spirit. Most people can pick up on a fraud a mile away. I know you are not a fraud; you're authentic. Furthermore, you know what the hell you're talking about. I rock with those T.I.P.s every day. They get me through."

Dr. T. smiled.

"Dean, great minds think alike. That's the part of the book I'm going to talk about today: The Intelligences."

Dean Baby smiled as he continued to work on his canvas.

"That's going to be so enlightening. Sis, I heard you and Dr. Sparrow Mack on the other podcast. That's my girl—her new movie *Friction Ridges* is fire. I'm so honored to be in the midst of women who are doing the *damn thing!*"

They smiled.

"But Dean Baby, do this *damn thing* on my face, quick fast in a hurry, or else I'm going to be late."

He chuckled, applying the finishing touches. *"BAM!* They're not ready for you!"

Dr. T. left a *fat tip*, got into her car—headed to the station. She pulled into the parking lot; she'd gotten a parking pass for one of the V.I.P. stalls. She glanced over to her right; there it was—Cassidy Gentry's parking area.

A sense of *"I've arrived"* came over Dr. T. 's spirit, as this caliber of interview was on her vision board.

"Hello, I'm Dr. T., here for the LIVE interview—"

"Right this way," the assistant led her to a room with a monitor.

What? No green room first? Dr. T. thought, taking a seat—she'd figured she'd at least get a chance to primp before going LIVE.

"Excuse me, will Cassidy Gentry be coming down to get me?"

"Your agent didn't tell you?"

"Tell me what?" Dr. T.'s confused expression said it all.

"Well, this is how Cassidy prefers to do her interviews, with a still photo."

Well, damn, if I'd known this, I wouldn't have gotten all glammed up, The Weight Breaker reflected mortification.

"So, help me understand. I'm going to be in front of this big monitor alone? Cassidy won't be able to see me?" she politely questioned.

Unbeknownst to The Weight Breaker, her questioning was viewed as prying.

"No, the viewing audience will be able to see you. However, you will see her image. It's easier that way… for her."

Dr. T. could feel her blood boiling a little bit. Yet, she realized that she had to be malleable—practice what she preached, not to view every unforeseen circumstance as weight. Then she deliberated, *Wait! I recognize this woman's voice!*

"Are you ready, Dr. T.?" the assistant asked again.

"Yes, I'm ready."

Dr. T. decided to simultaneously go LIVE briefly to tell her followers to tune in. The comments started to roll in…

Hi Weight Breakers,

Because you have been doing so well working on your intelligence's, I have a special treat for you today. I'm going to be on the Morning Show with Cassidy Gentry.

:That's amazing, I love Cassidy Gentry. You would be proud of me; I have set up my Weight Breaker Space and created a vision board—actually took it one step further by creating accountability partners. We are all working on this collectively, to get our vision intelligence on point. I am committed to doing the work, so I too can be a weight breaker!—Raina B.

:Since reading the book, I have reconnected with working on my faith. I still have a lot of room to grow, but I give God all the glory.—Ashtyn N.

Weight Breakers, I love the comments that are coming. You ladies are walking this thing out! I'm so proud of you, keep up the great work, stay tuned.

On the monitor before her, Cassidy Gentry's *still image* appeared. Dr. T. could see a small image of herself as if she was peering in a mirror. She caught herself furrowing her brow at the image not going on camera.

Girl, get your face together, she thought to herself. Cassidy's voice broke the silence,

"Hello, Dr. T., you look amazing. My makeup artist broke her arm, so I can't do it LIVE this morning. Is that okay?"

That's not what the assistant told me. She said she never does LIVE. Anyway, what else can I say?

This is perfect, *Cassidy*. Let's get started.

It took a minute for Dr. T. to get used to talking to the freeze-frame photo. However, she decided to roll with it.

"5, 4, 3, 2, 1... It is your *Morning Show* host, Cassidy Gentry, and today we have the distinguished honor to speak with physician, motivational speaker, and renowned author Dr. T. She is the author of the mega hit book *Think Like A Weight Breaker. Not Like A Weight Taker.* The book is in stores now by the host of the inspiring Chronicles of The Weight Breakers Podcast. She's all-over social media, journals, radio and television, inspiring wherever she goes. Give it up for this dynamic speaker."

Dr. T. straightened herself up in her chair, holding up the book.

Hi, Weight Breakers! Thank you, Cassidy, moreover thank you *Morning Show* viewers. I'm going to keep this very light, simple, however meaningful today, to jumpstart your morning. Turn to Tactic 4 in the book; this section will talk about The Inspirational Pathways or, better yet, T.I.P.s.

"Sounds interesting. Can you first tell us how you came up with these T.I.P.s?"

Certainly, I derived that I needed to have a new approach on how I managed each day. My hope is that over time, integration of the T.I.P.s will come as easily as tying your shoes, and will become an elemental part of your daily routine. The goal is to have the correct lens on how to view each day; establish a firm pathway to help deal with the weights of life; strategize on walking the modified way of thinking out; reestablishing the way you do things regarding your journey.

"Got it. So let's get started. The listeners are eager to dive right in."

Cassidy, T.I.P. 1: Unnecessary Distractions Go In The Trash Can! I have been told that this tip should be labeled as number 1—I agree. Originally, this T.I.P. was further down, so I moved it up.

"I've read the book; this has got to be one of the most beneficial T.I.P.s that we can review. I would put this one on the *trophy shelf* in your mind. I almost get physically sick when I think about how I almost gave up when an unnecessary distraction came into my midst to throw me off course."

We definitely are on the same page, Cassidy. If I would've stopped on my journey, or got sidetracked totally because of things that popped up unexpectedly, what someone said that was not so nice, or how the puzzles at the time did not seem to be fitting right regarding what I had worked so hard for, I would have missed out on abundance.

"Dr. T., I believe I can take this to the bank and cash it!"

Cassidy, if something or someone is not adding value to your headspace, moreover your physical space trying to cause you to fall off course, it is an unnecessary distraction. Do yourself a favor and toss "it" in your proverbial trash can.

"You are right, Dr. T. Inevitably, there will be things that occur that will attempt to distract you. What should we do?"

Cassidy, we should toss them in the proverbial trashcan ASAP! As soon as they come up, recognize them—disregard them. With each pound you lose, throw it in the trashcan—put the lid on tight! We are riding the proverbial weights of life and physical weight. *Bye-Bye!* Let me make it even more understandable, if the situation does not affect your family, health, your household, or your employment, it's not worth the energy or the battle. Don't dwell on it merely to dwell.

Dr. T. stated as she leaned into the screen further.

Cassidy, we all have to do a self-spot check on a regular basis. Life has an abundance of circumstances that evolve, so we have to make sure you have this T.I.P. of putting unnecessary distractions in the trash can, at the forefront of your mind. Weight Takers let unnecessary distractions fester, continuing *to brew*, clouding their focus. A raise of hands of those individuals who look forward to taking out the trash? No, seriously, if you haven't raised your hands, I may be a little worried about you. Nevertheless, whether you like it or not, you must take out the trash!

"What happens to *your trash* when you leave it in the garage or miss trash day?" Cassidy egged on.

We're on the same page, Cassidy. You know exactly what happens; it stinks up the place. I don't care how many air fresheners you try to use; it will *stink up the spot.* What I'm attempting to get at is that when you place distractions in your *proverbial trash can*, you must place that trashcan on the curb on Mondays, and not take *that garbage* into your next week, next month, next quarter, and definitely not next year. Imagine if the city dump would be in your garage, you would not be able to stand it. Weight Breakers recognize unnecessary distractions, and quickly puts *them* in the trash!

"Dr. T., this is amazing. I've read my autographed copy of *Think Like A Weight Breaker. Not Like A Weight Taker.* Furthermore, I'm so intrigued about The Inspirational Pathway, number 2, in which we should treat every day as if it is our birthday. What's up with that? Can you elaborate more?"

Dr. T. smiled, going on to share,

Well, Cassidy, it's pretty simple, I'm so glad you would ask about T.I.P. 2: Every Day is Your Birthday! Plain and simple, it is all about approaching each twenty-four hours that you are blessed to receive as your birthday, that will give you a new foundational hope for embarking upon each day.

"So, as soon as you arise from sleep, you should think of the gift of opening your eyes and seeing each day as your birthday? I like that concept."

Cassidy's freeze-frame photo agreed.

Yes, indeed; there are many who would beg to have that gift. The gift of another day. Psalms 118:24 said it best, *This is the day that the Lord has made, we will rejoice and be glad in it.* There are so many that were not as fortunate to awaken. You know that feeling that you have when you awaken, furthermore you realize that it's your birthday! You leap out of bed, with a smile, and you may *shimmy*—doing your birthday dance all the way to the bathroom to greet yourself in the mirror to brush your teeth. That is the feeling that we're going to strive to have each day.

"Dr. T., that sounds good. There are some days when challenges are awaiting at our doorstep, but knowing the grace that was given to you to see another day is priceless, and should be celebrated."

Cassidy, I did not know you were so deep. I agree that all of the weight breakers out there should write in your journal how you are going to celebrate each day as if it is your birthday! And please remember, some people would do anything for your worse day—don't forget that!

"This is good stuff, Dr. T. Please share more."

T.I.P. 3: Put "It" On Your Calendar! If "it" is on your calendar, you are more likely to do "it." So, what is it? It is time for you to meditate with God to get yourself grounded for the day. On my personal calendar is my prayer call that I have with the ladies in our prayer circle. Just like the scheduled meetings for work are on your calendar, you need to have a separate calendar on your phone, or if you are a person that likes to put pen to paper, write *it* down. An illustration, the time you need to: exercise, meditate, or take a soothing walk to clear your mind; put it on your calendar. Whatever it is, it is up to you as a reminder to take care of yourself, motivate yourself so you can identify the proverbial weights, meet them head on, handling them in a way that is not self-depleting.

I also decided to theme the months of the year putting motivation on each month for example: January the focus is Joy—how can I keep at the center of my core pure joy, instead of seeking temporary happiness?; February the focus is Forgiveness—how can I exude pure love, when I have felt slighted?; March the focus Maximize—how do I continue to revamp my thinking?; April the focus is Aspiration—what new visions can I put into place?; May the focus is Magnetic—how to I check in with myself to determine what I am attracting in my space?; June the focus is Just—how can I make sure that everything that I am associated with is fair and right?; July the focus is Jet set—where am I going to go to impact?; August the focus Adventure—where must I go to seek new exciting experience (i.e. travel)?; September the focus is Salute—how can I honor those people that support me?; October the focus is Optimistic—what do I need to put in my space to think and exude positive energy?; November the focus is Namaste—what can I do to enhance my ability to balance myself to relax?; and December the focus is Discipline—how can I evaluate my efforts that I've worked on this past year? Furthermore, how can I orchestrate a plan of order for the upcoming new year? With those monthly reminders, it shifts my mood—giving me focus.

In addition, one of the most important things I put on my calendar is a movement reminder. By putting the movement on your calendar, you are more likely to dedicate that allotted time for that endeavor; physical activity. That will help with the physical weight that tends to pounce on us due to inactivity.

"You know what I have been doing to deal with my weight issues?"

I was not aware you had any weight issues.

Dr. T. stated, a little perplexed, looking at the svelte *modelesque* image of the glamorous Cassidy Gentry. There was a pregnant pause before Cassidy went on to share,

91

"Well, what I meant to say is that I've been dealing with the proverbial weights all of my life, I have found putting words of encouragement on my calendar helps me out."

Cassidy, I'm so glad that you brought this up. If you have a favorite quote or Bible verse that is a reminder of the magnificent existence that God created all of us to be, you should put it on your calendar as well. It may sound a little corny, but it works. This activity of putting those positive thoughts on your calendar, even the daily decisions that are upcoming on our calendar, can move you to change and inspire. By those words, you've strategically planted in your space. If you're having a little difficulty getting started with something to write, consider this phrase I came up with to jumpstart—energize my day. I put it on my calendar—*Each day is a GIFT from GOD. I'm GRATEFUL and will approach the day with GRATITUDE to GLORIFY GOD. I will be IMPACTFUL and FULFILL my purpose in an attempt to make meaningful change and TRANSFORM my thinking towards my Vision, Faith and Resilience Intelligences. So, I can handle the proverbial/physical weights of life. I'm a Weight Breaker!*

"Dr. T., I love this," Cassidy's smile was felt through the still picture.

I knew you would. Even when days start out gloomy or if days are sunny, each is a gift. You can place the other T.I.P.s on your calendar privately to yourself, as well as your exercise, hydration, eating your healthy snacks, some *"me"* time. Weight Breakers only put things on their calendars that are necessary, cause self-growth, and maturation. Everything else needs to be put in the unnecessary distractions trash can.

"This is so good, Dr. T.; our viewers would love to have you on our Weekly Uplifting Segment. Please tell us about T.I.P. 4: Exercise *Your Intelligence Muscles* Each and Every Day!"

I would love to be one of your regular guests—there is so much self-work that needs to be done. In my motivational bestseller, *Think Like A Weight Breaker. Not Like A Weight Taker.*—you will find that the cores of the book and workbook are centered around Vision Intelligence, Faith Intelligence, and Resilience Intelligence. All are key to remember in every aspect of your day. Dig into the Intelligences, also alignment towards your ultimate purpose. This section is a great place to include reliance on the power of the Holy Spirit, versus mere self-reliance. GOD places intelligence in us so we can rely on Him for our vision, our faith, and our resilience.

"So, if something is attempting to distort your goals, you should evaluate whether it is aligned with your vision intelligence and exercise your vision intelligence muscle?"

You've got it. If an instance is attempting to cause you to doubt yourself or your circumstances, pump up your faith intelligence muscle. If there is a situation that will cause you to get knocked down or what appears to be failure in your eyes, exercise that resilience and intelligence muscle. You are stronger than you will ever give yourself credit for. Weight Breakers have their Intelligences at the forefront of their minds each day!

"I'm doing my best to enhance my intelligence. It takes a lot of effort; however, it is worth it. Now for one of the *Big Dogs*, pardon the pun, all of us need to hear about this next tip; especially me. T.I.P. 5."

Cassidy, you keep saying that, but I don't see that you have a weight issue. However, regardless of your weight, or BMI, it is important to give yourselves the best fuel possible to navigate life. Now we come to T.I.P. 5: Making Healthier Consumption Choices—*One Bite at a Time!* The more whole foods, straight from the ground foods that you can eat, the better. The proper portion of all foods is key in health and wellness, weight loss, and weight stability. In addition, proper nutrition is what you need to face the weights of life. Consult with a healthcare provider if your health needs warrant a special modified eating plan. Most of all, throw out the window the dirty curse word that starts with the letter "d"—diet! There is no such thing as a diet that will cause you to have permanent weight loss. What causes ongoing regulation of weight is a healthy lifestyle, which includes your input and your output. The input is what we are talking about now; what you are putting into your body. You can have most foods, along with certain meals in moderation. If you make a bad food choice out of dire need, do not kick yourself. Make better choices, ONE DECISION AT A TIME! Or even more granular than that is one meal at a time.

"So, Dr. T. are you saying Weight Breakers understand that they *eat to live, not live to eat*. The author of that quote is unknown, like most of us who grew up going through drive-thrus out of convenience, it's okay to drive through, but make better choices. It's okay to order in, but make better choices for your overall health, wellness, energy, along with stamina. I need to do that; I love the taco food truck that I eat out of at least twice per week."

Cassidy, you are absolutely correct. And I can't see you eating at a food truck; however I love them. Nowadays, with so many food restaurants, there are a multitude to choose from. We all know how many servings of lean meats and proteins and fresh vegetables to eat. Weight Breakers understand the decisions they make about what they put in their bodies matter. Weight Takers unconsciously eat, before long here comes the expanding waistline accompanied with upward numbers on the scale.

"Dr. T., you are so right. When people think of a healthy lifestyle, we think about all of the things that we will not be able to consume. What advice can you give?"

So, viewers, think about your favorite snack or favorite cuisine. When dietitians talk about a healthier lifestyle, they use the phrase *moderation is key*. Take a moment and think about the foods that you really enjoy. Before there was medicine, there were foods that our ancestors used as medicine. They would not only grow their own food, moreover they also harvested their own food—living off of the land, true farm to table living.

93

"Dr. T., you are so right. My grandparents had a farm. That is how they lived their life—farm to table. In the business of life, we often eat on the run. We realized we were hungry, and ate what was closest to use regardless if it was good for us or not. Before we knew it, we scarfed down our food without even tasting it."

Cassidy, so you are a farm girl too? In addition, know that along with enjoying your food, hydration is key, in the purest form possible. Standard information is to drink six-to-eight eight-ounce glasses of water per day. If you have certain medical issues, you will need to verify with your provider how much water you can consume or if you should be on a fluid limitation. Your cells, organs, tissues, along with your muscles need water in the purist form to properly function. It is a well-known fact that your body is sixty-percent water. Overhydration can be risky, even lethal. Therefore, stick within the guidelines of water consumption from your medical provider.

Come on, Weight Breakers, make those healthy balanced choices each day as to what you put in your body! To conform from a weight taker to a weight breaker about what you consume, keep tabs of what you are putting in your Magnificent Existence. I have identified all of those foods that come straight out of the ground, with no to little processing as my Weight Breaker Foods. Those are the ones that I attempt to consume in the majority. I have shared that I'm a *Post-It Note Queen*, and had resolved to put post-it notes on the Weight Breaker Foods to make sure everyone in the house knew what to keep their hands off of, what foods were reserved for *Mommy.*

"So, are you saying that we should identify those foods that are Weight Taker Foods—those are highly processed foods, high-calorie foods?"

Yes, The Weight Breaker Foods are those that have high nutritional value, that are in their purest form. Yet, there are so many food capturing apps out there, you have to find what works best for you. I find that I must identify the foods that cause me to gain versus those foods that I know will cause me to lose. I have been on most weight loss programs known to man; I've found that food choices with portion control work best for me. I believe that is a good, sound program that has tools available to make the type of accountability needed for weight loss to happen.

"So, what you are saying is that you can believe in yourself all you want, making some good choices here and there. However, if you do not have a sound plan, it will not be sustainable. How about if we could possibly replace the bad 'd' word of diet with discipline, we would be ahead of the game already—how does that sound?"

Cassidy, that sounds great. Consider this; there may be two different options for dinner that is prepared, one for the family, in addition a dinner for you. You can indulge in some of your delectable favorites from time to time, in moderation. However, know that you have to offset it in the rest of your day. Allow yourself grace. Just because you have one bad meal does not mean you *fall off the rails* completely. Get back up again quickly, that is where your resilience and intelligence comes in.

"This is good information. You just gave me an idea. We need to do a healthy cooking segment."

I'm game. I'd love that.

Dr. T. smiled as that had been something that she'd put on her vision board.

"Dr. T., we have a few more T.I.P.s, then we will be wrapping up this segment. Still, this is the one that I really feel makes a huge difference."

Agreed, Cassidy. T.I.P. 6: Movement Makes the Mission! This is literally *where the rubber meets the road.* It has been proven that daily movement=exercise are key to making an impact on your health. Discuss with your healthcare provider what the best exercise program is for you to start. It is hard to move towards the mission, without movement. Make sure that you get your physical examinations to see if there are any barriers to you being able to have meaningful movement with exercise. Use your smartphones or pedometer to track your steps. Studies have proven that ten thousand steps a day are a great start towards health and wellness. If you have physical limitations, speak with your healthcare provider about what options are best for you. To all the listeners out there, I believe adopting a movement that you can sustain, that you can have longevity with. I'm a walker, and I love to walk. However, I will be getting additional cardiovascular workout by getting on the elliptical, also participating in online aerobic classes. Whatever is best for your physical condition, get moving. Start small with low impact, then work your way up! Do not forget that certain activities around the house can be considered exercise. Seek the advice of your healthcare provider if you have specific health disabilities to determine what are the best exercises for you.

"Okay, Weight Breaker this next T.I.P. is what most of us women put on the back burner every day."

Yes, Cassidy, I love T.I.P. 7: Take Care of Yourself. This is a mandate that all of us women need to give ourselves permission to do. Find a way to really dig in, take care of yourself each day! That reiterates the need for self-care. It is a must. You have to love yourself. You have to get your physical examination yearly. You must get your laboratory evaluations done on a regular basis, furthermore getting your medications refilled when you are supposed to. That is all a part of loving yourself—self-care. That could be waking up earlier than usual to join a prayer call, meditate, get your coffee or tea, and just take a deep breath, take a walk, journal, or time to do crafts. For me it's time spent with family or to write. During my spare time, I write motivational self-help books, all which are a part of my creative outlet and self-care—"me time." It is a must that you carve time every day to love yourself. Some may be more direct in self-care. Transparently, it was that epiphany of self-care that prompted me to write the book, *Think Like A Weight Breaker. Not like A Weight Taker.*

"Agreed. I love to buy drugstore self-care products, special body washes, perfumes, colognes, hair products, just to take care of myself! Love on you; you are the only you that you've got! Weight Takers put themselves on the back burner."

Cassidy, you are so right, I get it. Most women have been a Weight Taker for the majority of their lives. Henceforth, it can be hard, with all of the hats that we wear, to really place a space in your life to love yourself. Weight Breakers make it a priority to not put themselves on the *back burner.*

"Dr. T., I know our viewers are loving these nuggets of wisdom you are dropping today. This next one is a little deep. Can you explain T.I.P. 8?"

T.I.P. 8: Cherish Your Systems is one of the most profound T.I.P.s.—Appreciate your body systems that are working hard on your behalf throughout the day—even while you are sleeping, to make sure you are able to exist at your highest capability—fully functioning. A lot of times we are not aware that the stressors, anxieties of life, fear, depression, with the lack of self-care we feel are emotional—we fail to realize the true impact that these emotions can have on our physical body. We are dispensed one body, the vehicle that carries us throughout this life. Furthermore, that vehicle is operated by precious body systems.

"Dr. T., I'm loving this series that you have been putting on your Weight Breaker Podcast. This next T.I.P. is what can really fill your cup up. Tell us about T.I.P. 9."

Cassidy, I come from a long line of givers. Remember this old phrase, "*it is better to give than to receive?*" Giving is a part of the reason that we are all here on earth. To give our gifts, to be a part of one common purpose—enriching others' lives as well as our own. So, T.I.P. 9: Forward Blessings! As a Weight Breaker, seek out ways to bless someone each day. Proverbs 11:25, *A generous person will prosper; whoever refreshes others will be refreshed.* Forwarding a blessing, I'm not just speaking about monetary and philanthropic giving, even though I'm called to do that as well. I'm talking about being a blessing through your time and energy.

"Can being a blessing be as simple as saying hello—a smile or a phone call?"

Yes; that simple gesture costs you absolutely nothing but time. Your action can cause a Weight Taker to be able to have the courage or strength to break that weight. You will never know how much you being the magnificent existence (m.e.), or the blessing that you are, will mean to someone else. People are hurting, hungry, separated from their families, alone, destitute, however you may be that silver lining to give them that boost to make it through another day. Many people sit back, wondering why some blessings bypass them. Now this is all up in your business, but I'm going to keep it real. I have found that you have to be a blessing in order to receive a blessing. It is at those times when I give that I feel most blessed. Weight Breakers are more likely to be individuals that understand that we all are in this together. Weight Breakers forward blessings!

"I love this one so much. You are blessed to be a blessing is what my momma used to redundantly say."

Dr. T. nodded in agreement.

This next T.I.P. is a lifesaver for sure. T.I.P. 10: Recharge Your Battery! Rest, purposefully unwinding are key to each day. It is advised to get at least eight hours of sleep—some people require more; some people require less. I have survived most of my life on a lot less, however I've found I thrive, more productive when I have adequate sleep. You have to rest, rejuvenate to be able to rejoice on your journey.

"I agree, I need my sleep."

Cassidy chimed in with an element of an exhausted tone coming through her still photo.

When I was young, I used to run on fumes—I realized how unhealthy that was. Now, I cherish sleep. Your body systems need sleep. Your cells need that time to turn over, becoming anew. With adequate rest, you are less likely to be agreeable to take on unnecessary weight. Other ways to recharge your battery throughout the day, such as sitting *in front of the computer all day for* work, is to put breaks on your calendar throughout the day. You may be able to steal away for five, ten, or fifteen minutes to meditate, go for a walk, or listen to music. We must all make sure that we recharge our battery. During sleep your cells in your body are able to regenerate, refuel your body. Pray, praise, read your Bible. Weight Breakers are mindful of the need to recharge their battery.

"Listeners, did you hear that? Ladies and gentlemen that are listening in, you need to recharge your battery. Get your rest to refuel. Many of us are walking around here *running on fumes*, that does not yield to a fruitful life."

Cassidy, you are so right. This next one that I will leave with you, then drop the microphone—exit stage left. T.I.P. 11: Weigh the Situation!

Everyone say it with me, *Weigh The Situation!* Regarding the proverbial weights of life, look at the scales of the balance. If there is something that is not aligned with your purpose, it is not worth tilting the scale. You know where to put it?

"Yep, Dr. T., we will put it in the *unnecessary distraction's trash can!*"

You may be wondering, what specific advice can be given to your readers to help them know how to do this? It's one thing to say, *put unnecessary distractions in the trash can,* but how can you help your reader recognize (diagnose) their distractions to solve their problems? This is all relative from the perspective of the reader. What I have identified for me as unnecessary distractions may be for me, may be different for you. So, I recommend gleaning to *the word*—biblical truths found in T.I.P. 1, if something causes you to steer away from your purpose, your truth= God's Word, it goes into the trash can.

This book is here to motivate uplift. Not a self-help book, but to work in adjunct to a life plan, changing what you are embarking upon. I fully understand that some people spend months or years in counseling working on these issues, but it may be a little presumptuous of you to merely say, *put your problems in the trash*. Therefore, there is no disrespect meant by that suggestion.

"Once again, you are preaching. Regarding the physical weight of life, it can creep up on us because we act like it does not exist. Take power over it—meet it head on. Regarding the Physical Weight of life, I have found that sometimes, you don't realize how out of control your physical weight has gotten because of the fear of the *truth scale*. I decided, instead of being intimidated by the scale in our bathroom, I would take ownership over it by weighing myself at a minimum weekly."

I totally agree. Even though some physical trainers typically advise people not to weigh themselves on the scale every day because it is discouraging.

"Personally I have found that I weigh myself more to keep myself in check, after losing almost fifty pounds, not wanting to take any chances. The ultimate goal is to grow in thought retention of new healthy habits, lifestyle. Physical weight loss cannot only be your incentive. Weight loss of the weights of life, in addition to physical weight are great. Your triggers for joy, peace—relishing each day is the plight."

Fifty pounds?

That's interesting.

Maybe in her teen years, Dr. T. thought to herself.

Cassidy went on to share, "I get it. Weight Breakers work on how to optimize each day, how to manage the risk of not addressing the proverbial weight and physical burden of life."

You're right on point, Cassidy. Besides, Weight Breakers know that they have to create new policies/procedures for their lives to be able to handle those two imposing weights. Come on, Weight Breakers, we must establish a new policy/procedure for the weights you confront. Take for instance, when you start a new job, when you are onboarding in your new role, you will learn your roles and responsibilities. There are policies/procedures on how your company operates. What you have to understand is that you are *your own company*.

"We should treat ourselves as a business?"

Yes, ma'am. You are your very own first business. That is why you need to attend to yourself, with just as much attention. So, consider drafting up a new set of rules on how to conduct your thought processes. Develop a policy/procedure for fostering your Vision Intelligence, Faith Intelligence, and Resilience Intelligence. Only P&P's that are inspiring, motivating, impactful, or moving are allowed in your weight breaker space. Start with creating new regulations on how you operate to walk your T.I.P.s out daily.

"Well, there you have it. This time with The Weight Breaker has been so uplifting. You can buy her book anywhere books are sold. *Think Like A Weight Breaker. Not Like A Weight Taker;* is a must-have, not just self-help book. Moreover a self-care book that will be *your best friend* along this journey called life. You have some great upcoming news. Dr. T., will you allow us to be the first to share that news?"

Definitely. For all you Weight Breakers out there, at a first read, it may seem hilarious, but take heed to the nuggets, and writing this book made me really think about the whole process of not being a Weight Taker any longer, level up to being a Weight Breaker. Weight Breakers out there, journal as to how you are going to walk out T.I.P.s (The Inspirational Pathway); have the correct lens on how to view each day; establish a firm pathway to help deal with the weights of life; strategize on walking the modified way you do things regarding your journey. I'm honored to be on this journey with you, moreover elated about your support. Stay tuned to The Chronicles Of The Weight Breakers Podcast, for upcoming events. Also, for more thrilling announcements.

"You heard it first on *The Morning Show with Cassidy Gentry,* have a great day."

Love you Weight Breakers, remember to upload glory, so you can download your greatness. Cassidy, thank you for allowing this phenomenal interview. We will connect soon.

"Cut!"

The video monitor was disabled, there was a pregnant pause. Looking around, Dr. T. sat there, happy about the interview—however, unaccustomed to not having human live interaction, the situation was not her norm.

KNOCK!

KNOCK!

The door opened; Penelope entered.

"Dr. T, thank you for coming. Please follow me. We will send you the email with the link for the interview so you can post."

Her voice sounds so familiar—Dr. T. kept thinking to herself.

"Thank you for being so kind. Have a great week. What is your name again?"

Her eyes lit up, seemingly used to being in the background. Surprised that anyone was even genially speaking to her directly, she eagerly replied, "Penelope."

"Well, Penelope, have a blessed day," Dr. T. exited the building.

A door opened. Penelope knew that it meant to *come in now*! She entered, welcomed with a harsh stare.

"Ssssstickkkk to theee scrippppt,. PPPenlope, how dare you tttalk to Dr. T. about nnnneeeding to llllose weight! I have nnnnever had a wwwweight problem. Also, I don't eat at food trucks or lived on a farm. And I have never put drug ssstorre perfume on my boddyy!" Cassidy's scolding dug into Penelope's spirit.

Your weight is that you are a fake and damn phony, you beautiful Barbie Doll ditz.

If it wasn't for me, you wouldn't have a career.

Penelope wished she could let her have it, just like always she tucked her tail between her legs like a cowardly pup, she retreated in her spirit.

Disappointment permeated her face like some cheap make up—this was the place she lived, being the voice that everyone loved, in the body that everyone despised.

9

CHRISTINA "CHAKA" BU

"THE ASPIRATIONAL"

[STAIN OR LIP TINTS—MORE COLOR LESS SHINE]

Midmorning in the Vietnamese restaurant, tables were being prepped, topped with freshly washed sparkling glasses—bleached starched napkins were being placed in the shape of a crane.

Christina was in the back of the restaurant, in the kitchen, in charge of "kitchen duty"—she finished staking the last of the piping hot plates, then on to wrapping the last of the spring rolls—readying for the lunch hour.

In an irritated natural manner, she noticed her sister, Ashley, inhaling a powdered sugar Danish that she purchased from the gas station, along with her Café' Caramel Macchiato.

"Damn, girl. You are eating that like it is *The Last Supper,*" she smirked at her arch nemesis since they were diapers playing with Fisher Price toys.

"Shut up, Christina; you're perpetually so shady—" Ashley, always a bon-a-fide *tattle-tale*, she spoke loud enough so their mother, in earshot could hear the taunting.

Their mother shook her head to ignore the continual annoying bickering, while she added extra chopped chilies, along with finely minced garlic—her secret signature ingredient to her famous spicy fish sauce recipe.

"Ashley, go to hell with your *bitchy ass!*" Christina yelled out into the stainless-steel appliances as she completed the last wrapping of the vegetable spring rolls, while she stuck out her tongue at her nettlesome sister.

101

Their docile mother slammed down the sharp knife, so sick and tired of her *two jewels' constant* fueling manner, attempting to get the attention of her beautiful bickering girls—mixing her native tongue with English.

"Cô gái Dừng nó. Girls, stop it right now! Love each other," their mothers' broken English attempted to cease the fussing daughters who could never get along.

Ashley huffed, shrugged past Christina, bumping her shoulder, while Christina continued to taunt snidely while stacking the plates, then went into the back storage closet where the non-perishables were housed—her reprieve, where she felt the most at home.

"Hey, man, give me a *cig*," she copped a cigarette from a dishwasher, took a drag, exhaled slowly.

"Go ahead, tell us *one*—" The men asked for a *pick me up*, something to light their fire to get them through the endless days of *busting suds*.

"Okay, here it goes. Ashley's ass is so big, when she went into the laundry room, she turned around, started a load of laundry on the washing machine—"

The men chuckled as they took a drag—

"If I could just teach *her ass* to press and fold, we could start a Vietnamese cleaners as well."

The men belted out of control.

"Christina, you are funnier than that guy, what's his name, *the little comedian*—"

"Oh no, by far—I'm not there yet. I have to get some more chops to hang with the *big dogs*. That's my dream."

Christina was startled when her father entered the room, his stern look proceeded his presence,

"What's your dream? Well, your dream should be to get yourself back in there, and get back to work! Dinh and Cuong, let her be; she has work to do!" Christina's father gawked with a disgruntled brow as he witnessed his daughter in rare constant form.

"Get your ass in my office, *now!*" her father fumed.

Christina had once again been caught in the act, running amuck being a *jokester*, she sat on the cold chair in his self-made office.

"Christina, I expect this from Ashley, but you're the responsible one—I rely on you. Get your head together—*this will all* be yours one day."

Christina was obviously not feeling the way she should feel with the offer. No gratitude or earnest gratefulness; only dread.

"Cha Thực sự, I have different dreams for myself—I want to make the world laugh—"

"You have got to be kidding me—get to work!"

Christina walked away, disappointed but not discouraged. She'd spent her evening hours on her headphones, listening to all of the great comics, from Redd Foxx and Richard Pryor to Eddie Murphy. She would study their timing, disposition, and felt that all she needed was an opportunity to get on stage to see if she really had *it*. If she got up there and totally flopped, then she would consider succumbing to being an heir in the Vietnamese restaurant business. That would make her father happy, causing her dream to crumble into a million little pieces, but it was what it was.

All I need is a damn break—Fat Tuesday's comedy show here I come.

Lunchtime came, the restaurant was bursting at the seams as usual. All hands were on deck, they were in constant need of some more reliable help.

In my father's eyes, our Vietnamese restaurant is a part of his legacy, because my father escaped Vietnam on a boat with his brother. During their tumultuous riptide journey, his younger brother drowned, leaving my father afraid—alone to wash ashore to make it to the land of freedom. He drilled the story in our minds as to how he ended up here in the United States, arriving in New York where he met my mother who was also Vietnamese.

Coincidentally, our mother's journey had mirrored my father's years ago. They hitchhiked across the country, ending up in California. My father had heard about and fell in love with California after hearing the 70s song, California Dreamin, by the Mamas and the Papas. They showed up here sleeping in their car, while working, saving up enough money to get a food cart to serve their authentic food. After some time, they were able to buy a small building across town, with word of mouth, this place that we have right here flourished.

Times were tough, we all lived in a one-room apartment. We ate Vietnamese noodle soup for breakfast, lunch, and dinner, until things really took off for us. Hell, I thought I was going to turn into a mother-

freakin' noodle. Now, we have a nice three-bedroom home, a beautiful front yard with a back terrace. The icing on the proverbial shit cake is a sister who I cannot wait to get the hell away from— inadvertently she's my muse. She is just so damn funny; I get a kick out of picking up my notebook just to write jokes about her.

Sometimes Ashley would laugh until she almost peed her pants. Depending on if she was hormonal, she would be a tattle tale, ratting me out to our parents. Either way, I love that shit. I love making people laugh. There was no feeling like it.

My dad and I were a lot alike, but he could not see it. He aspired for a life that took him across dangerous boat trips to land in New York, venturing across the country because of a damn song. Then there is me, who evidently got the gene to make "life" different, aspiring for something a little unique. It was as if he could not understand why I wanted this! It was like I was some alien, but he did not realize that I was his carbon copy—cut from the same cloth he was.

The lunch rush was on fire on that particular day. The cooks were on point, they were working like a well-oiled machine. Then there he came—*The Idiot!*

Looking around entitled, he belted out, "Hey, I've been waiting for my duck sauce. Where's my damn duck sauce?"

"Are you talking to me?" Christina asked with a furrowed brow.

"Gal, I'm talking to you," the irate customer proclaimed as if he couldn't eat his meal without duck sauce.

We don't have duck sauce, idiot.

"Hurry up and get it. I like to mix it with my sweet and sour to dip my eggroll—my damn eggroll is getting cold!"

We don't have eggroll's jackass. We have Vietnamese spring rolls.

I had to let him have it.

Christina craned her neck back with high irritation, spitting back, "I'll get your duck sauce for you, but you don't need me. With that nose, that sauce will make its way home. *Quack! Quack!*"

The onlookers let out a unison, *"Wow,"* as they were equally annoyed by the arrogant, entitled man who was clearly not going to be satisfied with service, even if Jesus was waiting on him.

"I need a manager, right now!"

104

"Better yet, let me see if I can call a taxidermist." Christina pulled out of her phone. "Hello, taxidermist? Yep, I've got your next *punk-ass duck* you need to stuff. He's on his way—"

The man's once egotistical demeanor was deflating as Christina went all in on his face, his clothes—without having any intel or information on the man—his love life.

Inadvertently, Christina turned the family legacy Vietnamese restaurant into a night at *The Apollo*. The man's once bold cheeks became humiliated, flushed. His entitled cruelty turned on him.

"I'll call the Pope because you're going to need him if you don't get your ass out of here right now—"

"Christina, enough!" Her father came raging from his office, Christina put her head into the *tortoise shell*—retreating towards the back. Her father apologized to the customer, promised to *comp* his meal, as well as getting him some piping hot fresh Vietnamese spring rolls to go with their famous fish sauce to dip them in.

Fuming on her way back, it was clear that her bold comments had caught the attention of a man who was eating at the restaurant that day. On her way to *the principal's office*, she felt a tug on her arm.

"Hey, little girl, you got *chops*. Have you ever considered doing Improv? Here, take my card."

Christina's eyes lit up, as if she'd been told she'd hit the Mega Millions. She took the card for the comedy club down the street, not only that, but behind the card was a tip for fifty dollars. She smiled, felt obligated to offer a response.

"I cannot accept this."

The man raised his hands in a surrender pose, as if to say, *you earned it.*

Christina responded, "I dabble a little, man. This would be a dream come—"

Before she could say "true," her arm was grabbed as she was briskly taken down the hall to her father's office by her stern patriarch.

He laid into her; his anger echoed into the walls of the restaurant. The wait staff turned on native Vietnamese music to bleed out the noise from the scolding in the back of the restaurant. Christina was asked to turn in her apron,

"Go home!"

She went into the bathroom in the locker room. Talking out loud to herself, she wished someone would hear her pain—the weight that she'd been feeling all of her life to live as her father wanted her to. She belted out to anyone that would listen,

"This is not my dream. All of my family wants me to become a part of the Vietnamese restaurant business circuit. They own several businesses. From restaurants, to nail shops, to hair imports; I just can't do it. I want to make people laugh; that is my gift. I'll be the first one to say that today, going *all ham* on that customer was not the right thing to do, but comedy is in me. It's bursting to get out of me. I can't help it. This is weighing me down so much—I cannot get it out. How much longer will I have to sacrifice my dreams?"

She found herself shaking in the metal fold-out chair in the corner of her father's office.

"Christina, get out of here! I can't look at you right now." Her flustered father's eyes, now bloodshot red from anger, moreover, downright being hung over with sleep deprivation from the continuous late nights, along with the early days that he put in to take care of his family.

She got up to leave, putting all of her dreams, along with her aspirations, into the cement brick steps that seemed to weigh her down. Any heroism that she felt moments ago roasting the irate restaurant patron, fizzled.

Yelling from his office, he said, "Christina, go by the store to get some more Bok Choy, Sambal Oelek, Rice Vermicelli, Vietnamese cinnamon, Birds' Eye Chile and fresh lime. I have a list for you, up front. Stay out of trouble. Go by Gadsden's, they got a new produce manager that's Vietnamese—he's made sure they're getting fruits and vegetables we can use so we don't have to go down to The Asian Market. It's good to have that grocery store close."

Still discomfited for her behavior, Christina relayed, "Father, I got you—"

"Christina, don't discount our blessings. You need to work on your resilience for your life; your future; also for your family. All of this is yours one day—all of it. Get yourself together! I had to pull myself up by my own bootstraps, now you have to do the same. Go, calm down and most of all get your head right!"

"My head right, are you serious?" she spoke under her breath while grabbing her backpack, that housed her *Think Like A Weight Breaker. Not Like A Weight Taker* workbook.

With each trodden step that she took, excellence evaporated out of her spirit, that weighed her down.

10

THE BLOG

"UPLOAD GLORY TO DOWNLOAD GREATNESS!"

[WORD.WATER.WALKING.]

Dr. T. put on her cute sweats with bling.

"Time to get into my word—Luke 1:37. The Lord is my Rock, that's my premise for the day," she thumbed through her bible.

She laced up her shoes, "I got my topic I'm going to lean into, now it's time to get my water ready," she pressed the button of the reverse osmosis water spout on her refrigerator, taking a gulp to hydrate her muscles, joints and organ systems. Her tired finger pressed the wall remote to open the garage door. With her arms extended above her head and leaning to the side, she stretched readying herself for *The 3W's.*

The morning cool breeze was cutting through her leggings, prompting her to jog a little to keep herself warm. She noticed the gentle sunrise peeking over a couple of clouds that looked like fluffy marshmallows in the sky.

If this weight will just come off, that darn Hashimoto's.

I know I can beat this; I will not allow this autoimmune disorder to trodden me down.

I'm confident that my 3W's—Word, Water, and Walking—will help me reach my goals!

She pushed herself to make it up the hill as she felt victory in her gut, although her now rubbery thighs wanted to give out.

Her arm accidently hit her iPhone, flipping! from her go-to gospel playlist to her audio version of *Think Like A Weight Breaker. Not Like A Weight Taker.*

Dr. T. smiled as she heard her voice,

You have to upload Glory to download Greatness...

It was as if her own words inspired her to determine what she would write about in her blog to day.

"My Weight Breakers need to hear about this to spark a change in their lives'. But before that, I need my pulse to come down," she felt her carotid pulse. "Great, I'm down to seventy-five," she strolled towards home, where she replenished her soul with more hydration.

In her mode to motivate, she sat at her desk in her home office to draft up her blog. Inspired by all of the inspirations that she had witnessed; in every ray of sunshine that kissed her cheeks, every breeze that blew through her hair, in every blade of emerald grass, in every hue of shades of amber leaves on the barked trees, moreover in every pallid columnar fluffy clouds, her soul aligned with her fingertips teemed with grace and glory. From her wits, she entered the words into her computer, thus into the atmosphere under the umbrella of her blog.

THE CHRONICLES OF THE WEIGHT BREAKERS BLOG

Hi Weight Breakers!

Warning, this Weight Breaker Blog is a little lengthy. I have been getting inundated about the concept of daily decision downloads—so here it is. I'm going to share with you about the concept of uploading glory, so you can download greatness.

In the book, *Think Like A Weight Breaker, Not Like A Weight Taker*, you will find the daily decision download samples. Weight Breakers, where are you? We are going to dive right in on how I determined why I addressed the weights of life the way I did.

She continued to wipe her brow, then wrapped her towel around her neck.

Every day, at each moment in time, we have a choice as to how we will respond to life. It all starts with what we have stored in our own personal cloud to draw from. With all of the positive inspirational verbiage we place in our personal cloud, by nurturing our vision, faith, and resilience intelligence with our daily inspirational pathway, or how we work on honoring our daily activities to refurbish ourselves, each day you will get a message from *the cloud* that is meant to influence your decisions.

She adjusted her monitor to get a better visual of her blog.

We have to put positive motivational affirmations into *the cloud*, so we can draw from them to address the proverbial/physical weights of life. Our mental cloud, what we plant into it, is key in how we handle the weights of life. You have to Upload Glory, in order to Download Greatness! Whatever is going on in our mental and psychological cloud has to do with what we put into it! Based on what we put into that cloud, our space, our being, is so very important. We have to upload positive affirmations, positive vibes—inspiring energy into our own personal cloud, so when we approach each day/situation, we are able to download what we need to combat all that comes our way.

She grabbed her bottled water, took a huge gulp, looked down at her sweatshirt embossed with rose gold-colored foil letters on front.

As you can see I'm wearing one of my favorite sweatshirts today. I'm posting the picture within the blog. See what it says? *Good Vibes Only*. That needs to be our premise. This is so very much intertwined with our intelligences that we have discussed. What we have envisioned for ourselves, the faith that we have—the resilience that we illustrate in our response to the rough patches of life, are based on what we sow into our mental space—being a weight breaker is a whole vibe in itself.

Don't forget, bad vibes are contagious!

She reached for her Bible, opening *The Word*.

It says here, in Philippians 4:8., *Finally, brethren, whatever things are true, whatever things are noble, whatever things are just, whatever things are pure, whatever things are lovely, whatever things are of good rapport, if there is any virtue and if there is any praiseworthy—meditate on these things*. That is what prompted me to orchestrate this section of the journey—tactics, called daily decisions.

She smiled at that thought, and took off her sweatshirt to cool down, as her fingers danced on her computer keyboard, now in her sweaty tank top.

We have twenty-four hours is derived into hours, minutes, and seconds. You can deny it if you want to, however every moment is an absorbed decision, after decision, followed by more decisions. As human's our state of mind affects our decisions. You have to upload Glory into your mind to download Greatness; to walk out your destiny.

You may be wondering, what are Decision Day Downloads? To put it bluntly, it is what is pulled down from our soul—the mental clouds that we approach each day with.

It is safe to say that most people enjoy a vacation. Destination to somewhere is on most of our radars as people, as a reward for hard work. Who would not want to jump on a plane right now, buckle up—fly off into a wonderful well-deserved vacation? I know I would. Whether you travel for business or pleasure, one of the gold standards that you hear when you choose air travel, after you board, the airplane attendants review safety features of the aircraft. What does the flight attendant tell you to do first? Yes, I knew you would recall, *Place the oxygen mask on yourself first—then assist others!* As people, parents, whether you are a stay-at-home parent, in school striving to start a career, or a busy full-time employee, we all have something so dearly in common—we all tend to place ourselves on the backburner—putting the oxygen mask on everyone and everyone arounds us, leaving ourselves *hypoxic.*

The presence of the world today has caused us to stop in our tracks, understanding the fragility of life. Moreover, life chooses what you are given, you choose how you respond! So, today we are kicking all professional titles to the curb, kicking all stereotypes to the curb, all the social economic status to the side—focusing on The Inspirational Pathway towards a healthier living, by making good daily decisions for ourselves, purposefully looking at the weight of life differently. We cannot control what happens in life, but we can control how we respond. So, how can we do that? I shared in the previous section that we can impact how we respond, that has everything to do with what we put in our mental cloud. What comes out of us is what we put into us! It's all about the messaging we tell ourselves; how we feel about ourselves.

Our demeanor, our whole presence, starts with our minds. If you peeled the purpose back of this podcast, like you were peeling a banana, at the center what I'm hoping you will find is the exudate of a Weight Breaker. You may be thinking *man,* she sure is spending a lot of time on this subject—yes, I am! It is so very important to understand this, getting this part down to a science. There is an old phrase that we were taught in grade school that is the foundation of my sweatshirt message *Good Vibes Only,* that phrase is, *No time for stinking thinking.* I cannot recall which teacher taught me that. It has taken me a lifetime to really get a grasp on that concept, understanding the magnitude of the power of the mind. We have to make sure that we put some good stuff into our mental cloud, so we can draw from that daily! You can get those *good vibes* from your daily devotion, motivational books, the Bible—all of which you can draw positive inspiration from.

She washed her hands, placing some blueberries, spinach, a fig with cashew milk with pea protein powder in her blender with crushed ice cubes. She pressed a pulse to make a green smoothie.

As I drink my breakfast, I want you to know I've packaged up some quotes that I have orchestrated for myself—hopefully, you also will be inspired. So, each day of this journey is not just a day, but a Decision Day Download from the cloud—Decision Day Download Declaration! I'm reiterating this until you get tired of me saying this.

Think about life so granular that you truly understand that each day is composed of little decisions that comprise the whole day. These upcoming daily downloads are meant to amplify your current goals, life, mission, and purpose on your assignment. Whether it is to lose weight or change the world, it starts with one decision at a time. Your health, wellness are imperative in facing the weight of the world, thus have to be your focus, *your jam!* Bottom line, you're what you think—what you say.

From this moment on, you're a Weight Breaker!

Stay tuned, I have something coming down the pike that is going to bring all of us aligned.

Remember to work on you. You see those clouds behind me in the picture I attached to this blog? You have to imagine that the work that you are doing right now is uploading glory, so you can download greatness.

What you put into yourself, is what you are going to get out.

If you put garbage into your spirit, you will get garbage out. That is a fact!

Love, Dr. T.

POSTED!

:You killed it today, girl. That Blog was fire. You have set my workout goals. You are my shero.—Tabitha B.

:Thank you, sis. I thought I was going to pass out on that walk/run. However, I'm so inspired by helping all of us achieve our goals.—Dr. T.

:Speaking of "pass out," you are going to faint when you hear about my marketing campaign proposal that I have for you. Remember, you told me the sky's the limit. *Right?*—Tabitha B.

:I can't wait; do tell.—Dr. T.

:Are you afraid of heights?—Tabitha B.

:Wait, what?—Dr. T.

11

PENELOPE KING

"THE SHADOW"

[LIQUID MATTE LIPSTICK]

"Go to camera 2. Zoom in...zoom in now on the building! Now, a voiceover of my pre-recording. Camera 2, zoom in on Cassidy's still shot with the voiceover playing. Cassidy's still photo is glowing, welcoming. Now cut to Brett. Brett, take it away. You've got one minute! Now the countdown: 5,4,3,2, and cut."

Penelope demanded, took a sigh as she stood in the sound booth.

"Great story, Penny! Oh boy, here she comes," Brett stated as he retreated to the back of the room *for cover.*

"P.P.P.Pennyy... wwwwhat wasssss thatttt?"

"I believe what Cassidy is trying to say is that she was startled that the picture you chose did not cast her in the best light," Brett said as he hid in the corner like a little boy who just got a lollipop from the doctor's office not trying to share.

"I I-I-I-ook f-f-fat, Pen-n--y-y," Cassidy spat out with her arms folded.

"Cassidy, I assure you that was a great headshot," Penelope said as she shrank in her *shadowlike* shell, doing her best not to make eye contact. She went on to render,

"Cassidy, I did the best I could—you know with your speech impediment..."

"S-h-h-ut T-T-h-e-e hell up! Stop taunting me!"

114

"No one is taunting you, but you have the look, Penny has the voice plus brains. With us working this out this way, our ratings have been through the roof," Brett spats shrinking—his kids private school tuition at the forefront of his mind.

Cassidy, in a spoiled manner, stormed out of the sound booth slamming the door. Stunned, they were left with an awkward pause between them.

"I don't know how much more of these tantrums I can take. We do all the work—*the bitty* still complains," Penelope was fuming.

"Nepotism at its finest," Brett snapped back quickly as he was editing the B-reel.

Penelope shook her head. All at once, her eyes twinkled with confidence to share her utmost desires of being a journalist. She never wanted to be famous or on the evening news, just *anchor-like* were her aspirations, that was a weight in itself. Because she'd suppressed her talent into a bottle of Yahoo—surrendering to being Cassidy's personal assistant, dry cleaning getter, being her toothpick to get the spinach out of her teeth toothpick before she went LIVE adjuster of the light to make sure *the imitator* could show her best side during photo ops. Although her dream was to not be famous, deep down she knew her calling was to be more than she was—a doormat to Cassidy Gentry.

"Brett, I was thinking about doing a piece on wellness. You know the author that *Cassidy* just interviewed?"

"Yes, Dr. T.—The Weight Breaker? She was just here talking about The Inspirational Pathway—I believe she called them *tips?* " Brett replied.

"Brett, you are right on the money. So, I was thinking that we should do more stories on subjects that matter, to help people—not just puff pieces about the latest boutique opening, or the hottest handbags—glam events. We need stories that can help women, empower them. Getting *Cassidy* to interview Dr. T. about the Weight Breaker concept took an act of God! Brett, you're so quiet. Thoughts?"

Brett kept his head down, not wanting to *rock the boat.*

"I'll clean up the sound bites. Sit down—chat with Douglas Gentry. You realize how sensitive he is about his niece. If it was not for Doug, I know for sure, she would not be able to even step foot on the nightly news," Brett stated as he put another pinch of snuff in his lip.

"I know that, but I did not go to journalism school to be the voice behind *the look* for this self-entitled, *grown-ass brat,*" Penelope quivered with her head leaning in to view the workmanship of Brett's editing skills.

"It's a job. Penny, don't bite the hand that feeds you," Brett replied while he clicked away—then played back the finished product.

"See, you sound great," Brett chewed with a smirk on his face.

For whatever reason, as this had been going on for several years, seeing Cassidy with Penny's voiceover made her feel *some type of way*. She watched the picture with screenshots of the boutique opening. It looked well done; however Penelope King was listed only as the editor—not the anchor when it was her voice, her words—her charisma that gave *the plastic fake anchor* her platform. She only smiled, took a pic—there was a voiceover.

She snapped back at Brett. "This shit is ridiculous. This ditzy blonde; I just can't take it anymore—"

"What do you mean? Sweeps week is coming up. You are not talking about *flying the coop*, are you?"

"I don't know what you call it, but I'm going to make some moves. I need my big break—"

"Well, up in here, Douglas Gentry only likes the sixes—size six waist and size six shoe. I really like you, Penny, but girl, you are... well, a little too plus-size to make it here. You are not *eye candy* for his type of marketing. You should consider a more invasive option. My sister got the gastric sleeve; you can't tell her anything now. She was three hundred pounds, now she's a hundred fifty wearing a halter top with daisy dukes."

Brett looked over at Penny, she had a clipboard in one hand, stressfully unwrapped a Snickers bar, bit into it with caramel nougat lingering on her lip.

"Girl, you are a lost cause. I cannot help you if you don't help yourself," Brett added, attempting to be motivating to his frazzled peer.

Penelope returned to her cubicle, not before passing down an aisle of pictures of Cassidy Gentry on the wall with sweeps week awards won for stories and voice overs that she had done. Douglas had made all of the employees at the network sign non-disclosures to render them voiceless on the fact that his niece was indeed an imposter—relishing in riding on the coattails of the talent of Penelope King.

For once in her life, Penny grasped that this was her life. She sat at her desk with a Twizzler in her mouth as she typed away, drinking her

116

Mountain Dew. She was mocking up the presentations, getting them ready for stories that she was shaping up for sweeps week. She received an alert on her phone from the Weight Breaker App, that prompted her to get to work on her vision board.

I need to get my damn vision board completed A.S.A.P.!

There is power in putting my goals out into the universe.

It's as if I eat sugary Weight Taker Cereal every day.

From outside where the cubicles were, Penelope watched Cassidy through the floor-to-ceiling glass of her corner office. She stood behind her onyx desk with gold-paneled feather wallpaper, talking to her ever-so-patient assistant who finished her sentences, beckoned to follow any *broken* commands.

I cannot believe I have allowed my life to come to this, I've sacrificed my soul, to do this?

Penelope opened up her compact mirror, saw not only residue from the Snickers bar in her teeth, along with a small piece of Twizzler in the corner of her mouth. She cleaned her face up while self-talking,

What have I become?

I'm a behind-the-scenes journalist, moreover an even farther behind-the-scenes anchor of the evening news.

I'm the brains behind the operation—overlooked based on me not being the package of what the perfect Barbie doll anchor should look like.

I graduated top of my class in journalism school. My story ideas have brought our network multiple awards. However, my physical weight has brought me to the place of not constantly having a seat at the table, but being in the background of everything. I make light of it with humor—sometimes painfully laugh along at the jokes, while I'm crying inside.

Do I have a shred of dignity left?

In my plight to get to this very space, I've worked at a car wash, flipped burgers at McDonalds, scrubbed toilets while working on my journalism degree. The funny thing is that, in those situations I had more dignity then, than now.

This what I am doing right now, is downright pathetic.

Penny's day had wound up—she was tired. Cassidy, along with the top anchors got on the elevator, Penelope got on. There was an awkward silence. She broke the silence. "Hey guys, what y'all getting into tonight?"

It was obvious that there were plans that she was not privy to, as everyone had changed clothes—seemed to have an unknown *code of silence* of where they were going to land for their evening outing. Cassidy's assistant broke the awkwardness when the elevator door opened, they filed in formation to get off.

"Penny, I'm sure you would be bored out of your mind. Big execs; pre-sweeps week stuff—"

Attempting to fit in, she broke the lack of relevant conversation. "I have no plans—I'll tag along," Penny nervously smiled with a clinging in the air, begging for acceptance.

She stood there out of place with the group. The car arrived; the clique of women got in. Penny was the last to attempt to enter, there was no room.

"Oops, sorry, Penny. If I had known you were going to come, I would've ordered a *bigger* vehicle!"

In her aura you could tell that life had completely been sucked out of her, along with any heroism she felt hearing her voice behind Cassidy's' still photo. She mustered up enough courage to put on a brave face, took her foot out of the car. The women left laughing, having a ball. They instantly started posting pics of them in the car on social media, with hashtags stating that pre-sweeps week was in full effect.

Penny walked back into the building, asked the bellman to hail her a cab.

A small tear tried to form at the apex of her sunken eyes, from the late nights she'd been putting in at the station.

Why am I not good enough to fit in?

That phrase crossed her mind a time or two.

Then she noticed *her comforter*, the one that she could control—the ice cream vending machine.

Penelope licked her lips, while her eyes zeroed in on the chocolate ice cream bar dipped in a layer of caramel, drizzled with chocolate sprinkled with almonds.

118

Her fingers shook like an addict, as she punched the buttons, her hands in eager expectation of receiving the treat to drown her sorrows, once again.

The spiral wheels that held the delectable, spun—delight arose in her chest.

Then all at once, they stopped turning.

"What the hell? Are you freaking kidding me?"

She gave the machine one good pound—nothing.

Penelope stood there alone, in disbelief—feeling slighted once again.

She considered, taking her robust fist that once held many a softball bat, to swing with all of her might shattering the clear glass, unhanding what she'd deserved.

If only I could be that bold about my life—my career?

Penelope pondered while she walked away from being duped by the vending machine.

"Can this day get any worse?"

A strong gust of wind came, she got into the cab,

"Where are you headed?"

"The grocery store—Gadsden's."

On the way to the store in the cab, she tuned into The Chronicles of the Weight Breakers Podcast as she bit her lip in eager anticipation of what was supposed to be an ice cream bar. However, she listened, attempting to find a granule of excellence that could seep into her withered soul.

12

PUTTING HER WORDS TO THE TEST…

"IS THE SKY THE LIMIT?"

[QUICK QUIVERING CHECK-IN]

:You are going to be fine.—Tabitha B.

:I cannot believe that your ass talked me into this. I can't do this!—Dr. T.

:Yes, you can. Explore a new mindset; isn't that what you say in your book? I need to make this happen in my own life!—Tabitha B.

:Yes, but this is my life that we are talking about. I know you wanted to explore creative marketing angles, but this is ridiculous.—Dr. T.

:Just let loose for once; think about all of the Decision Day Downloads. Put your words to the test. How do you put it, Download Greatness so you can Upload Glory, in your book?—Tabitha B.

:No, it's Upload Glory to Download Greatness. If you are going to quote my book ,get it right! Tell me again why did I hire you? Girl, I know I talk about the clouds, but did not think that I would be up there with them. I guess the sky is the limit?—Dr. T.

The hum of the single engine plane rattled Dr. T.'s nerves.

What in the hell am I thinking?

I'm so glad I only had a breakfast bar this morning, but I feel thunder in my gut already.

Dressed in her bright yellow flight gear, Dr. T. turned to the professional jumper guide.

"Are you sure all of these belts, buckles, and harnesses are tight?" She was shaking in her boots.

He smiled in a calming manner.

"Yes, Dr. T., you are secure. Take slow, deep breaths. Put your goggles back on," the jump instructor shared.

Dr. T. complied with the order, looking around at a few flight jumpers on the small engine plane. The bumps from the air paralleled her life: busy wife, mom, physician, author, being everyone's everything—soon-to-be a *pancake on the ground?*

What the hell? I feel sick to my stomach, she thought as she looked down over the beautiful green terrain of God's lovely countryside.

That would not be a player's move to vomit all over tarnation during the jump. Please, Lord, settle my stomach. Be a hedge of protection around me.

Flashes of her family raced through her mind.

I can't do this. What am I trying to prove? Her flight guide sensed her hesitation, stating to her once again,

"Breathe," the instructor soothed.

:Where are you, chicken? I've made it to *the hotspot*; go ahead—jump already. I see you have not gone LIVE yet. Let's do this!—Tabitha B.

That prompting played still in her spirit until she got a video call from her husband and son.

"Hello, mom."

The sound of her son's voice caused her to tear up. He placed her on speaker.

"Mom, you can do this, God has got you; remember that. You are a Weight Breaker, just like your books/podcast. Do this for the fundraiser, to help those women that you minister to with your motivation. Dad wants to say something..."

"Babe, you got this. However, if you want me to tell them to land the plane now, I will."

Dr. T. gazed at the robust clouds, knowing that every prayer that she ever prayed had transcended those clouds, catapulting their way to heaven, nestling themselves into the heart and ears of God—then the blessings came down. That presence of love resonated through the phone.

"Babe, I love you both for your support—I'm going to jump. You should see Tabitha at the landing spot."

"We love you too. Yes, babe, she is just driving up. You got this; I love you..."

Dr. T.'s son requested the phone back from his father.

"Let us pray, Mom. Father God, we pray for our family, protect Mom from dangers seen and unseen. Let her have the courage that she gives all that she encounters, to make that leap of faith. Protect her, keep her in the mighty name of Jesus, Amen."

"Amen to that, Son. Love you both. I'm going LIVE, then jumping."

CHRONICLES OF THE WEIGHT BREAKERS LIVE PODCAST

Dr. T. 's shaking, confident, empowered finger pressed LIVE on her social media.

She took a deep breath with the loud sound of the engine humming all around.

Hi Weight Breakers!

Yes, I am actually taking the leap today. It is because of my family's support that I have the courage to do this. This is all about establishing a new mindset to break weights, combating fears. I am terrified of flying, so the fact that I am up here, breaking out of my fears, is astounding. I do not recommend this to any of you; however, this is something I felt that I needed to do to break a weight in my life.

Dr. T. took a deep breath, still amazed that she was about to jump out of the plane.

My agent, Tabitha, encouraged this creative approach to message the Weight Breaker principles out. So, as you watch me do this, know that the sky's the limit. I want you to continue to prompt yourselves to engage with your Weight Breaker Journals. Get ready, sisters. You will not be doing this all at once, so relax—enjoy the ride in making an impact on how you see the weights of life. These will be topics that you will do daily. It is organized in a weekly approach, where you will be asked to explore the Decision Day Download topic a little deeper—search within yourself to see how it resonates with your life, align with your day download from the cloud, journaling to walk on The Inspirational Pathway to become a Weight Breaker.

Dr. T.'s lip's quivered with fear, however she pushed through.

We're going to explore a new mindset so we will no longer be Weight Takers! The details that I share about my personal journey are meant to be relatable because we all struggle. But, by no means are the depictions to render a stage to praise myself because praising ourselves doesn't stop the struggle; it only creates a new one. Some may wonder, perhaps maybe each day we should *explore* something; some weakness, struggle, or misunderstanding. I would like for you to explore awareness of: joy, clarity, bold expectation, confidence, foundation, and revelation. So, let's discover a novel or new approach to your purpose in handling the *mass* of life. Get ready, get your journal, refer to the daily decision download, put your T.I.P.s on your calendar.

Let's go! Weight Breakers, I am going to hand over my phone as we continue LIVE during the free fall. God help us!

Dr. T. handed over her iPhone, the door of the plane opened, the wind's sheer force knocked her back into the chaperone skydiver that she was now attached to. Her knees buckled, with her feet feeling like they were bolted to the metal bottom of the plane.

"Dr. T. you are going to be fine, don't be afraid. You have to trust me; I've been skydiving for over 25 years. Have faith. Do you trust me?"

"I guess, I have to. I'm up here now."

"I'm going to give you instructions. Listen carefully." Dr. T. nodded her head.

"Your legs will be tucked under me. Your head will lean back into my chest, putting your body into an arch. This arch will keep you stable in the free fall. You won't be able to hear much from me; however, we will communicate with the signals we went over. When I pull the parachute, it will feel like I'm pulling the brakes. We will jerk a little, but you will be okay," the jump instructor advised.

Dr. T. shook in her boots.

"One! Two! Three..."

They jumped, with gravity pulling them out of the plane, accelerating their fall. With instructed positioning, Dr. T. went from a fetal position to gingerly spreading her arms with legs out. The resistance of the air pushed back on them, evening out their speed. Her puckered lips now were crinkled then enfolded upwards to a smile.

This is what heaven must feel like, she thought to herself as she felt closer to her ancestors, even her father who'd recently made himself a home in heaven. She relaxed, taking in all of God's creation.

Look at all the beautiful landscapes, the colors, shapes, and geometry. This is something that only God could create.

She was breathless, as the views were breathtaking. Every hue of green, brown, gray, with blue imaginable was present in that space.

She continued on LIVE as the comments came in.

:That is beautiful. Be careful.—A Loyal Fan

:I'm so proud of you. I knew you could do it. Girl, you rock. Now get on down here; we have press waiting.—Tabitha B.

:Mom, I see you flying. Say hi to Grandpa for me.—Dr. T.'s son

:Babe, you never cease to amaze me. I love you so much. This jump is yet another jewel in your crown. Proud of you!—Dr. T.'s husband

:Dr. T, if you don't get your ass out of that sky. No really, you are my *Shero*. Drinks after this for real—not chai tea. I'm talking the hard shit—top shelf whiskey, straight up—no chasers.—Dr. Sparrow Mack

:Leave it to you to pull a stunt like this, but I get it.—Dr. Sophia Clark

:I have your book right here. I am doing the work. You are my inspiration. But, I'm not jumping out of any planes anytime soon—I'm a new mom.—Fawn. P.

:Dr. T., get it, girl!—Penelope K.

They reached a certain altitude that prompted the jump instructor to pull the cord. The parachute jerked the duo up a little higher—they glided. It was then in her core that she was able to sail into the winds of life as they gently nestled her, welcoming her into their aerial home. She felt a tap on her shoulder, and turned her head.

He mouthed. "Remember, when you land, you will extend your legs in front of you. We will run after hitting the land."

She nodded her head. She gave a thumbs-up to her instructor, holding the LIVE feed.

:Mom, you are almost there. We see you in arm's reach.—Dr. T.'s son

:Babe, you got this!—Dr. T.'s husband

:Why didn't you wear stilettos? Now that would have been a bomb-ass landing to catch on social media.—Tabitha B.

:You are doing your thing; so proud of you. Wish I could have been there for the landing. I'm here at the rehabilitation hospital with Luke. He sends his regards. We are praying for you sis.—Dr. Sparrow Mack.

BOOM!

Dr. T's confident feet kissing the ground was a momentous occasion. Instantaneously, she missed the *exuberant freedom* she had experienced during the free fall—addicted to the rush.

The tethered jumpers ran with accelerated momentum, then fell to the ground, still strapped to one another.

Hysterical laughter came over her, being terrified mixed with relief, yet now an unafraid empowered newly ordained sky diver.

Weight Breakers, I did it! I did it!

The Weight Breaker in wonderment of what she'd just accomplished, unbuckled herself from the jump instructor.

She ran to her son and *her King* with tears of joy sweeping over her cheeks. The other skydiver came over, handing her the phone that was still LIVE on social media.

Weight Breakers, oh my goodness can you believe it? I'm crying, don't worry these are tears of joy. I miss that feeling of freeness already. I uploaded joy, so I could download greatness. Weight Breakers, truth be told, I can't wait to do this again. This is pure God-gratification, I'm signing off, until next time.

Love, Dr. T.

Tabitha came up from behind her, tiptoeing through the marshy grass in her five-inch stilettos still connected with the social media commentary,

"Girl you did it. We have some more great news coming down the pike, so you stay tuned. The Weight Breaker will be in the building soon. It is going to be epic!"

Tabitha and Dr. T. enfolded, then the whole skydiving crew took a monstrosity of poses. Up above the clouds was the weight of Dr. T. 's fear of flying.

Furthermore, a yearning of wanting to continue to inspire with uploading glorious affirmations, so she could download greatness in every aspect of her life.

13

THE ABIGAIL LANCASTER

"THE VAULT"

[MATTE LIPSTICK-A SOPHISTICATED VELVET FINISH]

The Abigail Lancaster sat sternly at her onyx desk. Her office was cold, not in temperature—however, in the aura she casted. *The Abigail Lancaster's* rigidness was her trademark, the staple of residue left behind everywhere she went.

She exhaled deeply, hollowing as she wrote with her sterling silver Ampersand fountain pen. She signed checks, then pried her desk drawer open, grabbed her voice recorder, pressing RECORD. Her stern, matte lips with a velvet red finish spoke into the recorder.

"I appear to have a heart of stone, thought to be a fierce nose literary broadcaster, but the shell of the woman that I am came with time—the weathering of life. To my babies, know that Momma loves you. You will be well taken care of. Angelica, you are my complete joy. After your father died, it was only you and I—"

Abigail appeared strong, but when she made that statement, her quivering lip illustrated her falling to pieces internally. Images flooded her mind of her in the delivery room holding her baby for the first time. She thought back to her first husband, Andrew, who had been killed by friendly fire in the line of duty. She kissed his dog tags that always held a secret special place in her desk drawer, illustrating what her life could have been if she'd not been cheated out of the love of her life.

I imagined many days if Andrew would come back to me whole, safe and sound from the war. Would he be wounded? After his untimely death in battle, the only thing I did know is that every time I heard a knock at the door, my mind whirled back to the day when I got the news that my beloved was killed in an explosion on the front lines.

126

Can a widow have P.T.S.D. from such a horrific event? My answer is yes.

Her brow furrowed when she thought of the manipulations of Andrew's best friend who flew in to be by her side for the delivery. John, whom she would later marry, regretting every second. The conceptions infiltrated her fragile stoic mind, she'd never really allowed herself to grieve...

"My daughter, Angelica, you are strong and powerful beyond your own imagination. Follow your dreams while taking care of your little brother, Aaron Samuel 'Sammy', whom I lovingly call my *Ace*, I realize your stepfather, John, is quite a mess at times, but understand that I made him that way. I have taken all of my anger towards God out on John because God *took* my true love, Andrew, your biological father from us. He's been a good step-father to you both. After I'm gone, there may be things that are said about me. However, make no mistake, you both are my world—there was nothing that I would not do for you two. The demons of my life have simply become too unbearable; therefore, I need to go. Everyone around me attempts to get close to me, however I cannot let anyone in. It appears that I have a heart of stone—I don't know how to fix myself. The weights of life keep mounting upon my spirit, causing irrefutable damage—an incurable illness. Now I'm at the risk of losing it all due to this terrible disease, however for once I want to exit on my own terms. I am sacrificing myself, to spare you from witnessing me suffering. I love you."

Abigail pressed the STOP button, placed the recorder in her purse. She opened up the envelope on her desk, one that had been opened before. Her eyes welled up with tears when she thumbed through black and white pictures of a familiar man with a familiar woman holding hands, kissing, enveloped in each other's presence, laying in her bed. The man was her husband, John—the woman, her best friend, who was also her assistant—Margot.

This repulsed Abigail, moreover revenge set up in her spirit. But what is she to do? She did not have long on this earth. Abigail poured herself a stiff drink, stood at the window of her executive office watching the clouds roll in—her phone rang. She rolled her eyes, as she accepted the call.

"Speak!"

"Abigail, Joe here—"

"What is it, Joe? I'm not in the mood."

"I told you that our ratings were hanging in there on a wing and a prayer—"

127

"Well, what is it? I don't have all day."

"I have some good news and some bad news. Which one do you want first?"

"Joe, get to the damn point, *now!*"

"Your ratings went into *the shitter* really quick after the last tirade you displayed, going off on that new author. Turns out she has a very present following on her underground website—they have torn you to shreds."

"What's new? I say shit, *pissing* people off all the time; that's my M.O. Joe, why are you surprised? When you get *The Abigail Lancaster,* you get *Motherfucking Abigail Lancaster* and all the brash bullshit that comes with me. Everybody knows that," Abigail clapped lingering on her bourbon on the rocks.

"Well, now you're messing with my money. I need you to apologize on your show; kind of like the *beer summit* olive branch. You have to do this *one solid.* That will keep us afloat a little longer."

There was a pregnant pause. Joe got the clear indication that Abigail's stubbornness was a part of her package deal. "Abby, girl, I know you hear me."

"Joe, I'm not drafting shit. But what I will do is read the statement that you're going to draft for me, consider it, and think about reading it on air. Besides, soon none of this will matter anyway—"

"It matters, that is one of the biggest burdens of working for you. You don't think about consequences of your actions—always throwing your weight around as if you are immune to any casualties of *war*—"

"Slow the fuck down, Joe. You know not to even mention *war* to me," his ill-formed comment rips at Abigail's soul, she caresses the dog tags.

"I'm so sorry, I didn't mean to offend you—I know that you losing Andrew is still a sore subject. However, full disclosure—no one ever knows what in the hell to expect from you. It's like walking on constant egg shells. It's not what people are asking for, your brashness. Nonetheless, it's what you are handing out whenever you show up to add insult and injury, like putting your rudeness on a silver platter, magically thinking that it's going to turn into filet mignon. Not going to happen."

"That's the way that I am—"

"Well, that's nothing to be proud of, there is no heroism in your behavior. Somehow, you've let the excellence of who you are, become drowned out by your sarcasm. If you want to lose your show, keep acting like you've been acting, that's that!"

"I've said what I need to say. Joe, there is another call coming in from an unknown number. I'll catch up with you later."

Abigail took another big gulp of her drink, she answered,

"Hey, this is The Abigail Lancaster. Who is this? Speak!"

"Hello, this is Judge Regina Hinson—I have found your puppy."

"Found my puppy? That damn girl!" Abigail said, totally pissed off, then made a note on her post-it note to fire Marsha.

Then a confusing response came from the judge. "No, the puppy is not a girl—"

"I know what kind of puppy I have, missy!" Abigail collected her things, prepared to leave her *cement office*.

"Well, ma'am. What I was attempting to say is that I found your pup this morning, just now obtained the microchip information. I'm reaching out to you to see when it would be a good time to meet up so I can give you your pup."

"What side of town are you on?" Abigail said in a short response, still attempting to gain some self-control from the conversation with Joe.

"Midtown," Regi retorted, taken aback by the abrasiveness of the woman who she felt should be ever so grateful because she saved her canine. Not to mention, the damn dog almost cost her the job she loved.

"Perfect. You know Gadsden's Grocery?" Abigail replied as she took the bourbon to the head.

"Yes, I know it well. I have some shopping to do for our sons' school PTA bake sale—" Regi was eager to share, hoping to connect with The Abigail Lancaster; however, she did not see *the blaring lights* that indicated that would be an epic failure.

Abigail prided herself on being friendless. There were no sisters, no good girlfriends, no one to truly confide in—even more so now that Margot had betrayed her. All of that was a weight that hindered the stern-nosed woman from finding any sort of sounding board. She was *The Vault*—she liked it that way.

"Yeah, yeah, yeah, meet me there at seven. Don't be late!"

Abigail abruptly ended the call.

She grabbed her Mouawad 1001 Nights diamond purse, summoned her driver to take her to the Maserati dealer. It was clear that her arrival had been anticipated as she was greeted with a crystal flute of champagne, along with a warm, crisp white towelette that was handed to her with a tong. She was welcomed by Harlow, the head of sales for Maserati, whose time off was hours ago. He was insistent on handling the sales paperwork of Abigail's custom car himself.

The glistening fine automobile whipped around the interior, the circular drive of the dealership, into the showroom, filling the air with the Quattroporte's acoustics.

"Abigail, you would not believe *your baby*; it's beautiful." Harlow smiled with pride. Abigail sternly looking over the car, peering her head into the window taking a glance at the custom seats,

"Aaron and Angelica names embroidered in the seats—nice."

"Yes, I knew you would be pleased. A pre-birthday present, isn't it?"

Abigail furrowed her brow; she wasn't impressed by the extra attention she was getting.

"Well, we put the extra-protective covering over the entire body of the car. An asteroid could come down from the galaxies and wouldn't leave a scratch on this *baby*," astounding reassurance in his eyes.

Looking around eagerly in an ungrateful tone, Abigail demanded as only she could, "Where the hell are the keys?"

Harlow handed her the keys.

Abigail jumped up, leaving the dealer standing dumbfounded, she only heard muffles of his talk as if she were in a *Peanuts* movie.

"The Abigail Lancaster, you did the damn thing finally—didn't you," Abigail said as she got into the car, mentally checking off her *bucket list* fantasy car, before it was all over…

I might as well go out in style; she held back a single tear. Still enamored by the classic beauty that she was seated in.

Harlow went headfirst into showing her all of the amenities of the pristine vehicle.

"Ms. Lancaster, you see here. This is your 3D monitor, this is your rearview monitor, this is your sensitivity monitor. You have all of the details that you need to make this car all but fly into the horizon—"

"What's your name again?"

"Harlow," he smiled thinking how great it would be to get a five-star review from the celebrity radio host—

"Harlow, leave out all the buttery shit, I know all about this vehicle. Paperwork please!" she snapped as she galloped towards his office.

Harlow was taken a little off guard, picking up the pace to keep steadfast behind *the boss*.

I can't believe I chose to miss my little girl's piano recital to stay extra late to give Abigail Lancaster the Tour de France of her luxury automobile.

Abigail signed on the dotted line.

"Mrs. Lancaster, be careful. A storm is coming," Harlow stated as Abigail exited the garage of the upscale dealership.

She raised her hand in acknowledgement, left the dealership. Echoing in the atmosphere was the sound of the Maserati, with the tailpipes blaring out of the parking lot. She did handle the whip well, though it was way too much for her. The road was paved with fury, she let loose towards Gadsden's Grocery to pick up the pup.

A whimper of thunder blazoned in the distance. Sunset was not due for a while, yet columnar clouds were weighted with the declaration of something different on the horizon.

"Damn, I should have asked for some plastic for little Gadsden to protect my seats." Abigail looked at the console, attempting to turn on her radio.

All of these gadgets look like a spaceship. Abigail, you should have allowed the man to show you how to operate the car— stubborn me.

While messing around with the gadgets, she received a text from her assistant:

:Boss, you good?—Marsha C.

:Please have my Xanax called into Gadsden's Pharmacy. Just transfer the prescription. I need a full 30-day supply this time.—Abigail L.

131

:I'm all over it! Be Careful.—Marsha C.

:How in the hell did you lose the dog?—Abigail L.

:That is what I have been meaning to tell you. You see, I think your husband may have left the door cracked.—Marsha C.

Marsha's text was interrupted by The Abigail Lancaster's snapback text.

:Don't worry about it. Leave your keys with the entrance man at the gate. You're fired!—Abigail L.

Abigail dropped the phone as if she was dropping the mic. She flipped some switches, blaring out of the speakers came a podcast, surprisingly she listened in—

CHRONICLES OF THE WEIGHT BREAKERS PODCAST

Hi Weight Breakers

As promised, one of the first explorations of a new mindset is awareness…

Man, this chick is all up in my headspace. I will never allow anyone to know that I listen to this crap. I'm a closet listener.

Thank you for joining me on the journey through the skies during the skydiving event recently. I'm still exhilarated by the experience. This showed me that it is so good to explore the thought process of how we view the weights, or what we see as weights, in our lives. One quote that I absolutely love of Voltaire's is, *"Life is bristling with thorns, I know no other remedy than to cultivate one's garden."* How profound is that? To understand that there will be thorns, hard times, with circumstances that swell up into our lives. We must be on high alert for the thorns of life, recognize them, not to succumb to them; however, pluck them out. Write in your journal on how you can recognize, cultivate, meanwhile exploring your own proverbial garden! It's helpful that we know that the thorns will be there. You are exhibiting awareness that life is not going to be easy, nevertheless make each obstacle a stepping stone. That is part of cultivating your proverbial garden of life.

Abigail was attempting to get a handle on the car as she listened in with a stern ear.

We have some more exploration/soul-searching to do. Within each of us there is a soul, whether we want to acknowledge it or not—it's there. That is the full-disclosure between life and death. The light that you bring into the universe is your life. How are you nurturing that light? How does your light shine? Is your light a flicker that is barely noticed when you walk into a room? Or does it halo—illuminate, even after you leave?

It seems so cliché to state the common phrase, *your windshield is bigger than your rearview mirror.* Real life issues of unrest, concern, compounded with dismay can be downright debilitating. With that being said, understand the fact that looking forward is so very important. When you look forward, you are more likely to see the light that guides you into your purpose.

I need to be more aware to start looking forward. I think I can do that, Abigail thought to herself, feeling a conflicting waiver of confidence and despair.

Weight Breakers, we have to be aware that the eyes are the windows to our souls. The windows of our souls are constantly inundated with computer screens, social media, and television. To allow peace to resonate with the visions that are attempting to manifest in your life, sometimes all of those platforms of information that pound on our mental space can cause you to catapult towards looking backwards. Now, more than ever, it takes a conscious effort to control your scrolling thumb and put the phone and computer down to steer away—taking a moment to dredge your mind. Make the effort to quiet those whirling, unproductive thoughts that bustle within your mind. Take time to visualize how you are going to strategically look forward to purposefully control what inundated your mind! Weight Breakers, we are going to tell depression, fear, sadness moreover dismay that we are weight breakers, not weight takers.

I think I get while everybody is listening to this crap. I need to explore a new mindset, work on my awareness, Abigail humbly said to herself as she tussled with *the spaceship* of a car through the long streets headed to Gadsden's Grocery. She fumbled to turn the radio up to hear more.

Share how you can pause, seeing how good your life is. The fact that you are able to listen to this podcast, read the book, *Think Like A Weight Breaker. Not Like A Weight Taker,* you have signed up to shed proverbial weight and physical weight. Together, let us taste life in a new way—realizing that life is good. Expounding upon the idea of *tasting the goodness* of life, let's explore by making a vision board for yourself! Many may say, if you are a weight taker, there is no medicine nor cure. However, we boldly profess today that as sisters we are going to be guilty by association—unified in being weight breakers.

Love y'all,

Dr. T.

While gripping the steering wheel, Abigail pursed her lips,

"A vision board? You can't be serious; this sounds so elementary. Who has time for a vision board?"

She glanced at her wrist, noticing the time on her pristine diamond timepiece, wrinkled her nose.

"I hope this girl is not late!"

Abigail turned the corner, bending the new whip on its wheels. As the once blue sky began to beckon, a few dark clouds decorating the sky—the wind shifted.

14

GADSDEN'S GROCERY

"THE EVENT"

[WHAT'S BREWING INSIDE & OUTSIDE]

Regi

"Namaste. Namaste, my mother-in-law is going to make me catch a case," Regi pulled into the parking lot of Gadsden's grocery store, fuming from the text she received from her mother-in-law.

"Doesn't she know, today is not the day. And I am not the one," Regi closed her car door while she fumed out loud to herself.

Her *almost disbarred self*, scrolled through her phone to get a recipe for homemade cupcakes, while she sanitized her cart.

No, I'm not embarrassed to be a germaphobe.

She continued to scroll the internet, finding a simple recipe,

"Yes, this is it. Lemon cupcakes with buttercream icing. This is going to be a hit." Regi self-talked as she made her way down the aisles. She was a bit excited to attempt to resonate her *inner Martha Stewar*t to get the job done of reclaiming her title of mother of the year that her *monster-in-law*, Suzanne, attempted to strip away from her every chance she got.

Regi's Birkin continued to shift around as Troublemaker was inside her cluttered fifteen-thousand-dollar classic purse, making himself quite at home on the red silk inlet of the bag she gifted herself for her birthday last year.

"You want a treat?"

Troublemaker's eyes lit right up at the attention, with his perfect little puffy tail wagging with endearment. He engulfed the treat. Regi made her way to the end of the aisle, her eyes caught something.

Oh hell no, is this that damn book Dr. Clark wanted me to read?

Regi picked up *Think Like A Weight Breaker. Not Like A Weight Taker*. She opened it to the middle as she always did when she first picked up a book. Her eyes zeroed in on the words that seemed to leap off the page.

BARK! BARK!

Little Troublemaker alerted his new best friend that he wanted another treat, Regi obliged.

"Well, I'm not completely sold on this motivational feel-good stuff, nonetheless, this darn book is *every-freaking-where*—I cannot escape it. I'll get it, but when I'm ready."

Regi said as she picked up her phone, sent a text to The Abigail Lancaster.

:I'm here. Doing a little shopping. Let me know when you arrive.—Regi H.

:Who is this?—Abigail L.

Is this heffa crazy? Regi scowled in her mind.

:Regi Hinson. I'm the one you're meeting to get your dog at Gadsden's.—Regi H.

:Oh, okay. Be there in five minutes.—Abigail L.

Regi continued to shop on a scavenger hunt for: all-purpose flour; baking powder; salt; butter; sugar; eggs; vanilla extract; milk; and lemons. She received a text from her husband.

:You almost home?—Zachary H.

:No, at the store; going to make homemade cupcakes for the kids' bake sale.—Regi H.

:You mean from scratch?—Zachary H.

:*Damn skippy!!!*—Regi H.

:Oh, so you let my mom get to you, *Huh?*—Zachary H.

:Babe, I'm trying not to tell your mom to go straight to hell.—Regi H.

:I know you had a long day, so grab something from the bakery. Besides, don't forget your *Bomb-Ass* Pop Tarts a couple years ago, brought in the highest proceeds for the bake sale. That was epic, babe. Don't let Mom get to you.—Zachary H.

:Love, you know how to make me smile. I'm almost done; I'll be home soon. XOXO—Regi H.

BARK!

BARK!

"Shhh—Troublemaker! You're going to get us kicked out of the store."

Fawn

Walking down Gadsden's grocery store on aisle four, Fawn was on the phone dressed in her spandex leotards with a jean jacket. She was still dabbing tears from her eyes. It was hitting her that she indeed was officially *history* in the life of her NBA basketball player. She knew that she and Alyssa were now truly in *the trenches.*

Alyssa deserves a dad that's "all in." I should've listened to my gut about him, but I actually thought he loved me. Now, I'm officially off the dance performance squad. Then his fiancé came up to the spin class, threw it all up into my face.

Fawn was clearly distraught as she put on her shades, wiping away the weeping that continued to roll down her cheeks. She felt totally disoriented with her surroundings, unbeknownst blocking the aisle.

"Lady, you're blocking the lane. Which side are you going to be on?"

Abigail said in a curt way, not offering any type of empathy to a woman who was clearly distraught.

"Sorry, my bad."

Fawn blowing her nose into her Kleenex.

Fawn found her way to the baby aisle, tuning out the world, put her earbuds in, listening to her favorite...

THE CHRONICLES OF THE WEIGHT BREAKERS PODCAST

Hi Weight Breakers:

Ladies, we have talked about awareness, joy. Now, get your focus on clarity. Life can be like a merry-go-round. A merry-go-round would not be a merry-go-round without the motion going in a circle. As a kid, when you went to the amusement park or the county fair, one of the first rides that you spotted, and you wanted to go on, was the merry-go-round. They're fun to go around on. As a matter of fact, I bet most of you reading this book can attest that in their memory lockbox there is a memory on a merry-go-round. Up and down. Up and down, in the circles we went, we smiled with an unspeakable joy that could only be that of a child. When the merry-go-round stopped, for a moment we still felt the motion of a circumferential movement. We giggled, as our minds along with our tummies continued to swirl.

This analogy intrigued Fawn as she listened intently.

As an adult, multitasking through life can be like taking that ride on the merry-go-round. But not like when we were kids; we are not smiling. We are focused, gridlocked on projects with clenched teeth, due dates, deliverables—so much more. We have to make a conscious effort to stop and be still. Look to Psalms 46:10, *Be still and know that I'm God. I will be exalted among the nations; I will be exalted in the earth!* Trusting in Exodus 14:14, *The Lord will fight for you, and you have only to be still.*

The quiver in Fawn's spirit was a little more at ease with those words of comfort.

Weight Breaker, when we first attempt to stop and be still, our world may be whirling. But soon, we will realize in the stillness, our vision can be made clearer. What is the benefit of being still? Come on, Weight Breakers, a big distraction to your vision is if you are distracted by your expectations of others. I state it like that because, unconsciously as human beings, we place so many expectations on all of the people around us. We live with some level of expectation, thinking that everyone knows about or even considers reciprocity as a part of their DNA. We don't consider that there are different capacities that different people have. Each of us is dispensed with a certain level. Life, circumstances—the many things that life throws at them, it can adjust their capacity over time.

Fawn gathered herself together, arriving at the next aisle, thinking to herself,

I have to be still, allowing God to work. I have to trust in Him!

Some people feel that there are those who have a *selfish gene*—if someone did not grow up in a home of giving, has not had the chance to acquire it along life's journey, that time will offer you opportunities to grow in those areas if you allow it to. Just know, each of us were built to have the capacity to give, we have to be purposeful to unleash our giving spirit. That is where maturation in the spirit comes from. If you give a gallon, be good with giving the gallon—that's it. Don't expect anything, or a gallon back. Let it go. God sees it all. You were born to be a blessing to others. You are a vessel, however there can be angst with that, but understand the importance of it. Consider the quote by the great Martin Luther King, Jr. *"There can be no deep disappointment, where there is no deep love."*

Fawn took a deep breath, as she rolled down the aisle approaching the diapers.

Ponder on this thought, accept this, do not stop being yourself when you experience disappointment in people. Learn to move on. Look at Luke 6:30-35, *Give to everyone who begs from you, and from the one who takes away your goods, do not demand them back*. Weight Breakers, journal on how you cannot get hung up on the expectations of people. The only entity that should have expectations of people is the Almighty! Be generous.

Fawn paused with her hand on her cart, she stared at the diapers, realizing that indeed it was her and her daughter against the world. Although she wanted to be angry, bitter, even retaliate on the mishandling of her—God saw it all. God would have the final say of how everything would pan out.

Weight Breakers, it's okay. You can take your superwoman cape off. We are all human beings who have the same red blood cells (although different blood types) running through our veins. When one hurts, we all hurt. When one is hungry, we are all hungry. This whole thought process is about exploration of a new way of thinking or being in tune, more aware of what you are thinking with clarity—how it affects what goes on within your body. What you want to do with yourself in regard to your family, your health and well-being, your relationships along with your career. Pick one or more of them, visualize what that would look like.

She loaded her cart with the diapers with baby wipes, as she adjusted her earpiece.

By having that clarity, seeing where you want to be, how can those relationships be better? How can they thrive? How can my health and wellness be better? Psalms 37:5 *Commit your way to the Lord. Trust in Him, and He will do it.*

In addition, Psalms 32:8, *I will instruct you and teach in the way in which you should go; I will counsel you with my eye upon you.*

Weight Breakers, get clarity in those areas and execute on how you can make those ideas flourish. That is clarity, sisters. I'm not proclaiming to be a preacher, moreover what I can proclaim is that I'm a believer. Furthermore, we have to encourage each other.

Let me share something with you all. I was challenged with the potential vantage point change to really appreciate one day at a time. You need to have a vision for your future. In addition you have to stop to smell the roses. To truly embrace each unique second, minute, day, week, month, moreover each year.

A *B-Reel* of memories flooded Fawn's cognizance of tender moments of her with Alyssa, which caused a morsel of angst to evaporate from her chest.

Take this into consideration. I'm an avid flier, but not the best flier. Well, what I mean is that, if there was a teleport way to get me to my favorite vacation spots in the States and also abroad, I would be the first to be used in that experiment because of the mere fact of the amount of faith that I have to muster up to fly is profound. You all saw this firsthand with my airplane jump recently. I'm truly a *punk* when it comes to flying.

Ditto, me too! Fawn thought to herself with a vision of her holding on to her fellow dance squad mate's arm when flying to away NBA games on the jet.

I remember one day when we were ready to take off, it looked like an impending storm was in our midst, with blazing skies with lightning and thunder abound. However, based on the location of my destination, it appeared that we would be flying out of the torrential thunderstorms—downright bad weather. That took a little of the anxiety out of my belly. We took off into the black, heavy clouds, after an unflattering ascent into the heavens, I pulled my window shade up—shocked. The sun was shining brightly above the storm haze. It was as if the sun had no clue of the torrential rain that was pouring down on the mass of land beneath the clouds. Nor the lightning that was housed in those clouds was aware of the sun's shining presence. The idea of this is to appreciate all of the beauty of God's creation, Psalms 19:1, *The heavens declare the glory of God: The skies proclaim the work of His hands.* Weight Breaker, take a moment to look back over a time that you have experienced, or have gone through, when it looked like nothing but the storm was in your midst. Yet, in the middle of the storm was a ray of sunshine, or a blessing right around the corner. Journal about this *sunshine experience*; that will give you clarity.

Wow, that is deep. I'm going to journal when I get home. Fawn thought as she reached for a bright array of beautiful toddler barrettes.

These will look so cute in her hair; she beamed thinking of her daughter's beautiful curly locks.

Weight Breakers, even though you may realize that through the storms, the sun is still shining, so many times, we can become paralyzed in the nuances of our past. What somebody did to us. What someone said or did not say to us. How we were treated. Or what we did not have growing up. Or what we feel like we lacked. From people who were raised with two parents, a single parent, foster care, or in a group home, in the human experience, despite our race, character, or creed—we appear to have the gene in common, that is *The Lack Gene*. The Lack Gene, as I call it, is a perspective that we felt like we *lacked* something in the past or in our childhood. It is important to look back on experiences, viewing them as such—not crutches, entities to dwell in. You cannot build a dungeon of despair of what you didn't have. Alternatively, use those experiences as building blocks and see them as a launching pad towards your future.

Despite everything that Beckett put me through, I lack nothing because I gained a beautiful child.

Equally as important, knowing the future you are destined for will make room for you. In the Bible is a message about that I'm going to paraphrase, *God does not call the qualified; He qualifies the called,* 1 Corinthians 1:27-29. Each of us has a calling on our lives, whether we want to admit it or not. We have a calling. Say it out loud: *I have a calling on my life!*

I have a calling in my life, to help women lose weight—to be their best healthiest self. Fawn said in her inner voice.

One model of a life's calling is Dr. Vivien Thomas; his picture is one of my historical screensavers on my computer. He was a laboratory assistant that did not even have a college education. However, he was blessed with a gift that only God can give. He was hired as a laboratory technician, but his profound visionary skills for research and science caused him to be a pioneer for change in the cardiothoracic and cardiology field of medicine. He developed the procedure that saved "blue babies" by applying the skills that were God-given. He sharpened his astute capability, mastery of study to develop a protocol to fix babies that would surely have passed away without his intervention. To this present day, people with heart disease are able to thrive because of the surgical procedure that he developed, with not even a college education. Most people cannot even fathom that a person with barely a high school education could accomplish such greatness, creating the foundation of heart surgery. I'm here to say that your pedigree, education, and status do not define your purpose. God defines your purpose. I reiterate, He doesn't call the qualified; He qualifies the called.

God, I am called to empower women towards their health and wellness. Furthermore, God, I know that You will see me through this difficult time, Fawn began to stand a little taller as the word continued to speak to her, as it erased some of the uncomfortable memories of the event that occurred hours ago when *the mistress* showed up at the spin studio to flaunt her engagement ring.

Damn, abandonment still hurts. But as my grandmother used to say, what goes around comes around.

Weight Breakers, in this segment, I'm sharing a little bit more about Biblical truth about the purpose of our life. To know God, love Him—glorifying Him with our lives. Weight Breaker, spend some time with the divine, to understand—getting connected to that calling. God will place you in the right space, time to manifest your purpose.

The blubbering in Fawn's eyes had dried up and she appeared to be more upbeat as she maneuvered her way through the store, feeling like there had to be some purpose in all of the madness she was going through...

A.J.

A.J. arrived at Gadsden's, still fuming from the day's events. She was ready to get home, kick off her stilettos, grab a glass of wine—lay into Sean's chest to forget the crazy day she had.

"Excuse me, can you tell me where the bakery is located?"

"Yes, ma'am; it's over there to the back. On the right-hand side past the produce."

141

"Thank you," A.J. said as she looked down at a text message. It was from her mother.

:Anjali, I know you have been having a hard time lately with work and everything. I was listening to this motivational speaker; she said something that reminded me of you. She said that each of us is unique, we should treasure our uniqueness. Furthermore, have bold expectations with our gifts. That is what I want for you, Anjali. For you to be bold, also expect all the goodness that you deserve. Love you.—Mom

These endeared words from her mother took some of the heavy load off the day's burdens that she carried with her from the boardroom. A.J. walked through the produce, relishing in the fresh fruit and vegetables, reminding her of her mother's lovely garden that she harnessed to grow the produce in her own very backyard with her husband, so she could have control of the organicity of the pureness to let the Indian authenticity come to life in her cuisine that she cooked. That made A.J. smile.

She received a pic in a text message from Sean—her beau,

:Babe, this spaghetti sauce is on point. Can't wait for you to taste it, it's just like Italy up in here.—Sean G.

:I'm at the store getting the fixings for the garlic bread. I'll call you in the car.—A.J. N.

:Okay, can't wait to see you. Be careful, the weather is supposed to get *bad* in a bit. Drive safe my love.—Sean G.

A.J. made her way back to the bakery.

"Hello, excuse me. Can I have a loaf of your fresh baked sourdough bread?" she asked the bakery worker.

"Well, ma'am, they're all out on the display barrel. Is there not one to your liking?"

"I see that. However, I kind of want one fresh out of the oven—"

"Oh, *you* people!" The baker muffled under her breath, loud enough so A.J. could hear her.

A.J. pounded the bakery counter, "*You* people? Get me *your* manager now!"

On top of the day she had, when she heard *you people* in that derogatory tone, it sent her over the edge.

As the manager made his way over to the bakery, A.J. went all the way in on her heritage, that if her skin were a lighter hue, she would've received the fresh baked bread with no implication or resistance. The baker stood there with an opened mouth, baffled by the cussing out she received.

Clearly, the boldness that she displayed at the bakery is what she wished she would have shown in the boardroom today. Even more, what she wished that she had slammed into Scott, instead of choking under pressure...

Penelope

Meanwhile, Penelope piled cookies, candy bars, and chips into her full arms, having the audacity to open the pack of cookies, inhaling one before she even made it to the checkout of Gadsden's Grocery.

Rushing memories of exclusion blustered in her mind while she engulfed another cookie, wiping the heaping of sobbing saturating her cheeks. In her mind, the reel was playing over in real time how, once again she was *iced out* of everything at work. She felt *ghosted* on every level. Penelope was angry as she stood in front of the freezer section, seeing multiple gallons of ice cream that she desired to devour. She'd already gone down the cookie aisle and got her favorite Milano cookies.

"To hell with it," she placed a spoon in her carton of ice cream.

While she devoured the ice cream and cookies in front of the grocery freezer, echoes of Cassidy Gentry continually in her weighted mind.

"Sorry PPPenelope, no rrrooom for yyyou!"

Adjusting her earbuds to drown out the exclusion that pierced her heart earlier, she intently listened to THE CHRONICLES OF THE WEIGHT BREAKERS PODCAST on her iPhone. She was in her zone when she heard the words of the podcast,

Weight Breakers,

It has been proven human emotions such as: happiness; sadness; disgust, surprise and anger can overwhelm the human spirit. Yet, there is one emotion that is paralytic and can be the catalyst of so many other unproductive emotions, that is fear. Fear can cascade a multitude of actions to activate your nervous system and endocrine system to ignite the fight or flight system in which catecholamines are dispatched from your adrenal gland to cause you to get the heck out of somewhere, *ASAP,* to get to safety. Or if you can, give you the wherewithal to fight for your life. Still, to linger in a constant state of fear is not good for your body, mind, or your spirit. In some cases, the thoughts that penetrate our spirit and cause us to be afraid of taking the first step towards change are: What if I fail? What if I lose the weight, then gain it all back? Why should I apply for the position? I'm a minority, I will never get my dream job. Weight Breaker, these phrases are all founded in fear. Eleanor Roosevelt said it best: *You gain strength, courage, and confidence by every experience in which you really stop to look fear in the face. You must do the thing you think you cannot do.*

Penelope dipped another cookie into the ice cream, as onlookers turned up their noses at her lack of grocery store etiquette—*paying for groceries, then eating them, instead of vice versa.*

"What the hell are you looking at?" She peered at a lady who peered over her glasses at her display of lack of home training. The fellow shopper turned her petite nose up, bypassing the woman who was clearly on the verge of having a meltdown.

Weight Breaker, you have to have the confidence to face fear and not give it power. Yes, it would be nice if we got a heads up on those heavy situations—those instances that naturally we would be burdened by or ignite fear in our being. Wouldn't it be nice if we got a pre-warning about a meeting, a class, a situation, a family member's phone call, that presented itself with a sticker on the outside of the box that proclaimed *"Warning, this box is heavy?"* Instead of broadsiding us like life has a way of doing.

By giving us a heads up, you would think that life providing us with this common courtesy would allow us to be able to handle those events a little easier at times.

Yeah, that would be nice to get a warning about the shit that life hands out on a daily basis! Penelope ruminated, fuming from daily constant rejection due to *her weight.*

Circumstances will arise that will cause fear to fester in your belly. Strategize on how you're going to handle it. You won't get the warning that this issue or certain circumstance will be heavy. However, with a prepared strategy, you will conquer that emotion. Weight Breaker, fear has no place in your space. Think about a box with the following contents of the:

Weight Taker Box:

Negative connotations

Fear

Intimidation

Discouragement

Self-doubt

Covertness

Now think about a box with the following contents of; **The Weight Breaker Box:**

Confidence

Love

Caring

Concern

Kindness

144

Ladies, which box is the heaviest? You guessed it: The Weight Taker Box! You have got to give yourself permission, and the confidence, that you are going to choose the Weight Breaker Box!

This is deep. I've been carrying around more than the weight on my body. I've been carrying around all kinds of weight. That hit Penelope's spirit like a ton of bricks.

I've been carrying not only physical weight, but proverbial weight!

I have to do something about this.

Penelope placed the next cookie that she was about to eat back in the bag.

Weight Breakers, you need to re-consider which box you want to carry. This has to be something that you choose to do each and every day.

I want to carry the Weight Breaker Box, but how do I do that? Penelope pondered...

Christina

Christina was charged with going to the store, gathering some more vegetables for her family's restaurant. She had a heated argument with her father about her not wanting to follow *the legacy*—it was weighing her down. She spoke out loud,

"I cannot believe my dad doesn't get me. It is so heavy on me all the time to feel like I cannot live my life but must live the life of what my parents' dreams are. I guess what I heard while driving over here on XM is preparing me for what I have to do. Yeah, they were talking about exploring your foundation. My foundation is a rich legacy, but my parents don't want me to do anything with that foundation but build the exact same life that they had."

Christina made her way through the store as the podcast continued to play in her ears.

Great Weight Breakers, wanting the Weight Breaker Box is the right choice. Anyone who knows anything about construction is aware the foundation is the key to the stability of the building. If the foundation of a building isn't sufficient, the elements of wind and torrential rain have the potential to destroy the orifice.

Christina pulled her dark brunette straight hair behind her ears to listen more attentively, to the podcast as she fumbled around the store,

Ladies, when my husband and I looked into making our first home purchase, the first evaluation that we made of each potential property was the evaluation of the foundation to see if there were any cracks—any instabilities. I learned early on and was brought up in the church and into a strong faith. It was more or less a part of all that I knew, ever since I was a child in Sunday School. However, it was not until I faced obstacles as a young adult, challenges as an adult, along with experiencing the highs and lows of mature life—I feel that just like that building that had an uneven foundation I realized that my foundation had an opportunity to strengthen. My faith had to be strong, my vision had to be strong, if not it would be as if I was attempting to build a life on quicksand.

Christina pondered this whole exploration of what her foundation of her life was, while selecting from the fresh produce, reaching into her purse for the grocery list her father had prepared for her. She inadvertently pulled out the card of the man at the comedy house who wanted to give her an opportunity.

I can do this! I should do this!

Christina proclaimed while she loaded her grocery cart...

The Abigail Lancaster

Meanwhile, at the pharmacy of Gadsden's, Abigail stood at the check-out counter, Bart the pharmacist came over to serve her.

"Good evening, Abby."

"Bart," Abigail replied as she looked nostalgically around the grocery store, along with the pharmacy, as if that was going to be the last time she was there. Taking it all in—

"I got your transferred prescription; you're all squared away."

"Thanks," attempting to hide her shaking hand for her presumed ALS. Internally, she felt as if a knife had struck her heart with the fatal news regarding her health, moreover that she'd planned to end her life.

Bart rang Abigail up, noticing the normally all too stern woman was even quieter than usual. Peering over his glasses,

"Abby, are you good?" with a slight concerned glare.

She nodded as her shades shifted in the motion. That was how she lived her intense life—undisclosed. Her M.O. was to constantly hide exactly how she felt at all times—*The Vault*.

"I was thinking about your father the other day. Boy, we miss him around here—" he stated in a wistful tone.

Abigail purposefully ignored the comment, turning her head as to not let melancholy memories invade her space. Her eyes landed right next to the pharmacy consultation counter. Alongside the gift cards were a line of books. She zeroed in on the self-help book, *Think Like A Weight Breaker. Not Like A Weight Taker.*

She grabbed the book and thumbed through it.

"I can't keep those books on the shelf. I hear there are some good words in there; *food for the soul.* Judith raves about it," Bart replied as he placed Abigail's purchase in a bag.

"How is your wife?" She glanced over her Yves St. Laurent shades, finally allowing her bloodshot eyes of concern to reveal themselves.

"Well, she's been dealing with carpal tunnel, therefore reading is all that she's able to do—putting her knitting down—"

"Please tell her that I asked about her," the sincerity in her eyes resonated with Bart.

"I will. You all are like family to us, my dear. Shall I ring the book up for you as well?"

Abigail looked around to make sure no one was watching her, as if she were a part of a covert operation that would shame her anti-motivational proclamation antics she lived by, in which she blazoned on her radio show, while placing her shades back on her distrusting eyes.

"Ring it up." Abigail whispered, feeling in her soul that she had known for a long time that she needed to make some changes, but why now? When she'd recently resolved to end it all. She did not want her kids to see her suffer through her terminal illness. Moreover, she did not have support from her husband or best friend. That was long gone, since he decided to express his manhood in between the sheets with another.

Abigail placed the prescription into her purse right next to her *suicide note* that she had recorded.

"Give Judith my love."

Abigail left with a raised hand as her ring finger glistened under the florescent lights of the grocery store. She headed over to the wine and spirits section to retrieve her usual—Macallan.

Sirens began to blazon from the outside of the store…

Abigail looked around confused, taking down her designer shades over her nose to see if what she was hearing was authentic.

Regi paused, picked up Troublemaker out of her handbag, stroking him with a trembling hand as anxiety filled her chest, making it hard for her to breathe. The sirens unwelcomed to her ears.

Fawn was on the phone with her babysitter as she heard sirens.

Penelope grabbed the whipped cream from the freezer section; she was adamant that she was going to drown in a sundae, midbite when she heard the sirens.

Christina finally located the basmati rice, then pondered other items to purchase, unbothered by the sirens as her earphones were nestled in her ears.

A.J. grabbed a bottle of Shiraz 1972 wine she had decided to splurge on to celebrate with her *Bae*, after she finally received the fresh-from-the-oven bread that she felt entitled to. She called Sean to get an update on the from scratch Bolognese sauce.

 "Sean, do you hear that?"

"Yes, where are you?"

"Still at the store...wait there is an announcement—"

"Shoppers, can I have your attention please. This is Bart in pharmacy, we've just gotten notice that there's a weather *event* occurring. We all need to take cover now! Please follow the service workers to seek shelter!"

Many of the faces of the customers in the store turned pale as they looked around in confusion, sure that they were on *Candid Camera.* Some continued to shop as if Bart had not stated they needed to get to safety.

A.J.'s eyes got big, "Look, babe, not sure what's going on?" A.J. said as she grabbed her bottle of wine out of the cart, following the crowd. Her love asked,

"Baby, are you okay? I see a message scrolling across the screen telling us to take cover. Take cover where?" Sean said to A.J. as he stirred the homemade tomato sauce enriched with Italian sausage with basil.

"This is crazy; this must be a drill. I'll call you when I get in the car," A.J. said, keeping a strong hold on the bottle of the nice red Shiraz.

"Keep your phone on!" Sean beckoned of his love.

"I will. Excuse me."

A.J. said as she attempted not to bump into Regi on her way to take shelter.

"You're excused. I see you in those red bottoms, girl—nice." Regi commented, trying to keep calm while stroking Troublemaker.

A.J. give a polite smile as she walked by.

Penelope

Bart approached Penelope, "Ma'am, I apologize, but you have to leave the cookie section, follow me over to the shelter."

148

Penelope looked at the store worker with large doe eyes, as if someone had stolen her best friend. She carried the gallon of ice-cream with an open bag of cookies with her to safety with a spoon still nestled in her arm.

"But, sir, I have to pay for—"

"No worries, ma'am. I have to get you to safety," Bart commanded, focused on his responsibility.

The wind began to pick up—the store's fluorescent lights began to flicker uncontrollably.

Regi

:Zachary, there is some weird stuff going on with the weather or an earthquake. Are the boys at home from practice? Are they okay?—Regi H.

:Yep, I think it's just a storm. The boys are good.—Zachary H.

:A storm???—Regi H.

That caused Regi some personal torment. She felt like the air had been punched out of her chest. She was frantic, all of *the judgeship* that was nestled in every fiber of her being evaporated. She was that scared little girl that had nightly nightmares from a storm that shattered her youthful innocence long ago.

:Regi, baby take a deep breath. Everything is going to be okay.—Zachary H.

Regi's hand quivered as she typed back.

:K.—Regi H.

:I'm serious, Regi. You are going to be fine.—Zachary H.

Regi caressed little Troublemaker as she filed slowly behind the other shoppers into the storage area.

Christina

"Ma'am, excuse me—"

The grocery store worker tapped Christina on her shoulder. She turned around, baffled, took her eyes from the various basmati rice selections, pulling one of her earbuds out of her ear; a little startled.

"What's up, dude?"

"Sorry, ma'am. There's an emergency. We need everyone to come to the shelter," Bart guided.

149

Christina looked around, noticing all of the people filing into the back of the store.

"Ma'am? I'm not your grandma, buddy; I'm Chaka!"

"Well, Chaka, you need to follow me quickly. We need to seek safety."

Christina saw the back of his grocery store polo, as she followed suit. It was then that she noticed that there appeared to be pandemonium in the store, with a handful of patrons quickly attempting to get to a safe place, leaving their carts alone behind.

"Oh, hell. What's going on? Let me go LIVE. This may be something to get my Chaka followers amped up."

Christina's eyes related concern as she pushed LIVE.

"It's your girl, Chaka. Here at Gadsden's in Midtown, we are in the middle of mass chaos. What's going on, sir?"

Christina angled towards the man without permission to get his feedback. He politely pushed her LIVE feed away.

"I'm not sure, but you need to follow me quickly!" Bart demanded, clearly annoyed.

The grocery store floor began to shake as he picked up his pace, Chaka trailed. She turned the LIVE feed back towards her face.

"Well, you know how I do. I cause a ruckus everywhere I go—shaking shit up! You all be careful out there. It's your girl, Chaka, I'm out! Peace!"

PING!

:Christina, I saw you on *the gram,* are you good?—Ashley B.

:Yes, I'm good. At the grocery store for Dad. Are our parents okay?—Christina B.

:Yes, we're standing in the doorways. Not sure if this is an earthquake or I heard someone say this may be a tornado?—Ashley B.

:It can't be; we don't get those here. The earth is shaking—are you sure you weren't jumping rope?—Christina B.

:Forget you. Be careful, fathead.—Ashley B.

:Stay away from the windows. We're going to be okay, stupid. Right?—Christina B.

Fawn

Beckett, please pick up! Fawn pleaded internally as she was alarmed that her daughter's babysitter couldn't be reached. She knew that, about this time, Beckett should be at pre-game in the arena, which was near the sitter. His voicemail picked up,

"This is Beckett Trent "B.T." Blaze, make it do what it do."

Oh no, his voicemail. Do I leave a message?

Fawn bit her lip, decided to be vulnerable. This was an emergency. All of the *baby momma drama*, coupled with humiliation of having to deal with his fiancé randomly showing up at her studio, had no place in that moment. She swallowed her pride,

"Beckett, this is Fawn. I'm not sure what's going on with the weather. You may have left for the basketball arena already for your pre-game practice. If you can, please check on your daughter on your way home. I have to seek shelter—I'm having difficulty reaching the babysitter."

That brought Fawn to a light mist of one drip after another, she wasn't comforted by the small herd of individuals seeking shelter to hide from the unknown.

The shelter was a cement storage room in the back of the store. In that part of the country where earthquakes are common, basements were not a commonality and are deemed a death trap. The chatter amongst the people ranged from silence to slight whimpering, to outright crying, to a *BARK* here and there to break the tension in the room.

Taking Cover

Regi was taking deep, methodic breaths attempting not to become unglued. She looked as if she was at the beginning stages of labor in childbirth. This real-time situation she was experiencing seemed to mirror the turmoil of her past. Long ago she'd put that terror in her proverbial cerebral attic throwing away the key. She had hoped that *the cobwebs* would cover them so she would never envision that horror for a second time. The pup whimpered.

"It's okay, Troublemaker. You're going to be fine," Regi stroked the pup. She felt a tap on her shoulder and she turned her head,

Wow, there she is—The Abigail Lancaster.

I cannot act all new.

Regi struggled to keep her composure, not to let on that she was a little star struck.

"Hey, I'm Abigail," her designer shades didn't dare lower at all to reveal her human side to the humanitarian that saved her pup.

"Well, so nice to meet you—I'm Regi. This little Troublemaker and I had a great adventure today. He's quite a joy..."

Regi attempted to hand Troublemaker to Abigail—he nipped.

BARK! BARK!

"Hey now, little fella. It's going to be okay," Regi consoled the puppy, causing her a brief distraction from her childhood memory when a tornado ripped her family to shreds.

Abigail's jaw clenched in disdain at the embarrassment that the pup illustrated the lack of loyalty as she pulled her hand back—folded her arms,

"Why don't you hold him until we get through whatever this is?"

"No problem. The funniest thing happened today with Troublemaker—"

"*Troublemaker?* His name is Gadsden!" Abigail rudely interrupted, causing Regi's *Compton side* to want to come out, however she remembered Dr. Clark's coaching in anger management,

Namaste, Regi. Namaste, Regi.

"So, your name is Gadsden, like the grocery store we're in. Isn't that cute?" Regi stroked his cheeks, he looked up at Regi, totally endeared—not even noticing his owner nearby.

"Well, Gadsden and I had a wild day." Once again, Regi was interrupted as the room grew crowded. Abigail turned her back to Regi—she yelled out.

"Bart, there are too many people here. What in the hell is going on?" Abigail demanded of Bart who was doing his best to control the situation, getting the patrons to safety.

The lights began to flicker, the room shook a little. Bart scurried to corral everyone,

"Everyone, quiet down. I'm Bart, the pharmacist, we've been notified that an F4 tornado has struck the valley. We're in the safest place in the building. However, I'm going to move some of you into an adjoining room to give everyone a little more space. We've reached capacity in this room," Bart opened another area of the storage.

Abigail brushed past everyone to enter. Behind her, a few others filed into the secondary space.

Regi looked around, following Bart as she took methodical breaths while her husband was messaging her to make sure she was okay.

"Excuse me, can I have the Wi-Fi password?" A.J. asked in a clueless, entitled manner.

"Ma'am, I need to make sure you're safe first, then I can consider giving you the Wi-Fi password," Bart said as the winds picked up, seeping under the back storage door—whistling.

They arrived in the side room; Regi was in a panic. Penelope, A.J., Fawn, along with Christina all found themselves huddled right beyond the entrance to the room. Abigail was in the dark corner with her shades on.

Fawn started to cry.

"Hey girl, it's going to be okay," Christina attempted to console her.

"I'm worried about my baby. She's at the sitter—I phoned them earlier, but we got disconnected. Now, I cannot reach them."

Christina side-hugged the complete stranger, stroking her shoulder.

"Does anybody have a radio or something? We need to know what's going on," Christina belted out.

Bart brought in a small television, after leaving the weather radio in the room with the other employees and store patrons. He turned it to Channel 13.

A.J. sat in the corner crossing her legs. She realized she had enough battery life on her phone to use it as a hotspot to work on a document for work—her nose buried in her marketecture proposal. She pulled out a small flask to take a swig, she reflected on how she needed to save her ass due to her epic fail at today's all hands meeting.

"Anybody need a shot before I kill this?"

The ladies stared at her, bewildered. Then the room began to shake uncontrollably. The women sunk into each other around A.J., who was sitting. The whistling of the wind lessened for a moment. Relief filled the room while the women, as if on cue, began to do a round table of introductions.

Fawn, wiping her eyes, initiated the communication,

"Hey, everybody. I'm Fawn—I'm so sorry I'm a basket case, but my baby is at the sitter's, and she is my life—"

"Hello Fawn, just know it's going to be okay. We all will get through this. I'm Christina. I work at my family's restaurant—that's why I was here today. My dad sent me on an errand because I *accidentally roasted* a man that came in. He was being an asshole—I couldn't resist. I also go by my stage name, Chaka. I aspire to be a comedian one day."

"A comedian? Interesting," Regi quipped.

Christina chuckled as if she was on stage, getting ready to improv.

"*Y'all* are not ready for my comedy up in here," the ladies nervously laughed.

"Well, I guess, it's my turn. I'm Regina Hinson—"

A.J. squinted as she peered up at Regi.

"You're a Judge—*right?*"

Regi was confused about how she should respond. Could this be a person who was an admirer or someone who she had to place on her restraining list?

"Yes, I am—this right here is little Troublemaker, or better known as Gadsden."

The room began to shake again. The ladies pulled in closer together.

"Father God, keep us!" Regi belted out, in terror.

"We're going to be okay," A.J. stated, not looking up from her p.c. goes on to share, "I'm A.J. Nadkarni. I'm sorry, y'all, but my client said that I have to send him this document urgently, they are on eastern time, so, it's even later there. Regardless of a tornado, earthquake, or tsunami, I got to get this shit done—my ass is on the line."

Flashbacks of today's work debacle taking over A.J.'s cerebrum.

As if in an A.A. meeting, the ladies said in unison, "Hi, A.J."

Penelope stepped away from the group as the television flickered back on.

Bart came back into the room announcing, "Listen up. Cassidy Gentry is getting ready to come on to give a report!" He frantically adjusted the rabbit ears on the television—the picture went from static to scrolling lines to a picture of the Channel 13 logo. The winds continued to howl, picking up speed.

"Damn, is this TV from the 1970s? Foil on the antennas? Come on," Christina chuckled.

"Yes, it is!" Abigail replied as she pulled her shades down, zeroing in on the television that her grandfather had when he opened this grocery store in the 1970's.

Penelope motioned to the few people in the room to settle down.

"Everyone, could we please quiet down for about five minutes? I have to make this call!"

Penelope demanded the room.

"Yep, here we have it, Channel 13," Bart said as he smiled, stood back with his hands on his hips, seemingly amazed that he had gotten the old TV to work. He took off his pharmacy lab coat, hung it on a hook.

Cassidy Gentry's photo appeared on the screen, the women all looked up from their devices.

Penelope changed her stance, put down her carton of now melting ice cream and bag of Pepperidge Farm Milano cookies—morphing into a different mode, holding her phone like a megaphone...

"Live from Gadsden's grocery store while seeking shelter, it is yours truly, Cassidy Gentry—"

Everyone in the vicinity was startled. Regi glanced up from feeding Troublemaker a treat. A.J. stopped mid-keystroke. They all looked at the TV, then back to the woman in the shelter with them that looked nothing like the woman on the television screen. Their eyes darted back and forth as if they were watching a Wimbledon tennis match. Even the pup became dizzy from the bi-directional viewing, finally nestled in Regi's lap covering his eyes with his paw.

Christina began to slightly chuckle, looking around at the ladies.

"Damn, this is crazy—even the puppy can't believe this..."

Fawn wiped her eyes, walking up to the television, looked closely, glanced back at Penelope speaking, then back to the old dilapidated television, with her shocked mouth open.

"Everyone, thank you for tuning in. Once again, this is Cassidy Gentry, please listen to our weatherman Gary Black for updated information from The National doppler. It appears that we're getting impacted by a significant weather event. Therefore, it's imperative that you seek shelter now, follow the instructions that Gary gives you. Please be careful, we will have more news for you about this event as soon as we get it. This is Channel 13 News with Cassidy Gentry, signing off. Take it away, Gary," Penelope hung up the phone, grabbed another Milano cookie—took a big bite, wiped her chin,

"I'm Penelope King—I work for Channel 13 News," she remarked with a mouth full of sugary goodness.

"No shit. That was so dope. I always knew Cassidy Gentry was a fake. She always uses those still photographs during her *LIVE* interviews—now I know why," Christina commented as she began to put one earbud in her ear.

The room filled with applause.

"Now, that was clever. I must say, girl, you got some chops. I have heard of *ghosting* on radio, but never on television," sarcasm filled the room from with the icon radio host's vocal cords.

Looking around with solidarity, Penelope requested, "If you all can keep what you just witnessed under wraps, that would be much appreciated." Penelope continued to drown her sorrows by sugary carbohydrate loading.

The wind began to pick up more, the shelves on the walls began to shake. So much so that A.J. was determined to save her work, put her PC in her crocodile work bag. The ladies huddled into each other, side by side—they grasped arms like a Cuban link chain.

Regi began to shake uncontrollably, tears welled up in her eyes. Her mind rushed back to the great flatlands of Texas where, as a little girl, her only job in the tornado shelter was to hold onto her brother—she failed that task. The haunting of that experience enveloped every fiber of her being. The lingering evidence of her misgiving was the scar on her hand where charred glass from the tornado embedded itself there, rendering a daily reminder of her survival of the most horrific event of her life.

Fawn leaned into Regi, "Judge, everything is going to be okay. I wish I could reach my babysitter."

Fawn leaped up when she received a text.

:The baby is fine. We are in the shelter at the community center. Are you okay? Please don't worry.—Mrs. Mary

Mrs. Mary sent a picture of the baby cradled in her arms. Everyone appeared safe.

:Praise God! Hold her tight please Mrs. Mary. Let her know that her mama loves her dearly and will be there soon.—Fawn P.

"My daughter is safe and sound," Fawn belted out while clapping her hands. The ladies gathered around, she gently jumped up and down as she showed the pic of her beautiful two-year-old in the arms of Mrs. Mary. Her beautiful brunette ringlets were draped over her cheeks. Her binkie was hanging out of her mouth, as she laid comfortably on Mrs. Mary's shoulder. First, handing her phone to Regi.

"Judge, this is my daughter, Alyssa; she is two. That is Mrs. Mary, she's the best daycare provider in the world."

"She's adorable, please call me Regi. I have two boys, Isaiah, and Isaac, who keep me going. Cherish those moments because time goes so fast. Don't ever let your career get in the way of your family. In the past, I wanted more than anything to be Chief Judge, but family comes first."

Fawn smiled, "Yep, I hear that all the time. It's her and I against the world."

Another tear fell from Fawn's eyes, as Beckett Blaze had moved on completely.

I cannot believe he started a new life, abandoning his old one. Since the paternity test was 99.9% positive, he became even more distant. He even had the nerve to contest initial payment of child support, until I took him to court.

The wind began to pick up, howling—the ladies drew closer.

Christina's eyes widened, "This shit is getting really real. The wall looks as if it's about to crumble!"

She came closer to the ladies.

A.J. stood up.

"What is all the fuss about? Back in my homeland when I was a child, we had dust storms that were like tornadoes many times. They almost always passed over."

A.J. 's casual demeanor seemed to annoy the huddled ladies, especially Abigail who remained in the corner peering over her shades. Her isolated aura stuck out to Christina,

"What the hell is wrong with her? I bet she farts ice chips, she is so cold—"

Christina stated, attempting to cut the tensions of fear that the ladies were all feeling. She looked at Penelope who was back at devouring her delectable,

"Back to you, *Cassidy Gentry*. Why the hell do you let that imposter take all of your glory? I would guarantee you're a shadow," Christina stated, getting up in Penelope's business.

Penelope licked her lips, "It's a long story. Shadow? Do you mean from the *Think Like A Weight Breaker* book? Have you read it?"

"Well kind of *reading* the book, but I do listen to the podcast. You have the typical characteristics of *The Shadow*. Cassidy; yep—she's the Imitator. Moreover, I am an Aspirational—"

The ladies stood arm-in-arm.

"What in the hell are you all talking about?" Regi asked, confused.

"The motivational bestseller book, Think *Like A Weight Breaker. Not Like A Weight Taker*." Penelope shared.

That's the damn book Dr. Clark was trying to get me to read, Regi thought to herself, bent her ear to listen more, biting her lip.

"Hold on," Christina hooked her phone into a small speaker from her backpack.

"Ladies, this is The Chronicles of The Weight Breakers Podcast that was pre-recorded earlier today. It's so dope—"

The ladies leaned in to listen intently, to try to distract themselves from the chaos outdoors. They all settled on the floor in a tight circle, Penelope passed around her cookies.

"You want one?" Penelope looked in Abigail's direction.

Abigail held her hand up to decline.

CHRONICLES OF THE WEIGHT BREAKERS PODCAST

Hi Weight Breakers!

I'm so excited to share something with you today. It is so important to understand that you have to take time for yourself; be unapologetic about your private time. If you do not guard that time, it is up for grabs. I'm not by any means, implying being selfish. You need a lot of private time to collect your thoughts. Monumental tasks do not have to be obtained during that time. That private time could be spent exercising, journaling, meditating, going for a walk, or even plain outright doing nothing!

Quiet time? Are you freaking kidding me? When in the hell do I have time to collect my thoughts? I'm so sick of this motivational crap, Regi thought as she turned up her nose, although she continued to listen in.

It is in your private time that you are able to refuel. That revelation of the need for private time will allow you to regenerate, be a little more malleable. Being too rigid will cause you to break anytime something comes up against you. It will allow you to be more resilient. Let the lessons along with the revelations of your life shape you, polish you.

Too rigid?—I'd rather be too rigid than to be too soft. That's when you get burned, taken advantage of, the words of inspiration were clearly getting under Abigail's skin.

Imagine a diamond within the earth. When you first pull it out of the ground—in the mine, it looks nothing like the diamonds that we buy at the jewelers. They're malleable in the sense that they're nothing close to their potential. They're polished, manifested into priceless gems. Weight Breaker, you are a priceless gem, this comes about by being malleable—really being able to see your potential.

Priceless gem? That is what my mother is always telling me. I continually attempt to dull my shine, just to fit in with these cookie cutter out-of-touch assholes at work. Damn, she is dropping knowledge—as Sean would say. A.J. clenched her jaw at the thought of the continual microaggressions she experienced.

Ladies, journal on how you have evolved over time, even since starting this book. Consider this: before each athlete goes on the field, they will warm up their muscles, it is that stretching that allows their muscles to be more capable to withstand the contest of the event that they're going to be competing in. Will an athlete or team ever pick the players on the team, then send them out to play their first game or competition? No, they will practice. Will they simply do anything in practice? Or is it purposeful? I'm not indicating that there is an element of a perfect practice; what I'm stating is that we must make *efficient practice* key. Think about this. Even if you're not a basketball player, you know what a free throw line is. If you're standing at the free throw line and do not practice perfect form of your free throws, you will not make a free throw. Weight Breaker, you can see how we have walked through this exercise; we are practicing how we are going to implement. Walking this new way of thinking on a regular basis.

When we get through whatever the hell is going on outside, I am committed to practicing my timing along with my craft. I'm going to go back to the drawing board, dusting off my G.O.A.T. comic CDs and DVDs. Redd, Richard, and Eddie, I'm going to make you proud one day—Christina contemplated with pure self-gratification.

Weight Breakers, I have continually been told that I have thick skin, that I'm a little callused. I have built up that tough skin to make it through life. I'm viewed as strong because I was brought up to have the thought process of you must constantly represent yourself well. This thick skin does not make you inhuman or uncaring. However, you can experience so many obstacles, challenges, prejudices, with the weights of life that you can become a little numb to emotions and develop thick skin, as a form of a coping mechanism.

This *nugget* pierced Abigail's awareness as she reached into her purse, popped the pill bottle open with one hand as if she'd done that one too many times before—discretely slipped a Xanax into her mouth, swallowing hard as the room continued to rattle. She attempted to remain steady on her feet from the shaking foundation. However, she could not help but to ear-hustle. Abigail took her shades off, putting them in her purse.

The ladies looked over at her, attempting to connect. As the wind shook the building from the relenting storm, Regi reached out saying, "You can come over here, sit here with us..."

Abigail bit her lip, responding,

"I'm good."

That was the most she'd said in the entire encounter. The sound of her voice caused Troublemaker's ears to perk up in Regi's Birkin bag.

Weight Breakers, I'm going to share a story with you about one of the dearest people to me in my entire life. My paternal grandmother, she was my best friend; she lived to be just shy of 100. She was so full of life experiences enhanced by her sound reasoning. She was dropping pearls of wisdom. I was in my medical residency, and would go by my grandparents' house to make sure that they had groceries—whatever else that they needed. On one particular day, I went by to vent. I was absolutely exhausted; I was post-call then having to work in the grueling clinic all day. I had absolutely no reserve; I was downright tired. I went over to see my grandmother, I cried on her sofa. I told her that medical residency was too hard—I was thinking about giving up. I was expecting some grandmotherly love, hoping that she was going to console me. The words that she told me will forever resonate in my spirit. She said to me sternly, without consolation, *"Get up, go wash your face—get back to work!"* That revelation was tough love, that created more *thick skin* in me to walk into my purpose.

"Damn, that was cold. Her grandmother sounds like somebody I could hang with," Christina's levity momentarily filled the room with a sense of calm.

Ladies, if you're going through an uncomfortable space in time, you want to give up, get up—wash your tears, get yourself back on focus, so you can get back to work!

Even though life can cause you to have thick skin, you still have to walk in someone else's shoes so be considerate. The general definition of empathy is to identify with the feelings of one another. When you get out of your own vantage point, being able to look at what people are going through, it is really a gift of humankind. We can identify with one another, know that there is more than what is on the surface. We are all in this together; that causes us to want to see where our brothers or sisters need help, care, or concern. We are here on this earth to be a vessel to bless others. One of the ways that causes us to be resilient is to experience less than favorable times. Weight Breaker, it is so important to have empathy at your fingertips, to see a need—being empathetic.

I would love to have empathy for my monster-in-law; however, she makes it almost impossible. Zach and I have been married so long, that I'm not sure that her wish that her only son married a Barbie Doll will ever change.

Dr. Clark sure as hell can't fix this for me, because she cannot take the melanin out of my skin.

Nor would I ever want her to.

How can you have empathy for someone who despises you? Regi's mind whirled.

Ladies, have you ever prayed about something, then all of a sudden there is a subtle sign that occurs or an answer to the question that was in your mind? Those are what I call revelations. Revelations can keep you out of harm's way, letting you know that you are on the right path or the wrong path. Take heed to them. Looking for them can confirm if a friendship or relationship is worth the venture. It can steer you, to be your compass through murky waters.

God, keep my family safe. Help me have a breakthrough with that woman, my mother-in-law—Amen, is all that Regi could think as the room continued to shake, causing the lights to flicker.

The words of the podcast still rang in the air...

A Greek philosopher once said, *if you do not expect the unexpected you will not find it, for it is not to be reached by search or trial*. I gather that to mean that, just like we talked about in the vision section in reaching outside of the box, sometimes if you are not resilient and have faith, you will dare not to expect the unexpected. There are certain ways of thinking of life, of action, the end result. I agree wholeheartedly that action is required to move into your purpose and destiny. Resilience, as stated in the Resilience Intelligence, is being able to bounce back when obstacles come your way. When you are not resilient, when obstacles come your way, you can crumble, snuffing out your potential light. You could miss the fruits of your destiny. If we were to have all rosy days, would that not be wonderful? A raise of hands who would like that.

While holding on to each other, the ladies all raised their hands; even The Abigail Lancaster.

Weight Breakers, wouldn't it be awesome if when things were about to take a turn for the worse, we got a warning light to put our seatbelts on, like on an airplane? But life is not like that—we will face unexpected friction.

"Friction—*you Damn Skippy!*" A.J.'s blood pressure rose as she reflected on the *presentation-jacking* that her ridiculous work colleague portrayed at the office that day.

"Oh my, why are your panties all in a bunch? Girl, who pissed you off?" Christina solicited.

"*Shhh*, I need to hear this," A.J. replied as she attempted to glean as much as possible so she would not *choke* again in the boardroom—causing her to lose yet another big client attached with a hefty bonus, to her *less than peer* Scott—*The Jerk*.

Ladies, when you were forming in your mother's womb, your developing fingers pushed against their surroundings in the uterus that housed you.

In embryology class I learned that the pressure, abrasion around the fetus' fingers can occur. Those pressures cause friction ridges that will be known as your fingerprints. Those frictions help shape you into your identity. It is said that no two people have the same fingerprint. How marvelous is that? I told this to my dear friend Dr. Sparrow Mack, thus the muse for the title of her New York Times novel turned Box Office Hit, *Friction Ridges.*

The winds slowed up a little—the room got a little quieter. Penelope stood up; she received an alert from Brett.

:Penelope, not sure where you are now, but I think we should go LIVE with what's going on.—Brett

:I'm on it. I'm at the grocery store, taking cover.—Penelope K.

:Stay safe. I'll keep you posted on any updates I get.—Brett

"Christina, thank you for putting the Chronicles of The Weight Breakers Podcast on—this is good. Full disclosure, I got a preview copy of *Think Like A Weight Breaker. Not Like A Weight Taker.* when Dr. T. was a special guest on the show. The book revealed to me that I'm *The Shadow.* I did the entire interview while Cassidy was in her office getting a manicure and pedicure," Penelope transparently shared.

"No shit," A.J. sarcastically chimed in.

"Duh!" Penelope spat back as she smacked on another cookie, with crumbs nestled on the corners of her mouth.

"So, *Mrs. Shadow,* what do you plan on doing about it? Or are you just going to drown yourself in Pepperidge Farm cookies? Come on sis!"

Christina dropped some harsh encouragement on Penelope.

"I'm a work in progress," Penelope put the cookie back in the bag.

Listeners, even if you are knee deep in the Weight Taker phase in your journey in some areas of your life, it's okay. Remember this, it takes all kinds of people to make this world go around. Understand that statement in its entirety! You will run across several individuals in this journey called life. Every encounter you have is not meant to walk through your entire life with you. Please be okay with that. Having the right people in your corner to have your back is so important. Those individuals are key to what you need to make it through this thing called life. How does that person impact your life?

The women looked around at each other, with the realization that they had only met moments ago. However, they were hunkered down in safety together—with one goal in mind, to make it out alive together.

I've talked with patients, done television appearances, radio spots, talked with friends at happy hour, about health and wellness, the weight of carrying extra weight around. This discussion was a common theme amongst the women in my circle, my patients, friends, and colleagues—I truly take in that I was not in this plight alone.

Then God blessed me with the alignment that I always needed. And I realized, *Oh snap—this is my crew!* There was a vast sisterhood of women from all walks of life, religion, and economic stature. We all shared similar issues we confronted. Battling the proverbial weight of life along with the physical weight of life. I believe that you should become aligned with people organically, not forced. People who are a part of your kinfolk. Your kinfolk is your CREW or your council—you must take heed of what is in your circle. And keep in mind, there are supposed to be main actors in your life, with you as the protagonist and the leading actor/actress. The screenwriter, executive ordained producer is God—a reflection of God's journey for you. You have to stop doing random casting calls to allow *all* of *these extras* in your life—they can cause extra baggage, extra weight, extra heartache, extra drain—especially if God did not send them. Everyone that you meet, is not meant to stay. An old saying is that some people are present in your life for a reason, or for a season—use your discernment of who is who and which is which.

I miss my crew, Regi nostalgically thought about her HBCU sisters that she had been way too busy to connect with. In her mind, she envisioned herself with her beautiful sorors *stomping the yard* back in the day. *And I love that analogy of my life as if it is a script and I'm attempting to override God by doing my own casting calls, that stops today!* Regi confirmed to herself.

Weight Breakers your C.R.E.W. can be broken down into four sentiments. It can be broken down as such: "C"—Charter—what mission aligns you? You have a charter with those who are your fuel, whether it is on the surface or deep within your core. The charter is what your mission is. They're some that your charter aligns with only in your past; that is okay. Nonetheless, it is important that you have a crew that has a charter that is aligned with your future.

Then there is your "R"—Reach. Meaning how do you impact each other and those around you? If you have a positive crew, the mission's ideas and actions should not be self-serving; you should have a reach. Remember, stop attempting to cast people as characters in your story, if they are not aligned with what God has intended for your life—your box office hit, they are not supposed to be a part of the cast of your movie of your life.

Charter, aligned with the same mission? That's a good approach. Reach, that is my mission. That is my goal with my spin class—I've reached so many women, helping them on their fitness journey. Fawn smiled in that thought as she missed her dance squad since being kicked off the dance team.

Weight Breakers "E" is for Engagement. Your crew should genuinely care about you and be engaged with wanting the best for you. If your crew only tells you exactly what you want to hear, you cannot grow from that. The "W"—you guessed it—should be aligned with fellow Weight Breakers! Weight Breaker, please take inventory of who is in your circle. Ponder on this, your crew really matters, it's even in the bible. Consider the book of Mark in the bible. In Mark 2, there was a man that suffered with an illness that made him paralyzed. Furthermore, his body was made whole—he was cured of his paralysis due to the faith of his friends. Make sure that you have friends that will carry you during your tough times, willing to carry you to the roof and cut an opening in the roof to get you to your blessing. *When Jesus saw their faith, he said to the paralyzed man. So your sins are forgiven.* Amen!

The crowd huddled for safety chimed in, "Amen!"

This hit A.J. like a ton of bricks, *It's so hard to engage when I don't feel I can be my authentic self. I'm not sure I can ever reach weight breaker status, but it's worth a try. Also, I need to reevaluate my circle that is around me. I need to be with women that God aligns me with.* A.J. shrugged her shoulders with that contemplation.

Grab your crew, register to attend THE CHRONICLES OF THE WEIGHT BREAKERS CONFERENCE in two weeks. Tickets go on sale at midnight tonight—this is the first annual conference and it will surely sell out.

Sounds like fun, but not sure if I have enough P.T.O. to go to the conference.

Damn, I'm still hungry. I need to find out the location of the taco truck tonight.

Penelope, you are out of control, girl.

Ladies, there are yokes that need to be broken in your life. You need to explore: your new mindset; understand the intelligences; figure out how to cope with the weight of life, understand your momentum types, taking inventory and taking action, checking your connectivity storage reprogramming, downloading deep soul activities, upgrading your thought process, facilitating your firewall, silencing the unproductive noise, turning up the volume to amplify positivity, taking care of your body systems, most of all, taking care of Y.O.U.

Some of your favorite podcast guests will be speakers at the epic conference. There will be entertainment, food, in addition couture swag bags. This is going to be larger-than-life, ladies, designed especially for each of you. See you there.

Christina turned her podcast replay *OFF*.

Once strangers only moments ago, the newly familiar ladies looked at each other with interest, nodding respectively.

A.J. surprisingly spoke up, taking a moment from her computer,

"We should go!"

The ladies took this to heart.

"We should plan a girl's trip—to that conference. I'm talking old school—on the road," Regi delivered, as she unapologetically devoured one of Penelope's cookies.

"Road trip, hell yeah—*I'm down!* Check it, I'm going to wear this new halter I got from Las Vegas last year. It's going to be *On and Popping*," Christina yelled out with the pure visualization of *popping bottles*—with no regard that the walls were about to cave in with the torrential demise that was threatening to blow the house down as if the *three little pigs* lived inside.

"I'll work something out. Mrs. Mary should be able to take care of the baby. It will be good to get away," Fawn took a deep breath as if she was so relieved to have found a replacement for the dance squad she lost when she was fired. This felt like a new set of sister friends.

"What about you—missy? Can you get away or will you have to run that by Cassidy Gentry?" Christina instigated.

"To hell with her; she is not my mother. Yes, I'll be there. Come on, ladies! *Let's go!*" Penelope threw down the empty bag of cookies, put her hand in the center.

Christina, Fawn, Regi, and A.J. put their hands into the middle with consensus. Christina peered over at Abigail.

"Come on over here; you know you want to roll out with us—"

Abigail Lancaster shunned the proposal.

Suddenly, the room began to shake uncontrollably, the sky started peeking through a hole ripped in the roof off of the building. All the ladies, Abigail being the main one, huddled together to protect each other. The room swirled; the roof lifted off—the ringing in their ears from the roaring tornado penetrated every fiber of their beings. The tornado on the outside met *the tornadoes* on the inside of each of the ladies. Abigail's body was of its own volition. As The Vault of the shelter, she safeguarded the ladies, as the classical freight train besieged the store, shrilling their frightened ear drums, while echoing in their souls that would never be the same.

"Oh Lord, it's happening again, please God help me. I know I have not had the faith of a mustard seed, but if you get me out of this—I promise I will do better!" Regi belted out as the air was taken out of her lungs by the vacuum-like pressure of the tornadic forces. Regi's mind whirled back to being a little girl in the backwoods of Texas.

She never thought when she went to stay with her uncle and aunt for summer vacation, that her baby brother would be ripped out of the clutches of her little hands.

165

Her only job was to hold onto him in the storm shelter. However as the doors flew open, her brother four years younger than her, was ripped from her adolescent grip—her innocence right along with him.

Her lingering weighted scar was not only the one on her right hand from a nail along with a shard of glass that had been permanently lodged in her hand due to the event, moreover the scarring of her heart—that she was not able to protect the little brother that once looked up to her.

If walking heartbreak was a billboard, Regi was it. She hid it well in her juggling act façade.

15

THE AFTERMATH

"BRICKS, WOOD & BRUSH WITH DEATH"

[OUT OF THE RUBBLE]

Regi stood there looking at the rubble, "God spared us!" Those words coming out of her mouth surprised her.

Is this what a renewed faith feels like? She pondered to herself.

"This is Cassidy Gentry LIVE at Gadsden's Grocery in Midtown, we have all been impacted by the earth-shattering catastrophic event named *Declare*. This disaster came into our community and took our neighborhoods by storm. Please stay indoors, away from debris. Seek help with the authorities only if you or your loved ones are severely injured and truly in need of care. The emergency response teams are doing their best to keep up with the demand. I'm outside of the grocery store, surprisingly it's still standing. However, there is a lot of damage, so be careful everyone. Cassidy Gentry signing off. Stay tuned to Channel 13 for your up-to-date news on Tornado Declare," Penelope spoke as the shadow over the freeze frame image of Cassidy Gentry.

"Troublemaker, where are you?" Regi belted out as sirens rolled down the street, firefighters attended to those in need.

"Regi, what happened to the dog—*my dog?*" Abigail demanded in an accusatory tone, then proceeded to pull up debris frantically as if *it* was all that she had.

"Gadsden, come to Mommy. Come here right now!" Abigail pleaded.

The ladies sensed Abigail's inner terror, chiming in to assist.

"Come here, boy, you little stinker!" Christina yelled out.

"Troublemaker, come here, baby. I have a treat for you," Regi pulled out a treat to have on deck to make her hand ready, feeling

167

guilty as to how the pup was ripped from her purse during the event, immense guilt. This sense all too familiar to her, reliving the terror of how her little brother was ripped out of her grip years ago, the scar still on her hand to prove her loss.

Penelope asked the ladies, noticing that they were united in looking down, turning over rubbish. She had just gone off the air, imitating Cassidy Gentry once again, "What's going on?"

"The pup; he's lost—we've got to find him. Watch your step," A.J. said as she tiptoed in her heels over the broken boards with broken bricks.

"Come on, little doggy; show yourself!" Penelope yelled out, looking around.

"Mary, how's my baby? Y'all okay?" Fawn said as she looked around to join into the search effort, while finally getting a signal on her cell phone.

"Oh, she's fine. I tried calling you back but our phone went out. What was that? Do you know? They say it was a tornado, but I can't believe that. We haven't had tornadoes in these parts since before I was alive."

"Yep, that is what they're saying—a tornado. I know it was so scary, but God is so good," Fawn replied while looking for the pup.

She went on to dare to ask, "Did Beckett even call to check on his daughter?" She was hopeful, attempting to erase the incident at the spin studio, as she just survived the unthinkable.

"N.O.!" Mrs. Mary stated in a motherly way, as she inferred to the single mother—*get your shit together, forget that loser!* Her abrupt tone pounced on her through the phone, stinging Fawn's heart. Embarrassed that she'd dared to ask about the father of her child caring about his baby, she glossed over the painful response.

"Tell my baby that her momma will be there soon—*Muah!*"

Bart motioned for the women to come over where he was. "Ladies, I hear something," he cleared the rubble. Lo and behold, there was the puppy.

BARK!

BARK!

BARK!

Out of the rubbish, the pup scurried. Abigail snarl became a smile, as she knelt down to receive her pup. He ran right past her, pounced into Regi's arms, licking her all over her neck—giving kisses. Abigail looked disgraced, embarrassed to her core—moreover, alone.

The ladies all shifted their focus to their phones to connect with their families and loved ones to make sure they were all okay.

Abigail walked away from the group, not even concerned about her newly purchased custom Maserati that was still parked on the side of the building under the steel canopy. It was untouched from the storm, however just like the building had sustained an immense amount of damage—Abigail's soul was parallel for more than one reason.

The ladies noticed the change in aura around *The Abigail Lancaster* while on their respective devices, as Abigail looked up at the building that was wounded by the strange horrific storm. All at once, the hard shell of a woman began to sob uncontrollably. Abigail was barely able to catch her breath looking at what had become of the orifice.

"Hey, don't be sad—the pup is just a little frightened, he will warm back up to you," Regi stroked the canine. This response brought no comfort to Abigail, she walked closer to the damaged orifice. Regi came nearer to the obviously distraught woman, her cheeks flooded with tears, her hands shaking as she held her designer shades.

"I know you're in shock, but Abigail we all made it out okay. It's a store—I'm sure the owners have insurance," Regi attempted to console.

"Yes, I know they do have good insurance. This is my family's grocery store..."

The women's eyes were filled with amazement at that revelation. Abigail bit her lip, her bottom jaw began to quiver as she told the story of how her grandfather was an immigrant from Italy, building the store with his bare hands. Furthermore, how her father had taken over the family business, causing it to flourish as a grocer to provide wholesome, affordable food for the community, until he passed away. She'd hired management to keep this staple in the community. The account, with Abigail's transformation into transparency, took the women off guard a little. However, they stood by her side to soothe her.

She ambled through the wreckage, "Ladies before I was *The Abigail Lancaster*, I was little old Abby Gadsden..."

The women were dazed at Abigail's vulnerability as they gathered around her, embracing her. At first, Abigail had an illustrated unfamiliar discomfort with human connection—however on this day, that type of comradery was welcomed by her empty vaulted wayward spirit. The ladies had bonded in a unique way over The Declare Tornado. They stood there hand in hand, Penelope broke the silence,

"We should plan to attend that upcoming Weight Breaker Conference together."

"Let's hit that *weight breaker shit up* and light it up!" Christina beckoned in a loud, brash tone, while she snapped her fingers in the air.

"I'll see if my schedule allows for it," Abigail startlingly retorted, still enveloped in *her sisters'* embrace.

"I'm due for a girl's weekend—it should be fun. Let's get everyone's contact info so we can keep in touch," Regi orchestrated as the ladies pulled out their devices to exchange contact information, with Troublemaker comfortably nestled in her bag.

They all texted, called their loved ones while walking to their cars to go home.

"Abigail, let me give you Gadsden." Regi snuggled with the pup, attempting to hand him over, he huddled closer to Regi whimpering. That took Abigail back to The Vault of rejection.

Maybe he is better off without me, like everyone else, she thought to herself.

"You said you have kids, right?" Abigail asked in a genuine tender way.

"Yes, we have two sons," Regi smiled as she was eager to get home to her little *Kings*.

"Would they like a puppy?"

"Oh, I don't know. Dogs are a lot of responsibility—"

"Let me cut you off right there. Pups create a multitude of memories that you need to cherish while you can. Regi, look at him. Let's face it; he belongs with you."

"Well…" Regi hesitated. She glanced down into the beautiful, big round eyes of *the pocket pooch*—he pulled at her heartstrings. She felt that she had no choice. Moreover, in some strange way, she felt that the little four-legged being was already a part of her *crazy family* to begin with. He would fit right in.

CHRONICLES OF THE WEIGHT BREAKERS

Regi gazed into Abigail's eyes, there was a desperation that was hidden before by her opulent shades during the event. Regi felt exactly like *The Juggler* that she was, ready to rescue yet another stray.

"Well, if you promise to visit him from time to time," Regi stated jokingly.

Abigail laughed. "More than that—I'll even dog sit."

The women giggled as they walked to their cars. Abigail's Maserati was on the side of the grocery store, unscathed from the disaster.

Regi pulled some lone branches off her vehicle, checked it for damage.

Home, all the ladies went.

The women left the rubble so thankful for being able to see another day. The catastrophic weather event shook the bedrock community of the valley, making the national news.

Astute scientists blamed the recent wildfires that wreaked havoc on the area, cataclysmically resulted in the rare thirteen-mile-radius tornado that pounced on the valley—tearing down trees, disrupting power lines, and wrecking buildings. Furthermore, declaring new relationships combined with a new way of weight breaker thinking, yielding The *She Declares Crew.*

GROUP TEXT

:Hey, ladies. Today was wild and crazy. I know we said we would touch base later on this week, but I cannot let this day go by without saying how great it was to meet each of you. I have interviewed so many people, however you ladies are the most intriguing I have met thus far. See you all soon.—Penelope K.

:*OMG!* I was thinking the same thing. You are all up in my headspace like my split ends. Yes, let's do this! When and where? Cocktails must be involved.—Christina B.

:Yes, I'm down!—Penelope K.

:Let me know the date. I'll see if I can make it work. Let me know and my assistant will block the time.—Regi H.

:Your assistant? Damn, girl, you are not Michelle Obama. Are you serious? You're feeling yourself a little too much!—Christina B.

> *I hate being put on text messaging threads. I just met this chick—don't make me "Go Compton" on this girl,* Regi thought as she read the message.

:Yes, she is the only way I can keep my schedule intact. She makes sure I show up when I am supposed to.—Regi H.

:Give me a couple of days heads up so I can get a sitter. I'm there, I look forward to it.—Fawn P.

:I have an idea. I've been making calls to see how we can help the grocery store; with repairs and all. You gals game to get your manicured hands dirty to help repair the store?—A.J. N.

:You damn skippy.—Christina B.

:I love the idea. That would make a great story for Channel 13 news. This would be good for sweeps-week!—Penelope K.

:Will you do it—*Shadow*? Or will it be *The Imitator* doing the nightly news?—Christina B.

> *Oh no, she didn't. She is right though, but now is not a good time to snatch someone I just met. However, I'm not mad at her, because she spoke truth to power—I am a shadow, however I am going to break out of this,* Penelope said to herself while she had the nerve to be at home baking some Toll House cookies. She pulled them out of the oven pippin' hot, with *ooey gooey* goodness on the baking sheet.

172

:*Ha. Ha.* You got jokes? Remember, what goes on in *Vegas,* stays in *Vegas.*—Penelope K.

:Mums the word.—Christina B.

:Just looked at my calendar—I'm good for tomorrow. I'm there. What time?—Regi H.

:Can everyone meet at 10:00 a.m. @ Gadsden's Grocer?—A.J. N.

:I teach a spin class at 8:00 a.m., so that's perfect. Plus, I have a sitter. See you ladies then—this is exciting.—Fawn P.

:I'll go into the restaurant early to prepare. This is going to be so dope! I'll bring the champagne.—Christina B.

:Champagne? Too early in the morning for that. But, I'm looking forward to it.—Penelope K.

:This gives me enough time to make the homemade cupcakes for my kids' bake sale, drop them off, and I'll be on my way there.—Regi H.

:Abigail, you game?—A.J. N.

:Yes, I'm there.—Abigail L.

:Don't be showing up in red bottoms *trying to stunt to* do the work. I'm not going to call anybody's names out—Regi and A.J. wear some real clothes. Also, normal-ass shoes, with *your bourgeoisie selves,* please!—Christina B.

Oh no, she didn't, both Regi and A.J. thought simultaneously.

:I will be there in proper work attire.—Regi H.

:I have stiletto sneakers. Stop hating, I'm good.—A.J. N.

:Okay, ladies. Get some rest, see you in the a.m.—Penelope K.

:Did you all see that they named the event Declare? Interesting, isn't it?—Fawn P.

:I think we should call our group text The She Declares Crew. Thoughts?—A.J. N.

:Love it!—Regi H.

:Come on, The She Declares Crew!!! Let's go!—Penelope K.

:I'm all the way in.—Fawn P.

:Abigail, thoughts?—A.J. N.

:K.—Abigail L.

:Well, there you go; The She Declares Crew is in the building!—Christina B.

16

THE PODCAST

"EMERGENCY CHECK-IN"

[AFTER THE DECLARE EVENT]

Hi Weight Breakers:

I want to take a moment to do a self-check in. Enough about book sales, promotions, book signings; I want to check in on you. The Declare weather event has made national news. Fortunately, there were no casualties. Roll call; let me know how you are doing?

:Thank you for checking in on us. The event took us all by storm; pardon the pun. But we are good—A.J. N.

:It was scary. I've never experienced anything like it in this area since I've lived here. And I have been here a while.—Dr. Sophia Clark

:Dr. T., I cannot believe it. I'm used to that kind of weather in the Midwest, but not in *Cali*. What in the world?—Dr. Sparrow Mack

:We are good!—Regi H.

:The hardest part was being away from my baby during the event. Thank God, we are both doing well.—Fawn P.

:I cannot believe the damage. You think God is trying to tell us something?—A Loyal Listener

It is amazing that the name of that unusual F4 Tornado was Declare. Everything in my new book, *Think Like A Weight Breaker. Not Like A Weight Taker;* is about what you declare over your life. Declare means to say something solemn—in an empathetic manner, or to have possession over it. We, as weight breakers, must do that over our lives. That is what we are going to strategize towards when we come into our own, while walking out our purpose. So join us at THE CHRONICLES OF THE WEIGHT BREAKERS CONFERENCE, where we can expound upon exploring a new mindset. Register today; we will see you in the building!

17

REGI

"CUTE POOCH, KINGS & CUPCAKES"

[AND A MOTHER-IN-LAW FROM HELL]

After the event, Regi arrived home, she opened the door with little Troublemaker nestled in her tired arms, as he refused to go back in her purse when she got out of the car. Her family had been worried about her since *the event*, rushing over to be right by her side to greet her.

Zachary inspected his Nubian Queen from head to toe to assure that she was in one piece. "Regi, so glad to see you," they melted into each other's arms like a vanilla chocolate swirl ice cream cone.

"Yes, I'm fine, baby. Where are my little *Kings?*" Her voice echoed in the house.

"Mom!" Isaac and Isaiah came running to grab their mother's thick waist with both hands that were able to complete the circle of love of their giver of life.

Regi bent down, checked her son's over—they embraced, she looked upward,

"Thank you Jesus!" Regi bellowed, her heart fluttered with jubilee, with the sight of her family whole and healthy. This shocked her husband as he knew that his wife's faith muscle was sprained. Moreover, the longest she'd been in church was at their wedding, also only on holidays. That was one hill that he'd refused to die on, her arguments always made sense—she had the scar to prove it.

"Mom, you are choking me," Isaac giggled as his mother hugged him for dear life, struggling to let go.

"I'm sorry sweetheart. I'm just so happy to see my babies. Are you both okay? That was so crazy; the sky got so dark. I've never seen this happen before here. That is one reason why I decided to raise my

176

family in this part of the country," from the pandemonium, her purse jiggled.

BARK! BARK!

"Mommy...Mommy, is that the puppy from this morning? Wow, he's ours?" Isaac asked.

The boys took Troublemaker from Regi's purse, Zachary's eyes enlarged with concern.

"What in the hell are we going to do with a dog? We can barely keep up with the boys!" Zachary joked in his corny way, getting more eye-level with his enamored sons—who were truly enthralled with their *new family member.*

"I've ordered Chinese; is that okay?" Zachary took his wife's bags, led her to the bedroom where he sat her in the chaise lounge so he could go prepare her bubble bath.

"They say, with The Declare Event, we should prepare for some possible *aftershocks,* but we're used to that," Zachary articulated at the same time the boys rolled on the floor with the pup.

Regi smiled. "I met some nice ladies today when we were taking cover at the grocery store. You would never guess who?" She took off her heels.

"Who, baby?" Zachary asked as he filled the bath with eucalyptus bath salts, poured a glass of wine, placed it on the onyx claw bathtub rim.

"The Abigail Lancaster," Regi said as she disrobed, slipped her tired body into the bathtub.

"Really? I read somewhere she was a force to be reckoned with. I mean, downright rude. You were actually friendly with her?"

Regi shrugged her shoulders. "She was a little distant at first; it took some warming up to." She sipped her chilled South African Riesling. "As a matter of fact, that's her pup. She gave him to the boys."

"What?"

"Babe, don't worry; it's not that deep."

"Well, deep or not, I'm going to pick up the takeout. I'm glad the damage didn't come far up north so our roads are clear. I'll go pick up dinner, then stop by the mart to pick up some dog food. Remember, you made it out of that situation today. Don't get hung up in the *what if's* of life. That will cause worry, anxiety and doubt—that is a weight in itself. Are you good?"

"Yes," Regi responded in a concerned tone as a tear rolled down her face.

"Baby, what is it?" Zachary could pierce into her soul—knowing her well, he innately went into her inner core, spoke the words of her spirit. "It was a storm, wasn't it?"

Regi took another swig of her wine, nodded her head plummeting her entire being under water. She quickly rose out of the water with suds on her surface.

Zachery wiped the foam off his wife's face, and spoke life over her. "Regina, your mom called to check on you, since she heard about the storm on the news. She wanted to check in, making sure you were okay."

Those words made Regi shiver in the warm bubbles that surrounded her.

"Please, baby, what happened to your brother has weighed you down all of your life—that's got to halt. It wasn't your fault; you've got to stop blaming yourself, moreover continue opening up to Dr. Clark about it. There's some healing that needs to take place."

"Being in that storage room at Gadsden's brought it all back…" Regi's voice quivered.

"Regi, let it go—you can't keep carrying this burden. However, we need to do it, I want you to find peace within yourself. Whatever happened was God's will—right?"

Regi shook her head with agreement, as she wiped tears from her eyes.

"Babe, not sure what it needs to be, but you work so hard—you are drowning in the weight of work, pushing yourself so hard to be Associate Chief Judge. You've accomplished so much—is that too much for you?"

Regi, pulled her ringlet behind her ear sitting up in the tub, her heart pounding,

"Hell, no. It's not too much. It is what I've worked so damn hard for. I'm going to get that position if it is the last thing I do—"

"Hold on love, I'm on your side, calm down. You are going to get it, you are the right woman for the job—I just love you so much, I will not let you lose yourself at the cost of it all…"

Regi got it.

"Honey, I don't care if it is Zumba, reading a book, a girls trip or whatever—you need some balance. You are drowning, juggling way too much."

"My hero as always, attempting to save his broken wife," Regi gulped her wine with no class attempting to bypass the lump in her throat. She wiped the tears in her eyes and shared, "Zach, you're continually telling me about getting out with some good girlfriends."

"Yes, you need to do that." Zachary took the loofah brush, caressed his love's-tired arms. "You can't keep using the disconnection with your Howard line sisters as an excuse for not finding some new girlfriends. You need to let loose. You need that as much as we need you. *You* need you, baby!"

Those words resonated with the podcast that she heard earlier, Regi smiled as she lingered in that thought.

"Zachary, the ladies I met today are quite unique—you know, we clicked in a way. Penelope works for Channel 13; A.J. is an executive at a marketing firm; Christina works for her family's Vietnamese restaurant—she is also an aspiring comic; and finally, you know about The Abigail *Lancaster*. It was as if we were introduced on purpose. Does that sound stupid?"

"No, baby, that sounds like God had a hand in this. You never know, these ladies may be a good circle of friends from now until you're pushing each other around the nursing home."

Regi flicked bubbles at Zachary. He kissed her full lips, while she took her wet hand, stroking through his hair. They met eye to eye,

"Your ass better be in that nursing home with me." They shared a laugh at the visual.

The boys rushed into the master suite bathroom,

"Dad, come quick—Troublemaker took a pee on the floor in the living room."

Zachary got up. "Well, gotta go. Finish your wine, I'll clean up the mess. Afterwards, I'll pick up some dinner, then swing by the store to get some dog food."

179

Regi smiled, hearing the echoing of her kids' laughter that penetrated the Hinson family home.

"I'll get the boys set up for their baths. I'm laying out your favorite pajamas—the Gucci ones you like. When I get back, after dinner, we'll watch a movie, and slump on the couch."

"*Slump?*"

"Yes, *slump,* baby; as a family. The whole Hinson family is slumping on the couch."

The couple smiled at each other, their tested love of almost twenty years imbued every fiber of the home.

Regi got out of the bathtub and dried her melanin-infused curvaceous body; brushed her hair then placed her pajamas on her tired thick frame. She inspected herself in the mirror,

That was close, she thought to herself—the day's events settled in her the pit of her stomach.

:Regi, baby, you okay? Just checking in on you.—Mom

:Yes, Mom. We are all okay. Thank you for checking in. I will call you after dinner.—Regi H.

Regi rubbed some cold cream on her face pondering to her statuesque, intellectual, *Associate Chief Judge* self,

I have got to do the work to finally break the weight that I have been carrying around all this time.

Those words pierced the broken little girl inside of her. She looked in the mirror, staring back at her was little Regina as a child with tears in her eyes.

Regi is brought out of her past frame of mind by the beckoning of her sons,

"Momma," her sons ran in wearing their DC Comic pajamas, her inner joy kicked into the fullest.

"Look at you, *my Kings.* Thank you for being big boys today."

"Mom, an F4 tornado hasn't hit this area since1930—amazing, isn't it?" Isaiah rendered knowledge as his dimple flexed, while his bright perfect teeth spoke.

"What is amazing is that God kept us all safe. You boys and daddy are my whole world, I'm so grateful."

180

In came little Troublemaker, wagging his tail.

"Mom, we can keep him—right?"

"Yes, but we will share him with Mommy's new *friend*, Abigail. It's her pup, so she will dog sit from time to time. Is that cool?"

The boys were exuberant as they did their victory dance, their cheering echoed in the home, *"Oh, yeah! Oh, yeah!"*

The boys picked up the dog, walked out the room strategizing about what tricks they were going to teach the dog.

Regi smiled.

PING!

Oh, no he didn't, she thought as she read the text from Chief Judge Reynolds.

:I was expecting a more detailed brief from you today. Furthermore, the *shit-nanigans*—really Regi?—Chief Judge Reynolds

The text caused Regi's heart to lapse all over again. However, she knew she had to respond, or else she would be viewed as *weak*.

But what in the hell could I do about this now?

Not a damn thing!

:Regi, let's meet at 7 a.m. to review your synopsis, you are making it real hard for me to be a reference for you for the promotion.—Chief Judge Reynolds

:Got it; talk to you then.—Regi H.

Regi exhaled as she now could smell the aroma of food, *Zachary must be back.*

Damn, that was quick.

She grabbed her robe, arrived into the kitchen witnessing her husband fixing her plate.

Regi ate her Chinese food, played a round of UNO with her sons.

She excused herself, while her husband and son's watched WWE to see El Corazón battle.

I just don't have the energy to debate on why I don't want them watching wrestling—they wouldn't understand, too many memories.

Next she fell deep into her husband's chest to take a reprieve from being *The Juggler* that she was conditioned to being. She slept hard. Normally, she would be up all night contemplating her meeting with Chief Judge Reynolds, but not tonight. Just like the tornado, she declared something different for her life.

PING!

:Regi, did you make the cupcakes for the bake sale?—M.I.L.

Are you freaking kidding me? After all the shit I've been through today? My mother-in-law is going to make me catch a case, Regi thought to herself.

Before she knew it, she was tiptoeing towards the kitchen, trying not to awaken her household. She fumbled over all-purpose flour, baking powder, salt, unsalted butter, sugar, vegetable oil, vanilla extract, lemons, eggs, and milk, with a clenched jaw.

That woman, I swear. All she does is sit on her pedestal figuring out ways to judge me—

Hearing the ruckus of pots and pans clattering in the kitchen, Zachary looked at the Brookstone clock on the nightstand, he reached for Regi, nevertheless she wasn't at his usual arm's length. He got up, followed the noise towards the kitchen.

"Regi, baby, what are you doing?" Zachary asked as he came to the side of his wife.

"I've got to get these cupcakes ready for the boys' bake sale." Regi put the batter into the Cuisinart mixer.

"My mom got to you—*Huh*?"

Regi looked at him with a side eye, as she mixed the cupcake batter with a stiff arm.

18

FAWN

"THE LUMP IN HER THROAT & ELSEWHERE"

[SHE HAS TO MAKE EVERYTHING LOOK OK...]

After the event, it was downright pathetic that up until that point, there was still no response from the father of her daughter—in light of the catastrophic event.

"I'd at least expect Beckett to check on Alyssa. Damn him!" Fawn checked her phone once again to see if he'd texted with concern. She pounded on the screen door of Mrs. Mary's porch. Her heart fluttered with need to see her sweet baby with her own eyes dissipated with the appearance of her love's cherub face—this visual caused the lump in her throat to lessen.

"Hello, my beautiful girl," Fawn entered the child care provider's home with enough pull-ups and milk in her hands to stock the sitter for a year. She knelt down towards her daughter, she looked her over while lathering motherly kisses on her cheeks.

"She's been waiting for you. I didn't want you to worry. That's why I sent the photo," Mrs. Mary officially handed her over.

Fawn took Alyssa home, fed her daughter. It was pure bliss for her to watch her daughter eat. Simultaneously, she shuddered at the thought that only moments before, she wasn't sure if she was going to make it out alive to see her daughter again.

Thank you Jesus, for letting us make it through that event.

Praise God.

She gave Alyssa a bath, then gave her one of her favorite dolls to play with while she sat down, mapped out her week of fitness classes.

PING!

At last, it was an alert—a text from Beckett. Despite the blatant disrespect, her heart fluttered a bit. She had *the nerve* to smile. That was short lived…

:Please do not text me. You're making my fiancé uncomfortable! Don't you get it? I've moved on, I have a game tonight, I need to focus on what's important!—Beckett "B.T." Blaze.

What's important?

I can't believe this fool. He isn't even concerned about the welfare of his child after this catastrophic event.

I sure know how to pick 'em.

Fawn thought as she curled herself up in a ball, laid out on the sofa while watching her angelic daughter cradle her baby doll.

As luck would have it, she turned the channel and Beckett's NBA team was getting ready to play—there he was on the screen. She sat, paused on the channel as Beckett was stoically standing there for a pregame interview with the picture of Cassidy Gentry.

Two imposters…

"Thank you for tuning into Channel 13 News. This is Cassidy Gentry. Wasn't that tornado today a doozy? It will go down in the record books?"

Well, I'll be damned! That's Penelope's voice—Wow!

Fawn listened, realizing the voice over for Cassidy was actually her new sister friend—Penelope.

"Fortunately, there was only damage, no fatalities, and that is truly a blessing. Now, we have an interview with NBA All-Star Beckett Trent "B.T." Blaze, about the upcoming playoffs game tonight. B.T., what do you have to say about the game?"

Beckett's video was live, while Cassidy's traditional video was a still frame photo of her. He adjusted the microphone as he was seated at an interview table, leaned in charismatically. From his lips lingo came of how he'd perform in the game tonight to make sure that their team brought *it all home*—a "W".

"First, I want to say I'm so grateful that everyone in the valley is doing well. Furthermore, I'm grateful that everyone is safe and sound. That's my number one focus—"

That damn hypocrite! Fawn ruminated.

Fawn beheld her totally oblivious daughter who had no idea the man she caught a glimpse of on the television was her father. The man with the same nose, eyes as her, moreover the same beautiful skin. Unbeknownst to her, he denied her—cared absolutely nothing about her. His words hummed through the television, as they weighed heavy atop Fawn's chest, constricting her capability to take a deep breath. Her anger regarding her existing circumstances overwhelmed her.

This asshole gets to play the game that he loves. On the contrary, I lost my co-captain position on the dance squad because I broke protocol when I fell in love with this low-life. Talk about double standards. God doesn't like ugly. Fawn managed to take some deep breaths, trying not to have a full-on meltdown in front of her daughter.

Alyssa gazed at the television with familiarity. She crawled, then stood to touch the face of *her father*—she smiled. It was as if the sight of him was a *Christmas present* delivered from Santa himself. Fawn winced as her heart was pierced by witnessing her daughter longing for a male presence in her life. She was taken out of that stupor by an alert.

PING!

:Hey cousin, Beckett's on the news. See if you can get me some playoff tickets. Hook me up, cousin. Come on.—Cousin Paul

Really, Paul? This is truly ridiculous; he's going to make me block him, Fawn considered as she gazed at her phone with familiar disbelief.

The rambling of Beckett's interview antics penetrated the air.

"B.T., what skills do you think that your team will have to exemplify in order to make it to the championship?" Cassidy asked.

"Well, Cassidy, we have put in the work. Collectively, our talent will ready us to lean in—give them a run for their money. I'm confident in our coaching staff, plus our on-point defense will cause us to get a win," Beckett said as he concluded the interview, blowing a kiss to his fans.

The baby bounced with joy, thinking the show of affection Beckett was rendering to his fans was actually for her. In her innocence, Alyssa kissed the television screen with surprisingly confident endearment saying, *"Daddy?"*

"There you have it, straight from the power forward's mouth, All-Star, Beckett 'B.T.' Blaze. We're expecting a *W!* Go team, let's get that championship!"

Fawn rushed over to her daughter, she picked her up from the television, cradling her— stroking her back, "No, baby girl. He's your father; not your dad. DNA makes you a father—however love, care, coupled with concern makes a man a dad," Fawn fumed in a low tone as she watched. She was absolutely worn-out from the high and lows of the day. To add insult to injury, was the constant invisible lump in her throat, since the fall out with Beckett—there was an angst that penetrated her soul.

She put her baby to bed. A long hot shower is just what she needed, to cleanse her tired essence. She caressed her exhausted body. Her hands rubbed on her lean tapestry—when she got to her breast, she gasped,

"Oh my Lord, what is this?" Fawn totally freaked out—thinking back to being at her mother's bedside.

My mom passed away ten years ago from triple negative breast cancer. Please God, not me too…

She quickly grabbed a towel to dry herself off, laying on the cold floor of her bathroom. Her hands shuddered as she palpated over her entire breast. The lump was still present.

She swiftly grabbed her robe off the hook. Her hands quivered as she called her doctor after hours. The answering machine picked up—she hung up.

Attempting to calm herself, Fawn poured a glass of Shiraz, put on her oversized t-shirt along with her fuzzy socks—scheduled an online appointment. The first available was the next afternoon.

"Please, God, I need you *right now!*" she pleaded. She was lonely as she laid in a cocoon of blankets—she rocked herself into slumberland.

PING!

"Who is texting me?" her heart fluttered. "Is it Beckett?" She picked up her phone. It was the ladies she met today.

They want to meet up—nice.

"Should I go? I should!" Fawn replied to the text,

:I'm all the way in.—Fawn P.

I need to get my mind off this loser, Beckett. Moreover, my breasts. Help me God!

She turned the baby monitor up. The methodical breaths of her baby always soothed her way more than any red wine could. Within moments, she found herself drifting off to sleep.

19

A.J.

"COLD SHOULDER & COLD NOODLES"

[COME ON ANJALI, WALK IN YOUR TRUTH!]

After the event, Sean was in A.J.'s upscale condo kitchen cooking Italian—made-from-scratch linguini noodles, with his Cuisinart that he brought over.

A.J. entered through the door, completely spent from the day, that was layered with *the event* still lingering in her mind. Pleasantly, she was greeted with the whiff of marinara sauce. That caused the tight corners of her mouth to turn upward while she ingested the aroma of Italy.

"Sean, not *your slap your mamma fire* linguini? Babe, I'm trying to cut back on carbs," A. J. pleaded as she laid her briefcase on the counter next to the butler's pantry.

"Come on in *my Queen*—rest yourself."

She took the hand of her beau, with his sleeves rolled up. He took the pasta spoon with a nice taste of marinara sauce, blew it, then placed the wooden spoon up to his love's lips.

A.J. sampled the meal, her eyes almost rolled in the back of her head with the savor of the rich sauce embracing every single one of her taste buds. "Delicious."

He leaned into her, giving her a kiss. "Oh, baby, you haven't tasted half of it. I'm roasting the garlic cloves for homemade garlic bread."

A.J. kicked off her stilettos. "How did I get so lucky?"

"No luck involved here. We're blessed to have each other."

Leaning her head into his chest, she gazed up into his beautiful brown eyes while he continued to stir.

"Anjali, I'm ready and waiting for Scott—*he don't want none of this—,*" Sean said earnestly, without any undertone of joking.

"No, sweetie, I'm good. As you say, the higher you get in the corporate world, the more haters you get."

Sean nodded.

Sean fed his tired beauty, they sipped wine. Savory conversation was a delight in their impromptu date night.

KNOCK.

KNOCK.

KNOCK.

Both of their heads turned towards the door.

"Who could that be, are you expecting anyone?" Sean questioned.

A.J. shook her head, *No.*

She arose by opening the high-rise condo door. Her eyes widened. It was her mother, who invited herself in.

"Oh mom, I have your groceries, with all that we just went through with the event, I forgot to drop them by. I was going to call you—"

A.J.'s mother stood near the table, looking at the beautiful African American man who eloquently held a Baccarat wine glass filled with vino.

Unspoken, the mood shifted, and her mother stated two prolific words that A.J. had been dreading since she had been keeping Sean a secret.

"What's this?" Her mother's eyes were sincere with confusion.

Sean quickly stood, thinking he was going to be introduced—he smiled, his chiseled chin awaiting official greeting to the mother of the love of his life. However, A.J. succumbed to a peculiar mode. She walked over to the coat hook, grabbed his jacket...

"Sean was bringing me some paperwork. Thank you, Sean!" A.J. hastily handed him his jacket, escorted him to the door—closed it! Her neck became warm with alarm at what she'd just done, hiding her feelings like The Chameleon that she was.

Sean stood on the other side of the door, confused. A.J.'s mother invited herself to absorb the Italian feast that he'd spent all afternoon cooking from scratch for his love.

My scratch noodles are going to get cold. Damn! Sean thinks in dismay of how he'd been treated by the woman who he considered *his rib.*

A.J. sat across from her mother at her dining room table, where Sean previously sat only moments ago, she devoured the Italian feast Sean had labored over after a long shift in the E.R.

It was apparent that her mother, the *Tikka Masala Basmati Guru,* was a closet lover of Italian food.

Too embarrassed to reach out to Sean,

Damn, I really messed our relationship up!

Will he ever forgive me?

PING!

A.J. found herself enthralled in the group text with her She Declares Sisters.

:I think we should call our group text The She Declares Crew. Thoughts?—A.J. N.

:Love it!—Regi H.

:Come on, The She Declares Crew! *Let's Go!*—Penelope K.

:I'm all the way in.—Fawn P.

:Abigail, thoughts?—A.J. N.

20

CHRISTINA "CHAKA" Bu

"FLY BABY BIRD—FLY!"

[HER SISTER, HER ALLY?]

After the event, a couple of remaining co-workers at the Vietnamese restaurant were cleaning up, and prepped for the next day. The front door opened—in walked Christina.

Ashley jumped up leaving a bowl of pho soup, along with a spring roll, as soon as she caught a glimpse of her sister. "Damn, girl; I thought you got swallowed up by that twister, flowing into the galaxy headed towards Mars. It's so good to see you!"

The sisters often bickered with an oil-and-water relationship. Nevertheless, they were both relieved to be in each other's company.

Ashley hugged her sister around the neck so tight that she could hardly catch her breath.

"Sissy, are you okay—I've been texting you?"

"Enough already, girl. You act like you really love me. Calm down, Chica."

Ashley punched her sister in the shoulder as she let go of the embrace.

"Shut up, stupid. The whole restaurant felt like it was going to crumble in. That was so scary. We were worried about you when we couldn't reach you."

"The grocery store did not have good connectivity. I got the groceries, but the Bok Choy may be a little squished. Where are the parents?" Christina asked as she removed her coat, pulling items out of her pocket.

"Come over here, help me." Ashley handed Christina the dustpan.

191

"Daddy took Mom home right before all of this happened. The crew and I were locking up, then all of a sudden everything *went to hell in a handbasket.*"

Christina emptied the dustpan in the trash can. "I'm glad they're safe."

"What is this?" Ashley picked up the business card of the comedy club owner who made Christina a proposition.

Oh no. The card must have fallen out of my pocket.

She shrugged her shoulders.

Ashley gingerly came closer since there were other listeners in the now closed restaurant, folding napkins and filling the silverware containers with piping flatware.

"Daddy doesn't know about this, right?" Ashley pierced her eyes into her sister in a matriarchal way, holding the business card up of The Comedy Shop owner.

Christina felt *busted* for even considering the proposition of walking into her purpose. Her spirit shrunk; she thought her bratty, irresponsible older sister would surely rat her out to their tyrant of a father.

"Sit down right here!"

The ladies sat down across from each other in the red vinyl restaurant booth. Ashley opened her hands, extended them towards her younger sister. "Here, give me your hands!"

Christina obliged her sister with a curious brow; a little hesitant. "So, what's up now? Are you a therapist?"

"No, seriously, sis. Talk with me; give me your hands."

"Aw shit, here we go." Christina rubbed her hands to warm them, placed them within her older sister's palms.

"Christina, when you were born, you may not remember, but I changed your diapers. Fast forward to elementary school when I beat up for you—"

Their eyes came into agreement, stating in unison, "Ranger Callup!"

"Oh damn, I forgot about that." You could see Christina going down *memory lane*. Her hands were still in her sister's palms. She took a deep breath.

Ashley proceeded to say, "Remember all the kids that used to taunt you because of your lisp, because we were the only Asian family that moved into the neighborhood back in the day? I took care of *the problem* for you."

Christina, so not in her natural state, got a little misty eyed, sniffled, "Yes."

"Remember years ago, when we saw that baby bird being prompted to fly? We watched that bird lift off, falling over and over again. We thought it was the momma bird that was prompting the little bird to fly, all at once we saw the momma bird came back. We became conscious that the bird prompting the skittish bird that was afraid to fly was its sibling."

The demeanor of what her sister declared over her life took Christina by surprise.

"Well, the *gangster bird* trying to get its sibling to fly is me. You fly, Christina. I got Mom and Dad. They won't understand, but I'll hold it down. You are going to be on an HBO special one day," the women still held hands.

"Sis, I feel like I'm in an orbit between two worlds—the rice fields of Vietnam that daddy worked in as a little boy, versus our life now…"

"*Shh!* Baby sis, look in your hands." Christina pulled her hands away from her big sister's clutch. She opened her palm, there lay a Vietnamese origami paper bird. The girls stood embraced each other, laughing hysterically.

"Sis, you are going to be so big one day, you won't even have a last name—like Cher." Christina's eyes widened from the confidence that her sister had in her.

"For *reals*? There are not a lot of Asian comedian's out there. Maybe, I should just get in where I fit in—you know just forget all *this little comedy mess* as mom calls it. Me following my dream, well it is killing daddy—I just know it. I need to settle, embracing the family business—"

"Nonsense girl, live your life! So what, there are not many comedians out there that look like you—set a new motherfucking standard! Believe that! Plus, there is power in the tongue, which equals your words. So only speak power; you bridge that gap! Bà taught us that remember? Besides, when you buy us that mansion on the hill—it's *on and popping!*"

Christina is lifted by the power of the baby bird in her hand, she goes on to agitate,

193

"Ashley, when you move into my mansion on the hill, I'm going to have to have a separate room for *your big ole' donkey ass*. I may have to build on an extra guest house for your butt." Ashley playfully slapped her sister, while they prepped at the restaurant for the next day.

Ashley picked the card back up, handing it to Christina. "Call the man—set up *the gig* at The Comedy Shop!"

Christina accepted the card, went into the hallway, looking back at her sister,

"Ashley, thank you. You think I'm good enough?"

"Release that weight of self-doubt—call the man now!" Ashley demanded of her sister, spilling courage into her aspirational spirit.

Chaka called Ronnie, the owner of The Comedy Shop, the phone rang and there was panic in her being.

"Hello."

"Hey, this is Christina 'Chaka' Bu, we met at the Vietnamese restaurant. You gave me your card—" Ronnie interrupted.

"Oh, hell yeah. How are you? Are you ready?" His eagerness felt through the cell phone.

"Well, yes, I am," Christina spits out while biting her lip trying to exude the persona of confidence over the airways.

"I got an open slot coming up; you will get some stage time; we will see how that goes."

"I'm so grateful for the opportunity. Thank you. I will be there!"

"Cool, I'll text you with the details."

"Thank you!" Christina thought she hung up the phone, the sisters clasped hands, jovially jumping up and down yelling into the empty restaurant.

Unbeknownst to Christina, she had not hung up the phone,

"Oops, I'm sorry! I didn't mean to yell in your ear—"

"No worries. It's good to have an unjaded newbie fresh into their talent. I'm texting you now," Ronnie chuckled at *the fire* he felt in Christina's spirit.

Christina received the text with the information from the owner of the comedy club. She smiled, thinking to herself,

I'm on my way.

I just need to hit that stage; it's on and popping then.

PING!

"It's the ladies I just met! Wow!" She ran through the text thread, responding.

:Well, there you go The She Declares Crew will be in the building!!!—Christina B.

21

PENELOPE

"TACO & TUBE-SOCKS"

[A DIARY OF EVICTION NOTICES]

After *the event,* Penelope arrived at her rat-trap studio apartment after stopping at the food truck down the street to grab a grilled steak tostada along with tacos.

"Damn, are you serious?" she yanked the bright yellow neon paper, with red bold print on the outside of her weathered entrance. She tossed it on the end table next to her thrift store couch, along with the other growing abyss of unpaid bills.

Penelope disrobed, took a shower, putting on her high school softball t-shirt with grungy shorts—her go-to nighty—dousing herself with her favorite drugstore cologne as she stuck her tired feet into her tube socks. She laid on unwashed bed sheets, after dousing them with Febreze once again. A mismatched bedding set was her norm.

I need to get some quarters once the washing machine is fixed in the building.

It probably won't even matter, because I will be evicted by then anyhow.

She stared long around the room, gazing at the stained walls where some of the chipped wallpaper revealed the stale rose paint that laid underneath. The twin bed was next to the heating and cooling unit on the floor. Her window overlooking the alley was draped with a baby blue sheet secured with duct tape, surrounded with thumbtacks.

Instead of this broken-down studio apartment, at this stage in the game, I should have a mortgage and car note—instead of this and a bus pass and a broken-down car.

At least I don't still live with my parents.

Or rather I was forced to fly the nest when my mother ran off with her fourth or fifth husband to Mexico.

Damn, this is pathetic.

The constant drip of the faucet was the only sound that penetrated the quiet. Next to her alarm clock where you would expect to find a television, there was only a lonely radio. A piece of cheese fell to her dusty floor, as she saw *a fluffy scurry* in the corner.

"I see you," Penelope grappled a mouse trap attempting to load it, with crumbles of her dinner—

SNAP!

"Ouch, my finger," she dropped the trap rushing to get some ice for her pinched hand.

"You better hide—critter!" she wallowed in her unsavory space.

For Penelope to have interviewed all of the celebrities in the shadows of Cassidy Gentry, this was what her life consisted of—living in the slums, laying on a twin mattress, eating an okay food truck tostada, and wearing grimy high school hand-me-downs, relics from her teenage years. All of this after surviving an epic tornadic event.

She went to her olive-green refrigerator to grab a beer. The cold spirit penetrated her body, propelling her mind to the time that she was invited to Cassidy Gentry's Hollywood Hills home, adorned with all of the Emmy's she'd won for Cassidy, for a team builder activity. Cassidy's house on the hill, was definitely a stark parallel of the infested pit that Penelope was living in.

She received a text.

:What the hell? Who gave you the authorization to go off script today during the weather event?—Cassidy G.

Penelope was trying to unwind from being thrust into an earth-shattering event, seeing the eviction notice on the door, and already feeling unappreciated. Now this. She had to *check* herself before responding; Cassidy didn't like to speak due to her speech impediment. Penelope swallowed her pride that had been buried in the shadows of life—she replied,

:Cassidy, I spoke with the studio and they wanted me to go LIVE due to the catastrophic event. I got the green light from the studio to make it happen.—Penelope K.

:Well, next time let me know before you go live with my fucking face on it! I know you want to be me, but *damn!*—Cassidy G.

Startled, the text caused her heart to race a little. Penelope rarely had to come out of the shadows to become confrontational, so she was unsure how to handle the situation. She pulled at her oversized t-shirt, taking a bite of her tostada, licking the secret sauce off her hand before giving her best effort to respond.

:Okay, sounds good.—Penelope K.

Okay, sounds good?

You can't be that lame, Penelope.

Especially when all of the Emmy's that are in her home display case are from the stories that you crafted.

You are the talent.

Your personal self-dignity has so many holes in it, like Swiss cheese.

She self-talked with pure disgust of how she was weighed down by an unadulterated self-loathing coupled with poor self-confidence. She was ashamed that she would allow the imposter to talk to her in that way, even if it was by text. Although alone, infiltrated with constant humiliation, her funk was disrupted.

PING!

Her inner, lonesome self-felt a sense of inclusion by being included in a group text from her newfound sister friends from Gadsden's.

:I think we should call our group text The She Declares Crew. Thoughts?—A.J. N.

Penelope was agreeable, but would she have the courage to chime in?

:Love it!—Regi H.

The prompting from Regi caused her to look down at her tattered softball t-shirt from when she was donned the high school team captain, adorned with her favorite tube socks—taking the last bite of her taco. She was infiltrated from the past with confidence in the present moment.

:Come on, The She Declares Crew! Let's Go!—Penelope K.

:I'm in, all the way.—Fawn P.

:Abigail, thoughts?—A.J. N.

22

THE ABIGAIL LANCASTER

"THE TRAITORS IN THE CAMP"

[THE REASON THE VAULT CAN TRUST NO-ONE!]

After the event, Abigail walked up to her front door. She lingered before entering the cold empty house. The marble floors were spotless and shiny, causing her stiletto heels to echo throughout. She tossed her keys on the half-moon marble table with mahogany Queen Anne legs. A package addressed to her in a brown envelope caught her eyes as it laid on top of mail in her Kintsugi.

What is this? Abigail stood in a bare home that was free from her disjointed family. No loathing unfaithful husband; no ungrateful daughter (who was raised in a boarding school); and no little guy (her *Ace*, who was clueless that his father had spent most of his time in the downstairs man cave); just her with no one else.

She lingered in the mortified thought to be taken away from her son—after she would surely succumb to the terminal diagnosis she had been given.

Her mind reeled back to the consultation with the specialist illustrating on the view box where her MRI was housed—the progression of the disease that she'd googled, now confirmed.

"I can't leave my baby—my Sammy, my Ace!" Those words escaped her lungs, leaving her breathless.

She dropped to her knees with the image of the one child that she was connected with clouding her vision; a premonition of him standing at her graveside alone while they lowered her into the ground. She shuddered at the fact that, soon, he may be in life unaided without her—a life where he would be surrounded by every material *thing*. Yet, he would lack the tender comfort of his mother's love.

It was so unusual for Abigail to shed any tears. She tended to harness all her emotions, placing them in her proverbial vault to lock them away. She viewed showing her feelings as a display of weakness.

She grabbed the envelope from the Japanese artifact pottery that was purposefully broken—then mended with lacquer dusted with powdered gold. The irony was that in that vessel, breakage repair was a part of the history of an object that was beautiful, instead of something to disguise—like its valiant owner Abigail did on a regular basis. Her Kintsugi was a parallel to her soul, without the repair.

Seated on the floor, she opened the envelope. In her hands was the anticipated evidence that she'd received earlier that day, that her husband had been having an affair with her best friend/personal assistant—Margot. Seeing additional more graphic pictures caused the pit of her stomach to wring into knots. Each picture illustrated the entanglement that her husband, who she fortunately had a prenup with, had found himself once again in. Nonetheless, this time, she felt the betrayal was double the sacrificial lamb because this *God-forsaken* treachery was by the only individual she felt was in her corner, besides her young son—Margot.

Why, Margot? Why?

Damn you, John! Always getting into some Lewinsky shit!

Abigail proclaimed to the heavens, knowing that her husband had been out philandering, but now with her best, overall and only friend, since childhood. Margot knew where all the bodies were buried, along with her every woe. It was clear she used that intel to plot against Abigail—making her way into her home, infiltrating her life. Stealing her man, attempting to steal her family—her life.

She heard the garage door lift. She wiped her eyes, put the package encroached with infidelity in her purse—quickly pulled herself together.

In came Margot with Abigail's son, Aaron Samuel, who they called "Sammy" for short—which Abigail affectionately nicknamed him "Ace."

"Mommy!" Sammy ran over to his mother; she melted like butter into his small arms—he looked around.

"Mom, where's Gadsden? Here puppy, where are you?" Sammy went over the doggy bowl near the bay window of the opulent kitchen.

I cannot bear to tell Ace that I all but gave his pup away.

Or the truth is, that his pup did not like his mom, and would rather go to a complete stranger, than come back into my arms.

How pathetic?

I'm that pathetic.

"Ace, he's fine. He is away on *a vacation…*"

"A vacation?" Ace echoed, curiously.

Abigail hugged her son, while giving a snarl at Margot with the look of, *I see you, heffa.*

Margot totally oblivious, grandiosely pranced in the house like she ran the Lancaster vestibule—as if it were her own.

"Don't worry Ace, momma's got you. Also, your dog is just fine, we will see him soon."

"Oh my god, Ace did the cutest thing when I picked him up from school. He blew a kiss to his teacher as we were leaving. He's a little charmer like John. Girl, you better watch him."

Abigail gave Margot a side eye.

No, I should've been watching your bitch-ass!

How dare she call my son the nickname I have for him!

Is she serious?

"Do it again, Ace, show your Momma!" Margot prompted little Sammy as she took Abigail's purse, coat, and briefcase, sat her down. She placed a to-go box of food in front of her, beckoning her to eat.

She's got one more time to call him that! He's Sammy to you! Abigail wanted to ring out into the kitchen, however *the key to her vaulted voice* was misplaced.

As if in a fog with muffled activity all around her, Abigail, as if being thrust in an out-of-body experience, was still going through the motions. She picked up the plastic fork, she mindlessly swirled her noodles in circles—completely zoned out.

"Abby?" Margot snapped her fingers in front of her face. "What's with you girl? Are you listening to me? John's going to be late; his flight got delayed. Are you okay? That event today was crazy, wasn't it? I was at Bergdorf's picking up your suit when the ground started moving around. We didn't know if we were in an earthquake, tornado, or what—it was petrifying."

201

"Yep, I felt it, too," Abigail spoke in more of a growl fashion, than sisterly words as she used to, with the images of the skin-to-skin photos of her cheating husband with her whorish best friend relished in her mind, causing her to almost feel sick to her stomach.

"Mommy, we had to sit under our desks when the teacher said, *Take Cover!*" Little Sammy said in an animated tone as if he was excited about the life-risking event.

"Ace, I'm so glad you are okay. Mommy is tired, I'm going to go to bed," Abigail rubbed her pride and joy's head purely defeated,

Abigail excused herself from dinner while her son ate, tended to by his *Aunt Margot.*

"Aunt Margot, can I have some apple juice?" Sammy asked.

That time it was like taking an icepick to her mental tires as Abigail felt deflated, hearing the endeared way that her son rendered to the *backstabbing jezebel* who played the role. Who should've won an Academy Award for acting like her best friend all of those years.

"Yes, you may, my love *Ace*," Margot rubbed his beautiful chestnut ringlet hair that was in a fauxhawk, and gave him his cup.

Hearing Margot call her son, by his nickname caused a reckoning in her spirit—Abigail disappeared into the scenes of the mansion, melting into the chaise lounge, wanting to erase all that she had found out, but it was right in her face. She was The Vault; she had suppressed all of her emotions arcane into her soul—that she did not have the combination to.

I can't believe that bastard. This is some real sister wives shit!

PING!

Her cell phone text alert chimed, pulling her back into the land of the living,

:I think we should call our group text The She Declares Crew. Thoughts?—A.J. N.

:Love it!—Regi H.

:Come on, The She Declares Crew! Let's Go!—Penelope K.

:I'm in all the way—Fawn P.

:Abigail, thoughts?—A.J. N,

She began to draft up a long reply,

202

…

I just don't want to communicate right now! She thought, while she deleted her response.

She mustered up enough energy, responding only,

:K.—Abigail L.

Later that evening, Abigail was awakened by John stumbling home in a drunken state. Apparently, he had done more than merely landed; he had stopped by a bar to participate in his usual shenanigans. It appeared that Margot was still in the home. She could hear Sammy's carousel night light playing soothing music to calm him to sleep. There was distant scuffling with whispering, scolding undertones of Margot's voice getting closer and closer to the master suite. With one eye open, Abigail pretended to be asleep as she witnessed Margot bringing her husband into their bedroom.

No, this heffa is not coming into our room.

The Vault lay still. His *side paramour* pulled the sheets back, then she took his shoes off, quietly positioning him next to his devoted, cold vault of a wife. The harlot closed the door, her five-inch stiletto steps echoed down the hall.

Yuck!

The aroma of *five too many* straight-up scotches filled the vaulted ceiling in the master suite—nauseating Abigail's nares. With the pit of disgust in her gut, she rolled onto her side, ensconced her head with an oversized down pillow.

He rolled towards her; she inched away not even wanting his thumbnail to graze across her skin.

That low down dirty bastard.

Is this really what I have resorted to?

Loneliness?

Despair?

Humiliation?

Why did my real first love have to die in that godforsaken war?

Why have I put myself in a position to settle for paying for companionship—accepting a loveless marriage?

Abigail had consistently spoken coldness over her life. Thus, that was exactly what had manifested, alongside the millions of dividends.

Yet, in Abigail Lancaster's case, The Beatles song, "Money Can't Buy Me Love," held ever so true.

23

GADSDEN & THE COMMUNITY IN SHAMBLES

"THE COMMUNITY COMES TOGETHER"

[WE SURVIVED!]

Hi Weight Breakers,

This is a short check-in on you and your families after the catastrophic event. I want to take *the temperature* of all of you Weight Breakers out there to make sure you all are okay. Yes, we have work to do, on ourselves. Conversely, when *Declare* hit our community, we were not expecting *her*. *She* showed up and showed out, shaking our world to its core. Take time to breathe, check in on family, call someone you haven't called in a while, tell someone you love them because tomorrow is not promised. Hug on each other, love on each other, most of all, be kind to each other.

Dr. T. got into her car, starting the ignition adorned with her volunteer bright t-shirt with the orange vest draped over it.

Come on out, join me in midtown today, at Gadsden's Grocery. I will be joining a group of volunteers to help clean up the debris from the damage. Guess what? They will be distributing food to the neighborhood. They've always been there for our wonderful community.

Don't forget about the upcoming Chronicles of The Weight Breakers Conference, we will be connecting to determine how to be Weight Breakers, not Weight Takers—to have a purpose-filled life. The Weight Breaker movement is donating to rebuilding our community. Let's go, people. Meet me there, at the address of Gadsden's that I put in the chat.

Love , Dr. T.

24

THE SHE DECLARES CREW & THE COMMUNITY

"THE SISTERS BOND OVER VOLUNTEERISM"

[GIVING BACK IS THE NEW SEXY!]

"Ladies, over here!" Dr. T. stated with her bright orange vest on.

The women seemed to arrive slightly staggered, nonetheless greeted each other casually as they walked over to her along with the man with the bullhorn who was controlling the traffic of bodies showing up to volunteer to clear debris at Gadsden's Grocery.

"I have your volunteer t-shirts right here. Ma'am, I recommend that you wear tennis shoes. Those stilettos are not going to work out here." He handed each of the women their shirts, giving them instructions on what was next.

Bart came over to the ladies. "You heard Dr. T. Put on some regular shoes. We have to make sure you are safe."

Regular shoes—what the hell are those? A.J. said to herself as she glared at Bart sideways. She removed her heels, placed her stilettos in her bag.

"I guess giving back is the new sexy?" A.J. said as she scrunched her nose, grabbed a pair of scissors attempting to *zhoosh* the standard volunteer t-shirt up—*laser cutting* the back out.

"Now, that's better. I can *rock* this!" A.J. pleased with her impromptu style hack.

Regi was on the phone as she walked up to other volunteers receiving their t-shirts.

"Thank you, Judge Reynolds; I got it. I sent you the updated document this morning. Let me know if you have any questions. Okay, great! Goodbye." Regi concluded her call, going on to inquire, "What did I miss?"

"He's passing out t-shirts," Christina said as she took a deeper look into Regi's natural coiled tress, pulled something out of her hair, moreover smelled it,

"Is this cupcake in your hair?"

Regi laughed, "Yep, from scratch. Kids bake sale."

Fawn was approaching on the phone. "Okay great. This afternoon at 2 p.m., Medical Plaza. I'll be there." She was handed a t-shirt.

"Where is Penelope?" Fawn asked the group as they were attempting to gather themselves into volunteer mode, following the instructions.

"Penelope is *shadowing*," Christina said jokingly.

"Oh, giving an interview?" Regi smirked with her response.

"Christina, you are so funny. You wake up shady—*Huh?*"

The women swiftly stepped into work mode—they operated in familiar unison. As the day progressed on, other volunteers noticed their natural comradery,

"It's so good to see best friends working together. How long have y'all known each other?" was the redundant question that The *She Declares Crew* was asked. It was as if they were involved in a sorority or even *sisters from other misters*, the way they gelled together—which was a rare divine orchestration.

The truth of the matter was that even though they came from different walks of life, *The Declare* weather event had caused the women to quickly form a bond. They talked about what was going on in their lives, furthermore encouraged each other to change their mindset when meeting any adversity in their lives. They also bonded over their appreciation for the *Think Like A Weight Breaker. Not Like A Weight Taker* lifestyle—supported each other in doing the work to grow.

As they picked up debris, they identified their momentum types, some more reluctant than others. They talked about what that meant. To their surprise, Abigail, *The Ice Queen,* as Christina affectionately named her, chimed into the conversation as well. It was a great day helping to clean up the store. The day wrapped up with them disinfecting their hands, while eating box lunches.

They all discussed going to THE CHRONICLES OF THE WEIGHT BREAKERS CONFERENCE again—they fully committed to the trip.

"Ladies, love you all, but I have a doctor's appointment. I've got to go," Fawn let slip out of her mouth to her new sister-friends.

"Everything okay?" Regi asked in a motherly tone.

"Oh, yeah. Just a quick check-up—my annual," Fawn quickly backtracked not to let on that she was indeed going to get checked out for the lump she discovered in her breast while in the shower.

"Smooches. *Muah!*" Fawn drove away.

"See you ladies; I have an appointment as well. Happy Hour next week?" Regi said as she got into her car.

"Now, that's what I'm talking about. I need to tip a real bottle, not this plastic water bottle. Let's decide in the group chat when and where. Cool?" Christina sassed.

A.J. took off her flats putting her stilettos back on,

"There that's better," she smiled while tiptoeing to her vehicle that was parked next to Abigail's Maserati alongside Penelope's *ride*.

"Yes, this is my *hooptie*," Penelope said, feeling a little embarrassed.

"No shame, girl; it reminds me of the car I had in college," Abigail said in a sisterly tone.

"You hear what you said? In college. I'm a grown-ass woman," Penelope said as she dusted off the hood of her ole' reliable Pinto.

A.J. walked over to Abigail, they both looked at Penelope, seeing all the potential in the world. "Well, what do you plan on doing about it?"

Penelope shrunk a little.

"I have not thought about it, I need to figure it out soon." Penelope transparently uttered.

The ladies nodded in agreement.

Just then, Abigail's phone dinged with a text,

:This is Dr. Ransom, give me a call as soon as possible. I have some news to share with you.—Dr. Ransom

Abruptly, Abigail exited stage left, got into her Maserati, sped off.

A.J. and Penelope stood there, polar opposites—yet so close on the magnetic energy. A.J. wanted to blend in so much that she projected a different image as The Chameleon. Penelope, with so much talent bottled up, resorted to being most comfortable with her— dimming her light=*The Shadow*. The ladies waved goodbye to each other—tossed smiles, got into their cars.

Later that afternoon, Fawn found herself with her arms raised while her chest was pressed close upon the 3D mammogram machine. After that, she was sent right over for an ultrasound; the mass she had felt while in the shower was indeed there—a biopsy took place. Based on the imaging studies, the preliminary diagnosis was breast cancer, until proven otherwise, which would take a while to get the official report. The idea of *The Big "C"* caused Fawn's *heart to stop*—her mind went straight to,

My God— what is going to happen to Alyssa, if I'm not around to raise her?

Her father does not claim her—wanting nothing to do with her.

Lord, this cannot be!

Fawn got misty eyed. "What are my treatment options, Doc?"

"Well, we'll know definitively after the biopsy results. To be honest, the imaging looks suspicious of cancer. However, we won't know until we get the official report. Let's not jump the gun…"

"Doc, what if it is, you know—cancer?"

"If it is non-invasive, that may require radiation only. If it is invasive, then chemotherapy, possibly surgery we will know more soon."

That was a lot for Fawn to process all alone. As the physician was speaking, the only thing that surfaced in her mind were flashes of her daughter, along with various phases that she may or may not be able to see of her daughter's future. The news troubled Fawn deeply. The doctor gave her a Kleenex.

"Listen, Fawn; let's get the results back. There are treatments and therapies that will allow you to get through this—to live a long prosperous life. We need to get the results first. I'm here for you, furthermore I will be with you every step of the way." The empathetic doctor went on to ask Fawn, "Can I pray with you?"

"Yes," Fawn responded, she reached for the doctor's hands.

"Dear Heavenly Father, we thank you for our sister, Fawn. We ask that you come into this room and cover her along with her family.

We pray and claim that this mass will be benign or non-invasive. Moreover, if it is cancer, that the treatment will heal her body. We pray she will have no adverse-effects. In addition, she will live her latter days with her daughter and that they may be better than her former days. In the mighty name of Jesus. Amen."

Fawn was comforted by the doctor's declaration over her life. Now what she realized, more than ever, was that she needed to speak life over herself.

Fawn decided to keep the troubling news to herself until she received her final pathology report. From the doctor's office, she went straight to Mrs. Mary's to pick up her daughter. The ladies were going to meet for drinks after work, but Fawn couldn't muster the ability to hide what was behind her eyes, that she knew that she possibly had breast cancer.

:How about High Pockets for drinks in Bel Aire? The Happy Hour special is *Bomb!* Bring your *Think Like A Weight Breaker. Not Like A Weight Taker* books.—Christina B.

:I have a briefing near Bel Aire that I'm wrapping up. Sounds good. I need a cocktail. Giving back is the new sexy, right?—Regi H.

:I can reschedule a meeting. See you there! I believe happy hour is over at 7, so let's plan to meet at 6. Is that doable for everyone? Penelope, you game?—A.J. N.

:I'll be there, but a little late. —Penelope K.

:Come on! Roll call, Abigail? Are you game? —Christina B.

:Are we really bringing our Weight Breaker books with us? I've been working all day with my face glued to a computer analyzing dockets, I'm so not up for reading any damn thing. Let's do a book club or something later to be all intellectual. I need a mental break.—Regi. H.

:Ditto. It's been a long day.—Penelope K.

:Abigail. Oh Abigail, are you there? —Christina B.

Even though sisterhood had been laid at her feet, Abigail was still stale—a little reluctant for new female friendships. Especially at the news that her only and very best friend had proverbially stabbed her in the back in regard to her husband.

Should I go? Abigail wondered while sitting at her cold onyx desk going over the details of her last will and testament or rather what she liked to call her "Life End Push." She endeared the activity of determining how her assets would be distributed as her *L.E.P.* She scanned the document without responding to the text message thread.

Despite the lack of response regarding the sisterhood outing, the ladies filed in to meet at High Pockets. Onlookers would have never guessed that theirs was a blossoming friendship. The cocktails, appetizers, mocktails kept coming—this caused the ladies to feel that *The Declare Event* had provided them with a new lease on life. Through all of the devastation it was a blessing, furthermore the silver lining of the disaster. Their chance meeting had provided them with a wealth of support coupled with a resource of resilience boosters that they all seemed to need in their space.

"Okay, you all, I know we said this is not going to be a book club, but I'm intrigued about doing the *Daily Decisions*," Regi shared.

The ladies agree that they could do that.

"Yep, let's start small. We are going to start, don't quote me, but Dr. T. said that we need to *Upload Glory to Download Greatness*. What I take that to mean is to really clean out our mental matrix of negativity, working on redesigning how we think about ourselves," said A.J.

She then excused herself from the table, rushed into the ladies' room stall, not realizing that next to her was Fawn, who had arrived late and was washing her hands. A.J. *puked to the high heavens.*

Fawn heard A.J. in the neighboring stall, whispering, "A.J., is that you? Are you okay?"

A.J. emerged, went to the sink, washed her face, gargled with the mouthwash she kept in her purse to disguise the aroma of her frequent purges. She presumed that *this unfavorable behavior* would not allow her to blend in with the world.

If anyone found out about this, I'd be labeled as weak.

Therefore she had to blend in, as she assumed the position of The Chameleon that she was.

"Yep, I'm good. I think it was some questionable sushi I had at lunch," she replied, not wanting to let on that any and everything that had to do with self-accountability stung her stomach in a way that was so unsettling.

It weighed her down so much that it led to her self-injurious, bulimic episodes. Moments earlier, the conversation at the happy-hour table reminded her of the weight of allowing work colleagues to trample all over her. Moreover, because of her self-hatred, not allowing herself to be loved by Sean. The disavowal of her relationship had eaten at her spirit all day. She kept pounding herself with guilt,

I cannot believe I treated Sean that way. He's been so good to me, accepting me—loving me for who I am.

It's all too much for me to bear.

Although weighed down with the issues of her health along with the pending breast biopsy, Fawn didn't want to let on about what was going on to any of the ladies. She gave A.J. a side hug, stating, "I hear a little damn pesky stomach bug has been going around. Or better yet, you could be pregnant. You are not *preggers,* are you?"

The ladies let out a chuckle as they left the ladies room arm-in-arm. They approached the booth.

"Look who I found sneaking around in the ladies' room," A.J. said as they were eager to see Fawn.

"Sorry, I'm late, ladies. So much is going on." Fawn presented a *mirage* of a smile.

"Ditto for all of us," Regi said as she took a bite of a tomatillo salsa-filled warm tortilla chip, going on to explain the rationale for being the first to devour. "We didn't say grace, but I had to dive right in! I'm starving."

"So, who would like to bless the food? I'm not so good at stuff like that," A.J. asked.

Since the encounter with her faith in the event, Regi opened up *the box* of prayer more in her daily life. Surprisingly to herself she stated with authority—her faith resilience had been a work in progress,

"Let's hold hands. Father God, we thank You for being God and all the blessings that You have bestowed upon us. We praise You for Your magnificent existence in each and every one of our lives. Guide us, Lord; protect us, Lord, we ask that You keep us and our families safe and healthy. Thank You for keeping us unscathed in the tornado and that there were no fatalities. We ask that You cover each and every sister here and watch over our new sister, Abigail. Please continue to give her peace and protect her. In the mighty, matchless name of Jesus, Amen."

The ladies' eyes were turned upward when they heard, "Amen," from Abigail who at the last minute, decided to join the ladies.

The women jumped up to greet Abigail, who showed up way too overdressed.

"Girl, *Abigail,* where in the hell have you been? Are you trying to *ghost* us?" Christina belted out.

"I've been on my way here, nosy. Now move over so I can sit my tired ass down," Abigail commanded in her natural *The Vault* bossy way.

The ladies sat, ate, and moreover talked about their childhoods, their relationships, spouses, families, and friends.

A lady walked by as she was leaving the restaurant with her dinner date.

"Y'all need me to take the pic?" She stated to the ladies as they attempted to take a group photo with A.J. 's selfie stick—it was an epic failure. They all laughed, the stranger coming to their rescue, taking the picture for them.

She handed the iPhone back, "Seeing you ladies makes me miss my college girlfriends! Stay in touch—true friendship is priceless."

The ladies snickered because they were an organic, divine sisterhood of Weight Breakers who had yet to come into their own. People could sense their connections; it was all based on declaring a new mindset and way of thinking about their lives. The world would never have guessed that they met only days before. Look at God!

The women's relationships flourished as the countdown to the conference ensued. They had all gotten *their Think Like A Weight Breaker. Not Like A Weight Taker* books, listened to The Chronicles Of The Weight Breakers Podcast, overall they looked forward to their road trip to the conference. They all became engaged in the book, also pursued the daily decision downloads, exploring new mindsets, taking inventory, taking action, checking their connectivity and storage reprogramming.

Not to their surprise, Abigail sometimes showed up then sometimes not to their impromptu happy hours, mani-and-pedis, or participating in their group texts.

Regi went back to see her counselor, Dr. Sophia Clark. Dr. Clark looked over her glasses, twiddled her pen with her fingers, and she took a deeper look at Regi.

"Regi, you look different—well rested, are the night terrors still there?"

Comfortably laying on the couch, Regi replied, "They are a little less frequent."

"How's the puppy? Did you return him to its rightful owner?" Dr. Clark inquired further.

"Yes and no. He has been gifted to our boy's; they love him like he's a part of our family."

That made Dr. Clark smile as she realized that there had been some breakthrough with her client.

Regi rolled slightly, reached into her bag, pulled out the *Think Like A Weight Breaker. Not Like A Weight Taker* book—proudly showed it to Dr. Clark. The book had a life of its own.

Dr. Clark grabbed it from Regi and saw that it had truly resonated with her, as it was thoroughly highlighted along with dog-eared. Dr. Clark thumbed through it; her eyes looked up at Regi as she gave a slight smile. "Regi, you are doing the work. I'm so proud of you."

"Dr. Clark—I'm The Juggler. I'm everybody's everything, that can be overwhelming, moreover exhausting. I know you have heard of the conference coming up, right?"

"Why yes, ma'am! I'll be one of the speakers. I'll be tag-teaming with another panelist. I'm honored that I was even asked to be a part of it. It's going to be life-changing."

Regi smiled for the first time in Dr. Clark's office. She had originally felt that coming to this office was a *death sentence*.

"Dr. Clark, I don't even let my mother-in-law get under my skin like I used to. She still gets on my damn nerves, but I have more self-control since the event."

"You seem calmer, more collected than usual. I love seeing that in you, Judge."

"Transparency moment; I believe I owe it to this group of friends that I have."

"Oh really? You've been connecting with some of your HBCU alumni?"

"Well, I still remain in close contact with my Howard crew, but this is a new set of friends that I met during The Declare Event a couple of weeks ago. We were hunkered down trying not to be consumed by the tornado. We've committed as a group to become Weight Breakers."

"That is so nice, it's amazing how the most unlikely situations can cause you to connect with people—"

214

"When I was in the midst of the tornado, it was exactly like the dreams I've been having all along, but now, it seems like I have a different perspective on them. It was as if the divine was preparing me for that recent event. My husband commented the other day that he was glad that the night terrors were less frequent."

"Regi, this is such good news. I'm so proud of your progress. I know you have a hard stop regarding your time today. I'll see you in a couple of weeks. We should make sure we run into each other at the conference."

Regi felt better, however not fully convinced of the grape grand *Kool-aide* that Dr. Clark was giving out.

Regi left Dr. Clark's office as she marked on Regi's chart,

PROGRESS NOTE:

Judge Regina Hinson appears to be making great progress.

Significant improvement regarding her anger management.

Progress is no longer stagnant.

Positive letter of improvement to be drafted to Judge Reynolds,

I believe that she can handle becoming Chief Associate Judge.

COMMENTS/RECOMMENDATIONS:

Drastic improvement of her three intelligences:

vision, faith & resilience!

Next session with her will be her exit session.

I'm so proud of her progress.

As time went on, the women filled their group chat with excitement about actually having some girl time—a road trip. They established a cadence of daily check-ins about life, addressing issues that they were facing. Of course, they had their fair share of happy hours, and also even began a low-level book club on their own—in which they discussed nuggets and pearls that they had discovered while working from the book. More importantly, they supported each other.

Abigail, depending on which way the wind blew, would sometimes grace the women with her presence, or not.

Although she never really shared much of her own personal business, the ladies were correct in calling her *The Vault*.

Penelope was still *The Shadow*—giving all her talent away to the entitled imitator Cassidy—who benefited from her gift. Regi continued to *juggle* everything in her world, she tried her best to keep all of the spinning plates rotating all at once. While A.J. persisted at being *The Chameleon*—her goal to blend in, no matter the cost.

Christina continued to practice her aspirations of comedy. Daily she inundated her notebooks about her life events, infusing them with comedic twists to them.

Collectively, interestingly enough the ladies' environments whirled with the weights of life, they struggled to shed a pound or two before the conference.

Fawn kept her pending biopsy results to herself, continued teaching her spin classes as if there was nothing going on—*The Mirage*,

"Hello ladies, it is your spin cycle coach. Today, we welcome some of my friends to join in!"

The class went into a pandemonium. Regi looked like a deer in headlights when she walked her thick body over to the stationary bike, placing her bag on the counter that housed the resistance bands. She was ready to let go of all of the pent-up energy she held onto inside.

Christina was all game, with enthusiastic youth on her side.

Penelope entered with a Snickers bar in hand and old softball uniform on, clearly missing the memo of what kind of class it truly was.

A.J. came straight from the office with slacks, her feet adorned in stilettos. "I had no idea what *spin* meant—my bad. I'll be cheering you all on from the back, while I work on my computer," A.J. retorted. She found a chair to sit down—opened her laptop and started to type.

Regi heard, as she walked by, "Girl, that's Judge Hinson. I may have some warrants pending. I'm going to the back." Regi turned her head, looking around—the voice seemed to dissipate into *the sea* of women.

The workout ensued; it was an epic fail. The ladies quickly found themselves out of breath, falling off their bikes. A.J. was still sitting back in *the cut* working, she cheered for her sisters while being on the sidelines.

Abigail Lancaster showed up at the end to lend support.

"That is *The Abigail Lancaster*," many said as they huffed and puffed to get through the workout.

Although Fawn was dealing with her own less than favorable circumstances, she was beginning to accept her uncertain fate. She'd been managing her absentee relationship with the one love of her life, Beckett "B.T." Blaze. Moreover, dealing with the recent news that she possibly had breast cancer. What she was certain of was that she was still able to pull air into her lungs. Furthermore, she was still able to move her legs, getting the class full of focused women to celebrate their bodies. Sweat, motivation, accompanied with a few light curse words penetrated the air of the spacious hardwood floor mirrored-wall fitness studio.

"Okay, ladies, great work with your stellar effort today! I'm reading awesome motivation books along with some of the new ladies who have joined us today, who are in my self-proclaimed book club. Please say hello to: Regi or rather, Judge Regi; to Penelope from Channel 13 News; aspiring comic Christina Bu from the famous Vietnamese restaurant; A.J., a VP of Marketing; and last but definitely not least is The Abigail Lancaster! These ladies have shown up, because we know we must address the physical weights of life."

"Well, if all of these powerhouses are in this building, who is running the city?" a *smart-aleck* spin patron stated as she stepped off her bike.

"Show our guests some love!"

All the ladies clapped. Many who were in *the know* got up and went over to The Abigail Lancaster, who arrived with a tray of green smoothies in her hands, accompanied with her trademark smirk on her face, to see her new sister friends.

The patrons left however The She Declare Sisters remained in the studio, wiping their necks.

"Damn, just looking at you all is making me sweat," A.J. stated as she shut down her computer, she grabbed a smoothie taking a huge *swig*, it was so cold an ice chunk hit the back of her throat like a glacier.

"Brain freeze," she winced.

"Girl, shut up; that's what you get—you didn't do a damn thing but finger curls on your computer," Christina said as she jokingly swatted her with a towel.

217

"Gather around, Weight Breakers, I have some news!" Abigail said as she continued to hand out the smoothies.

Regi turned her nose up, hesitantly taking one.

I don't know about this green stuff? Yuck, but I'll take a swallow—Wow, yummy.

Christina eagerly took a smoothie while Penelope was handed one by Fawn. A.J. grabbed hers, as Abigail dispersed the tray that housed enough of the healthy green goodness for all of the participants.

"All the smoothies are the same. They have kale, pineapple, banana, blueberries, with lime juice. Strangely enough, this smoothie is called The Weight Breaker. I could not resist; enjoy," Abigail said as all the women were enamored by her vulnerable generosity.

"So, where have you been, stranger?" Christina cut the elephant in the room into bite-size pieces. She waited for an answer, taking a sip with her pinky stuck out—head cocked to the side, the jokester always.

"Well, *Mrs. Smarty Pants*, that's what I'm going to share with you all. I have a proposition," Abigail said as she took a sample of the green drink herself.

"Aw shit! What is it?" Regi snapped back.

"It might sound a little crazy, but how about we go to THE CHRONICLES OF THE WEIGHT BREAKERS CONFERENCE side-by-side?" Abigail proposed with self-pride, as if she was Amelia Earhart—the first woman flying.

"Girl, bye. I thought you were going to say something profound. We are already rolling out. Girl's trip in full effect! You would've known that if you had shown up for the last happy hour."

Abigail seemed a little crushed, she started typing on her phone.

:Abigail, I have secured the transportation. Their driver will be Mr. Cecil, he's *on the mature side*, however he's my *top shelf* employee—Jose`

:Great!—Abigail L.

"Okay, well, how about this, we ride together. It should be fun," Abigail shared in a concerted effort to do anything to regain the ladies' trust along with gaining buy-in, as she had been a *no-show* for most of the get-togethers.

The ladies agreed to meet at Gadsden's for the pickup before heading to the conference. The ladies formed a circle, with green smoothies in one hand, placing their opposite hands in the middle.

Christina counted them down to say, "She Declares Crew—on three. One, two, three—She Declares Crew!" The ladies screamed to the heavens, their proclamation echoing off the mirrored walls and bounced off the hardwood floors.

That spin class not only caused the ladies to sweat out their impurities, nonetheless sweat out some of the weight that they had been carrying in their very own lives.

Regi appeared to be souring a little as she realized all the time she'd spent stressing over her responsibilities. Since exercising a new mindset, she'd been able to take control over *her own ship*—which caused her to be more present with her family.

Maybe I can have a balance between work and life?

It's really too soon to tell, however I'm going to work at it.

One of the biggest pills to swallow for her was the one constant weight of the guilt that she felt about her role in her little brother's untimely death years ago.

The icing on the proverbial *weight mud-cupcake* was the profound weight of her mother-in-law's disapproval of her.

Despite all I've accomplished, my monster-in-law could never swallow the fact that I was not the daughter-in-law that she had in mind for her son—the heir to the Hinson family financial legacy.

Through reading *Think Like A Weight Breaker. Not Like A Weight Taker.* with The She Declares Book club sisters, her troubles seemed to dilute a little bit—not totally vanished like she wanted them to.

The constant weights that were ever present in her life before, however became easier to carry on her back. Her She Declare Sisters seemed to be the right filler—not a substitute, for her HBCU crew that lived far away.

Things were looking up for Regi—The Juggler.

Fawn appeared to be hitting her own stride, she realized that she had to fend for herself without a help mate. She took inventory of her life, and she determined that she could make it on her own. She was angry that Beckett had the nerve to ask for another DNA test when she petitioned for child support. However, she had the sense to do what she needed to do. She remained hopeful that the lump she felt in her breast

219

was a blocked milk duct. She had to wait several weeks for the final results of her breast biopsy. In the meantime, she continued life in eager anticipation of how her life would pan out—she presented as if everything was okay—The Mirage.

She dropped her daughter off at the sitter, finished her cycle through the park while listening to The Chronicles Of The Weight Breakers Podcast. Afterward, she returned home, enjoyed a long hot shower. She stood in front of her bathroom mirror—stared at her body in her statuesque reflection. A nagging sensation started at the back of her neck as she gazed over at some of the belongings Beckett had left behind. They were always a reminder of the hope she had that he would stop his philandering ways, suddenly awakened to be a good man—coming back *home*. She spotted his clippers. Fawn picked them up, clicked the side of the clippers—they began to buzz. She raised her shaking hand, looking at herself in the mirror, she recalled the comments Beckett used to tell her, *"Baby, your hair is so gorgeous,"* echoed in her mind. Before she comprehended it; she shaved her head in anticipation that she would have to have chemotherapy. Although she had not had her final pathology report read, she was devastated about the impending report but told no one. The weight of that stressed her spirit. She could feel her mind starting to spiral:

Will I live to see my daughter grow up to become the beautiful girl that I prayed that she would become?

Will I have to have chemotherapy or radiation?

Will I lose my breast?

Will I die?

Who would take care of my baby?

If I survive this, will I ever have love again?

The answers to those questions swirled in her mind, moreover they wouldn't leave as easily as the hair that now laid in her bathroom sink. I am The Mirage.

A.J.'s romance with her beau steamed up a little, but she was still keeping it quiet, after she pleaded with Sean to take her back following the disrespectful denial of their love. She began to slowly but surely embrace her ethnicity, but she was still being judged by her mother about denying her heritage.

She was still quietly waging her battle with bulimia; taking things one day at a time. Her work schedule was picking up, it seemed that the more work she was doing, the more she was putting the focus on what made her an outcast. Nonetheless, her goal was to take her place in *the good old boys club.*

A.J. arrived at the salon, she spotted a beautiful Nubian queen across from her, who had decided to go blonde.

"Can you do that to my hair?"

"Yes, I got you."

She chose to go all in, as she signed up to erase as much of her culture as possible. When she left the salon, her beautiful cinnamon skin was in stark contrast to her new blonde lowlights,

Now, that's better, she thought.

She walked through the office the next morning—people were dropping their phones along with papers when they spotted *the new* A.J. with her new hairstyle. All of the people of color who saw her as the one person of color in their Fortune 500 company c-suite—who could relate to her, saw A.J. fade more into The Chameleon. An example of a person who tried to strip away her beautiful culture to become a part of the majority.

"Baby, what are you doing?" Sean asked when A.J. arrived home to flaunt her highlights—he'd long forgiven her disownment of their love to her mother.

"I'm doing what I have to," A.J. said as she sipped her wine while she dove into her steady work.

The weeks progressed on; it was the day before the ladies were to leave for the trip.

"Penelope, great job on the diversity and inclusion story."

Penelope blushed at the compliment regarding all of the hard work she'd put in, especially knowing that she was in dire need of a promotion.

"You really have skills. Have you ever thought about spreading your wings a little bit? Possibly going to another network?"

That caused Penelope's heart to stop a little. "Frank, have you heard they're firing me?" Her chest felt flushed—it was written all over her face.

"No, nothing like that. It's just you're so talented. You have a true gift—"

Penelope remained seated, startled in the sound booth. Frank got up, went to the door, shutting it.

He leaned in, as if he wanted to impart a revelation to *The Shadow*,

"Everyone knows what you do for Cassidy, you've been doing an excellent job. Despite that, did you really have this in mind for what your life would look like?"

His words made Penelope shrivel with the weight that she now had been exposed; her insecurity was being seen by everyone. She reached for the mini-Snickers that were in her pocket, and started to unwrap it nervously.

Frank smacked it out of her hands. "Penelope I'm old, furthermore I won't allow you to disrespect me or yourself anymore. It's time to step out of the shadows. Own up to your talent!"

That brought her into a downright ugly-cry with snot bubbles to boot. Frank, the lead janitor, had been with the network since he graduated from high school. He provided a ray of sunshine to the studio, always checking in on everyone in a grandfather type of way. He handed his white handkerchief to Penelope—she blew her nose in it.

He patted her on the back. "Sorry for knocking the candy bar out of your hand. I see so much more in you. I expect more from you. Do you understand?"

Being without parents from a young age, to Penelope and others around the studio, Frank had been like a grandfather or a dear old uncle. He was always known for giving great advice. Penelope's father had passed away from lung cancer and her mother was an absentee—running from pillar to post, man to man. Penelope had no one except for Frank along with the new sister friends—*The She Declares Crew.*

"Pull yourself together, little girl. You've got some decisions to make."

"Thank you, Mr. Frank." She gave him a proper hug.

He unlocked the door, continuing his work. Penelope picked up the mini-Snickers bar placing it in the trash can. Penelope pulled out her compact mirror to wipe her eyes, gazed at herself, then glanced at the poster of Cassidy Gentry that was glistening with lights around the frame.

"She is *she*, because of me," Penelope finally said out loud as she felt the shadow lift a little in her spirit.

I've got to break this weight.

This is not healthy for me.

She thought as she prepared to go LIVE within the Shadow of Cassidy Gentry once again.

:Ladies, are you all packed?—A.J. N.

:Yep, we got it. This weekend is going to be on fire. I'm doing my gig tonight. I'll let you know how it goes.—Christina B.

:What gig?—Fawn P.

:Oops. I'll fill you all in later. —Christina B.

:I'm all packed.—Regi H.

:Me, too.—Penelope K.

:Abigail, are you still good?—Regi H.

:We are meeting at Gadsden's at 8 a.m. Ladies, please don't be late. If you are late, you will be left!—Abigail L.

:We will be there on time. Abby, please leave the stick at home. Don't pack it!—Christina B.

:Stick?—Abigail L.

Christina pressed SEND on the text messages to her crew, while she stood in the green room getting ready to go out on stage at the comedy house, already in comedic form.

:Stick up your butt. *Ha! Ha!*—Christina B.

As soon as her name was called, the room echoed with applause; she was in her element. The lights welcomed her to the stage. She filled the room with her comedic twists on her life nuances, leaving the audience in *stitches*. She left the stage like she was leaving her mother's womb for the first time—she felt alive.

"I told you all she was a *gut buster*. Give it up for Chaka Bu! You're going to see your name on the marquee here one day," Ronnie, the owner and host of the stage proclaimed. The crowd went wild.

Back in the green room, Chaka sat reveling in what she had accomplished. There was a knock on the door—in walked Ashley. Christina's eyes lit up; she didn't realize her sister was there to support her. "May I speak to the Mark Twain Prize Award Winner, Chaka Bu?" Ashley said as she entered the room with a bouquet of Twizzlers.

Chaka embraced her sister. "Sis—"

"I wouldn't have missed it for the world. Little sis, you killed it!" Ashley said as she hugged her little sister for dear life, like she was oxygen.

"Ashley, I hope you're not mad about the jokes made about your butt, girl," Chaka jokingly stated as she succumbed to the endearing embrace.

"Girl, me and my *big ole' butt* are honored. You were off the damn chain! I'm so proud of you. Don't be shy; open your Junk Food Bouquet," Ashley said as she removed one for herself.

Ronnie was originally standing back to allow the sisters to have their moment, but he stepped forward after their embrace.

"Chaka, you were excellent. You have great raw talent—that's hard to find. So many people come out here saying they want to be a comedian, a lot of them are pure horseshit. They want fame, with their name in lights, however lack the grit along with the talent to make it. You, on the other hand, you've got something—the *'it factor'*. Your demeanor, and stage presence are impeccable. You're a natural, however I'm going to work with you on your timing. You rushed your cadence a bit. *Linger* the crowd a little more, give them *a cliff* to hang onto; they live for that shit. Keep them begging for more. I'm convinced you've done this before—"

Ronnie adjusted his fedora hat, sucking on a toothpick.

"No, man, just in real life, around the restaurant." Christina honestly gave her authenticity of wanting to live out her dream.

"Girl, you got chops. A few more times opening to get *your beat* down—you'll be headlining soon. You remind me a lot of myself back in the day."

"I do?" Christina was a little surprised.

"Yes, I was born down in *NOLA*, in the grit of the city. Well, I did not have a good home life. For the lack of better way to say it—*my papa was a rolling stone*. He was never really around, but when he was—boy there was some trouble. What I've lived through, no child should have to—"

With each word, Ronnie relived the horrors in his eyes all over his face as he sucked on a cinnamon toothpick.

"Man, I can remember when I held up two gas stations at the same damn time right smack dab next door to each other, I did my best to not be my dad, however I ended up imitating him. By God's grace, I caught a case, did my time—got out to make a change in my life."

"I'm so sorry," Christina identified with the strained relationship with the patriarch of the family, her empathy grabbing him out of his delinquent nostalgia.

"You know what, it was because of those hard times that I leaned into comedy. Look at me now, I have my own business, hopefully opening another," pride exuded from his face, him going on to share,

"I watched the crowd—you had them on the edge of their seats. Not once did I see them rolling their eyes, shifting in their seats. You made them want more," Ronnie nodded in approval of the new *comic gem* he'd found.

"Yep, I could sense as soon as they saw my ass walk on stage, they were saying in their mind, *Motherfucker—your ass better be funny*." Christina's transparency was refreshing.

Ronnie in agreement reassured, "The audience laughed so hard many of them could not even finish off their hot wings during your set—you have moved the needle little girl!"

Ronnie kicked back as he'd just given the *green comic* a chance, contrary to so many epic fails, he may have won the jackpot with Chaka.

On the contrary, little did Christina know the destitute plight that Ronnie did not share. His birth name was Walter, the namesake of his father. He despised his father, therefore taking on the name *Ronnie*. It was a strategic effort to distance himself from the man that gave him life—that he loathed. However, all of that tainted history he kept under his fedora.

"I'm going to put you on our website to get some marketing around you. Can you come by my office next week to sign some paperwork? I want to lock this agreement down—you've got authentic chops, not that gimmick shit. Moreover, giving people The Asian Experience, a fresh point of view," Ronnie inserted.

"For sure," Christina beamed with enthusiasm.

He looked back at Christina, "When you blow the hell up, don't you forget about me!"

"Never that!" she waved, with Ashley by her side.

"You may have rolled up here on a faded bus pass, however mark my words, one day you will have a driver to all of your

225

appearances in the future—that's for sure," Ronnie said as he leaned in for a side *chummy hug* from Chaka.

"See sis, I knew you could do it!" They left The Comedy Shop, drove home in Ashley's beat up car.

As they approached the house, they noticed items being thrown, flailing through the air from the front door of the family home.

"What the hell?" Christina said as she turned to her sister who was driving.

"Oh shit. That's Daddy. What is he doing?"

"That's all my stuff, Ashley."

"No way!" Ashley put the car in park, the girls jumped out discombobulated by what they witnessed. Christina ran to start collecting her stuff.

"Daddy, what are you doing?" Ashley rushed up to her father; acting like a toddler who was throwing a tantrum.

"I told her not to do that comedy stuff, she defied me. You cannot live here!"

Flying past her head was her suitcase. Christina gathered her belongings.

"Come on, Daddy. Give me a chance. I'm really good." Christina pleaded with her father.

"Get out!"

"Sis, here take my keys, let me work on dad." Ashley proclaimed as she attempted to soothe her sister, simultaneously calming their father down. Ashley rushed to her father's side. "Come on, Daddy; don't be like that towards Christina. She meant no harm. She has dreams—"

"She defied me," their father proclaimed as he continued to strew Christina's items across the lawn.

Christina gathered all of her personal effects. Along with the mismatched luggage set, she had been weighted down by her gift. Her aura suffocatingly big with concern, while noticing the bloodshot eye, along with pulsating temple, that her father wore on his tired face. With each flail of Christina's personal belongings, it seemed to kill her father slowly but surely.

With her father still fuming in the yard while Ashley endeavored to quiet him down in her rearview mirror, she drove around for a while with tears in her eyes, before she knew it she ended up inside the family's Vietnamese restaurant. Bewildered, she cried herself to sleep.

At the crack of dawn, she went in and prepped the entire restaurant, like she had consistently done: folding the napkins crisp, pairing the cutlery, julienning the vegetables, refreshing the dishes, she made sure the bathrooms were clean. She took a shower in the back near her father's office, not before leaving a thank you for Ashley along with her car keys in an envelope on her desk. She texted her sister.

:Hey, Ashley, thank you for your support. I laid your car keys on the desk. I'm headed to the conference; I'll figure out my living arrangements when I get back. Love your big fat head to pieces. It's time for this baby bird to fly!—Chaka B.

:Okay, be careful. Remember to soar, little birdie. You got this! I'll handle *the parents.*—Ashley B.

Christina caught a taxi with her two large suitcases stuffed with everything that she owned. As planned, she arrived at Gadsden's parking lot. Most of the ladies were already standing there.

"Hey, ladies!" Christina jumped out of the taxi as if nothing had happened, looking completely like a vagabond.

Regi was finishing off a granola bar, texting Zachary. "Has anyone heard from Abigail?"

"Nope," Penelope chimed in. Out of the corner of her eye, she noticed a Mercedes bus approaching. "Look, here she comes."

"*Damn*, we out here like that?" Christina uttered, putting her fingers in her mouth—rendered a sexy whistle. "That joint is on fire. Now, that's what's up!" Christina nodded to her own rhythm.

"Yep, exactly like Abigail." A.J. pulled out her compact, applying another coat of foundation.

"This is going to be nice," Fawn drew nearer to the crew from behind. They did not see her arrive—she rocked her fresh cut.

"What in the world? You better work it Sinead O'Connor! Girl, that *cut* is *blazon—nothing compares to you* girl!" Regi stated as she gave Fawn a much-needed hug while she rubbed her short tress.

Fawn smiled; she appreciated the much-needed love.

"Look at you *dripping*. I'm going to need an icebox to sit next to you with that bracelet. Is that from your *boo*?" A.J. asked.

"No, from my ex—*the baby daddy*. I got it, so I might as well wear it." Fawn extended her wrist to allow the ladies to see her *ice*.

"It looks like the gang's all here, except Abigail," Fawn stated out of concern.

"You see that luxury truck? She's pulling up," Penelope's eyes bulged out of their sockets.

"Yep, looks like we're going to be riding in style," Christina remarked, smiling ear-to-ear, not letting on the tumultuous highs and lows that she had experienced within the last twenty-four hours, basically getting evicted from her family legacy.

"Speaking of style, Christina, we're only going to the conference for the weekend. You look like you're going to be moving in—what's with all this luggage?" A.J. added as she took inventory of Christina's persona of a *bag lady,* looking her up and down.

Speechless for once, Christina laughed it off as she stood in front of her suitcases holding everything that she owned inside.

There was probably some front lawn grass mixed in as well.

The luxury van pulled up; the door opened. "Good morning, ladies, are you all The She Declares Crew going to THE CHRONICLES OF THE WEIGHT BREAKERS CONFERENCE?"

The women nodded in agreement as they stepped towards the vehicle.

"I'm your driver courtesy of The Abigail Lancaster. She sent transportation for you because she will be traveling separately, to meet you at the venue. My name is Mr. Cecil. Let me help you into the van, I'll fetch your bags." He tipped his hat as he smiled—there it was, a shiny gold tooth right smack dab in the front of his mouth. He looked like he was knocking on eighty years old, but he was *dapper to the nines* with a golf hat, bowtie, and vest. He loaded the ladies' luggage.

"Well, I'll be damned. Abigail is a no-show again," Regi said, irritated.

"I'm good. Abigail or not, we're about to turn up," A.J. boarded, gladly turned her *out-of-office* setting on.

"Excuse me Sir, did she say why she wasn't joining us?" Fawn asked out of concern.

"Welp, she said an important meeting came up at the last minute. She had to go ahead of you ladies. Rest assured; she'll meet you there."

"I'm glad we made our own reservations, dealing with Abigail's flaky ass. You all got your hotel room confirmations—right?" Regi asked while taking roll call.

All the ladies confirmed.

Mr. Cecil gave directions,

"Each of you has a gift basket, courtesy of Mrs. Lancaster. We want to have a good time on the road, however let me know if you need a restroom break. You don't want to miss the VIP reception."

"VIP reception? Aw, *hell yeah!*" Christina belted out, acting *all new*, doing a rendition of the *cabbage patch* with a sprinkle of the *stanky leg* topped off with *the WHOA*.

"Yes, ma'am," Mr. Cecil said with a smile. He went on to share, "You ladies have full access to the sound system."

He demonstrated how to operate the music, along with sharing the contents of the mini-bar.

The women cut completely loose, going down the highway.

They popped some champagne, turned on SIRIUS, The Chronicles Of The Weight Breakers Podcast was playing.

25

THE PODCAST

"THE CONFERENCE HYPE"

[THE TIME HAS COME...]

Hi Weight Breakers,

Ladies, the time has come. It is the last call, all Weight Breakers; this is your moment. Get your crew together, your sisters together, your downright Weight Breaker Crew; we are waiting for you to get refreshed moreover rejuvenated. Someone once said, *You never know who you are until you meet yourself,* truth be told, that's a phrase that I put my own twist to. This is a time for you to actually meet yourself, find out what makes you tick, to get to know what you need to surround yourself with to let your gift thrive. The goal of this conference is to give you the tools to prevent succumbing to being a weight taker. You will be in the midst of fellow Weight Breaker's just waiting to manifest. And when you lead with a *protective shield* to hinder the negativities of: self-doubt; gossip; friction or anything that cannot build you up to *stick* to you. The goal is that you will have a different hunger down in your belly—a hunger for peace, love, hope, thriving, excelling, and walking out your calling. The ideas that you will embark upon, will be substantial—something that you can sink your teeth into to help with all the weights of life—which is a form of self-care. The pearls that you will glean are not just for you, however they are for generational weight breaking. Weight taking can deter your destiny so we want weight breaking to bubble up in your spirit, so you can release it into the world. The peace of being a Weight Breaker, is priceless, however it is not without cost—you will have a *new address* that some folks will not be comfortable with, that can result in *hateration*. However, don't let that intimidate you from the challenge of evolving into your best self, it's worth it. So who is this conference for? For those, who wonder if and how they can truly walk into their purpose; for those who have restless nights wondering is this it in life?; and for those who simply want to be the very best version of themselves. Weight Breakers, if you are so busy weight taking, you won't have room enough to receive the bestowed blessings that God is attempting to shower you with.

It would be nice to have a specific code or combination to being a Weight Breaker, or hire a mentor or coach to help you morph into one—it all leads back to you! No one can do this for you.

The ladies yelled out in pandemonium on the luxury ride, sipping their champagne, leaving their comments on the chat of The CHRONICLES OF THE WEIGHT BREAKERS PODCAST.

:We are on our way.—Regi H.

:Conference, here we come. You all are not ready for us!—Chaka B.

:I can't wait!—Fawn P.

:I really need this.—A.J. N.

:Weight Breakers, let's discover some tools to help us navigate this thing called life, for real. I need some tools.—Penelope K.

:I'm honored to be a speaker this year. Ladies, you are in for a real treat.—Dr. Sparrow Mack

We will be shouting out crews coming to the conference. We got word that there is a group of ladies coming from the valley. A special shout-out to *The She Declares Crew* that is coming in, as well as all of you ladies coming in from all over. You may arrive as weight takers, however we will all leave as Weight Breakers!

Love, Dr. T. The Weight Breaker

The ladies let out huge screams, "That's *Us!*"

They danced, celebrated their *me time* that had been long overdue.

Mr. Cecil wanted to tell the ladies to be seated. However, the jovial innocence that was displayed touched his heart, so he smiled at the women in his rearview mirror.

26

THE CONFERENCE

"SIS, BREAK THAT WEIGHT!"

[WITHOUT RESERVATION]

"This is *nice*—"

Christina's mouth was wide open, like a fly catcher, as she walked into the regal hotel lobby with shimmering gold flecked white marbled floors, mahogany wood pillars, golden arches—the air diffuse with bergamot jasmine. She was touching everything like a kid in a candy store.

"Girl, please act like you've been somewhere before," Regi snapped in a motherly way.

"But, I haven't—that's the problem," Christina chuckled as she stuck her tongue out at Regi.

Chaka went LIVE on *The Gram* with her alter ego in full effect, "It's your girl, Chaka, out here in these streets doing big things. Stay tuned for more info to come. Thank you for the love you showed me last night at The Comedy Shop. I'm out—*Peace!*" Throwing up two fingers, she blew a kiss to her followers.

Each of the ladies walked up to their individual counters to check-in.

Fawn looked around, determined to have a good time. Briefly, she thought of when Beckett had whisked her way to this very hotel for a romantic weekend, which seemed like decades ago, but was not. She looked down at her bracelet as she approached the front desk to check in, catching a glimpse of the rocks circling her wrist—it glistened.

At least I will always have those memories, she thought to herself.

"Hello, I'm Fawn Paige, I'm ready to check in—"

Adjacent to her, approaching the desk was Regi, whose aura was that of regalness—a Black Card atmosphere surrounded her.

"Hello, I'm Judge Regina Hinson. I should have a king suite—"

"Hello Judge, thank you for joining us today. Do you have your confirmation number?"

"Yes, here it is," Regi showed her phone with the confirmation number.

The clerk input the information into the computer—her brows furrowed.

"Ma'am, can I see the card that you secured the room with?"

Regi was irritated, handing over her card.

"I'm so sorry, Judge; I cannot find your reservation—"

"Well, I'll just make a new one—" Regi was clearly fuming, attempting to decide if she was going to have to *check* the hotel clerk.

"I'm sorry, ma'am, the entire hotel is sold out for the week due to THE CHRONICLES OF THE WEIGHT BREAKERS CONFERENCE.

"This is a bunch of *bullsh*—"

Regi turned her head—A.J. tapped her shoulder,

"Girl, I know I made my reservation—I have the confirmation to prove it. It was canceled, what the fu—"

A.J. filed in behind Regi startled by the rest of the crew storming over to them—totally *pissed off.*

Christina, Fawn, Penelope, Regi along with A.J. were about to come unglued, fuming at the hotel clerk—about to combust.

"Are you damn serious?" the crew spat in unison.

The clerk gave the disgruntled ladies a printed-out list of hotels nearby, while other hotel guests were jovially checking into the *conference hype.* The ladies were devastated, embarrassed— downright ready to *throw down* in the lobby of the luxurious hotel, baffled.

Although Penelope had secretly spent *her last* to come on the trip, the cancellation with the option to downgrade from the luxurious five-star hotel would put *extra coins* back in her meager bank account.

I just know by the time I get back to my rat trap apartment, that slumlord will have all of my shit on the curb, Penelope thought to herself, mustering up a smile.

POOF!

"There you are, *She Declares* Weight Breaker Sisters; you all took long enough getting here—"

The ladies swiveled, it was The Abigail Lancaster—adorned in a full full-length Gucci smock, tortoise shell shades. Her svelte legs wore ripped boy shorts. Her garb accentuated with snakeskin gladiator open-toe sandals, her neck along with her wrist in a completely an *iced-out façade.*

Nothing about her illustrated her deflated internal enmity towards John and Margot—*The Back Stabbers, she internally sang in her O'Jays voice.*

Regardless of what is going on within, in her exterior she was *feeling herself,* with her standard smirk.

"Abigail," her crew belted out. The ladies went over to greet *the breath of fresh air,* after being totally embarrassed without reservations to boot—besides two seconds from being escorted out of the five-star hotel.

"Girl, where in the hell have you been? Nice bus you sent for us though. However, our rooms are all *jacked-up!*" Christina projected in a boisterous tone, as if she were making a public service announcement, like she had no home training.

"*Shhh*, not so loud, Christina. What do you mean?" Abigail acknowledged with a fully loaded smirk.

"They say we don't have our rooms, so we're about to make phone calls to see what's nearby. I'm on the phone with one hotel now," Regi stated as she put her other finger up to her ear to cancel any background noise out.

"Regi, hang up!" Abigail commanded, going on to address the manager of the hotel. "Excuse me, Barbara; these ladies are residing with me. I have *the usual* suite, correct?"

"Yes, the three-bedroom with the view of the veranda. I don't see Margot. When will she be arriving?"

"She won't be!" Abigail's tone caught the clerk off guard; usually, Margot was always there to handle the arrangements.

Abigail's temporal artery palpated at the thought of Margot and John,

To hell with them…

She shook the thought off, she asked Barbara, "Are we good?" Abigail Lancaster kept her stoic demeanor.

"You are all secured using the same Black Card! Dexter, please show The Abigail Lancaster along with her distinguished guests to the penthouse," the manager beckoned to the bellhop.

"Distinguished guest?" Christina mocked; her head cocked.

"Penthouse?" Penelope gulped.

As if on cue, hotel staff appeared with sunrise mimosas on deck, a quiet hyped pandemonium ensued—while murmurings of,

"There is The Abigail Lancaster," sprouted from all around the lobby. Cell phones slyly took pics going LIVE on social media.

The ladies sipped their mimosas jovially, except for Regi—she peered at Abigail, with a calculating untrusting mind.

What in the hell is this lady up to?

The She Declares Crew arrived in the opulent three-bedroom penthouse suite—adorned amid marble floors. The kitchenette with stainless steel Viking appliances, accented with Onyx countertops.

"Abigail, this is out of control—this *joint* is on fire," Christina emphasized as she looked around, animated.

"There you go again, letting all the flies into your mouth," Regi blurted out.

"Okay, ladies, we're not in high school. The master bedroom is mine, but please make yourself at home in the other two spacious bedrooms. They each have two large king beds, while the other has a spacious pull out. Have at it, gals!"

The ladies disembarked with instructions from the *principal*. They began to run around like elementary school kids staking their claim on their room choices. Christina and Fawn roomed together, while A.J., Regi, and Penelope slipped into the other together.

"Hey, *Golden Girls*, how's your room?" Christina belted out like the true comedian she was.

"Golden Girls? I'll show you some Golden Girls," Regi turned on the radio system, blasting some Chance the Rapper, freestyling in the middle of laying their bags down.

"Hey. Hey." The ladies shook their *tail feathers*, as they danced, rapping along to their own unique capabilities.

The music pumped, they had a war of the generations, they danced like they were a part of a Flash Mob.

Abigail, slipped out of the room.

They proceeded to open their dynamic gift bags nestled on their opulent bedding. They pulled out their blinged T.C.O.T.W.B.C. t-shirts in them,

"Yes, THE CHRONICLES OF THE WEIGHT BREAKERS CONFERENCE t-shirts are on fire, it matches my new pumps I got yesterday," A.J. realized that she did not have to dress this shirt up.

PING!

Penelope was the only one near her phone, the other ladies enthralled in cutting a groove along with pulling out the items in their *swag* bags.

:I was able to score all of us PRIME VIP tickets to the reception. Get ready now!—Abigail L.

"Hey y'all, Abigail just texted us," Penelope alerted, facing her phone to her friends.

"I didn't even know she left the penthouse," Regi turned her nose up.

"OMG y'all, what are PRIME VIP tickets?" Fawn asked.

"Only those tickets that allow you top shelf access to the celebs—the roped off part of the VIP Experience."

I've always been on the other side of the velvet rope, while Cassidy had PRIME VIP tickets.

This is a first.

Penelope thought as she applied too much blush to her full face, having no clue as to what she was doing. She was excited, responded to the text for The She Declares Crew,

:We will be ready!—Penelope

"Girl, you are looking like Halloween over there, A.J. help Penelope out, please," Christina attempted to assist.

A.J. unhanded the brush from Penelope, an applied more foundation, with a bronzer over it,

"There that is better," A. J. rendered. Penelope smiled as she placed her favorite shirt on.

"Ladies, time is getting away from us. Let's finish getting ready!" Regi quipped.

The ladies raced to their rooms—foundation, blush, mink eyelashes, eyeliner, flat irons, thongs, body shapers along with multiple bustier's flew through the air—the ladies wreaked havoc on their living quarters bathroom, placing their diva couture on their excited bodies of various shapes and sizes to *represent*—having a blast.

"We need to *bounce!*" Christina summoned.

They looked trendy, downright beautiful with their hair flowing, *drip* generated from their sisterhood. They didn't walk, they glided in uniform steps with one another, looking like the trailer of the box office hit *Charlie's Angels*.

The women arrived at the venue of the V.I.P. reception, their glossed lips of their mouths dropped in amazement.

"Damn *Weezie*, we've moved on up!" Christina stood in the doorway of the opulent experience that awaited her on the other side.

"Come on ladies, we belong here," A.J. prompted as they entered together, damn near holding hands, headed straight for the bar.

They sipped their drinks, as they were flabbergasted by all of the Who's Who that walked by.

"Is that Viola?"

"That can't be Reese?"

"You sure that is not Kylie?"

"You have got to be kidding me, is that Angela?"

"Is that *B*? Girl, stop! You know I'm a part of *The Hive!*"

"Girl, I'm about to faint."

237

Then a man who looked like he just stepped off of a GQ magazine came over to the ladies,

"Excuse me beautiful ladies, are you The She Declares Crew?"

Christina sprung in front of the ladies, introducing herself as the leader of the pack,

"Why yes handsome, I am the president and C.E.O, of this group," she stuck out her hand for him to give a kiss.

He planted a warm smack on her hand, he felt he had no choice.

The ladies fanned themselves, recognizing Christina's *game.*

"I have been summoned by The Abigail Lancaster to escort you to THE PRIME VIP section of the event space. Please follow me," he held out his arm, Christina slid her desperate arm into his.

I might not be homeless after all. This could be my sugar daddy, she giggled in her presumptuous thought.

"So player, do you have your own spot or do you live with your mama?" Christina intrusively questioned, the escort's head pivoted looking down at her while he raised an eyebrow at the rambunctious question, shaking his head—all about fulfilling his duty.

The gentleman unclasped the rope, as he assured the ladies were secure in the roped-off VIP section.

While the upper echelon *schmoozed*, mingling amongst themselves, The She Declares Crew was smitten with the VIP lifestyle.

I can dig this, Penelope thought to herself.

They giggled, talking amongst themselves while seated on the plush leather couches snapping and getting their groove on to the LIVE cover band.

Reverb from the microphone, redirected the attention of all attendees of the event.

Dr. T. took the microphone for an impromptu announcement,

"So, let's contribute to The Chronicles Of The Weight Breakers Foundation, we are going to help restore the township that was impacted by The Declare Tornado that ripped parts of our area to shreds. Let's go, people!"

An impromptu fundraising effort due to Dr. T.'s plea—one million dollars was raised for the community that was hit by the disaster, within an hour.

"Damn, this is so dope. One million dollars—that's going to be me one day. Being able to write big checks for charity," Christina spoke in an endearing manner.

"Girl, you will be able to, sooner than you think." Penelope supported that vision for her sister friend.

"Speak truth to power," Regi supported that ambition.

The ladies partied, until the accent lights went off, and the bright *"I don't know where you are going, but you've got to get the hell out of here"* lights came on.

"Y'all, we kicked it with both feet—" Christina *cheesed* from ear to ear.

"This was nice," A.J. smiled.

"I really needed this," Fawn endearingly shared.

"I can dig this." Penelope embraced feeling included.

"Okay, ladies, we need to head back to the suite," Regi said as she started to yawn, pressure from Chief Judge Reynolds had been getting the best of her lately.

"Y'all I'm not twenty years old anymore," hearing in her spirit the other night from her husband,

See Regi, I told you—you could not hang!

"Regi, okay Golden Girl, you take your *geriatric ass* back to the suite. Who wants to go hang out at the bar? Who's with me?" Christina prompted, eager to let loose.

"I'll go," Fawn agreed without hesitation, ready to down some shots as a strategy to forget the lump in her breast; the abandonment of the love of her life, most of all the weight of having to deal with all of it alone.

"Come on. Let's go get a nightcap," Fawn and Christina wrangled themselves towards the bar that served up top-shelf liquors.

"To us!" Fawn and Christina toasted, as they sipped, feeling the burn of the shots. After thrice rounds, they were *nice*.

"I have some sidebars I need to have about the conference, so I will see you ladies later in the room," Abigail stated as she grabbed the arm of another Greek god of a man that was chiseled like a statue.

"There she goes again," A.J. watched Abigail disappear in the sea of *Who's Who*.

"Well, ladies, looks like a slumber party is in effect," Penelope stated as she locked arms with her sisters—they strolled back to the penthouse suite.

The ladies returned to their suite, ordered room service, dressed in their PJs, while they played the hotel's complimentary high-end board games.

"Y'all are you serious? Checker's dipped in gold? What?" Penelope proclaimed as she set up the checkerboard.

They even got in one good game of charades that was an epic failure because the cocktails had truly kicked in.

"Girl, stop. You are so stupid—you got me over here almost peeing my pants," A.J. laughed hysterically, snorting.

Fawn and Christina stumbled their way back to the penthouse, after the bartender revoked their bar privileges, finally arriving back to the penthouse—*bent*.

"We have a long day tomorrow—*man down*! I'm headed to bed," Regi yawned.

The penthouse was quiet, somewhere in the night Abigail returned. All the women slept hard.

KNOCK!

KNOCK!

"Oh my goodness, who could that be?" Regi wiped her eyes, as she removed one eye from under the sleep mask, startled by the beckoning at the door.

Am I the only one that hears the knocking?

Those damn girls, probably still out or hung over.

"How may I help you?" Regi cracked the door.

"Ma'am, Abigail Lancaster scheduled an in-penthouse custom breakfast this morning. Can we come in to set up?"

The chef prepared a breakfast made for the queens that they were.

Before the women was a delicious spread of Belgium waffles, home fries, scrambled eggs, fresh-squeezed orange juice with varieties of coffee and to top it off jumbo shrimp and grits. The room smelled incredible.

As if on cue, when the food was totally prepared, Abigail entered—floating towards the table.

"Girl, you have a glow about you. Did you get *lucky* last night?" Christina heckled.

"It's just good to see you all—let's eat, but first we must say grace—"

This caught the women by surprise, they gladly obliged. They ladies held hands bowing their heads, Abigail led the prayer,

"Dear God, Thank you for everything. I am so grateful that you have made us understand that—*We Can!*"

A few silent moments passed, the ladies all peeked from behind their sleepy eyelids looking around to see if Abigail was done with her prayer.

She was.

The ladies looked at each other, stating,

"Amen."

It was the most befitting straight-to-the-point prayer, moreover meaningful for The She Declares Sisters.

"Let's eat," Abigail summoned.

Weight Breaker
You Matter!

She declares

For I am the Lord your God, who holds your right hand, who
says to you, Do not fear, I will help you'

Isaiah 41:13

27

THE CONFERENCE

"TAKING INVENTORY & ACTION"

[OPENING SESSION-YOU MATTER!]

"Dr. T., let me touch you up before you go out on stage," Dean Baby blew off his brush of concealer, took some of the shine off her nose—planted a gloss on her lower lip,

"She's ready!"

He signaled to the emcee, while unleashing the cape off the bestselling author, podcast host and motivational speaker.

Smiling with eager anticipation, the emcee pulled the microphone to her mouth, announced with unriveting excitement.

"Welcome to the stage, the author of the bestselling self-help book, the life-changing motivational book, *Think Like A Weight Breaker. Not Like A Weight Taker*. Everybody give a warm welcome to your very own Weight Breaker, Dr. T!"

The sea of motivated ladies went into a pandemonium, roared with excitement. The cover band version of *I'm Every Woman* started to play—the women went wild.

Clapped their hands.

Grooved, straight *cutting a rug*—they were in a zone.

The She Declare group had front row seats—truly *vibed* with the uplifting ambiance of the room, as THE CHRONICLES OF THE WEIGHT BREAKERS CONFERENCE began...

Hi beautiful Weight Breakers,

Okay D.J., cut the music! I can't hear you, are there any Weight Breakers in the building?

The sea of energized women raised their hands full of weight breaker energy.

243

Let me tell you about a Weight Taker, who we all know so well. She was born into a space in which Weight Taking was a part of her being, it was as if she was riding in a *Weight Taker-mobile*, just going throughout life carrying her own weight along with everyone else's. This overwhelmed her. Then she decided she needed to Take Inventory and Take Action—that Weight Taker was me.

The women held on to every word. Many nodded their heads, identifying with being a Weight Taker at some point in their life.

This is our opening session; The Chronicles of The Weight Breakers Team is all over the room with orange shirts on—raise your hands team! We are here to do our best to make this the most powerfully engaging conference that you have ever been to. Are you all ready?

I can't hear you all. Are you all ready?

A sisterly unified, *"Yes!"* echoed off of the walls of the grandiose ballroom event space.

Okay, ladies, let's get started, we are going to take "what if" out of your vocabulary, because "what if" is a weight in itself. What if I chose to lose weight?; what if I allowed myself to put myself first for once?; what if I went back to school?; all of the "what if's" are weight in itself. While you have breath in your body, "what if" is kicked to the curb, some people would do anything for your worst day—so the fact that you are here able to move into your future is priceless, and there is no room for "what if". Keeping this Weight Breaker energy going, grab your workbooks in your swag bags; we are about to make some things happen. I want each of you to know that you matter to God, to the world, and most of all you must know that you have to matter to yourselves. Take the fact that you matter to God and to this world out of your blind spot, it should be in your purview.

Cling to this nugget found in Isaiah 41:13, *For I am the Lord your God, who holds your right hand, who says to you, Do not fear, I will help you.* Now get your books out!

The women were now seated with their *Think Like A Weight Breaker. Not Like A Weight Taker* books handy, positioned in their laps.

Tactic 6 is that of Taking Inventory and Taking Action. You may be wondering what does that mean? To put it bluntly, you need to focus on getting up and getting to work! For *we are* the barriers and the bridges of what does not work in our life and what could be so prosperous in our life.

Now it is time to do the work and take action. You will be asked to take inventory of what is going on currently in your life. We must complete tasks that are aligned with the decision day downloads. How many of you all have been working on your daily decision downloads?

The hands went up.

We cannot just identify a problem and blindly think that it is going to disappear. Let's be real in what we are really talking about: the proverbial and the physical weights of life.

Take time to act out how you are going to make an effort to visualize the outcome. Journal in the back of the book about an area of your life you want improvement in. What the ultimate goal would be. We are going from Talking About it, to Taking Inventory and Taking Action. Get your journal handy to help if you need more room to write. These will be quick responses that you will provide. Keep those experiences that you have had bubbled up in the forefront of your mind and you will give a short response on how to take action.

The ladies inscribed in the book, as a large box was rolled out on stage.

Can I get a volunteer from the audience? Okay, you right there in the front row, in the purple shirt! Yes, you!

Penelope was shocked that she was singled out, this never happened to her.

I'm always an outcast.

Moreover, she was being pulled up on stage.

You don't have any physical ailments that would prevent you from swinging a hammer, do you?

"No, not at all," Penelope replied, in the back of her mind she thought,

If you call being overweight and alienated an ailment, then maybe I do have an ailment.

Tell us about yourself.

"Hello, everyone. I'm Penelope. I'm a behind the scenes journalist. Combined with being an even farther behind the scenes anchor of your evening news."

"I can't believe she's telling all her business—" A.J. scoffed, while she *clutched her pearls.*

"She needs this." Regi endeared as she winked at Penelope as if to say, *you got this sis!*

"I'm the brains behind the operation of the network. I'm often overlooked based on the fact that I don't fulfill the ideal of what the perfect *Barbie Doll* anchor should look like. I graduated top of my class in journalism school and my stories have brought our network multiple prestigious awards. My physical weight has brought me to the place of not continually having a seat at the table but being in the background of everything. I make light of it with humor—sometimes painfully laughing along at the jokes that make a mockery of me, while I'm crying inside. Due to a chance encounter with some ladies, I started to think about myself in a different light, also because of the book *Think Like A Weight Breaker. Not Like a Weight Taker*. This caused me to understand that I've been creating the momentum type of The Shadow in everything that I do, which is a weight. I'm going to work on creating a firewall to not allow the bullshit in! Also, if you have people in your crew who gossip about other people, just know that as soon as you are out of their presence, they are doing the same thing to you. Therefore, you should have a firewall up regarding those types of people. And ladies, please do not be alarmed by the firewall that God puts up for you. There may be times that you were not invited to an event; you may feel the exclusion from a group; count it all joy—that was God putting up a firewall to protect you from individuals that were not aligned with your purpose."

The sister friends in the audience nodded their heads, identifying with all that Penelope was sharing.

Penelope, I commend you for your transparency. Quick question. Are you ready?

"Yes, I am," Penelope belted out into the room, as the ladies in the audience cheered her on.

Well, you see this box right here?

"Yes!" Penelope replied, her eyes intrigued with what the *actual ask* of her would be.

After each 'I' phrase that I state, your response is to SWING at the box. *Okay?* Here are some goggles.

"Got it!" She said with the mediocre confidence that she wore like a garment.

"You got it, sis. Go!" Penelope's crew yelled from the front row, while she smiled, getting her muscles ready for the swing.

Okay, with my Weight Taker here, we are going over some goals that we need to really focus on. I'm going to have you repeat after me. Every time you hear me say the "I" phrase—*SWING!*

I will not be idle.

SWING!

I will dig my heels in.

SWING!

I will take inventory of areas that I may need to improve on.

SWING!

I will unveil my inner being.

SWING!

I will approach the encumbrance of my life's journey.

SWING!

Damn, I'm swinging with all of my might—still not making an impact in this big box. I can swing; I used to be captain of the high school softball team, Penelope disgustingly thought of herself, a little shell-shocked by her subpar skills.

She appeared to be a little embarrassed, holding the hammer in her disappointed hands—it seemed to mirror everything that she was attempting to chip away in her life. In many areas of her life, she would try with all of her potency— making little to no impact. The encounter in front of the audience truly illustrated to her inner core that she needed to take inventory on how to move forward with attacking the mountain of a box, which represented so many obstacles, barriers, disappointments, moreover the challenges in her *shadowed-shelled life.*

Penelope, stop! The command from The Weight Breaker startled Penelope, feeling ashamed as if she were hearing in her spirit,

See, you really are not good enough, at ANYTHING!

Her negative self-talk was disrupted by a penetrating question from Dr. T.

Are you here alone?

Isolating anxiety overcame Penelope as her default address in which she solemnly lived was being alone.

The big room started to feel small with her head shrinking into her shoulders.

"Yes," Penelope replied. Penelope's She Declares Crew turned, looked at each other, disappointed in her response.

Christiana belts out, "What are we, *Chopped Liver?* Girl, we got you…"she began to walk towards the stage to rescue her friend from public humiliation. Regi stopped her.

"She's got to do the work herself. We have her back, but she has to go through this." Regi clapped her hands as she yelled out, "You got this Penelope!"

This brought Penelope out of her stupor. She raised her head, turned towards Dr. T., with her shoulders now back straight; a mild case of confidence coming over her, a light bulb went off in her mind,

247

"No, I'm here with my crew; The She Declares Crew."

The ladies exuded excitement as *the tortoise* took her head out of her shell.

How many of them are there?

"Well, there are actually five others, but four that are here with me this morning."

Okay, call your crew up here with you! Shane, get those four hammers.

Shane came on stage with four additional hammers, handed one to Regi, one to Fawn, one to A.J., also one to Christina. They put goggles on, so they could be fully protected while present to assist their friend.

Okay, ladies, Penelope has picked you to have her back—to help her conquer this box. So, every time that I say the "together statement" you all, *SWING!* Everybody spread out; we don't have time to go to the emergency room.

The ladies spaced themselves out as they held their hammers with intensity in their eyes, as if to say, *Box—you don't want none of this!*

Ladies, when you hear me declare *together*—you will swing. Alright, She Declares team!

Together, we will not be idle.

SWING!

Together, we will dig our heels in.

SWING!

Together, we will take inventory of areas that we may need to improve in.

SWING!

Together, we will unveil our inner beings.

SWING!

Together, we will approach the encumbrance of our life's journey.

SWING!

Together, we can be the change that we need to make.

SWING!

Together, we can encourage one another.

SWING!

Together, we can keep the momentum of taking inventory and taking action.

SWING

Together, we can celebrate the shedding of proverbial and physical weight by taking inventory and taking action.

SWING!

BOOM!

The once mountain of a box was now in pieces—smashed to smithereens by the group's unified effort.

The ladies celebrated their heroic feat. However, they were a little puzzled; especially Penelope.

There's nothing inside?

Ladies, take your seats. Give it up for Penelope along with her *She Declares Crew*. They were the bomb, weren't they?

You know what we learned from that? Penelope alone had *the tool* needed to break down the box. However, when she was aligned with like-minded people, with tools like hers that exhibited various strength levels, *they* were able to break the weight of the box—overcoming the challenge together!

The challenge was never about the potential of what was inside, it was about realizing that if you want to be a weight breaker, you have to align with weight breakers!

The room was overwhelmed with applause.

Let me reiterate, each of you have the tools to be Weight Breakers. However, we are going to see how to use your tools effectively. There will be instances in which you will develop synergy or a combined power in your life when you align yourselves with people that can assist you, guide you. More so, when you need to break some shit down.

These are the peers that will help you with adding sugar, water, or even bring the pitcher when you are given these yellow beauties—lemons. When you are handed them in life.

Dr. T. rose up her hand with lemons in them.

So what do we do with these lemons Weight Breakers?

"Make lemonade."

That's right, you make *mother-freaking lemonade*.

The room went into pandemonium, The She Declares Crew hugged their Weight Breaker, Penelope, celebrating her epiphany that she also had sister friends that were ride or die for her. And that would help her break down the barriers, insecurities, along with strife in her life.

The women took their seats.

The premise of the conference is to not be idle. Many of us have turned on our *"I don't give a damn anymore"* engines, thus we're idle—not moving. That is not what we were designed for. When you are idle, the engine is running, spinning its wheels, a whole hell of a lot of energy burnt up, being wasted with no movement towards progress.

The women in the audience belted out, convicted in their spirit,

"Amen."

"Hallelujah."

"You said that!"

"Preach, sista!"

Ladies, think about this analogy, that your life is your own proverbial garden.

What are some of the thorns that need to be cultivated out of your garden?

What are they?

Or better yet, who are they?

Ponder on some things that have been weighing you down that you need to let go. Think of, at most, three things that come to mind.

Reflect on how those things have weighed you down over time.

How will you take action over what is weighing you down?

A lady belted out in the audience, "Do the work!"

You are absolutely right, our sister; we have to do the work. First, we have to be real with ourselves about this. This is called, taking inventory.

Now, think about how you can solve these three things if money were not an issue. You may be wondering, why are we doing this? Well, there are issues that we go through that could be handled in a simple way. Some could even be solved by writing them down while visualizing how you may solve them. Once you can see them, you realize that you do have the power to overcome them.

Sometimes, what you may think of as a cumbersome event, may be a lesson or a stepping stone to the next phase of your life. More importantly, when you begin to take inventory, just like Penelope grasped, of who she wanted to come up with on stage to help her with the weight that she was confronting.

Penelope hugged her sisters, giving them love for their support.

You realize that you are not alone in this.

The ladies clapped.

In addition, you heard me mention in the book about *your crew*—it is important that you identify those allies in your life. Those individuals that do not drain you and are able to invest in you as you invest in them. It is such a blessing to have at least five people in your life that fit that bill. If you can, list five in your journal. In your action column, write ways how you can continue to foster those relationships. Keep in mind that there are people that were a part of your core that you kicked out of your life for the wrong reason, you need to forgive them. Everyone say—forgive!

The ladies in the crowd followed suit.

Be honest with yourself. What are some things in your life that need forgiveness? Map out a couple of quick steps that you can implement so you can start working on how to get forgiveness in your heart.

Now we are going to go a little deeper in standing under the principle that you matter. How many of you know that you are unique? Say I am unique!

"I am unique!"

I like the sound of that. Now, take a moment and take inventory, about your uniqueness. What are two top unique character traits about you? What makes you one-of-a-kind? How can you use those unique character traits that you have to walk into your purpose boldly? That is the way that you can take action, regarding how to use your unique gifts.

The ladies were deep into their workbooks, intrigued while jotting down their own unique character traits, coupled with how they could incorporate forgiveness in their world.

With that being said, what makes you unique is that you are being born into this world to enhance the earth with your gift.

Since you are God's gift to the world, this next task should be relative to embrace. I know I'm hitting you with a lot in the opening session, but it is a part of doing the work. Because you are a gift, you have to find a way to lean into the words of First Lady Eleanor Roosevelt, "With the new day comes new strength, along with new thoughts." This quote is so profound. Think about how you can put this into action.

251

Take time out of each day to allow yourself to celebrate life, with your new beginning. Be creative.

"Now, that is one that I'm going to put into practice starting today, because life is too short. Celebrating every day as if it is my birthday," a single tear rolled down Fawn's face as she thought,

I can't leave my daughter.

God, please let the breast biopsy results be negative!

How many more birthdays will I have?

Regardless, I'm going to celebrate each day with my daughter, as if it is my birthday.

I'm going to beat this.

Each of you are strong women. If you think back over your life, you can remind yourself of when everything was *hitting the fan*—all of us have seasons like that we've gone through.

"Amen," many women identified.

When it seemed like there was no way out, you leaned into something greater than you—that's faith. I call those faith over fear moments. Ponder on the character traits you got you through that difficult time. So many times, we focus on the things that we do wrong, our weaknesses, how we wish we were different in a situation. Let me see a raise of hands if you do that?

The entire auditorium was filled with raised hands.

Now, Weight Breakers, close your eyes for a brief moment, do a *look back* and shout out, at minimum, three of your successes on which you were strong, having positive thoughts that got you through a tough situation? I know there are so many; however, name your top three.

The women obliged, doing the work shouting out to the brim of the auditorium.

"Vision."

"Faith."

"Resilience."

I love this. You women are strong, and those successes that you had based on your strength are the building blocks to where you are—right now in this very moment. And I have noted that you all have been working on your intelligences'.

Now, let's think of this, what does it solve when you kick your own self when you are down, forgetting the characteristics that brought you through tough times?

Many women in the crowd belted out, "Absolutely nothing!"

Yes, you are right—absolutely nothing! We are going to download the practice of not being so hard on ourselves, to change that destructive behavior.

What does that look like for you?

How are you going to purposefully substitute those feelings?

Be intentional in how you are going to do this. We are going to dig our heels during this conference to take inventory of all ways in which we think.

Most of all, as of today, we have pressed the DELETE button on ALL negative thoughts that attempt to distract us, from who God called us to be. Everyone say, DELETE!

The eager women nodded in unison, while they followed suit.

"DELETE!" The building was filled with the word.

Ladies, henceforth you are going to press the DELETE button on ANY negative self-talk on; about how nobody cares for you; idiotic ideas that you don't matter; and garbage that attempts to infiltrate your beautiful mind.

All of that comes from the enemy—you do matter.

What you do is keep being your authentic self, taking care of yourself, furthermore doing good for people—all of this is a part of your divine purpose.

The women were eager, they listened on for more tools.

Finish this sentence. I matter because...

Write your response in your journal.

The women's heads were down as they completed their tasks. They were affirmed, as the verification that they mattered in this big, magnificent, complex, awestruck world.

We are only going to look forward to it. By looking forward, you build a bridge over what may seem impossible. Give three ways that constantly being stuck in the past hinders you from moving forward. Think about how you are going to keep your eyes focused on your future, also how you are going to dig your heels in to do that.

I need each of you to schedule quiet time for your mind to clear—pondering how you are going to be focused. How do you create that quiet time in your hectic life? How can you do a better job in doing so? What is that designated space for you to focus on how to do so? I like to call that the Weight Breaker Space. Think about a realistic way that you can commit to that quiet time. Plan it—make it happen!

The women's pencils were almost dull from their writing as they *tapped in*. Furthermore, their ink from their pens was almost dry as they manifested their purposes on paper.

Sometimes, it can be difficult to create movement regarding issues in your life. What are some of the tools that you can use to *GO* and create movement regarding your health and wellness goals along with peace of mind?

To really activate this, it is important to know what you will need to do to continue to move forward when obstacles come your way. For example, this may seem simplistic, however I wanted to commit to drinking more water and a friend blessed me with a water jug that encouraged me to drink water based on the time of the day. That water jug keeps me accountable. A part of my daily decision, pure hydration is key. I strategically use this tool to help me.

How many of y'all can commit to drinking more pure water?

The hands are raised all over the building.

In addition, one of my goals, in understanding that I matter, is what type of food I am putting in my body. I have structured my meals to incorporate eating green vegetables and fresh fruits.

"Do Starburst count, they are *fruit?*" Penelope joked to Christina.

"Girl you are out of control. Hell no, Starburst candy does not count as a pure fruit. You are a hot mess," Christina snapped back.

I'm definitely not perfect, and I am not saying that I always wake up on time, however I have calibrated my morning alarm to alert me as to when I should awaken to start my workout. Each of us are fully capable of doing some of the work, to show ourselves that we matter to ourselves. Just like we have discipline at work and all of the other mundane activities of life, we must provide ourselves with discipline to invest in ourselves.

"That's right, Dr. T."

I'm glad you agree. Think about a time in which you demonstrated strict discipline on a project at work or at school. What was it and what did you do? Recall that scenario like it was yesterday to meditate on it. This is you taking action!

"Yes!" one lady yelled out in the audience.

I see your spirit awakening. Furthermore, in carrying out that project or activity, there was some sense of joy that you held when you completed that task. We have to have a sense of Joy towards how we approach the fact that we matter. If joy is not the foundation, the effort will be fleeting, like smoke from a blowout birthday candle. It is so important to act on your daily decision with joy. Everybody say—joy!

"Joy!" the crowd yelled to the atmosphere.

Count it all as joy. What in your life causes you ultimate joy? Generally, what brings you joy can lend to your legacy. Take inventory and look around you to see how you can enhance your legacy by helping others. It does not have to be a grand gesture like writing a check. It can be as simple as serving within your community, giving back with your time. Let it be aligned with your authentic self and your God-given purpose. Finding our purpose requires some quiet time. That can be very hard for us *Bad Ass Boss Chic's* who wear many hats, to make it through. Do you hear me?

Some of the ladies raised their hands.

All of this seems like a lot, however it all ties into how your sacrifices, your heroism, your excellence illustrates that you matter. In the midst of all of this, you must also take time to be still, relax, recharge and meditate.

Today, ladies, think about how you can schedule time for being still. Being still does not equate to not taking any action. It equates to having a moment to take a breather, allow yourself to become aligned with your own peace.

We have to remember to first enjoy our blessings to meditate on our whole being along with the changes that we need to make to live to be our best. What are the circumstances that cause you not to be able to be still? Lean into the Bible verse, *to know that I am God and I will be exalted.*

Amen, everyone.

"Amen," the ladies belted out.

Weight Breakers, you must carve out time every day to begin to make prayer and meditation more purposeful. Take a moment and list five things that you are thankful for.

The ladies began to transparently share out loud while they wrote.

"My health."

"My kids."

"My job."

"My house."

"My family."

"My friends."

"This conference."

Dr. T. smiled.

Ladies, thank you for sharing. Please note that by acknowledging what you are grateful for, that is a part of taking action. Gratefulness gives you the fuel to continue to take action. Furthermore, each day is an opportunity to walk into your purpose, to lose proverbial physical weight; be healthy, and accomplish your goals.

The ladies continued to scribe in their journals.

Let's think about what effect not taking inventory in your life will have on you?

A lady from the back yelled, "You will be living aimlessly."

Dr. T. nodded her head in agreement.

You are absolutely correct. If you take inventory without taking action, what are you doing?

"Nothing! You won't accomplish anything," another lady on the left side of the room yelled out.

You are unquestionably accurate. Let's do something a little fun. Are you all ready?

"Hell yeah!" one lady aggressively responded, while the others clapped.

Any self-proclaimed cooks in the house?

The ladies began to applaud.

Case in point, you go to the store to buy the ingredients for one of your favorite recipes. What should we be making, ladies?

"Some five-cheese macaroni and cheese!"

Okay, ladies, we are trying to break some weight. Let's go basic, like a good old-fashioned healthy salad. Shane, would you mind bringing out the cart?

The table was rolled in, with a chopping block.

So, ladies, what makes a good salad?

The ladies started to chime in:

"Lettuce."

"Tomatoes."

"Cucumbers."

"Onions."

As each of these salad ingredients were yelled out from the audience, Dr. T. held the vegetables up in their whole form.

Okay, this is a pretty basic salad, or is it?

"No."

What needs to happen?

"You need to cut the vegetables up!"

Weight Breakers, what does that equate to?

"Work!"

That is correct. We have got to do the work.

Dr. T. replied she cut up the veggies. She walked to the front of the stage as Shane rolled the cart off.

There is a lot at stake here, in the fact that you matter. Your fundamental beliefs about yourself are key in all of that. I'm going to hit you with a couple of questions to ponder as we wrap this session up, they are all in the Taking Inventory & Taking Action section in the book.

What are ways that you can speak to your vision and your faith each day?

How can you become agile and help you on our journey through life?

What is the advantage?

How do you qualify persistence?

What does persistence mean to you?

How can you do a better job manifesting persistence in your life?

Who are some people that undeniably show you accountable love for being persistent towards your goals?

These are all the ingredients that you need to be Weight Breakers—these all require work!

The ladies' body language jovially agreed.

Weight Breakers, I want to share with you one of the final messages of the day from me that I want to marinate in your spirit, that is how to respond when things don't happen the way you feel they should.

257

"You better preach, sis!" a lady on the right jeered on.

I am no preacher, but I feel you. So, let's look at something that we all hate to face, "closed doors."

The women were in agreement that it was a topic that caused them pause in their day-to-day lives.

Listen, all the doors that have closed in your life, think about the times when those closed doors led to a better blessing around the corner.

"Amen."

"Hallelujah!"

"Praise God for closed doors."

"I think about those blessings during quiet time."

I hear all of you. I'm glad you mentioned quiet time. Think about the value of serene time. How can you incorporate tranquil time in your day? Think about some areas of your life that you need to have more vision, faith, and resilience surrounding your quiet time? What are some of the experiences you felt like you would not get over? What are some cycles that need to be broken in your life? What steps are you going to do to plan your down time? What areas in your life can you ease up on a little? What are some of the profound blessings that came into your life by being a blessing to another?

The ladies were exuberant at the questions that were being proposed to them.

Dr. T. dug into their souls.

The whole foundation of THE CHRONICLES OF THE WEIGHT BREAKERS CONFERENCE is to share that we will do this together, and that we matter to this world—that is why we are here.

Now everyone stand up, look into your sister's eyes along with her spirit. Repeat after me, some of the mantras that Penelope exuded while she was on stage with her crew at the box *beat down:*

Let's not be idle.

Let's take inventory of areas that we may need to improve in.

Let's unveil our inner being.

Let's approach the encumbrance of life's journey.

Together, we can be the change that we need to make.

Together, we can encourage one another.

Together, we can keep the momentum of taking inventory and taking action.

We are Weight Breakers and not Weight Takers!

The women cheered, as they hugged their accountability partner's.

You all sound wonderful, however don't be surprised that the fact that you are becoming a weight breaker may make some people uncomfortable being around you. They are so used to you being in the box of living as a weight taker. For the lack of a better way to say it, they just don't know how to handle the empowered you! Be prepared to prune *your garden*—removing the weeds that have attempted to overpower the beautiful flower in you. Now embrace your fellow weight breaker sister's.

The women nodded, also readily embraced their neighbor sister friends, cheering each other on.

Now, ladies, this conference is all about you. Overall, how you're going to prompt yourself to walk into the depth of your new dimension. You're going to commit to continually taking inventory and taking action. We can do this, one tactic at a time! Give yourselves a round of applause.

The women's energized cheers filled the room. The music began to pound, keeping the room upbeat and engaged.

In your bags, you have a charm to go on your bracelet. The first charm is a hammer for taking action and taking inventory. So, when you leave this conference, the goal is to venture back into your lives with these charms wrapped around your wrist as a reminder of your new mindset of taking action and taking inventory. To remember that you and only you can *hammer down*, making those changes in your life, just like Penelope did. Furthermore, you will recall that, at times, you will need to call on your very own Declare Crew to beat down the walls of your life with you.

We will have a thirty-minute break and then we will have an energetic speaker that is sure to make you want to check your connectivity and evaluate your storage reprogramming. Okay, ladies, we will see you in thirty minutes. Go out and check out the vendor booths.

Much love, see you after the short break, Dr. T.

The women followed suit, and collected their belongings, many saving seats to come back to the main grand ballroom for the next speaker.

"What did you ladies think?" Abigail prompted.

"That was phenomenal. I can't believe I was up on stage with my big self-hammering away at that box," Penelope replied as she tried to suck *it* in. "It felt so

259

good not to have to be The Shadow this weekend—I have my *She Declares Crew* right by my side to have my back. I feel free," Penelope exhaled, releasing *her pause* in her life to take action, while taking inventory on her life.

The ladies put the hammer charms on their bracelets, putting their adorned hands in the center of themselves with their charms.

"Okay, sisters; Weight Breakers *We Can,* on three. One. Two. Three."

In unison, The She Declares Crew yelled out, "Weight Breakers, *We Can!*"

28

THE CONFERENCE

"CHECK YOUR CONNECTIVITY & STORAGE"

[WHAT ARE YOU PLUGGED INTO?]

Beautiful Weight Breakers!

I'm sure you all are still hyped up about the last session, Taking Inventory and Taking Action; I knew you would be. Now, ladies, I have a real treat for you. You may have noticed that in your swag bags you were blessed to have the book, *Friction Ridges* by Dr. Sparrow Mack. Look in your bags and hold them up.

The ladies followed the instructions.

This book is truly a testament of how, if you take inventory, along with taking action in your life, you can make it through life. Moreover, if you check your connectivity and storage programing, you can accomplish your goals.

So, without further ado, I have the author-screenwriter, Dr. Sparrow Mack, author of the box office hit, *Friction Ridges*. She was on my Weight Breaker Podcast recently. Today, we are going to talk about Checking Your Connectivity and Storage Reprogramming. If any of you are a Chronicles of The Weight Breakers Podcast listener, or have read my books, you realize I like to keep my followers engaged. So, what does Check your Connectivity and Storage Reprogramming mean to you? We have microphones set up, so go to one, just one person right now, you'll see why in a minute.

Surprisingly, Fawn was the first one at the microphone.

Hello, Weight Breaker, what is your name?

"I'm Fawn Paige," Dr. T. began to scratch her head, remembering the name.

Wait a minute—you won the first signed copy of my book, right?

"Yes, that's me," Fawn smiled, running her hand through her short *do*. She was adorned with a camouflage t-shirt that had *BOSS* embellished in bling—her tennis bracelet haloed the room. She was endeared that Dr. T. remembered her.

Dr. T. ran over to her, gave her another mic so she could hold it herself.

So, Fawn, tell us a little bit about yourself—what does checking your connectivity and evaluating your storage reprogramming mean to you?

Fawn put the microphone to her lips, as if to confess. Her sisters looked at her, surprised. "Hello, Weight Breaker Sisters; I'm Fawn."

"Hey, Fawn."

"Most people who meet me see me as perfect. I'm a personal trainer, however mostly everyone would describe me as upbeat, free-spirited, and completely optimistic. Some recent events have rocked my world. I found a lump in my breast and while I'm attending this conference, I'm waiting on my biopsy results—"

Fawn disclosed to a public audience what she had not had enough courage to share with her family or closest friends.

"What the hell?" A.J. stated; her eyes bucked at the disclosure.

"I cannot believe this," Penelope proclaimed, standing with her mouth open.

"What the fu—?" Christina arose from her chair.

Her She Declare Crew looked at each other dumbfounded that Fawn would make this sensitive public announcement, without changing this earth-shattering news with them privately first. They watched their sister reveal her truth to a room full of *strangers*.

"During this crucial time in my life, I realize more than ever the importance of checking my connectivity. Meaning, what I'm allowing myself to connect to. My space needs to be pure, sound—uplifting. After reading *Think Like a Weight Breaker. Not Like a Weight Taker,* I recognized that I had been taking on weight for far too long. I needed to shed some of the proverbial weight of life. I had been allowing myself to be The Mirage—not being my true self. I realized that I needed to start taking inventory, also taking action. I checked my connectivity along with my storage program!"

Hold on, Fawn. I know we're all about THE CHRONICLES OF THE WEIGHT BREAKERS CONFERENCE, but we're all sisters here, right? So, my sister, we are lifting you up right now in prayer. Come on, Weight Breakers, gather around this sister.

The room moved, surrounding Fawn.

Please extend your hands towards your Weight Breaker sister.

The women in the spirit-filled room stretched their hands towards Fawn.

We come before you God no longer as Weight Takers God, but Weight Breakers. God, we come to Your throne of grace, asking for healing for this sister right now, Lord. We ask that You bless her transparent spirit, guide her heart, touch her home, watch over her family, sustain this young woman. It is crucial what her needs are, Father God we know that You are a crucial God of more than enough. We thank You for her, moreover the life that she has led; the lessons that she has learned, and that You led her here for such a time as this. We claim this in the mighty, matchless name of Jesus. Amen.

Do we agree with our sister, Weight Breakers?

The women applauded between wiping their eyes, extending their hands. Dr. T. hugged Fawn, going on to say,

Ladies, we need to FOCUS ON GETTING CONNECTED TO THE RIGHT POWER SOURCE! I say that boldly because we have to do that boldly.

Fawn made it back to her seat with her crew, they hugged her. She was wrapped in their loving embrace.

I should have told them earlier, she thought to herself among tears.

Sisters, check your connectivity—storage reprogramming; you may be connected to the wrong things. Did you hear that? You may be connected to the wrong source. Checking your connectivity is a way to make sure you are aligned to your mission. Now, it is time to do the work on looking at your connectivity. You will be challenging what you are connected to. Be aware of what you are saturating your space with. Let's clean the cobwebs out of our attic in our mind! Archaic ways of thinking, unforgiveness, and moreover drama are taking up valuable space. This distorts your focus to meet weight head on. *Sync up* with the right ways of thinking—not just any source.

The women shook their heads in agreement.

There is a saying, you are what you eat. But more importantly, you are what you think. We are going from checking out on life, to checking your connectivity—storage reprogramming. The goals of this session are: recognizing your power source; knowing where your charger is; recognizing when you are low on battery life; identifying the situations that zap your battery life; realizing how powerful you are when you take care of yourself; releasing some of the things you have been holding onto that are taking up space; considering the joy by releasing the weights by checking your connectivity to monitor what you are storing, therefore what you need to reprogram.

The ladies were ready to listen.

Weight Breakers, I have a real treat for each of you. Back to our speaker, who is going to share some nuggets with you. Give it up for my friend, Dr. Sparrow Mack.

263

The room went into applause as Dr. Mack arrived on stage.

"Please, ladies, sit down; it's not that serious. I'm just a down home girl from the other side of the tracks, who worked hard to become a doctor turned author and now I'm making movies. With all of that said, my life is a testimony. Everyone say it with me—*Testimony!*" Dr. Mack beckoned to the crowd.

The listeners obliged.

"Now take a moment, turn your phone into photo mode as if you are taking a selfie. Look into your beautiful self. Look deep into that person, into your reflection, into that mirror or in your image from the phone. Cancel out all background noise surrounding you. Take this one moment for you. However uncomfortable that it may be, you must take this moment to look deep into your own spirit. Once you have tuned all of the noise of the world out of your mind, focus on yourself for this moment. Repeat after me, *I'm the Bomb"!*

The women yelled out, *"I'm the Bomb!"*

"Your divine purpose in life is to live at your maximum potential. And by saying that you are the Bomb, you are professing to be blessed and highly favored; Optimistic of God's guidance; a Magnificent existence of God's reflection and Bountifully filled with God given gifts. Each of you are the *BOMB! You are Brilliant, Optimistic, Magnificent and Beautiful!"*

The women went into an uproar as The Weight Breaker, Dr. T., joined Dr. Mack on stage.

"This is so good, let me take a moment to level the playing field for all those in the audience, we are all God's masterpieces. Now, I want you to say out loud, I'm a Magnificent Existence," Dr. Mack encouraged.

"I can't hear you; say it again," Dr. Mack asked of the ladies.

Thank you for approaching that topic, now, let's break this concept down together. Do you know that there is no one else like your unique self? Your thoughts, your time in space, was created from The Divine. From before you were a being, God knew your place in this world—moreover what your assignment would be.

From this moment on, instead of referring to yourself as *me*, refer to yourself as a magnificent existence! What do you think about that, Dr. Sparrow Mack? I know you have been very transparent about your path. Especially surrounding your best friend, Luke—with all of the complex dire circumstances surrounding him. I know you have a lot to say about this. Do tell.

Dr. Sparrow Mack let out a deep breath, a little flustered; however, deciding that it was a wonderful moment for true transparency.

"Dr. T., you are so right, exactly like you talk about in your book. You should take a moment, reflecting on how you're going to exercise your magnificent existence today! By grasping that you matter, seek God's counsel creating a covenant with the Holy Spirit for your destiny. Cancel out the plans of the enemy, debunking negative self-talk that caused you to stumble. In addition, realize by knowing that you matter, you cannot be complacent. You need to take charge of the gifts that God has entrusted each of us with. What is one gift that God has given you that you are going to nurture?"

Thank you, Dr. Mack; you're giving powerful words straight from the book. That is good. Ladies, get into those journals, writing out one gift God has given you that you are going to nurture?

The ladies willingly wrote in their journals.

Regi was still attempting to really get in the groove of all of the motivational *hoity toity*.

Fawn and Penelope dove right in.

A.J. was *semi-listening*, not totally unplugged from work, still checking emails on her iPhone.

Christina was getting all of her seat neighbors hyped about the activities.

Dr. T. went on to share,

Okay, ladies, it is oh so very important that as Weight Breakers, you realize *where your charger is!*

There are three hundred sixty-five days in a year, fifty-two weeks in a year, thirty days in a month, four weeks in a month, and seven days in a week. Twenty-four hours in a day. Sixty seconds in a minute. However, there is only one today! How are you going to make this day count regarding your well-being by tasting and seeing how life is good for today—recharging your spirit? Look at Psalm 34:8, *Taste and see that the Lord is good.* God wants us to have a gratifying life. In order to do that, we must refuel and recharge. What can refuel you is to be that person that enriches the world. How are you going to connect with that source to be an enrichment to the world? One of the ways we can do this is to fully recognize when you are low on battery life. Nevertheless, we must remember, in this *microwave* type of society, we need to be in tune with the fact that our creativity is the paint on God's canvas.

The crowd was amped—stoked on *100!*

I want everyone to go on social media to post, #ImAWeightBreakerNotAWeightTake#CheckYourConnectivityStorageReprogramming.

"Dr. T., I have known you for years, you truly are a Weight Breaker. When I wanted to give up on being both a physician and thought that I could not be both a

265

physician as well as an author—you put my self-doubt to rest really quick. Do you remember what you told me?"

Dr. Mack, I sure do, my sister. When you sent me that text telling me that you felt like you had to choose one over the other, I said the devil is a lie! You are called to be more than one thing. We all have a measure of faith combined with gifts. Therefore, that is why we are going to agree to bind all negative thoughts, to bring forth the fruit that was deep down within you!

"Dr. T., you sure did! You got me told—in line really quick! That is a part of checking my connectivity; making sure that I have sister friends around me that pour into me. In addition, reevaluating what I store in my mind—reprogramming my thoughts towards a higher thought process that is motivating."

Dr. Mack chuckled into the microphone.

"You see, there is, at minimum, at least one seed deep down within your being that is ready to flourish. Don't water seeds that don't benefit you by bringing a negative influence in your life. Water the seeds that will allow you to grow as a person—that is a part of God's vision for you. Sisters, you owe it to yourself to thrive. Let me tell you about something a little personal. There was a recent moment where I was burning the candle at both ends, and needed a little help to get through. My publisher recommended that I consider a ghostwriter. I met with her with a full two texts in hand, thinking that she could help me consolidate two documents. From that first meeting, it was unreal—I was taken aback by how the ghostwriter was super creepily intrigued with the manuscript—"

How so?

"She kept uncannily interjecting herself prematurely into my writing space and creativity—"

Wow, that's crazy!

"Jarringly for sure. Sis, *bright red flags in neon lights* went up profoundly in my mind, as she went on to share that she was tired of being *Farnsworth.*"

Who's that?

Dr. T. asked with a raised eyebrow.

"You know, like Robin is to Batman."

You said that cacophonously.

Dr. T. stated, looking around to make sure that her audience was safe in the space with Sparrow's past.

"Girl, every time I'm with you, I need a dictionary to keep up. Are you a walking thesaurus?" Dr. Mack clapped back with sarcastic humor.

The women in the audience hesitantly chuckled, while looking around to see what Dr. Mack was looking around for.

That lady really had you shook up Sparrow? I usually don't see this side of you.

Dr. Mack took a deep breath,

"The ghost-writer got super excited—kept telling me about how she did not want me to forget about her *when I blew up.* I spoke with the publisher, and informed her that her recommending this ghost writer was definitely not a good fit because of the *warning lights* God gave me about this lunatic."

What did the publisher say?

"The publisher was agreeable, very apologetic that they recommended her. Enough about that because just thinking of this person gives me the *heebie jeebies.* The moral of the story is that when your spirit points to red flags, believe them. I even had to get a restraining order on her; she kept showing up at all of my book signings— to stare at me and tell me how we could work great together."

Oh, my, that is awful. I'm so glad that part of your life is over.

"Let's hope so. I have a security detail with me at all times now. Just be aware of the red flags that you see regarding those that are way too eager to infiltrate your space quickly, what you download into your mental cloud, and who you are around. That is manifested by what you are linked up with and what you were storing in your mind," Dr. Mack's lip quivered, she then added,

"My husband said I am a magnet for *broken birds* with my name being Sparrow and all—"

I get it. First, Dana stalking your ass and trying to impersonate you, then this ghostwriter chick. Girl, I need to screen everyone you let into your space. Better yet, let me get out the prayer oil.

The ladies high-fived.

"Oh my goodness, you are so right. From that day on, it has not all been rosy, but I have not looked back. I cherish those words and continue to push forward with a new perspective. I have enhanced the time I spend with my family by really making sure that I'm connected with the right power source, for me it is God. In addition, kicking out all of that negative self-talk; that is why I love the Daily Decision Downloads you provided in the book. And just to be clear, I don't have anything against ghostwriters, however for my projects thus far, I have not used one and won't be any time in the near future. Each and every word of Dr. Sparrow Mack's work is written by me."

Dr. Mack, you got it, girl—you are so talented, God's got you. That is what those daily affirmations are for, for you to upload glory so you can download greatness. Turn to your workbooks, find those daily decision downloads, I want you to dog-ear that part of the book—make sure before your beautiful heads hit the pillows in the hotel room, check out that part of the book.

Now, Weight Breakers, think about a time when you were at your best, on your grind, the wheels of your thought processes were jelling. You were thinking fluid—able to meet encounters head on. More often than not, if this was done in a healthy fashion, with balanced rest at your core, you were able to not only complete the task, but relish in the fruits of your labor. Resting, sleeping, along with recharging your internal battery will allow you to do that. Realize the possibility of how powerful you are when you take care of yourself.

"Yep, as we all know, possibility means *a thing that may* happen. There are so many possibilities for our lives; we just have to be aligned, getting ourselves together so we can charge forward to our destinies. This reminds me of a time when I was paralyzed in fear…"

Dr. Mack please share.

"I was studying in my parents' home, then gunshots rang from the streets. I ran huddling myself in the bathtub. It was a horrifying experience. I found myself almost a hermit over the next few days, then one day God delivered me from fear to get myself back aligned with my destiny, which was not to be locked up in a house surrendering my dreams. In order to walk into my purpose, I had to trust God, study hard, and do what I could to get out of those circumstances that made me feel bound."

Girl, you have been through a lot. A drive-by? The layers of you keep unraveling.

"I know, and I have the scars to prove it. However, I had to change my vision for my life, which took a lot of work," Dr. Mack added with a blessed spirit that surrounded her.

We should think of positive visions for our life. Take out your phone, ladies, find a picture in your photos that illustrates when you were living out your legacy. A picture where you were serving your community—giving back. What did you do? How did that make you feel? In the words of the beautiful poet, artist, actress, and dancer—Maya Angelo, *"Your legacy is every life you touch."*

"I totally agree, Dr. T. If we are no longer to be Weight Takers, we have to release some of the things we have been holding onto that are taking up space! Because if we don't, we cannot fully plant our legacy."

Yes, indeed. We must realize that those things hinder our connectivity. We can get distracted by having doors closed in our faces. Yet, what I have fathomed is that when God closes a door, look for the window that He has opened. I would even go so far to even say that God may close the door, to have you remain in the room a little longer to glean additional insight so you are fully prepared to walk into your destiny.

In many instances, if you get the blessing, the job, the spouse, becoming a parent too soon, you may not be equipped to handle *the heat in the kitchen* for the lack of a better way to say it. There is a blessing *in the meantime*. Everyone said, in the meantime!

The crowd belted out, "In the meantime!"

Read, focus on your wellbeing, relishing in the time of enhanced *learney period.* Yes, I did not misspeak, I said *learney*; it is the learning period in the journey. Hardships will come, causing a cloud on your current state but understand they do not define your whole existence. Joshua 1:9 says, *Be strong and be courageous: do not be frightened or dismayed, for the Lord your God is with you wherever you go*. During those times that can be viewed as hard, you are very well learning something.

"So, Dr. T., how do we do that? A raise of hands, we are moms, wives, partners, daughters, everybody's everything. How do we do this?" Dr. Mack asked as she began to walk around in the audience to connect.

Let's think about how we can create a roadmap of how you're going to connect with yourself, being: more fluid; malleable, and purposeful. Be specific, write it down, making it clear. Set deadlines; put *it* on your calendar!

"Ladies, this is some good stuff. If I had some of these pearls earlier in my life, things may have been different—I would have made better decisions. Dr. T., can I be a little more transparent?"

Yes girl, but hold on. I still can't believe that I jumped out of the plane recently. I did that jump for all the Weight Takers that listen into The Chronicles of The Weight Breakers Podcast, to encourage them to overcome their fears. Full transparency, I could not have done that jump without you all. How hypocritic would it be for me to continually preach to you to overcome your fears, when I had fears of my own that I was not willing to overcome? It started with one of the first airplane rides I ever took. Let me level set, on that flight, little did I know that I was flying into the eye of a torrential storm. I was so scared that I even asked to hold the hand of a neighboring passenger, who happened to be a pastor. There was a seat between us. The pastor, at first, reassured me that everything was going to be okay. Then his tone changed when the plane appeared to toss and turn in the air as if it were a paper airplane. His prayers became a little louder. We landed safely; I tell you I had lost all of my embarrassment because I was downright scared.

"I hate flying; that's why I drove six hours to get here," a lady yelled out from the back of the room.

I agree. I don't want to discourage anyone from flying. However, with full transparency, during the midst of that storm, I vowed to myself that I would never fly again. Nevertheless, as anyone knows me, since that proclamation, I flew too many times to count—it's a part of how I spread the good news of weight breaking. Just like that bumpy flight that occurred out of nowhere, life can be that way. Moreover, you all saw my LIVE feed when I jumped out of the single engine plane—what was I thinking?

"Girl, I know you are bold, but seriously—knowing you, I was shocked that you did that. Besides, don't we wish that there was a sign that would come on first before any issues arose to tell us to *Buckle Up*? Before any family crisis, drama among friends, or escalated issues at work, don't you wish a sign would appear that said, *buckle up, here goes some turbulence*? God will put the right people around you, even building structure through the new people you encounter during those turbulent times. Moreover, I cannot believe that you took that plunge—skydiving. I'm still tripping over that!" Dr. Mack added.

I can't believe it either. You bring up a great point, that is so true. Issues can occur without any warning, that's why it's so good to have good connectivity. I have found that I have to carve out time in my busy schedule to pen those individuals in who really care about me; that is so important.

"In my fold of people that are a part of my core is my husband, Weston, who is so supportive of my endeavors. Our relationship is not perfect at all times; however, we work at our connectivity—what we allow to be stored into our marriage."

Sis, you and Mack are cut from the same cloth—a relationship that is ordained by God. You share all of the challenges that you are faced with on your life journey, especially some scary situations with your best friend—Luke. I don't want to be a spoiler of the book *Friction Ridges*; however, can you share how you worked through some of those circumstances that you talk about in your best-selling novel, now a box office hit?

Her face told it all—Dr. Mack appeared to be a little hesitant to ride down those cobblestone, horrific memories in her mental dungeon. However, she went on to share.

"Let me tell you something, my life has been no *crystal stair*—quite a doozy. From looking down the barrel of a gun, escaping the backwoods, searching for my best friend that was presumed dead, to so much more. What all those catastrophic events taught me was to seek to consider the joy, in all circumstances. The pursuit of joy is the grace that God has given me to see another day. That, in itself, caused me to do whatever I can to release the proverbial weight and physical weight by checking what I am connecting myself to. I have had to seek counsel, read motivational books; moreover, reevaluate the circle of people I allow into my space. I had a mentor, a chief surgeon that always warned me about who I let into my space."

The one you lost in the tragic plane crash?

270

"Yes, that news still haunts me. However, it is because of the lessons that he taught me, that I realize that I am always grateful to see another day."

A surgeon that died in a plane crash? Zachary's relative, who was a surgeon, died that way—interesting, Regi thought to herself.

That struck A.J. to heart as she realized that she would surround herself with people that were anything other than what she was, suppressing her culture. Her fantasies of being able to go out into the sun not lathered by sunscreen, as to not get *too dark*—so she could fit in. The Chameleon remembers herself standing in front of the television, placing her young arm, as a child, up to the television actress' to try to imagine her skin not so melanin thick.

Penelope realized that she also allowed her space to be centered around Cassidy Gentry, who caused her to feel less than all the time. She was three times Cassidy's weight, yet she felt the weight of being in the shadow threefold. Penny, what her mother affectionately called her when she was hung over on Xanax mixed with tequila—which is not advisable. While preparing the standard meal of fried bologna sandwiches for dinner, swallowing in pity of yet another failed marriage, once told Penny that she felt that her favorite hobby must be *being a wallflower*, she must be addicted to loneliness. Penelope allowed that lie to become her truth. Owning the idea of being a misfit—The Shadow.

Regi felt the weight of constantly worrying about her awful connection with her mother-in-law, compounded by the clasps of the grips of a tornado long ago that ripped her life to shreds—causing her to be the *hanger on of all things*. She juggled so much at all times because if she ever stopped juggling, *the pause* would cause her to catapult into the storm shelter, watching her little brother's hands being ripped from her into the ominous sky. Every effort to forget that day, caused her to keep several plates always spinning in the air—The Juggler.

Chaka had not connected with anyone, except for the recent acceptance of her sister, who helped nurture her dream of becoming a comic. If she went after her ambition and failed, her father would be right. In her heart of hearts, she'd rather die than not live in her truth of becoming one of the comic greats of all times. She'd prove them all wrong—rendering a new meaning to the American dream for women of Asian descent. She wanted to turn The Aspirational way of thinking into manifestation.

Fawn's connection of investing all of her hopes and dreams were washed away from her. To add insult to injury, the biopsy results held her fate. Would she live to see another day, responding to the upcoming treatment regimen? If she was not okay, how would her aging mother take care of her baby girl? If she did make it, would she ever find love again? However, the way to cope was to always make everything appear as if everything was okay—The Mirage.

Dr. Mack went on to share,

"When you get the epiphany that what you are feeding your soul is not serving your purpose, that is a whisper from God to make some changes. What are some whispers from God, the higher power, that you have noticed in your life, that caused you to check your connectivity and reprogram the way you think about your overall life? It is so very important to connect with like-minded people or a group that has innovative ways of thinking, moreover are aligned with your purpose. It has been said, if you are the smartest one in your group, you are in the wrong group. Hopefully, within this segment of the day is one of the foundational aspects of our life."

Dr. Sparrow Mack, you are so gracious for taking time away from your promotional tour; the continued appearances for your box office hit, *Friction Ridges*; to grace us with your presence. Ladies, give her a round of applause.

The ladies followed suit.

"Dr. T., I would like to take a moment to say thank you to each and every one of you. I'm humbly honored to be present in this room with your exuberant energy. I write fictional stories; however, I have never written an autobiography. Yet, I will embark upon that. One of the highlights in my life is to be in this space with you Weight Breaker sisters today—this is a part of a bucket list item for me. I sincerely love each of you. Take this word to heart: *if you can believe it, you can achieve it!* Dig deep, check in with yourself to see what you are connected to, who you are connected to."

Sparrow bit her lip, cautious to tell all.

"Let me be transparent with you, I had a wonderful employment opportunity that appeared to be so great many moons ago, when I was in clinical practice. Unfortunately, I had to part ways with that clinic for many reasons. One example was that my colleagues started having a steamy affair—coupled with practicing medicine unethically. I'm so grateful God got me out of that situation. Unfortunately, one of those physicians expired in a horrific small engine plane crash in which he was the pilot, along with his wife whom he philandered on throughout their marriage. It was so sad. The point of the story was that God saw what was going on in that clinic before I even knew what was going on, causing another great job to be in pursuit of me. In which I would be surrounded by the right type of people. Now, repeat after me. I will be a Weight Breaker, surrounding myself with other Weight Breakers."

The ladies obliged.

There she goes talking about that physician again who died in that horrific plane crash. I wonder if they are talking about Zachary's relative? The circumstances sound so familiar, Regi ruminated.

Dr. Mack went on to share, "It is so vital to do this because each of you are so essential to your mission here on earth. Much love with exuberant blessings, Weight Breakers!"

Dr. Mack blew kisses, then waved as she exited the stage.

Ladies, send our Weight Breaker sister off to her book tour with a round of applause. So, ladies, you are getting tools to break that weight. In the first segment, you received a hammer charm to remind you to take action, after you take inventory. Now being passed around to you are *connectivity symbol* charms, to remind you to check into your connectivity. Don't lose your charms; please keep them close by.

The ladies eagerly placed the charms on their bracelets.

From this section of the day, you should have journaled about how you are going to Check your connectivity, furthermore how to program what is going on within your mental cloud. In this section of the book, you have done the following: recognizing your power source, knowing where your charger is, recognizing when you are low on battery life, identifying the situations that zap your battery life, realizing how powerful you are when you take care of yourself, releasing some of the things you have been holding onto that are taking up space, considering the joy by releasing the proverbial weight and physical weight by checking your connectivity, while monitoring what you are storing. In addition, what you need to reprogram in your life.

Can't wait to see you all in the next session,

Dr. T.

"I'm so glad I connected with you ladies—" Fawn turned towards her sisters.

"Hell, you didn't connect with us. That damn tornado brought our *Weight Taker asses* together," Christina pronounced with her quick wit.

The ladies enveloped each other as they giggled.

"Why in the hell did you not tell us about what is going on with you?" Regi scolded Fawn.

"Because by me saying it out loud, that would make it real," Fawn bit her lip.

The ladies gathered around, "We love you girl," A.J. stated, while she solicited a group hug surrounding Fawn.

GROWL!

"Damn Penelope, is that your stomach?" Christina joked.

"Yes, when is lunch again? I need something sweet to *tide* me over," Penelope questioned as she pulled out a Snickers from her purse, taking a bite with a nugget attached to her bottom lip.

With irritation all over her face, Regi grabbed the candy bar from Penelope. Her eyes told it all as they bucked.

"We are supposed to be breaking weight up here, and there you go—really? Come on, ladies. Let's go over to the healthy snack table—see, grab one of these apples."

"The only kind of apple I want to eat is one dipped in caramel, draped in dark chocolate with crushed walnuts on the outside. I'm a lost cause—"Penelope's negative self-talk was interrupted by her sisters.

"No, you are not a lost cause. You've got this, Penelope. We are *your connectivity*, so you can make better decisions. We got you, girl—we will not allow you to continue to self-sabotage. Besides, how are you going to catch a man *that looks like a whole delicious snack,* if you always have sugary snacks in your hand?" A.J.'s firmness was received with love as Penelope grabbed an apple, along with a package of almonds.

"Is this better?" Penelope questioned the *food police.*

The ladies nodded in agreement, encouraging their sister that *she can*, while they ate their healthy snacks—continuing to connect.

29

THE CONFERENCE

"DOWNLOADING DEEP SOUL ACTIVITIES"

[TABITHA'S EMULATE LIFE...]

Welcome back Weight Breakers,

Next coming to the stage, we have Tabitha Blanko. She is a phenomenal broker agent to *The Stars*—negotiating their six-figure contracts, securing their multi-million-dollar book deals. You are going to hear it first at THE CHRONICLES OF THE WEIGHT BREAKERS CONFERENCE how she is dipping her toe into the sports arena along with other creative ventures—she's *One Bad Sista!* This phenomenal *shero* has a revealing message to share with you. In my book, *Think Like A Weight Breaker. Not Like A Weight Taker*, I talk about Downloading Deep Soul Activities—this lady right here has done just that. She has done so by breaking through barriers that are unimaginable, her story will cause you to grip your seat. She is the epitome of what *digging deep* looks like. She pulled herself up with God's grace—manifesting a bountiful purpose for her life. Please give a round of applause, for the amazing Tabitha Blanko.

The Weight Breakers stood to their feet as billowing hands clapped for Tabitha.

"What's going on ladies, you all are so beautiful. I feel like I can be very real with you. I've read the book—I'm doing the work. I realized I had been carrying some weight around with me. Behind the red carpets, the handbags, the shoes, furthermore being in the green room of every major studio, I was The *Emulate* momentum type. I've been living The Emulate life."

Tabitha echoed into the microphone.

People in the audience gasped at that revelation, as they had seen Tabitha on every magazine cover, most recently the *Forbes* article—she referenced how she could negotiate *the damn paint off the wall.* Furthermore, she had the reputation of *always keeping it real,* in a high-class way.

She took a sip of her bottled water, placed it on the podium, acquiesced while she surveyed the audience to determine if they were ready for her unveiling. She commenced, as she paced the stage, while Dr. T. stood in the background.

"I'm going to tell you a story about a young girl who lived in a trailer on an open field of land. She loved pretty things; she would look at magazines imagining what her life would be. She found some white spray paint to paint an old chandelier that had been tossed out into the trash. Bolting the junky refurbished chandelier to the ceiling of the one-room trailer, I can see it just like it was yesterday. It gave her a sense of gratification, after she secured the fixture with duct tape to the top limit of the raggedy orifice in which she lived with her sickly mother. Everybody say duct tape!"

The women looked around at each other, as they shrugged their shoulders at the odd request. They complied—uncertain of its significance.

"Duct tape?"

"Way to go. Now, listen further—the young girl would take old rags, quilting them together orchestrating throw pillows. This is going to get really deep, ladies."

The She Declare Crew sat on the edge of their seats, as well as all of the other women in the crowd. There was silence—you could have heard a pin drop with the ladies listening intently. Tabitha began to get really vulnerable—a tear formed in the apex of her eye.

"So you may be wondering about the origin of this story. Let me backup, as a teenager this girl's mother became pregnant, while being the babysitter for a middle-class couple—need I say more. After her family became aware she was expecting, because the girl was not willing to disclose who the father of the baby was, in fear of shaking up the bedrock community, she had the baby alone—surviving by becoming a waitress. Fast-forward to when her very own daughter was an adolescent, in between homeless shelters, *couch surfing* with friends—the woman and her child landed in a trailer park. Her mother began to have *spells* of stomach pain that worsened—ultimately she was diagnosed with stomach cancer. The young girl became *a nurse* for her dying mother, she fed her; gave her medicine whenever they could *scrape* enough money to get it. She would hold her mother's emesis basin while she threw up daily. The young girl had the love of her mother, however was taunted daily at school for her tattered torn clothes. She resorted to finding food for her family inside local restaurant dumpsters. The one joy in her life was when her mother was having *a good day*, the two of them watched *I Dream of Jeannie* along with *Bewitched*. The young girl loved the magic of Tabitha—the good witch. She would imagine that by wrinkling her nose, magically she'd disappear out of their destitute circumstances."

Tabitha rendered a wistful chuckle.

The audience was prompted not to leave the speaker *hanging* alone on her nostalgic transparent bid for some humor in the sad story—snickering along with her.

This story brought a smile to Christina's spirit, "Damn, those shows were my *jam*. I used to sneak, watching them in the back of the restaurant when I was supposed to be working when I was a little girl. Back in the day, I'd imagine I was

Jeannie being rescued from a bottle by a fine-ass *Denzel-like* astronaut. The icing on the cake was that Captain Nelson would fall in love with me—taking me home to live happily ever after," Christina kiddingly stated.

Penelope scolded, attempting to listen intently, *"Shhh*, girl, you are a hot mess. You're not Barbara Eden. Be quiet; the woman is trying to talk. I need to hear this. We're not in Cocoa Beach."

"Yeah, Chaka, shut the hell up with your comedic shenanigans; you're always doing way too much," A.J. stoically rendered, positioning her body to take better notes.

Christina snapped back in a gesture, she placed her hands together in the genie prayer pose, then twitched her nose, her sassiness felt by her seatmates.

Tabitha stepped to the front of the stage, "Anyone out there ever imagine what your life could be, when you were a little girl?"

Hands raised.

"Stand if you have ever fantasized about things you did not have, especially when you were a little girl!"

Women stood all over the building. In many of their eyes, you could see they related all too well with the origin of Tabitha's story.

"Look at your seat neighbor, don't leave any of your sisters hanging, repeating after me—We are Weight Breakers! We are going to download new information. We are going to work on activities to work deep into our soul. We can do this!"

The ladies followed instruction—they high-fived.

"Okay, ladies, buckle up; the road will be a little catastrophic. There is more to the troublesome story. In this young girl's *imaginary life*, she wished that she could twinkle her nose and be immersed in the *fancy schmancy* magazines she read living a life of grandeur opulence. *POOF,* she desired to change her circumstances in the blink of her eyes—but she couldn't. A life of destitute loneliness, coupled with despair was *her address.* All of the kids at school had their own computers; however, she was determined to change her life through learning as much as possible. She'd walk to the library to use the free computers, reading almost every book in the library on various topics. This girl had grit, determination, a vision that she felt deep down in her soul."

Tabitha's eyes seemed to be reliving the moments she was talking about, empathetic about the girl she was referencing or, possibly, much more.

"This young lady even had the ingenuity to create a home economics project called, *My Real Life,* in which she'd blog regarding high fashion along with decorating trends. Those subjects were such a stark contrast to her actual real life living out of the trailer. She lived for that class. Many times the joy that was on her face abruptly disintegrated as soon as she got home. There were alcoholic tirades that occurred in the trailer by her mother's abusive boyfriend. She would put the pillow over her face to hide herself from the domestic violence eruptions, all the way up until—*a hollow grave."*

One woman gasped loudly, as Tabitha wiped tears from her strong cheekbones.

"You may wonder, how could her dreams come into fruition? Throughout time, by *downloading* a new vision for herself. She had a vision for her life, although she had no idea how she could make any of her *dreams come to pass*. Through her creativity, deep down, she knew *it* would happen."

The women were awestruck by the hardships of the story.

"One day, while looking at the shell of the trailer, she had an endearing smile, as she recalled wanting to lighten the mood for her mother, therefore she started to paint the interior of the dingy, mildewed trailer all white. She found a chandelier in the trash, also dressed up the interior of the trailer while attending school—ramping up her followers. Her mother couldn't afford to shower her daughter with material things. However, she managed to shower her with faith. Adorned around her mother's frail neck was a beautiful necklace with a cross pendant—the most cherished item that her mother had. That little girl's name was Savoy."

Tabitha touched a necklace around her neck, holding it dearly.

"Then *that solemn day* occurred. Savoy returned home; she was preparing her mother's medicine. She walked towards her mother; she was unresponsive. She recalled the horrific memories of attempting to bring her mother back to life by doing C.P.R that she learned in health class. She didn't know what to do, so she called the man that owned the land that the trailer was parked on. He came by, retrieved Savoy's mother's *body,* telling her he that he was going to take her to the hospital to get help."

The air was thick with emotion as Tabitha painted the picture of the story,

"Long worrisome days went by, however there was no word of what happened to her mother. She walked in her flip flops to a payphone, calling the landowner and he said, *Oh, forgot to call you—your mom didn't make it. Please vacate the trailer in forty-eight hours,* then he hung up the phone. The girl was standing there three miles away from home when she received the startling news. Left with no choice, she walked back to the trailer crying all the way. She found a can of cold pork and beans, sat on the couch—cried herself to sleep. Then the unthinkable happened—*BOOM!* The trailer was struck, it shook, it felt like an earthquake, her vision swirled as the only home she knew toppled over. She was able to climb out a broken window, becoming conscious that the trailer was being bulldozed by the landowner who had a shotgun ready and willing to aim and fire at the orphaned teenager. In surrender pose, she pleaded for his grace, as he fired a warning shot in the air. She noticed on the ground the keys to the old beat-up old Chevy that her mother had parked out in front of the trailer."

Some women in the audience could relate all too well with the illustration of abandonment.

"Grabbing a plastic bag throwing anything she could in quickly, afraid that the twelve-gage bullet had her name on it, she cranked up the dilapidated car where the floorboard was half missing driving off. With no driver's license, in addition no official driving lessons she felt like a thief on the run, however a run to nowhere. The only things in the front seat of the frantic insecure motherless fatherless girl with tears rolling down her face, were tattered clothes; a couple of books; cans of beans and her scrapbook she had entitled, *MY Real Life.* With tears flooding her face. There was one thing that she was propelled to do and that was to place a marker to honor her mother. She found a rock that she put a *white finger nail polished heart* on to mark the spot she and her mother called home. She held onto the necklace around her neck, which was her mother's, got back into the car and drove. Pleading for God to provide a breakthrough to pour down from Heaven, as she drove the car that felt like it could fall apart at any minute with less than a fourth of a tank of gas. The scared child was on a road to nowhere, when the clouds opened and rain burst through the dark sky."

The Weight Breakers listened in, as they shed tears of remorse for the deserted girl.

"Her tattered windshield wipers didn't do a good job in clearing the view for Savoy to drive safely in the darkest of nights. It was raining so hard. Redundantly, she prayed out loud for God to help her as she maneuvered the rundown car on the slick roads. The bottom of the raggedy car was rusted, which caused a clear view of the road through the bottom of the car. The torrential rain soaked her feet through the rusted floorboard. *I have no idea which way to go, God,* she belted out to the heavens. Just then the steering wheel commenced to escalate in vibration—this caused her to panic. *What now, God. Please Lord, I can't take much more!* The car started to jerk, it stalled out, bringing the car to an abrupt halt. *Oh no, what do I do now? Walk—was* the word that came into her broken spirit."

The women in the audience clutched their proverbial pearls of the unknown that this innocent young woman was walking into—in alone destitution. Tabitha's eyes told it all,

"With no umbrella in hand, she figured she would find a gas station; possibly more gas would get her to a safe place to land. In the downpour of rain, she set out to walk into the dark of night to find gas. Tears rolled down her young cheeks, appearing to be equivalent to the water that was pouncing on her from the dark night sky. Then, out of nowhere, it began to hail. At first, in the stark night, the ice coming down from Heaven looked like diamonds. She even held her hand out to see how many she could catch in her youthfulness—smiling briefly. Hard rain pellets hit her face; her feet scuffled along the hard uneven pavement losing one of her flip flops. The ice began to cut her young supple skin. The *diamonds* started to rain down steadfast. Pressure from the hail pounded on her body. She ran, tripped, falling on the sidewalk. Getting up to run again, she noticed a side door on a house that had a covered awning. She was hesitant to go on anybody's porch, but she was desperate for relief from the storm. She realized that the gate had been left open, she hustled up to the house to seek out safety from the golf ball-sized hail. Between the melodic sound of the rain coupled with being absolutely exhausted with a growling hungry gut, her innocence was cold drenched, resting on the door. Suddenly awakened as the door she was leaning against opened, her face fell hard against cold marble. The girl went into the house— in awe! Her young eyes were not sure if she was dreaming or not. She looked around at the immaculate crown molding and the marble floors; amid antique beautiful furniture. It appeared to be an abandoned family home. She rummaged through the pantry, found some tuna fish—devoured it like it was Thanksgiving dinner. Mid-bite, a noise rumbled upstairs. Grabbing a knife, in her bare feet she tiptoed upstairs, treading with caution. Her heart pounded almost outside of her chest, anticipating what she would walk into. A huge master bedroom door was cracked, her scared eyes peering into the room. Her pulse decreased as she witnessed an elderly man, his aged hand uncovered the blanket on his body, when rolling over making eye contact with the young terrified girl, he fairly uttered, *"Come on in, girl, don't be afraid. I won't bite. What's your name, young lady?"*

The ladies in the audience were now seated on the edge of their seats as they awaited the unveiling of the canvas that Tabitha painted.

"The young girl was petrified, but hesitantly replied—*My name is…Tabitha*?" That was the only name that Savoy could think of sharing—she felt her mother guiding her lips.

The women in the audience gasped with tears in their eyes.

"There *Tabitha* stood in the opulent master suite of the lonely multi-million-dollar mansion, a stark contrast to the dilapidated trailer that was now demolished, bulldozed into a million little pieces along with the history of Savoy Middleton. In that moment, young Savoy evaporated like dust at the feet of Mr. Blanko, taking on a whole other identity—a caregiver to take care of the wealthy gentleman. Both individuals, in that moment, emulated the pauper and the prince. Although brought up on the opposite sides of the tracks, felt a unique bond—the bond of abandonment. Both of them longing…"

Intrigue filled the room, as The Weight Breakers hung onto every word of The Emulate standing before them.

Tabitha went on to share,

"Quite often Mr. Blanko would tell me, even up until I was a young lady, that I was an angel that showed up out of nowhere, *willing* him back to life. On that fateful day, of our chance encounter, he was the lucky one."

The Weight Breakers were in absolute tears in the audience. All writing utensils dropped, Kleenex was being passed, there was a real human connection going on.

"I cooked, cleaned the mansion from top to bottom on my hands and knees, while nursing him back to health. Even to the point where he was no longer bed-ridden. He was honored to take on the role of guardian for this young girl, raising me. I read every book in his opulent library, while he took me out on the golf cart teaching me the business—he managed liquidated foreclosed companies assets. Mr. Blanko shared with me that he grew up in a Jewish working-class family. His grandfather came to the United States not even being able to speak English, whose family immigrated from Russia through Ellis Island, in which he changed his name from Blinov. He also revealed his Romanian heritage on his mother's side. He taught me how to make Pelmeni that he liked to eat alongside Beef Stroganoff with Syrniki's. Furthermore, holidays were filled with memories of his mother with piping hot Sarmale on top of polenta. To top it off delicious Colaci."

Smiles filled the atmosphere, as they felt the aromatics of the story.

"Mr. Blanko's first endeavor in business was being a *dumpster diver*."

The women in the audience were startled at the thought of the billionaire mogul, drudging through garbage by the expressions on their faces.

"Please don't judge, you never know someone's story. As a young boy he would wake up early in the morning before sunrise to sort through what others had discarded—taking soda along with beer bottles from and dumpsters. With the money he was able to earn, he contributed to the family household to help keep the lights on in the dilapidated row house. His hustle was very real, he had to put cardboard in the souls of his shoes, moreover was finally able to buy some sneakers by taking a paper route."

Tabitha smiled at that thought.

"When he was not in school or at his multiple after odd school jobs, he was a pure lover of literature. He did not have a library card, so he would spend time in the library daily reading every book he could get his hands on. The books that attracted his spirit were those that pertained to business. Then one day, he stumbled on a magazine that resonated—Forbes Magazine. Before there were vision boards, he wrote on a piece of newspaper he got out of the library trash can—*I'm going to buy businesses to sell parts of them.* It was simple, straight to the point. He was able to attend community college, by financing his education with multiple business ventures, including working in the cafeteria; note transcribing for fellow students, moreover starting a small cleaning company—to clean dorm mates' filthy dorm rooms. He

281

survived, by any means necessary. He plunged his entire being into empowering words that was housed on the raggedy worn vision statement in his wallet, he networked, negotiated into his billion-dollar empire, later inviting a little abandoned teenager on that journey. That girl was me, Savoy Middleton, I would have never guessed that God would be so gracious to land me to be what I am now—Tabitha Blanko, agent to the stars!"

The ladies applauded; tears streamed down their faces—they were on that journey with Tabitha.

A.J. was balling, her crew comforted her.

"Sis, are you okay?" Regi rendered concern with her overwhelmed reaction.

"I feel like that story was all about me. I'm constantly attempting to be someone else; The Chameleon." Regi embraced A.J. like a true sister would, she handed her a Kleenex to wipe her eyes.

Dr. T. stepped to the front of the stage,

Any questions for Tabitha Blanko?

Surprisingly, A.J. raised her hand, the microphone was brought to her.

"Good afternoon, Weight Breakers, my birth name is Anjali Jagruti Nadkarni. I go by A.J. because I feel that it's more acceptable in the corporate world. The story that you shared got me all choked up. With every word you spoke, I saw me," she fell into *the ugly cry* that encroached upon her.

Take your time. You will no longer be The Chameleon; you have all the power you need to walk into your purpose. You've got this.

"Thank you, I feel like this is a safe space to share," A.J. smiled.

 It is. Go on, child.

Dr. T. said in a motherly fashion.

A.J. glanced over at her She Declare Crew—they encouraged her on,

"Yeah, A.J., you're *The Bomb Girl!*" Christina belted out like they were at the Apollo, with A.J. on stage to perform. Her sisters gave her a look to pipe it down a notch.

A.J. mustered up the courage to share a bit of herself. "I'm a Vice President of Marketing. I've worked so hard for upward mobility in my company. Despite all I've accomplished, I'm sad to say the firm isn't representing culture and diversity very well—moreover it's pissing me the hell off!" A.J. let out a big sigh as if weight was released with those words.

The women in the audience obviously identified with her; they were nodding in agreement. Empowered, A.J. stepped forward—faced the crowd, asking them all with a newfound force.

"Have you ever had to deal with microaggressions?" She questioned the plight of women who were all there to release physical and proverbial weights themselves.

Weight Breakers, for those of you who said they have; I feel your pain. For those who don't know what microaggressions are, they are actions along with statements of subtle discrimination, against a population of individuals. In many instances against minorities, or those thought to be minorities.

"Dr. T. you are so right. In my company the microaggressions are *out of the wazoo* daily. However, when I faced microaggressions, I pathetically remained quiet, because I'm attempting my hardest to be *Americanized*, which is such an added weight, because I feel like I must deny my own culture to fit in," A.J. in full vulnerability uttered.

Multitude in the crowd identified with the words being verbalized, A.J. went on to identify,

"People just don't know how to take me or what I am. I'm asked if I'm Latin, Mexican, Indian, Arabic. All are beautiful cultures and races. But I'm in denial. I've worked hard to temper my dialect so I can sound like my male American colleagues. Conversely, in my mind, I keep hearing my mom saying, *Anjali, be proud of your heritage*. My mother's self-pride of our culture is a constant ringing in my ears, echoing in my heart. I have recently met a friend who let me know the importance of being proud of exactly who I am," A.J. paused as she got a little sick to her stomach. She took a deep breath, so she wouldn't purge on the microphone, making a complete fool of herself in front of the crowd.

Dr. T. encouraged her to breathe—she mouthed to her,

A.J. We are here for you.

"To cope with my self-identity issues, I started to practice some unhealthy habits. I heard about this book in the midst of pure chaos, decided to pick it up, *Think Like A Weight Breaker. Not Like A Weight Taker*. The book caused me to realize that my momentum type is The Chameleon. I've been making the wrong daily decisions to attempt to change my appearance, as well as my overall demeanor to fit in. I need to be accepting the beauty of who I am—who God called me to be. More importantly, I needed to start to Download Deep Activities so I could also be a Weight Breaker, no longer The Chameleon Weight Taker!"

A.J. threw her hands up in surrender pose.

Wow, you've got some spunk. I love it—

Dr. T. weighed in.

"Can I say one more thing? I've needed to get this off my chest for a long time."

Go ahead, you have the floor.

A.J. dug deep into her spirit, beckoning Anjali to the surface. She cleared her throat,

"Listen to me clearly! YOU CANNOT TOUCH MY HAIR!"

The women of ethnic descent applauded; the room was in pure pandemonium.

You could feel the weights lift off the women of different hues of brown as they rallied their sister on.

Wow, A.J., you've got *it* sis! Don't ever forget that! This woman is powerful; let's keep this momentum going, Weight Breakers. Tabitha, take a stab at providing Anjali with support—pour into her.

The women took their seats; the uplifting spirit was a buzz in the room.

Tabitha, held the mic to her lips.

"Dr. T., I love that you have been speaking in this part of the conference regarding downloading deep soul activities. Furthermore, Anjali, what a beautiful name, don't hide behind A.J. anymore! You have to FOCUS ON GETTING CONNECTED WITH YOUR INNER SOUL! Anjali, you are beautiful, intelligent, besides I can tell you are such a gift to the company you work for. Walk in your purpose, honor your culture and who you are!"

Tabitha came off the stage to give Anjali a hug.

Dr. T. chimed in.

Weight Breakers, one of the ways to do that is to realize that you were made for motion. You are made for taking steps! All motion starts with taking the first step. First steps can be scary, causing anxiety to overwhelm your spirit. When negativities flood your head, speak that verse out loud. Lean on Philippians 4:8, *Finally, brothers and sisters, whatever is true, whatever is noble, whatever is right, whatever is pure, whatever is lovely, whatever is admirable; think about such things.*

The women were agreeable with the bible verse, picking back up their pens—writing in their journals as she shared more information.

I imagined that God has a notebook and has a pen that He uses to write in His notebook. With that pen, God wrote out the divine purpose of all of the beings that

He created. What do I believe that God writes in pen? I feel that it would be his love that He has for us; that is the forgiveness that He has for each and every one of us; moreover the salvation that is readily available for all of us, if we so choose.

The women nodded in agreement.

When you think of something written in pen, you think it is final. That's why I'm so glad that God's love is final for each of us. With that security, I pray that you release all of your fears, knowing that your purpose is already written by the almighty hand of God. In addition, if we step out on faith, trusting that if you take heed to God's voice, you're able to walk into your purpose. And most of all, our purpose along with our future is written in pen. You hear me ladies?

"Yes!" The group surrendered to the air.

Without going deeper within your soul, figuring out root causes of things at the core of an issue, action is a waste of time. Digging deeper equips us on our excursion of life. We are going from derogatory thinking to Download Deep Soul Activities: Reflection, Meditation, Concentration, Projection, Determination, Restitution, and Demonstration.

Dr. T. proclaimed as she walked around the room.

I use this analogy all the time, reflecting on a time when you were in a tough situation, then out of the clear blue sky, a solution came, a raise/promotion or unexpected accolade on your job, an unexpected gift, an unexpected phone call. Those are the whispers of God, telling you that you do matter! A phrase that I coined is—*You are the only you in the universe, made especially for your journey.* Sis, you better *Shine*—you are a unique, limited edition. Everyone say shine, with me!

"Shine!" The roar of the ladies was full of empowerment.

"Can I chime in?" Dr. Sparrow Mack entered from the side of the room to render additional insight.

"First, ladies, I applaud you for releasing the weights surrounding you. Tabitha, you are the bomb, I am so proud of you for sharing your story—being so vulnerable. Just like Tabitha, I may get a little misty eyed when I talk about this next topic, since it surrounds the matriarch of my family, my grandmother. One of her favorite colors was orange. This is magnificent because it combines the majestic regal color of red, with the color yellow, which has been known to be associated with joy along with happiness. Those two vibrant colors have been associated with so many adjectives, including joy, creativity, determination, and encouragement. Most of all, vigor coupled with endurance; according to color wheel pro/color meaning. In order to be vibrant, having joy, creativity, determination, furthermore to be encouraged—it is key to have a clear mind. It is those actions that my grandmother would always instill in me when I wanted to give up. I can hear her like it was yesterday challenging me, '*Little girl, you better grab that joy that God has bestowed upon you!*' In her will,

285

she *gifted* me her favorite orange coat, in a debacle, someone stole it from me. I was absolutely devastated; however God gives beauty for ashes."

I remember that coat, I was devastated when it was taken from you.

"I know you were, then by a chance encounter, I was given an orange prayer shawl by the family of a person that I resuscitated in the airport. I'm a true testament of how God will restore everything that the canker worm attempts to devour."

Anjali raised her hand as she still held the microphone.

"May I add something?" Anjali asked.

Yes, please share.

Dr. T. solicited The Chameleon coming into her own.

"Dr. T., I have found that having a cluttered mind, as a natural way of life, robs a person of their joy. As high-powered women, we are constantly multi-tasking to get things done," Anjali added.

A.J., I'm going to start calling you by your proper name, Anjali. You are so right. Furthermore, for self-improvement to enhance your well-being, an unclear mind is a form of self-sabotage. We must meditate, find that space to meditate on connecting with our soul. In addition, as Weight Breakers, we need to allow time for concentration—that is what I use my *Weight Breaker Space* for daily.

Think about a time when you had a goal or inspiration that most people thought was impossible. What was it? What did you do to attempt to accomplish it? In the same token, what are the possibilities that you have towards your health? Is it to obtain a well-controlled blood sugar? If you have concentration, opportunities can manifest.

"This is good stuff, thank you. So, you may be wondering, what about Projection? You have got to project what you are at your core. So many times, we try to cover our own uniqueness up. God made us all very unique," Tabitha shared.

Do you think He wanted to have a bunch of carbon copies of Dr. T.'s running around here? No! We are all beautiful in our own unique way. So Tabitha, be the very best version of you. Anjali, be the very best beautiful Anjali that you can be.

Tabitha walked back towards the front of the stage; her eyes lit up when they got to the next download of deep soul activity.

Come on, Weight Breakers, Determination is key. I gave you illustrations from my life about how I was raised, therefore, what I was determined to be. Visualize *your end result*. It is one thing to make a vision board but take it to the next level, my notebook that I kept was kind of like a scrapbook. However, over time, I realized that it was actually a vision board or roadmap. What does your vision feel like to you? What does it taste like to you? Or how do you expound upon that vision? How do you sustain that vision?

Tabitha smiled as she went over to the end table on the stage, held up a tattered binder. She shared, "You see, it all started here! In this very dilapidated book—my form of a vision board."

I had no idea you made vision boards; me too. Some of the most beautiful souls that I have been in contact with make vision boards. Having that vision board in your face can keep the focus at the forefront of your life. That is where the Weight Breaker T.I.P.s in the book come from. One of my favorite T.I.P.s is to view every day as your birthday.

The ladies high-fived each other.

Christina belted out, "Hell, yeah. I can do that. I can pop bottles every day, as if it's my birthday!"

Weight Breakers, I want each of you to do just that in downloading new ways to approach your day. That puts special care into each of your days, to cherish each day should be viewed as our birthday, until it is no more. It means that each day is enriched with new beginnings with new promises.

There was an old commercial for a donut company, where the employee on the commercial would wake up every day and say, "Time to make the donuts," in a monotone voice, you could hear the weight of his task that lay ahead. Let's attempt to be the polar opposite of the man that was dreading life because of the mundane he experienced in making donuts day after day. How many of you remember that commercial?

The hands went up.

"Let's not approach life in that way," Tabitha stated, then she went on to share,

"Life is to be filled with restitution. The proper definition of restitution is restoring something that is lost. So, by going deeper, you can find out what is missing in your soul. When you do that, you open the door for restoring—releasing weights. So you won't have to wake up every day to say—"

She tilted the microphone towards the ladies in the crowd.

"Time to make the donuts!" they belted out as if on cue.

"You better preach, as my mother used to say," Penelope said out loud.

The She Declare Crew high-fived each other.

Tabitha settled the crowd down.

"Okay, ladies, let's wrap this up. The last and final effort in downloading deep soul activities is to demonstrate. Everybody say demonstrate!"

"Demonstrate!"

The women obliged.

Thank you, Tabitha, for that segue. Once us Weight Breakers peel back the layers of *you* and sort them out, you'll be able to demonstrate who you were actually called to be. Weight Breakers, journal about your Download Deep Soul Activity, how you are going to walk this out—Thinking Like a Weight Breaker and Not a Weight Taker!

The women follow suit.

Dr. T. concluded,

Weight Breaker, we have walked through Reflection, Meditation, Concentration, Projection, Determination, Restitution, and Demonstration. You now have what it takes to download deep soul activities, taking on the world. Give it up for this powerhouse of a woman, agent, broker, Tabitha Blanko! Are there any parting words that you would like to impart on the women?

"Yes, ladies, it has been a pure joy to be in this space with you today. I'm so grateful to have had this day with you. Hopefully, there was at least one nugget of encouragement that will assist you on your Weight Breaker journey. I'm going to be completely honest with you. Although I have this to emulate couture life, I'm a work in progress, doing the work daily; the tactics are a part of my mode of operation," Tabitha added.

The women stood, applauding. Tabitha went on to surrender to her fellow weight breakers,

"I stand here to applaud each one of you. There are things that I need to complete as well. I've always wanted to honor my mother with a home decor line. I have drafts from when I was a little girl, in that trailer that I got up out of the attic. I want you ladies to hold me accountable, by checking in with me on social media! Let's go, ladies," Tabitha blew kisses to the attendees while she exited the stage.

Don't forget your *download charm* to go on your bracelet! We are going to have a quick break, then on to hear from some beautiful inside out subject matter experts. Weight Breakers, I am so proud of each of you. Many blessings, I will see you after the break.

Love, Dr. T.

30

THE CONFERENCE

"UPGRADING YOUR THOUGHT PROCESS"

[YOU ARE WHAT YOU THINK, WHAT'S IN YOUR MIND?]

Vivacity exuded the Grand Ballroom, where the conference was being held, from the impetus of the day's speakers. If you were to look down from the balcony on those women's lives, you would have seen stay-at-home moms, executives, women who survived various health ailments, and domestic violence overcomers. Moreover, you would have witnessed the interaction of Weight Takers shedding the weights of lives with their profound exhales, smiles, laughing, along with wiping off weight taker tears. For in that moment, the common thread that bound them together was to be there for each other—as they peeled the proverbial and physical weights together.

Hello Weight Breakers,

I hope you enjoyed the vendors. Let's settle down. I'm sure your bellies are full, moreover your spirits are even fuller. We are going to talk now about Tactic 9: Upgrading Your Thought Process—Inside and Out. As you can see on the stage, we have Dr. Sophia Clark, psychologist along with Dean Baby, makeup artist to the stars.

The crowd gave a loud applause, as they recognized Dr. Clark from being on the nightly news as the psychoanalyst alongside Dean Baby as he graced the red carpets alongside his celebrity clients.

"That's right; she did say she was going to be here," Regi remarked, not sure whether to smile or hit the nearest exit, regarding her regular couch sessions with Dr. Clark—even though Regi had made some progress.

"You know her?" Penelope questioned Regi.

A little taken aback, not wanting to let on that she had seen the psychiatrist/psychologist, Regi cupped her hand over her mouth, said into Penelope's ear,

"Yes, I'm seeing her for therapy," Regi owned up to her downfall—misplaced anger from years of being the juggler to cover up her pain.

All the ladies ear-hustled with bugged eyes. Penelope responded,

"We knew Abigail would need therapy, but little perfect Judge Regi? No, not you. You're pulling our leg—you and therapy don't even go together…"

"Perfect, my ass; you best be quiet. Listen please, before I go *ham* on you," Regi butted in to snap back.

Penelope bit her lip, she shrank in her seat as well as the others in the crew.

I'm not as perfect as everyone makes me out to be, Regi pondered to herself as she attempted to calm down to see how she could upgrade her thought process. She folded her arms.

Weight Breakers, I need a volunteer, Dr. T. eagerly requested.

Chaka stood, making herself known, already walking towards the dais.

"Go, Christina," Fawn belted out; finding it hard to contain herself.

"You've got this, Christina!" Anjali cheered.

Regi and Penelope reassured her by their applause.

Come on up, take this empty seat right here on stage. I really have loved your energy throughout the conference. I believe that you will fit right in with this panel.

Dr. T. further instigated.

Tell us how you feel about this session, Upgrading Your Thought Process—Inside and Out. That can help you on your journey.

"Well, I'm Christina Bu; I work at my family-owned Vietnamese restaurant. More than that, my real calling is to be a comedian. My stage name is Chaka, which I equate to power."

Her new sisters stood in agreement, cheering her on. Chaka smiled.

"I'm here with my crew right there on the front row." She pointed to her She Declare sisters; they blew kisses back to her, Regi's arms still folded.

"My aspirations far exceed *the plan* for my life that is a part of my family legacy, in which my father has established for my sister and I—to run the family restaurant. I'm going to be a *Star* one day; I have a gift to share with the world. My future goal is to live out my dreams. I plan on making it on a wing and a prayer—I know I can do it. My friends keep asking me if I have any well thought out strategies—I don't. I have faith that my gift will make room for me, causing everything to fall in line."

I'm sure it will, Chaka. You got this, weight breaker—

"But wait, I'm not finished," Chaka interrupted.

Dr. T.'s eyes prompted *The Aspirational* spirit—nodded her head for her to continue.

"When you see me, you see a true hustler. By day, I work in the family restaurant. By night, I put in work doing *my little comedy thing,* as my momma calls it," Christina got choked up.

Her crew was a little taken aback since they had always seen Christina as a jokester. Her garb was the life of the party, even when not appropriate. Her vulnerability, coupled with her seriousness, was refreshing—surprising.

Dr. T. gave her an endearing side hug, prompting her to go on.

"There is a huge weight in having to hide my gift. However, in *my book club,* we are reading your book, *Think Like a Weight Breaker. Not Like a Weight Taker.* I have come to the realization that I'm The Aspirational momentum—I'm good with that. However, I need to work on upgrading my thought process, to have a business plan to collaborate with my ambitions."

Dr. T. stepped in.

Chaka, I am so proud of you for knowing who you are, along with what gifts God has placed in you. Let's do an exercise—*you game?*

Chaka, irrevocably, was all in.

"Hell yeah, I'm game. Let's do *the damn thing!*" Chaka belted out, provoking the crowd to go wild—her energy on fire.

Okay, ladies, we talked about connectivity. We are connected to this Weight Breaker sister right here. Ladies, we are upgrading our thought process by speaking life into the dreams of our sister—Chaka. Ladies, rise to your feet. You stand right here. Weight Breakers, point to Christina on stage, repeating after me.

Chaka, God hears your aspirations!

Chaka, you are not alone!

Chaka, you are strong!

Chaka, walk towards your purpose!

Chaka, your purpose will surpass your pain!

Chaka, keep being a servant. God sees your effort!

Chaka, your parents are proud of you. They will come around!

Chaka, by upgrading your thought process, aligning the business with your talents, success is around the corner!

Now everyone give your sister a round of applause for her transparency.

Dr. T. affirmed to Christina, to walk into her purpose as Chaka. The women sounded off in pandemonium to support her as she smiled from ear-to-ear.

"I'm overwhelmed by the love along with the interaction from the crowd. From my sisters right over there," Chaka prepared to leave the platform, but was beckoned to remain by the weight breaker.

No, stay up here; this is where you belong, we are going to call you Chaka. Get used to being on stage. Moreover, I'd like to introduce everyone to Dr. Sophia Clark, world renowned psychologist. Dr. Clark has written many articles, has developed world renowned therapies that are being used in universities with curriculums throughout academia—on how to upgrade your thought processes. Her work has been noted as life-changing.

Life-changing? Regi folded her arms saying *that word* in her mind, leaned into her seat. She made eye contact with Dr. Clark on stage—piercing with disdain...

Dr. Clark recognized Regi's tension through the cluster of women, she winked at her. Penelope leaned into Regi, sensing her hesitation to listen on.

"Judge, just listen. We all have something to learn; that's a part of life," Penelope's encouragement started to crack at Regi's guarded exterior.

Also adorning the stage is the wonderful celebrity makeup artist Dean Baby, who has made up every face from award shows to the White House.

The flock of ladies in the audience went wild because of the *lit* panel.

Dr. Clark chimed right in, going into psychoanalytical mode.

"Thank you for that wonderful introduction. I believe that your book said it best regarding the need to Upgrade Your Thought Process to focus on walking into your potential. That is so key. I have been observing the engagement of the participants—I applaud you. So many times I listen to individuals who come to lay down on my couch to reveal their hurts, pains and challenges—combined with their truth. Nevertheless, I feel like I learn more about myself with each person I *help*. That is why I know, for a fact, that this encounter that we are experiencing here together today is unique. So many times the world hits us so hard, with all of these images of what our lives should be, that we forget about our uniqueness—the gifts that set us apart. Furthermore, let's not get started on social media—with its airbrushed illusions. Upgrading our thought process is right on time! Thank you for this opportunity to share a little about myself, I am Dr. Sophia Clark—a woman of God, daughter, sister, friend as well as mentor. I am honored to be the psychologist and psychiatrist where my goal was to dispel the myths of mental health. I have found that it is important to have a valuable blend of clinical background, business acumen with dedication towards promoting health and wellness within the community."

She appeared to force the words out of her mouth.

"I have had proven success in defining as well as executing health plan strategies that strengthen clinical teams. I have been described as a decisive leader with strong relationship building skills and a motivator who quickly identifies issues, develops solutions, and builds high performing culture. I leverage a positive, collaborative management style that builds a culture of employee engagement with collaboration that manifests across the organization."

Damn, is she giving a job interview, or trying to drop some knowledge, Chaka thought to herself, looking at Dr. Clark sideways a little.

Dr. Clark went on to transparently share,

"I did all of this, while fighting a personal battle—being a woman of color that faced the battle of fibroids head on (also called leiomyomas or myomas). It is common knowledge that fibroids are noncancerous tumors of the uterus that may cause heavy menstrual bleeding, pelvic pain, bowel and bladder problems, furthermore interfering with fertility. I have undergone hormone therapy to shrink the fibroids, ultimately having to resort to the surgical intervention of a myomectomy, however my daunting journey with fibroids did not stop there. The real issue, for me, with fibroids started when *they* returned with a vengeance, leading to: one intrauterine invasive procedure to debulk the fibroids only for them only to return; a failed attempt at The MyoSure tissue removal procedure. However, all along I kept working, attempting to make sure my patients were doing well—living their best lives possible, while I was severely anemic. I'd even suffered some *mom-shaming*, as well as taking on rude comments about my growing abdomen—which I would have loved to have been filled with a bundle of joy, however I was filled with fibroid tumors."

Regi sat on the edge of her seat, thinking back at the unsisterly hurtful comment she made towards Dr. Clark in her office.

"Ultimately I'm contemplating a hysterectomy—all within a matter of four months causing me to hemorrhage, while attempting to be a wife, as well as a career woman. I am not unique, the story of fibroids impacting women, and even more so women of color, is a topic that needs to be focused on as well as solutioned. Focus areas on topics of discussion in some of my literature is mental health, how it impacts women with fibroids—understanding risk factors that predispose women to uterine fibroids; determining the role of new treatment intervention addressing fibroids by establishing strategies for the prevention of fibroids. In addition, complications from fibroids. A raise of hands of women who have dealt with fibroids?"

Surprisingly, hands went up all around the room.

"I'd experienced multiple emergency room visits, hospitalizations, my life was filled with being so anemic I could hardly stand—I was determined to exude self-advocacy to get the help that I needed. You see ladies, many feel isolated dealing with this, just know that you are not alone. This did not start with us, look at the bible, Mark 5: 25-34—the story of the woman with *the issue of blood*. I'm here for you, please reach out to me, my contact information is in my book, to get more information regarding fibroid treatment options. Let's exercise, eat clean, and get our checkups to make sure that we are doing all that we can, especially when we are attempting to preserve our fertility."

Dr. T. patrolled the stage, looking at the fervent women beckoning their destinies.

Regi's demeanor is a little less guarded, as she had not realized that Dr. Clark had gone through all of this, in the midst of attempting to help her.

Weight Breakers, you are so right; we are more than what's on social media—and thank you for your commentary on fibroids, Dr. Clark. That topic is going to be on one of my upcoming live podcasts in the future. We are more than what our families may have been and more than *their curses* have been. We are more than any negative thing anyone has said to us! We are upgrading our thought process to Think Like a Weight Breaker, Not Like a Weight Taker. We are going from undermining what our potential is, to upgrading our thought development...

"Not to cut you off, Dr. T., but I guess I just did—*my bad*! I love that in this section of the book you talk about keywords: earn, target, demonstrate, attain, outperform, surpass, and extend. Write those words down. These are now words that I put into practice. I see you, Dean Baby. What do you have to add?" Dr. Clark solicited.

"This is a great segue into my notes I have prepared to share. Hey, everybody, it's your boy, Dean Baby. Ladies, you've earned the right to be your best self-possible. You have to understand that you all work hard for your families, but it's just as important that you work hard for yourself! You need to work hard to rid yourself of the weights that so easily beset you. Dr. Clark Weight Breaker, your thought process must be targeted! It has been said that if you don't fill up *your cup*, you won't have anything to give. With that being said, your target has to be to fill *your cup* or rather your inner vessel. If you don't, life will be draining. A raise of hands from those who feel drained?" Dean Baby added.

Some women stood in agreement with those words that resonated with their souls, while different hues of hands were raised in unison of experiencing outright exhaustion.

Dr. T. was invigorated to expound.

It definitely is arduous to feel good about yourself when you are sapped, leading to depletion evolving into self-pity. Self-pity can make you feel like you don't matter, but

294

you do. The source of life is the way you can fill up *your cup* without reservation. List three ways in which you will thwart yourself by pouring into your own space filling up your own cup with invigorated thoughts—rescinding self-pity?

The ladies wrote as Chaka raised her hand.

"I see you, Chaka. How do you think you can demonstrate that you are upgrading your thought process?" Dr. Clark petitioned her fellow panelists.

Chaka took a big breath.

"Well, I'm no expert, but I try to exercise a resounding viewpoint to specifically have a clear exchange of information, and you have to demonstrate that daily. This is key in every aspect of life. Each day I wake up to evaluate how I can effectively enhance my communication skills. Sometimes, or if I am being truly transparent, all the damn time, my *in-your-face* communication layered with my humor gets me in trouble. Nonetheless, I'm being my authentic self. Ultimately, I clearly articulate my clear thoughts; helping me demonstrate the goals I'm striving for."

Chaka was comfortable at the microphone. The panelists and emcee nodded in agreement.

"Look at *our* Christina getting all confident—that should be you up there, Penelope."

"Yep, it should be. But, at least I broke down the box with my crew's help."

The ladies snickered from Penelope's comment. *However, I have to be fully persuaded in my comfort level with upgrading my thought process, in hearing my voice along with seeing the vision of me articulating my talent. Baby steps, Penelope. Baby steps,* Penelope thought to herself.

Dean Baby cleared his throat. The attention was drawn to him as he had been sitting there with his finely manicured hand raised, causing the pinky ring to sparkle brightly.

"My bad, Dean Baby. I know you have some nuggets to drop on these dynamic women. Let's have it?"

With his eyebrows raised, he clapped back.

"Clearly, you ladies, in upgrading your thought process, have forgotten basic panel etiquette. My hand has been raised for five damn minutes..." Dean Baby whipped.

The crowd let out a gigantic laugh that echoed in the room.

295

Well, *alrighty* then, you got us in check. Go on, Dean Baby, speak your peace.

Dr. T. smiled wholeheartedly.

"So, Weight Breakers, when upgrading your thought methodology, you have to commit to attaining a new thought process, sort of like an *embryonic development*. This new way of thinking has to orchestrate in the *womb of our mind*. Whatever you have worked hard for, you are on the brink of achieving. You are close to accomplishing something, so go out and give your life your best self! You have to understand that God will not be outperformed by anything going on in your life! Joy is abundantly available for us to receive. The Bible speaks of unspeakable joy. Joy is a place that a lot of us do not have *the address to* and have to mature in. This is so much a part of what can be birthed and pushed into the world as your innate gift," Dean Baby asserted.

Dr. Clark agreed, delving into psychological acumen, delivering, "Preach, my brother, you were all up in my headspace. I highlight multiple sections while I read *Think Like A Weight Breaker. Not Like A Weight Taker.* When I deliberated about upgrading my thought process, I used to think about only one goal that I strived for. However, life is so much more. It's a compilation of events, happenstances, goals, triumphs, and failures layered with victories! There are several thought processes and goals that are a part of our journey. What are your thoughts about that, Dr. T.?"

That is why it is so important to not *just talk about it, but be about it*. Many times, when we look at the good things that happen to us and celebrate. On the other hand, when something bad happens to us, we sometimes don't find the lesson in that experience. There's something to be celebrated in both—that's the only way to upgrade your thought process.

Dr. T. went over to the open seat and copped a squat, resting her legs.

"You are so right, Dr. T. I tell my clients to view those things that happened as steps on a ladder or, better yet, stairs to a different opportunity. That caused a change in the thought process about looking back and feeling self-pity and getting stuck dwelling in it. All experiences are steps in that journey; it's our perspective to see them as stumbling blocks or launching pads. Dean Baby, I see your hand. I'm upgrading my thought process, working on *my panel etiquette*. You wanted to say something else, my brother?"

"Dr. Clark, you've got a little *shade* in you; I like it. Yes, there is a cost to everything and life will have obstacles. Think about the cost of not walking into your purpose. You will never know what can become if you don't try and you have to do this with grace and being good to yourself and one another."

Dean Baby gave more insight. He stood and then walked the stage, or rather glided the stage.

"People will forget what you said, people will forget what you did, but people will never forget how you made them feel. Not my words, but those of the prolific, magnificent Maya Angelou. Ponder on this quote, implanting this in the forefront of your thought process of how you treat people. Girl, I love me some Maya." Dr. Clark walked the stage as well, not to be in the shade of Dean's opulent beauty and knowledge dropping.

"Can you share with us about being *kind?*"

Yes, can you and Dean drag that whiteboard over to me? Thank you.

Attendants brought the whiteboard out, and on the board Dr. T. wrote K.I.N.D.

Does anybody know how we can align this acronym with upgrading our thought process?

The women started yelling out:

"Knowledge?"

"Impart Information?"

"Nonjudgmental?"

"Divine?"

Thank you for your prompt thoughts on this acronym, I see you have been reading. I am going to break down how we have to keep that in the forefront of our awareness. You must honestly keep in cognizance that before you say anything, determine is it, K.I.N.D.?

"Hell, that makes sense. Who doesn't want to hear something kind?" Christina whipped.

The room was approving.

I hear you, however, it's a little deeper than that. When you do or say something, we need to know does it impart *knowledge?* Are you genuine; coming from a place of love? Is the comment that you are about to state necessary for the recipient of the comment's health and well-being?

Dr. Clark added in,

"You should ask yourself, is what I'm about to say going to help develop this person in some way?"

I agree, will your comment boost and build another up?

Dr. T. declared as she walked through the cluster engaging them, while writing on the whiteboard.

Chaka was right at home and put the microphone to her lips,

"I love this. I'm such a newbie to comedy. As a matter of fact, I did my first stand-up right before I came here. I've grounded myself in one of the tips I follow from the book, and that's to put *IT* on the daily calendar. For me, it is time. Find private time to breathe, inhale, and exhale—absorbing peace. When I achieve that, I can have more energy to be kind."

Dean Baby smiled,

"I think it's in the Bible that Jesus modeled alone time—quiet time—for the specific purpose of praying and having quality time with God and to meditate. Well, the comedian is on point again."

"I am by far not Jesus. I have not parted the Red Sea or turned water into wine, and I am amazed that God gives a heathen like me any grace whatsoever. However, I'm grateful that God loves even the little old imperfect me. And Dean Baby, you are so right, time alone in prayer and meditation is key to making sure you can deeply connect with your soul. To add a little more, the comment should *impart information*, be *nonjudgmental*, and if the *divine* were listening, which He is, would He be pleased?"

Chaka beamed with gratification; the audience rendered a sincere applause.

Dr. Clark, you have more to add on this?

Dr. T. inquired, putting her marker down.

"Yes, I tell my clients that you have to be cautious about who they invest in because of these principles. You have to align with people who practice that same K.I.N.D. method of thinking. There are so many self-proclaimed experts on any topic under the sun—it is dangerous if they do not have the same main beliefs."

"Amen, you better preach; we are about to have some church up in here."

Dean Baby verbalized in a whimsical manner.

The ladies high-fived. Dr. T. strode towards the apex of the rostrum.

Well, Weight Breakers, we have laughed, cried, while we embraced each other all day. Your homework assignments are laid out in your Weight Breaker Journal. Let's Upgrade Our Thought Process so you are going to Think Like a Weight Breaker, Not Like a Weight Taker, by journaling regarding your experiences currently. We have talked about how you have earned the right to upgrade your thought process, you need to target the areas you are to converge on, you need to demonstrate your new way of thinking that you have obtained to deal with weights of life so that you can outperform the bad that has come into your life—surpassing your wildest dreams. Once you have all that goodness that you harnessed, extend it to others. Dr. Sophia Clark, Dean Baby—last but definitely not least, our special guest, Christina "Chaka" Bu!

Love, Dr. T.

The three gratefully took a bow, then exited the stage.

Dr. T. and Dr. Sparrow Mack left for book signings. Dean Baby for a makeup demonstration.

Christina ran down to her *Posse* where they jovially embraced their sister.

"Girl, you did so well. You're a natural; you belong on a stage," Regi remarked as she gave her an additional side hug.

"Christina, or rather Chaka, I can see why you're going to be in *the game* real soon. You have talent layered with natural stage presence. Now, all you need is a business plan," Anjali proclaimed of her new sister friend.

"Bravo. You were amazing," Penelope genuinely celebrated.

The Weight Breakers collected their *upgrade your thought process* charms. The women's swagger was a little buoyant, as they felt that their perspective of the weights of their lives had been lifted. They declared from The Chronicles Of The Weight Breakers Conference that they can walk into their purpose, they mattered to God, they will break the weight of their lives, and so much more.

31

THE CONFERENCE

"FACILITATING THE FIREWALL"

[MONITOR WHAT COMES IN YOUR SPACE!]

Hi Weight Breakers

You've listened to the podcasts, bought the book, traveled here to THE CHRONICLES OF THE WEIGHT BREAKERS CONFERENCE, moreover had transparent demonstrations on how to shed that weight! This session is all about getting you to understand that, in order to prevent you from spiraling back into becoming Weight Takers, we have to build a firewall to prevent all the *Bullsh#t* from coming in, infiltrating our goals. When weight taking ideas, issues, or people come into your presence, if you plant yourself with a Weight Breaker mindset, the Weight Breaker Firewall will cause those negativities to bounce off of you—just like if you were a bug zapper, those poor insects don't have a chance!

I have one impromptu special guest; you all are going to love this. Unless you've been in a cave for the past 10 years, you've heard her on the airways daily *telling it like it is* regarding literary works, movies and impactable news. She's one bad chick, a force to be reckoned with. Please put your hands together for The Abigail Lancaster.

The ladies were awestruck by the celebrity radio host. Eager to hear her snap back antics style of display.

"Oh, it's going to be on now!" Chaka snapped, settling in her seat.

Her She Declares sisters didn't know she was going to come to the stage as *the closer.*

"Girl, this is going to be interesting," Regi leaned into the women.

"I know, right. What the hell! This is motivating as all out, but Abigail Lancaster? I think I'm going to need some ibuprofen," Anjali rubbed her temple.

"Look at the trail behind her as Abigail walked up on stage,"

300

"What trail?" Fawn craned her neck to see.

"The ice chips coming out of her *cranky ass*," Chaka billowed out a laugh, which caught Abigail's attention, causing her to shrink in her chair.

Abigail positioned herself on stage, she gave her snarl look at Chaka.

"Dr. T., from the mixer last evening, to today and all of the information shared, I would love to have you on my show...soon: The Number One Syndicated The Abigail Lancaster Show," Abigail crossed her legs just so you could see the crimson on the bottom of her shoes.

"Damn, that was a shameless plug for her show—always trying to floss," Regi threw some *shade.*

"Girl, you know she is always on the grind, hustling—with self-promotion," Anjali egged on.

"Hush, silly. Abigail is trying to speak," Penelope requested of her *peeps.*

Abigail saw her crew chatting on the front row while she tried to speak, peering at them over her spectacles. Penelope shrunk with embarrassment.

"Anyway, people truly don't believe that women can support one another, we have to continue to prove them wrong. Speaking of that, I'm here this weekend with *my crew*. Ladies, stand—"

The ladies were a little taken aback from the shout-out, from the *Ice Queen*—surprised she shared her stardom with them. They felt special.

That caught Dr. T. by surprise.

What Abagail, you *rolling with* a crew these days?

"I know that is not me. I truly believe that God brought us together through that catastrophic event recently; they have been a true blessing," Abigail transparently revealed.

Abigail no offense, but you usually are solo, except for Margot—

"Let me stop you right there, all that appears is not what it seems," Abigail's temple pulsed.

Well damn, I thought Margot was her girl. I guess I'll move on...

Dr. T. got the clue to move on to give a synopsis of what brought the ladies to this portion of the conference.

Weight Breakers, I'm not going to repeat everything that was said today because the panelist shared some great nuggets earlier.

By working on all of those problem areas, you can build a fortified, strong life. You've realized that you have to hold onto Psalms 18:1-2, *I love you, Lord; you are my strength. The Lord is my rock, my fortress and my savior, my God is my rock, in whom I find protection. He is my shield, the power that saves me, and my place of safety.*

"I love that verse—" Abigail prompted.

That verse lets me understand that I am not navigating through life in my own brawn, which lifts weights in my world. Moving on to be a Weight Breaker is the reason I orchestrated this workbook, exercise, journal, daily decision, or maze navigator through the inspirational pathway; it was not to be felt to be as mundane.

We are all such a magnificent existence that we have to get aligned with our purpose to walk out this thing called life to our very best ability. Ponder on the circular diagram that depicts what I like to think of as our own personal solar system life of movement around us. Life is going to happen, so how are we going to nurture our intelligence in the facets of vision, faith, and resilience to cope, while conquering the mountains that lay ahead of us? I shared this awhile back on one of my impromptu podcast's—the reception of that concept was wonderful—looking at the world's circumstances through this lens.

The goal of this close-out session is to focus on how to block and tackle anything that attempts to infiltrate your space. The key is to not let the *BS (BAD STUFF)* in!

"Bad stuff? What are we in, kindergarten? It's called bullshit!" Abigail snapped on stage, getting buy-in from the crowd who raised their hands in the air.

"Girl, Abigail needs to pipe down. What was in her water bottle?" Anjali inquired.

"Probably some Gin—*don't hate,*" Chaka responded.

"What are we going to do with you—girl?" Regi catechized.

"Love on our sister—leave her alone, let her speak her peace." Fawn added, redirecting towards the stage.

Be your own gatekeeper! Being your own gatekeeper fuels the Weight Breaker in you! We will focus on the following regarding protecting your Weight Breaker mentality. We are going to go from having a frail protection of our mental and physical space to having a Firewall Projection. The goals of this tactic build that: Fence; Limit, Barricade, Hurdle, Protect, Roadblock, as well as Circumvent.

"I agree—in many instances, with God's help, you'll be able to know who and when it's time to garner from someone. Furthermore, when to mentor as well as when to be mentored. This helps to build that firewall," Abigail invited the conversation to continue with her *The Vault barrier* seeming to melt while she was on stage—her rare vulnerability shining through, as if the conference had the four-digit code that caused her to open up.

Abigail, the osmosis of your words I pray are infiltrating our sisters. Moreover, full transparency; this was very hard for me. I prided myself by having an open door; I felt like it was the human thing to do. But everybody cannot have access to you. Everyone say access!

The ladies followed suit.

By controlling access to yourself, you are able to weed out things that may be a distraction. This helps you to remain focused. By protecting your accessibility, you must understand that you sit at your Heavenly Father's feet—that should be honored. By tapping into your gifts, you need to x-ray—examine your surroundings, to see what is needed to nurture your gift. Work on that gift, talent, capacity, ability, moreover the genius that you are; your forte. How about praying and asking God for direction on how best to use the gifts he's given you? See where He actually wants you to use them so that you're not just vainly doing *good things for good reasons*, but actually serving an eternal divine purpose. Don't offer access to yourself, just for the sake of not being lonely.

"Weight Breakers, please continue to take notes as we finish strong in this conference. Promise me that you will *hurdle* those situations that attempt to get you off track—that behavior enhances your firewall. Weight Breaker, protect your head space to enhance that firewall! Weight Breaker, build that roadblock to anything that comes to distract you! Your firewall is to realize how you can be more malleable in life. Protect that capability. Weight Breaker, circumvent all that is meant to thwart you! Perceiving that you indeed have a friend out there willing to support you. For those who do not have kind words or support, better known as *haters*, continue to shine; they're watching! Everyone say firewall!"

Everyone followed the command of Abigail, belting out the word "firewall!"

Little Abby, girl you've been up and through the *Think Like A Weight Breaker. Not Like A Weight Taker* book!

"You damn skippy, on my third pass through the book," Abigail smirked, going on to share, "I must admit, I was a little apprehensive about even picking up this book, I bought it right before the horrible event that just happened in the valley. However, this book caused me to change my mind about doing something that could have had an awful impact on my loved one's recently—I'm grateful. Moreover, one of the reasons that I am a The Vault, as you say, is that I've been *burned* by people I've trusted."

I'm sure we can all agree with that. Can't we, everyone?

Dr. T. solicited the room, where women were *testifying* with hands held high to the heavens.

Abigail raised her expression when she painfully confessed,

"I have introduced couples; they've gotten married and I've not been invited to the wedding or the baby showers. They've gone on with their lives without even a thank you. I only know what's going on with them by seeing *updates* on social media."

"Hey, I can see the pain in Abigail's eyes. Is she okay?" Fawn whispered to Penelope; her crew concerned, with the blatant transparency Abigail was showing—raw to the core.

"Also, there have been people who have begged to be a part of my circle. I have connected them since that is just the kind of person I am. They've gone on to write books together, start businesses together, orchestrating conferences together. I heard about all of their collaborative shine through *the grapevine*—with no acknowledgment of how they got connected, through me. I even had a so-called friend in the past who didn't speak to me for several years, after I had my kids. At the start of our friendship, we both started out with fertility issues. However, I ended up with two kids. To this day, she has had none, terminating our friendship because I was able to give birth—so ridiculous. I've written millions of dollars for charities, furthermore supporting people that I know wouldn't even give me a drop of water if I was thirsty. All of this summed up, why I guess I've been labeled The Vault—all locked up. For me, navigating through life is easier this way."

Dr. T. gave a warm embrace to Abigail.

"Damn, our sister is *constipated with bitterness.* She's going to need some ex-lax superstrength—" Chaka is always the comedian.

"Girl, be quiet. Have some empathy." Regi snapped.

That was not your crew. There will always be those individuals who are opportunists, don't give up on sisterhood. I see you here with some sister friends. See, God will restore all the hurts of the past, aligning you with those you need to be with.

Abigail smiled, going on to say, "Weight Breakers, from this point forward, we have permission to prevent negativity—all those things that are preventing you from walking in your purpose. Now say, I have permission to block negativity!"

"I have permission to block negativity!" the assembly verbalized.

"Journal, making it very clear—all up in your face to yourself as to how you are going to have a firewall around your vision, faith, and resilience intelligences. Yell out how you are going to do that!"

The crowd excitedly affirmed Abigail's proclamation,

"I'm only going to let the good stuff into my spirit!"

"I'm going to be a fence around my mind!"

"I'm going to limit negative influences in my life!"

"A barricade will be around my soul!"

"I will hurdle any undo stressors that attempt to infiltrate my life!"

"I am going to protect my being—making a roadblock to any negative intake in my life!"

"I will circumvent any strategies that are meant for my distraction from God's guidance!"

Dr. T. and Abigail smiled at the feedback from the audience, looked at each other as they felt that firewall vibes from the crowd...

These ladies got it; they are Weight Breakers!

"I agree. They are on the ball; nothing can break through their firewalls!"

Ladies, give it up for *The Abigail Lancaster!*

"Can I say one last thing?" Abigail looked a little sentimental.

Yes, the stage is yours.

Dr. T. stated as she stepped back.

"Ladies, I want you to know that everything you heard today is just words. Everyone say just words!"

"Just Words!"

"However, to make meaningful change, those words have to manifest into action. Promise me that when you walk out of this encounter, you will carry your momentum and move into your God-given purpose. I may not ever see you again, but I want you to know that I am rooting for each of you. Weight Breakers, on Three."

"One!"

"Two!"

"Three!"

"Weight Breakers!"

Abigail Lancaster dropped the microphone, reverb echoed in the auditorium as she exited stage left, leaving the ladies a little startled, holding their ears.

Dr. T. concluded,

We've talked about becoming Weight Breakers, however just know that Weight Taking is a part of the journey to becoming Weight Breakers. Weight Taking is a part of the season in your life, not the destination—this should not be a permanent place where you reside! There should be growth in the *weight taking period*. If you linger in that stage of life, you will find yourself as a weight taker mimicking Weight Breakers—when indeed you have everything in you to be a Weight Breaker in authenticity. You first have to see yourself as a Weight Breaker—on a regular basis, check in with yourself to evaluate how you see yourself!

In addition, who you are around is a reflection of how you think of yourself—moreover your life's purpose. The bottom line, don't just be in the midst of weight takers to have people around, your purpose for your life deserves better than that. You should constantly want to advance regarding how you show up in the world—seek out books, conferences, groups that are aligned with your purpose—to keep you on the rails of the Weight Breaker track. I want everyone to enjoy this beautiful resort, the sun, the beach, the new sisterhoods that you will cherish for the rest of your life! Before we go, you have one last assignment. I know you have noticed that there are barrels around the room. Also in your journal's you have cards that tear out. If you feel compelled, put your response as to how you are going to explore a new mindset, take inventory and take action, check your connectivity, download deep soul activity, upgrade your thought process, and have that firewall present. Please enter your contact information on the bottom because there will be accountability teams reaching out to you, if you mark the box that gives permission to do so—just to check in. Remember, when you enter a room, the only weight that should be seen is the weight of your name. Henceforth, when your name is mentioned or you enter an orifice, you will represent sacrifices, heroism along with excellence. Your name will elevate, reflecting a new mindset.

You may recall, in the movie *Forrest Gump*, when he talks about the box of chocolates, well Weight Breakers, whatever you get out of your box of chocolates, you are going to handle it with vision intelligence, faith intelligence and resilience intelligence, because you are no longer taking on unnecessary weight. Weight taking will be in your rearview mirror.

Run Weight Breaker, Run!

Many blessings and say it with me, Think Like A Weight Breaker. Not Like A Weight Taker! Get your firewall charms that are being handed out. Celebrate this new phase in your life with your crew, there is no heroism in thinking that you can do this alone. I want to be an eyewitness to how this conference and you becoming a Weight Breaker has resulted in: job promotions; entrepreneurship; mended relationships; enhanced self-care; being equip to handle unforeseen change; you being set apart in favor; thriving in your uniqueness; not allowing other people's influence to categorize yourself as weight taker; being able to unsubscribe to being a weight taker; having that agape love yourself while being a light to others causing them to want to break weight; realizing that weight breaking is an ongoing journey; to not be distracted by campaigns out against you; being capable to disrupting thoughts that don't align with who and what God called you to be; being that person to use all the tactics learned to address weight taking on the spot; and most of all—finding your specific key down in your core that unlocks our predestined purpose. Ladies, you are ordained to drip *weight breaker sauce* everywhere you go. Ladies, get up so we can go through our Weight Breaker Pledge,

The empowered Weight Breakers stood in unison all over the grand ballroom.

Repeat after me,

This is The Weight Breaker Pledge,

I am a Weight Breaker, not a weight taker. So what does that mean? It means that each day, I'm standing under the promises that God gave me ALL the tactics I need to break the weight of life. Take a front seat and watch me approach each issue: boldly, resiliently, encouraged, abundant, kind; elevated and restored! My intelligences shines so bright, that I will draw weight takers to me—to encourage them to break the weights in their lives. It is not by accident that my magnificent existence is here on earth, so world look out—this is only my beginning!

Now Weight Breakers, get to work!

Love you all.

Some in tears, some hugging, and others clapping to the high heavens felt years of bondage being lifted up off of their being, ready to sprinkle *Weight Breaker dust* into their perspective worlds.

Regi smiled from ear-to-ear, thinking about how she may have been wrong about the whole motivational thing being *hoity toity stupidity*. She was seeing that there were others that were *juggling* all of what life threw at them with grace, not total frustration that they took out on everyone. She imagined herself *running with* her firewall, as if she were an extra in the Forrest Gump movie.

Fawn felt full of hope as her sisters realized that it was more than a coincidence that brought them together, but a pure divine intervention. She was also relieved that she didn't have to go through the possibility of breast cancer alone. Furthermore, she could release the weight of being *The Mirage*, making everything appear that it was all good when it wasn't.

Chaka felt empowered by the powerhouse speakers, embraced her talent wholeheartedly. However, she needed to put a business plan in place, but also develop her acumen, so she wouldn't be alone with *aspiration* in her career path. However, have a business plan to align with it.

307

Anjali understood what her mother as well as Sean had been attempting to tell her all along. Her brilliance was in her uniqueness, not in the blonde highlights masking her beautiful tress. She didn't need to purge because of her denial of herself; it wasn't who God had called her to be. Leading her to know that she was not *The Chameleon;* however, a uniquely beautiful individual.

Penelope understood that there were women she could confide in. That they would help her step out of *the shadows,* into the light where she was supposed to be. She deserved more than *a shadow* in this thing called life.

Abigail walked over to her crew after *her performance.*

"How did you like it—the panel?"

"Well, you showed up and showed out, *The Abigail Lancaster!* Damn girl, you are a Weight Breaker *AF#!*" Chaka said in her snarky sarcasm.

"Please call me Abby; my friends do," with weight lifted out of her eyes, she opened her arms to embrace her sisters. They were astonished with her warmth.

"Well alrighty then, Abby. You really shared a lot of great information. That was so dope," Chaka gave a side bump to the now transparent true sister friend, Abby.

"You really were vulnerable; I'm a little shocked—" Regi stated.

"I am really trying to do better with that, being this way is like fitting a square peg into a round hole. I've got to break out of being The Vault—" Abby shared.

"I'll help you—" Regi came close, "Pinky promise?"

Abby smiled.

"Pinky promise," the women's pinky fingers locked declaring a new way of looking at their life's journey.

"Look at y'all, acting like you are in elementary school–so cute," Chaka smiled.

"You Miss Chaka were phenomenal." Anjali added.

"Now, you were such a transparent beautiful Indian sister—Anjali," Chaka replied, turning towards Anjali.

"Yes, that is my name is Anjali—I'm proud of it!" sass exuded for her melanin infused pores.

"My goodness, Penelope, you really showed your power. We will not allow you to be in the shadows anymore; that stops today!" Regi commanded.

"Fawn, why did you not tell us?" Penelope asked as her eyes began to mist.

"Not now, we will talk about it later. Is that cool?" Fawn asked.

The women nodded.

Abby cuts the moment, "It's happy hour time. Drop your cards in the buckets *so we can blow this popsicle stand.*"

"How about happy hour after we get our books signed?" Regi strangely remarked; since she was the one who didn't want to even buy the book at first. However, after the words of the conference hit her spirit, she was a new fan.

The crew arrived to get their books signed and their *eyes bugged* when they saw the line wrapped around the building.

"Are you serious? This line is ridiculous," Regi's impatience on her sleeve.

"We have nothing else to do. Let's get in line; it may be fun," Penelope beamed.

The ladies got into formation. They started taking selfies, discussing the *good nuggets* they had learned. Furthermore, they were going to show up differently in the world from that point on—as Weight Breakers, instead of weight takers.

Abby engaged in text messages, "Ladies, I will catch up with you all later—" Leaving abruptly.

"Where in the hell does she think she's going?" Regi asked, seeing the back of Abby leaving, once again.

"This line is crazy. I vote we *bounce*—grab some appetizers, I heard there is a *bomb* happy hour across the way. I need a drink," Chaka—not needing any buy-in.

"I'm game," Fawn kept one eye on *the gram.*

"I'm down. Plus, later maybe a little shoe shopping—this hotel is connected to the Luxe Shoppes," Anjali primped, glossing her lips.

32

CONFERENCE DEBRIEF

"OVER COCKTAILS & THEN SOME..."

[WE ARE EVERYWOMAN, THEN "THE ICE" FLEW AWAY...]

The ladies did not want to miss *The Bomb* happy hour. As the ladies waited to be seated for drinks, Regi caught a glimpse of a woman helping an elderly lady up from her chair in the hotel lobby. Regi noticed that they rumbled with many bags, attempting to enter the elevator. She rushed over to help hold the elevator door open for them.

"Let me get that for you and your mother," Regi endeared.

"Oh, you are so sweet, dear. This is my daughter-in-law, but I consider her my daughter." The elderly lady smiled, while her daughter-in-law guided the elderly woman. "Mom, watch your step," the daughter-in-law said as she got her *m.i.l.* into the elevator gripping her shopping bags.

"Thank you," the elderly lady touched Regi's hand that held the door open. That touch gingerly saturated Regi's spirit of what she did not have, the love of her mother-in-law—she teared up a little.

A crucial conversation has to happen with my monster-in-law, but how? This has weighed me down too long.

In retrospect, she and her mother-in-law never talked to each other, they talked at each other. If Regi said black, Mrs. Suzanne said white. If Regi wanted to have her Ketchup in the refrigerator, Mrs. Suzanne argued, what's the point, at the restaurants, it's on the tables. Regi wanted her blinds tilted upwards internally, while Mrs. Suzanne wanted them angled downward to have the light hit the floor just right. And worst of all, damn pillows—Regi likes to shake her throw pillows, parting them down the middle. Mrs. Suzanne like her pillows fluffed and spread out. More than mother-in-law and daughter in law, they were lemon juice on an agonizing paper cut. Each of their arguments were cliffhangers to the next WWE battles.

She collected herself in her thoughts, rejoining her crew, who were now seated nestled in chips, salsa with fresh guacamole.

Fawn reached for a chip to dip into the salsa. Her elaborate tennis bracelet wrapped around her toned svelte wrist glistened in the light, catching a hold of all onlookers—Chaka taking notice, craning her neck back.

"Well, okay then, *Miss Icebox*," Chaka said as she nudged Fawn.

"Don't trip. I got this from my baby's father before I told him that I was pregnant. My baby along with this bracelet are the only good things I received from the collateral damage from Beckett Trent Blaze's sorry ass."

The ladies went into motherly concern mode, speaking one right after the other.

"Fawn, come on. Why didn't you tell us about *The Big—C?*" Penelope asked.

"Yes, girl. What's the damn plan man? Surgery? Chemo? Radiation?" Regi insisted.

Fawn bravely tried not to cry. "Not sure; I had the biopsy right before I came."

"So—that's what's up with the hair?" Anjali said with no filter; kicked under the table by Penelope.

"Ouch!" Anjali grabbed at her foot. Her face now softened with more empathy. "Mademoiselle, don't get me wrong; you're definitely rocking *the do*. I didn't mean any harm."

"I wanted to get ahead of it. Not sure. A few nights ago, I had a couple of drinks, the baby was in bed—then I found Beckett's clippers that he left at the house. I just wanted to be…"

"Proactive?" Chaka offered.

"Yes, proactive—do you like it?" Fawn said with a newfound confidence, rubbing her tress.

"I thought about the whole Amber Rose thing, but my head is too big," Regi laughed at herself, with the visual of her olive skin rocking the low-cut Caesar cut.

Chaka zeroed in on Penelope after the kick under the table. "Well, since we're being all transparent, Penelope, it appears that you are a *g.a.i.t.s.*" she said with a smirk.

"A gate, like wrapped around a backyard, connected to a fence—do share?" Penelope questioned as she took a sip of her cocktail.

"Well, a *g.a.i.t.s.* stands for someone who *goes all in too soon*. Being in the shadow so long makes you feel like you have to rush into being accepted. We got you, girl; just the way you are—with your big *ole* head."

The two women shared a shoulder hug.

"Shifting gears—Regi, I noticed you helping that lady with her mother onto the elevator. Did I witness a tear roll down your cheek? What's up with that?" Penelope inquired.

"You all don't understand the weight to carry around when your own mother-in-law feels that you are *the absolute bane* of her existence—it's horrible. I can't do anything right in her eyes. When the only thing I do from the bottom of my heart is love her son, and her grandsons with all of my soul. Besides that, what the hell is wrong with loving the melanin in my skin?"

"That is horrible, besides in this day and age interracial couples are everywhere. Is she caught back in the movie *Loving?* That's crazy. You want me to put *paws* on her? I mean, your mother-in-law can meet these *gunning in-law's.* You want me to put that *Nina* on her? I'll *refrigerate her!*" Chaka piped in, flexed her muscles, kissed her biceps.

"So you are The Incredible Hulk?" Regi solicited.

"If you're not careful, I'll turn this table over, becoming emerald green on y'all," Chaka cocked her fingers in a *pistol move*. "I'm *100!*" she went on to say.

"Damn Chaka, she dislikes me, disrespecting me always. However, that doesn't mean I want to *sell tickets* to see you *waxing that ass.* I need *RESPECT;* that's all. No crazy shit—I mean it. I better not find out that you harmed a hair on her hateful little head you hear me, with your crazy self?"

Chaka shrugged her shoulders.

"Speaking of *crazy,* where is our new bestie, Abby? She's always *dipping out* on us. That gets old. I hope that she understands it takes more than a Black Card for her to make friends," Fawn added.

"Hell, I don't know what you're talking about. Shit, I'll be your best friend, your side friend, your *Boo* if you got a Black Card!" Chaka hooted. "I'm just saying, Sista's, I could *Ball* like this every day if you asked me. I'm down for the cause. I'm trying to make some *bands!*"

"Girl, you are so damn ridiculous. Do you wake up like this?" Anjali asked.

"Yes, every day—my Sista." Chaka egged on.

"So, ladies, what's next? What are we into?" Anjali tussled her hair, pouting her lips while she took a selfie to send to Sean.

Regi looked around at the group. They were nothing like her Howard Crew or even her stiff fellow judge colleagues, except for *Miss. Frigid Bloomers*—The Abigail Lancaster, but she felt at home with this assembly of *affirmative estrogen*. Thinking about the day they met—she smiled.

"What the hell has got you showing all thirty-two of your perfectly veneered, capped teeth, looking like Chester Cheetah?" Chaka snickered at the judge, "You are going to leave orange paw prints everywhere with that grin."

"Seriously, ladies, I'm just thinking how nice this is. Who would've ever thought that only weeks ago, when I felt the weight of the world on my back, on the way to see my therapist for anger management?"

"I knew your perfect ass had road rage tendencies."

"Be quiet, Chaka; you're going to make my eyelashes come unglued," Anjali beckoned.

"It's just nice, is all I'm saying—"

"Just say it, your honor; you love our *crazy asses*," Chaka belted out, sipping her drink all the way down to the bottom—slurping.

"Girl, do you have any home training?" Fawn stated.

"Well, frankly, my darling, I don't give a damn—I have no home training because I don't have a home to go back to. Remember, kicked out!" Chaka's eyes bugged, as she forgot that she had not been that transparent with the group yet, but the liquid courage was kicking in.

Oh shit, I let the cat out of the bag, Chaka thought as she took a sip of water to dilute the straight-up vodka.

The ladies turned a little side eye.

Regi went on to lend an endearing chatter, swiftly changing the subject. "I can't believe I didn't tell you all about what happened right before The Declare Event; the day that we met..." Regi related the story of the dog shitting in the courthouse.

The roaring laughter at the table cut through the restaurant noise.

"*Stop*, girl, you are going to make me pee my pants." Penelope buckled over, holding her belly—giggling to the point of snorting.

"Damn, *Miss Piggy!*"

Penelope bumped Chaka due to the pig comment, feeling comfortable enough to confess that she was thinking about the gastric bypass surgery so she could get herself together.

Anjali, let her sisters know about her insecurities with race, what she had been experiencing.

"*WHOA!* I thought I was the only one messed up. You are as jacked up as I am." Chaka guffawed.

Abby arrived at the table. "Is there room for me?"

"Where in the hell have you been, *Ghost?*" Regi folded her arms disapprovingly of the last guest to the happy hour.

"Regi, I think you call it, *making moves*," Abby unapologetically expressed.

"*Um, hum*!" Regi gave it right back to her with an attitude. "Why are you putting me on blast like that? That is not even in my verbiage," Regi responded as she sipped her wine with her right pinky out.

"No, for real. We're supposed to be here together while you keep leaving when we're trying to bond," Penelope imparted.

Abby ignored the ladies, getting all up in her feelings, and ordered another round of shots. "This is a work trip for me, I have a small confession to make—"

The ladies were all ears.

"Promise you won't get upset with me?" she pleaded.

"*Heffa*, if you don't spit it out. I'm going to choke you," Chaka belted out.

"I canceled all of your room reservations right before you got here." Abby wrinkled her nose, in an entitled way—daring the ladies to snap back.

The receivers of the news were not amused, especially the judge.

"I knew your *control freak ass* had something to do with our rooms being canceled." Regi gave a straight attitude; swirling her wine down to the last corner.

"Well, since we're confessing shit, I feel like I'm on the Dr. Phil show. The reason I brought such a big-ass suitcase that you all were giving me hell about moving into the hotel, is that my father kicked me out of the house since *I was found out at* the Comedy Club," Chaka shared.

Most of the women were empathetic, but Regi, being the *mother hen,* said, "Christina, 'Chaka,' or whomever the hell you say you are, it was about time you got your grown ass out of your parents' house anyway. I mean, come on! I'm with your dad; get on your own two feet," Regi delivered unsolicited advice, not backing down on tough love.

Without looking up, Abby said, "I've got a guest house out back. It's yours for six months, then my nephew is coming to town to start film school. You can crash there if you want. Is that cool?"

"Hell yeah, that's more than cool! That's *Christmas! That's what's up*. Thank you *Mrs. Claus*." Chaka, in her joking way, grabbed Abby around the neck, planting a big wet kiss on her cheek.

"Yuck, back the hell up. We're all Weight Breakers now, but the sloppy kissing stops now, dammit!" Abby wiped her face, then she went on to reveal, "Well, since we're confessing, most people have no idea that I also come from meager beginnings." Usually after a few cocktails, Abby would wear her emotions on her sleeve telling of her inner core. Sometimes it would be taken well, sometimes not. She felt that once people got to know her real self behind the dividends, they rarely stuck around unless they needed some cash—that was a weight within itself.

The ladies craned their necks back at the possibility that Abby would get even more transparent than at the conference.

"You know Gadsden's, where we were hunkered down? That was my first job."

"You mean Miss *hoity toity* used to bag groceries? *Damn!*"

"Yes, I did. That's what made me who I am today. My grandfather started with selling fresh produce on the side of the road, then delivering produce door-to-door out of his truck. That is why I continue to send checks to the store on a regular basis—to support keeping good wholesome food within the community."

The ladies were endeared by the beautiful nostalgic story with the *Ice Queen,* for once, seeing the softer side of the *banded tyrant.*

She confided that things had not been going so well, furthermore she desired to leave her husband. She dared not to let the entire cat out of the bag—the fatal diagnosis. She covered her hand slightly, shaking, while she simultaneously texted.

"Now, any of you other silly girls need more of my advice?" Abby said, full of herself a little as always in her vaulted way.

Irritated, not drinking any of *The Abigail Lancaster Kool-Aid,* Regi delivered a sarcastic, "Girl, bye, with that—"

Just then, their attention was drawn to rambling over the microphone on stage. It was an amateur comedian who obviously had one too many vodkas, failing tremendously at improv.

Chaka turned her nose up. "Who the hell is this guy?"

With a nudging undertone in her voice, Abby said to Chaka with full confidence in her ability, "Chaka, why don't you go on stage to show 'em how it's done?"

Chaka had a flashback of her stand-up at the comedy club when she brought down the house only days ago. She nodded, biting her lip.

Man, I can rip this guy to shreds. Chaka dusted her shoulders off, giving a disapproving *stank-eye.*

"Girl, are you going to let him disrespect *your craft* like that? Show him what you're made of!" Regi added on to Abby's challenge.

"I'll go up to introduce you," Penelope offered to Chaka, so out of character for *The Shadow.*

As the drinks continued to flow, Chaka took another shot, slamming it down on the table—then popping her knuckles like she was ready to *whip some* ass on the playground.

Chaka winked at Penelope. "Let's go!"

Chaka and Penelope boldly marched up to the stage. Penelope took the microphone from the drunk amateur; the reverb sound shocked all surrounding the bar.

Anjali slumped down in her seat as to not be seen with the rowdy group. "Aw, shit, they're going to get us kicked out of here."

Regi smiled. "This is going to be on fire. Man, I need this; besides, I got their *get out of jail free cards* waiting. Let's have a little fun," Regi said as she downed the last corner of her wine, then poured another glass, holding it up high to toast the girls.

"Ladies and gentlemen, hang onto your hats. Welcome to the stage, from our She Declare Crew, one of the funniest women that you will ever hear—our girl, Chaka!"

"Give me the microphone, *nephew*," Chaka commanded of the amateur night at the Apollo act performer, booting him out of the way.

Chaka took the mic—Chaka was born. Her comedic chops roared.

Once again, her alter ego *killed the game*.

"I'm Chaka Bu—I'm out!" she mimicked, dropping the microphone.

The audience went into a roar with a standing ovation.

The She Declare Sisters ran up on stage, even Abby, to congratulate her with sisterly kudos. The other slimy comedian exited stage left, stumbling out of the venue with his tail between his legs.

The D.J., as if on cue, began to play "I'm Every Woman." Grabbing the microphones, way off-key, they got their groove back just like *Stella*.

Regi was in a groove.

Penelope was cutting loose.

Anjali *waved her hands in the air like she did not care.*

Chaka reached into her bag of *swag hip hop repertoire*, teaching the ladies a thing or two.

Fawn was feeling her tress, with *Amber Rose aura*.

Abby stood nearby with her hands folded, tapping her toe to the beat discreetly.

PING!

317

Fawn looked down at her phone; she'd placed settings to alert her when Beckett was on the Gram.

This fool is out there kicking it in the Hollywood Hills.

This troubled Fawn. Penelope noticed in the middle of ending their performance on stage. "What's wrong, girl?"

Fawn took a deep breath, struggling to get the words out, shaking her head. "It's Beckett; he's living his best life while I'm struggling—facing God knows what with the biopsy results—"

The loud, pounding music began to have a disco vibe. Penelope grabbed Fawn's hands, canceling out the music.

"To hell with all-star B.T! We're going to celebrate life. We claim you're going to be fine. Let's let loose. We're going to go back to the room. Let's have *A Jammy Jam*."

"*A Jammy Jam?*" Regi craned her neck, attempting to stay on beat with her two left feet. It was obvious she was counting off the beats in her head to imperfection; she hadn't *cut a rug in a while*.

"Damn, girl; I thought all *Sista's* had rhythm. You're about to lose your culture *black card*." Chaka bent down as if she was picking something up off the floor. "Yep, I now have your *card*," she said as she convincingly did the *WHOA!*

Regi sisterly slapped her.

"Oh, I want to exhale, but I can't." Fawn raised her hands to the heavens on stage, caught the glimmer of the twinkling of the tennis bracelet in the lighting. Her mind returned to this very hotel when Beckett and she had spent a romantic weekend; back when things were good.

As a matter of fact, the jewelry store where he bought this tennis bracelet should still be here on this property. Fawn thought that as she left the stage, walking over to the waitress while her friends were having a good time, dancing the night away.

"Hello, is there a high-end diamond gallery on the property?" Fawn asked while wiping the sweat off her brow.

"Oh, are you trying to *ball* like that?" the young lady asked with a smirk on her face, clearing the tables.

"Just wanting to get some more studs to go with this bracelet I got there a while back."

"Yep, it's in the luxury mall. As a matter of fact, now you don't have to access the mall from the outside anymore. Last year they completed the tunnel; it's a hop, skip, and a jump away."

"Cool." Fawn went back to their table, leaving her portion of the tip for the bill.

Her hurried movement caught her sisters off guard.

"What are you doing? Remember, we are VIP—this evening is *comp*," Abby said as she sucked the olive off the toothpick from her dirty martini. "Where are you going? Back to the room? I'll go with; I'm too old for this shit. I need my beauty sleep," she said in a motherly tone, inviting herself.

"No, I have a quick errand to run. I'll be back in the room shortly," she replied, prompting Abby to sit back down.

The other crew members noticed that Fawn was leaving, and came over to see what was going on.

"Fawn, where are you going? We all can bounce," Chaka said as she grabbed her backpack.

"Yep! We came, we slayed—now it's time for some cigars by the pool," Anjali said.

"Girl, we don't smoke," Regi stated.

"What about a hookah? You all are so boring," Anjali rendered like a schoolgirl with a temper tantrum, folding her arms—pouting her lips.

Fawn held up a pic of her baby daddy hanging out—*balling'* in a *Champagne Room* with his boys, she placed an alert on her social media settings to track when he was LIVE. "While I'm staring my mortality in the face, I need to make sure my daughter is okay. I'm going by the jewelry store to see what I can get for this bracelet—"

"Nope, not a good idea. *Bet on black*, girl. You better mark my words; you are making a big mistake. You better listen to this Golden Girl of The She Declare Crew!" Regi admonished, going on to say, "I'm only a parent to my two sons at home; you all are grown. I'm about to go to the room, and take a hot bubble bath, then secure a nightcap."

"Me too; us *Golden Girls* will catch you all in the room. I have a quick stop to make before I go to the penthouse. I'll see you later, *Blanche*," Abby put on her shades at nighttime.

"Oh, so you got jokes. Okay, *Dorothy*," Regi hammered back.

319

Abby smirked, "Take your ass on, *Rose*."

Regi laughed, "You better watch out, *Sophia*."

The women *snapped on each other*—playing a lightweight version of *the dozens,* staggering their separate ways, vowing to meet up in the hotel suite soon.

Chaka yelled out to Abby, "Seriously, Abby. Be honest. Do you have a man *hemmed up* in here—in one of these rooms? Come on, girl, at every *beat* of this trip, you're pulling another one of your disappearing acts like you constantly do."

"Lest I remind you once more, I'm *working* this weekend. I'm *The Abigail Lancaster,*" the icon snapped back, putting Chaka in check.

Once again, they saw the back of Abby as she was off to do what she did. Regi decided to head to the room, while the remainder of the crew scurried behind Fawn.

Regi soaked in the tub, eating chocolate-covered strawberries while sipping on another glass of chilled Riesling. She could easily relax after she video called her family.

Meanwhile, Fawn exuded a new found authority in her stride over the catwalk to the Luxe shoppes. Slightly behind Fawn were Penelope on her left with Anjali on her right. They appeared like soldiers going to war—with *game time* in their faces.

"You all, slow down. I can't feel my pinky toe," Anjali said as she attempted to be regal in her five-inch stilettos that she had been wearing all day.

"Anjali, bring your ass on; always trying to *stunt* with your shoe game. I told you to wear some *regular* shoes," Penelope championed as she could see the fire in Fawn's eyes. Although not knowing Fawn long, this was the first fervor she'd witnessed in The Mirage—not wanting that spunk to fizzle away. The ladies trudged onward, hurt feet and all, arriving at the store that housed couture diamonds.

"This is it—" Fawn uttered nostalgically. In her mind, she visualized moments of yesterday when Beckett brought her to that very store to *shower her* wrist with diamonds, to prove *his love.*

Fawn turned towards her allies. "Wait, should we go in?"

"That decision is up to you. What do you feel like you should do?"

"I feel like I need to know how much this damn bracelet is worth, so I can get compensated. It's only me who is consistently taking care of my daughter. Now that I'm sick—" Fawn catechized her friends, who had her back, while fighting the tears exuded from her ducts.

I know this is not what Dr. T., The Weight Breaker, meant when she instructed us to break the weight.

What the heck, I'm here now—I don't have anything to lose.

"Hello, may I help you?" a sleek woman with the name tag Aster neatly on her lapel, asked.

Penelope nudged Fawn in the back, prompting her to spit her words out.

Nervously, she stated, "Hello, my ex-boyfriend bought me this lovely tennis bracelet. I wanted to verify its value before I gave it away... to charity."

Fawn winked at both Anjali and Penelope.

Aster analyzed Fawn's wrist, holding it gently, "Beautiful, I see our insignia. This is one of our pieces. Would you mind taking it off your wrist?"

"Why certainly," Fawn took her tennis bracelet off that appeared to weigh a ton by the amount of lift her wrist had in its absence. She handed it to Aster with glee in eager anticipation.

Aster retrieved her diamond magnifier, brushed her lavender pixie cut back—peered down through her oversized red tortoise shell glasses onto the diamond bracelet. "Fine. Hollow. Dazzling. Well-cut—a unique piece with distinct diamond cuts, with the dazzling clasp of our marquise diamonds. This is a beautiful piece. You did well, darling. You mean you want to give this away?" Aster said as she allowed the magnifier lens to fall from her eye, unhanded.

"I'm moving on," Fawn said confidently.

"Would you mind? I will need to do some analysis to see its current value—I will be back shortly," Aster went to the back of the store.

"This is nice," Chaka emphasized, "When I make it, I'm going to get that big iced out Cuban chain right here. Man, this is beautiful."

The ladies gathered around, enamored. They noticed a three carat canary diamond earrings next to a black diamond neck chain.

"You mean people spend this type of money on a bracelet?" Penelope said as she noticed an alligator eighteen-carat yellow gold bangle that was on sale for two thousand dollars. "Girl, I'm going to put this on my vision board," she said in total admiration.

I think Cassidy has one of these? Penelope coveted.

"Ladies, look at this engagement ring. It's a canary diamond, five-carats total with one-carat, pear-shaped baguettes on the sides. A girl can only dream…" Anjali pressed her forehead against the glass. Her admiration was disrupted by a gentleman that came from the back, that boldly stood at the door. The ladies continued to eyeball the beautiful jewelry—window shopping.

"Sean has good taste. I can see him getting me this ring; it's nice, sexy—elegant, most of all it would look so good on my svelte hand. If he got me this, you couldn't tell me nothing—"

"Ma'am, I have some good news for you," Aster interjected, interrupting *the window-shopping spree.*

Fawn smirked, along with her crew right by her side—for the good news. "What is it?" she smiled, thinking about all that she could do for her daughter with whatever dividends the tennis bracelet could provide.

Aster questioned, "Fawn, is it?" Her demeanor is more formal than when she exited moments ago.

"Yes," Fawn's shoulder square with hers.

"Well, I'm happy to share with you that this beautiful bracelet is worth forty-thousand dollars without tax," she said in a stern manner without the bracelet in hand.

Fawn's crew gasped; they moved in around their sister holding each other's hands—then excitedly exhaled.

"Damn, girl, you were walking around with the freaking lottery on your wrist—you didn't even know it," Chaka jeered.

Forty Thousand Dollars. Forty Thousand Dollars… Fawn thought to herself, standing there like a deer in headlights. Her mind was a B-reel with all that she could do with the money.

Get out of the small apartment, into a nicer neighborhood.

Put my daughter in a better school.

Help my parents out.

Put the rest up in a college fund.

I need to hock this, getting the money really quick!

"Oh my Lord, are you serious, Aster!" Fawn replied with a relieved *Thank You Jesus Smile* on her forlorn face, her hands now shaking.

Penelope grabbed hold of her friend, "Be cool. You see, everything is going to be okay—"

Anjali stood back, surveying the perimeter, with an eyebrow raised, speaking out, "So, what's next?" Going into business-mode.

Aster winced, looking back at the gentleman who had the body build of The Rock at the door. He nodded to her as if to give permission to share the *news.* Aster went on to say, "Unfortunately, Fawn, there has been a lack of payment for *the said jewelry*. Therefore, we will have to confiscate the tennis bracelet."

This news was too much for her spirit; her vision tunneled to black—*Lights Out!*

Fawn fainted.

Fawn awakened in the hotel room with the ladies fanning her.

"What happened?" She looked around, she reached for her wrist, realizing that her worst nightmare was actually true. *The Forty-Thousand-Dollar Dream* had evaporated off her wrist. She did not even remember her crew all but carrying her inebriated self-back to the hotel, wiping her tears the entire way.

"Yep, it's gone!" Chaka confirmed, shaking her head.

Penelope sat on the couch next to Fawn, keeping a cold compress on Fawn's head, letting the sisters know, "She's waking up—"

Anjali was on her computer working. "Is she okay?"

"What is all the *damn ruckus*?" Regi entered into the living room of the penthouse, removing her *Fly Diva* eye mask, bundling her robe around her curves.

"They took Fawn's bracelet that was worth forty thousand dollars!" Chaka shared.

Regi shook her head. "Wait a minute. I need some coffee to digest this. Anjali, can you get some brewing? I need some caffeine to comprehend."

"Coming right up," Anjali pressed SAVE on her PC, making her way over to the kitchenette. The room filled with the aroma of coffee beans as the women were still bewildered; in shock with surmountable surprise.

"Well, we need to go down there right now to get the bracelet! Let me put on my suit. Where's my briefcase? Somebody, get me a cup of coffee!" Regi insisted, attempting to wake up as she appeared to walk in circles. It was as if she was leading the charge in getting her army aligned to take *the hill*.

"No, *General*, it is not. Besides, the crew tells Regi the real deal," Anjali quips to the group.

Penelope chimed in with a play by play. "Listen Regi! Let me tell you what happened. We go to the jewelry store, Fawn hands over the diamond bracelet, the diamonds are analyzed, Beckett's *punk ass* had stopped making payments on the bracelet, furthermore, the jewelry store confiscated it! The icing on the diamond shit cake is that, Fawn fainted, now we are back in the penthouse—"

"What?" This caused Regi to pause, as she now realized that there was nothing that could be done, due to the actions of Beckett's lack of payment. She dropped her briefcase, kicked off her shoes and took a large sip of her coffee. After which, she curled up into a ball, draped a throw blanket over her tired body. Regi then scolded Fawn like a mother, "I told you all to *let sleeping dogs lie*. That's what my mother always told me."

The full aroma of the coffee filled the air, perking Fawn up. She gazed at her sisters, bewildered. "Please tell me that I didn't lose forty thousand dollars!"

"Welp, hate to be the bearer of bad news, but your ass basically gave away the money. Who does that?" Chaka jokingly stated.

"Shut up; you were one of the main ones egging her on," Anjali thumped Chaka.

"Yes, the bracelet has gone *bye-bye*," Anjali said matter-of-factly without any comfort—with her hands thrown up into the air.

Fawn began to wail uncontrollably.

Regi grabbed Fawn, and shook her,

"Little girl, pull yourself together? Did you realize you had an extra forty thousand dollars this morning?" Regi asked.

"No," Fawn replied, rubbing her eyes.

"Were you going to make it through this season of storms in your life with God's guidance, before you knew the worth of the tennis bracelet?" she further interrogated as if Fawn were on the witness stand.

"Yes."

"Well then, it is settled. All money is not good money or God-ordained money."

"Bump that, dirty money or *stank* money. *Forty G's?* Come on."

"Be quiet, Chaka. This is life; not a damn joke," Regi commanded.

Chaka shrunk.

"What was this weekend about? What were us surviving The Declare Event about? We have to break ties, family curses, bondage, yokes, moreover weights that have been placed on our lives. Fawn, get yourself together—you will get through this! So, get off this couch, go wash your face, get your shit together girl! This loathing stops right now!"

The ladies stood up and surrounded Fawn with a huge embrace.

"It's just like I was watching a movie, got up and went to the ladies room, then returned to the theater—only to see that another movie is playing—" Fawn let out a sigh.

Then there was a knock at the penthouse door. Penelope left the *Waiting to Exhale* hug to answer the knock.

"Abby, you forgot your key?" Penelope cracked the door with Chaka behind her.

"Thanks for disappearing on us again," Chaka said as she opened the door wider.

Behind Abby were Dr. T.—*The Weight Breaker*, Dr. Sparrow Mack, Tabitha Blanko, Dr. Sophia Clark, along with Dean Baby.

"What the hell?" Chaka belted out.

Dean Baby snapped his fingers, entering with boldness. "*Hey, I'm here for the pajama party.*" He entered loudly with signed books, brandishing big couture gift bags for the ladies.

"Coffee, for real? This is the Golden Girls room. Regi, why? Where's the champagne?" Abby protested.

"Come on, ladies; it's time to turn up!" Tabitha came into the room, she pranced to her personal playlist on her own Bluetooth speaker.

"Hey, ladies; we got *Swag* for days and personally autographed books for you diva's," Dr. T. stated.

"My brother Luke wants to know which of you ladies is single?" Dr. Sparrow Mack asked while hammering away on her cell phone.

Penelope jumped up, "I am!" She rendered in desperation.

Dr. Mack smiled at Penelope. "Okay, I'll let him know."

"Hello, Regi," Dr. Clark stated.

"Hey, Doc, good to see you."

The women embraced. The mood in the penthouse suite went from somber from the ambush at the jewelry store, to jovial times filled with selfies, champagne, plus laughter.

The Abigail Lancaster took centerstage, after summoning the penthouse staff to prepare late-night delectable for her crew.

"I was *dipping out,* as you would say, to coordinate with all of these ladies, also the gentleman to make sure you would get one-on-one time with them."

The ladies were totally enamored.

"Let's go out on the veranda around the fire pit."

They grabbed blankets while exiting out onto the terrace where they were met with a blazing fire.

Dr. T., The Weight Breaker, jumped right into conversation, highlighting each of the Tactics the conference walked through.

"The tactics will strengthen your bonds with yourself, in addition to those around you. Simply put, what you speak to yourself, declare over yourself, is what you will attract—what you will become."

Regi, Anjali, Penelope, Chaka, and Fawn were seated in the swivel-back patio chairs around the glistening flames with blankets warming themselves amid smores that the house chef provided with cinnamon graham crackers, marshmallows, Godiva chocolate, in conjunction with dessert wine.

"Ladies, Abby thought so much about you to assemble us all together. That is how much she cares; a testament of what kind of woman she is."

The ladies nodded in agreement at Dr. Clark's comments.

Dr. T. stood. "First, thank you for being the dynamic woman that you are, supporting the Weight Breaker movement—I appreciate you. I have been in communication with Abigail, I feel that this is one of the most important interactions of the conference—that is, with you ladies. Is it okay to share your survey results, leading to an intimate discussion?"

"Hell, yeah. Let's go!" Chaka hyped, while the others nodded their heads with their eyes lit up like Christmas trees.

"Okay, Chaka—our beloved Chaka, you are The Aspirational. You aspire for so much in life, without a well-thought-out plan."

"Yep, that's me. However, I'm breaking that weight after this weekend," she answered back.

"That's good to hear. Now, Regi—"

"Oh, so we're really doing this?" Regi asked as she semi-nodded off, as late nights had gotten the best of her.

Dr. T. signaled yes with her head, as she went on to endear, "Regi, your survey said that you are *The Juggler*; you attempt to be everybody's everything—that is so much of a weight on you."

"You better preach," Regi agreed.

Dr. T. added, "Fawn, you have been a *Mirage* all of your life, always attempting to make sure that everything always appears to be okay, even when it is not."

Still wiping her eyes from the tennis bracelet heisted off her, she replied, "You are all up in my headspace."

Dr. T. turned her head towards Anjali, "Anjali you have been scored as a *The Chameleon*; you do your best to blend into everything."

"I can see that," Anjali responded.

"Penelope, you are *The Shadow*, always in the background, allowing others to shine."

"I own my *Shadow* tendencies." Penelope took a bite of the delectable smore.

Dr. T. turned towards Abigail, shaking her head, "Abby, girl, we go way back—you're such a *tough nut to crack*—you're definitely *The Vault*. You keep everything locked up deep down."

"No comment," Abigail turned her nose up, giving her signature snarl.

"Sweet Tabitha, Sis, I am still dumbfounded by your story. You are so brave—your scars are your truth. Your survival momentum is *The Emulate*. You've lived a different kind of life; however, you sustained this as a part of your path.

Dr. T. leaned into her friends; their longevity of friendship went beyond the others in the room.

"My girl, Dr. Sophia Clark, you are the most reasonable person I know. The momentum type that you carry is that of *The Reasoner*, everything has to make sense *down to the tee* or else it is not allowed in your space."

"Why thank you very much; I consider that a compliment," Dr. Clark aligned. "Why are you all up in my business? Remember, my friend, I know *where all of the bodies are buried*. Don't you forget, *Missy*."

The women gave a side hug.

Dr. Clark looked her friend over. "So, Dr. T., you are analyzing us all up the *wazoo*. What is your momentum type?"

"Full transparency, I am a combination of all of the above; that is why I am so complex. There are times when I fall into each one of the momentum types. That is one of the reasons why I was prompted to write this book, just to lend to all that read the book—to help others with how to navigate through life. Dean Baby, I did not forget you. This applies to men as well."

Dean Baby pondered. "Depending on the circumstances in my life, I feel like I have evolved into various momentums. I love this self-awareness movement. When we know ourselves, loving what and who God called us to be—we are more equipped to walk in our purpose. Overall, that's a beautiful thing."

Dr. T. smiled at Dean Baby. "Should we go ahead with making our announcement?"

"Why frankly, *my darling*, I believe so—"

"I've been working tirelessly with Dean Baby on a new Weight Breaker product line. Drum roll, ladies."

The ladies slapped their thighs, emulating the drum roll. Dr. T. held up a beautifully decorated box, along with Dean Baby smiling.

"Introducing *The Chronicles of The Weight Breakers Declare Lip Lacquer*. The purpose of this lip care line is to nourish the lips; moreover, the movement is to remind ourselves that what we declare over our lives comes out of our mouths."

Dr. T. handed a lip lacquer that was the affirmation of each of the momentum types to The She Declare group—the ladies were enamored with the ornate packaging.

"Pause!" Dean Baby belted out. The ladies looked around a little bewildered, coming up for air while diving into their sleek swag bags. He goes on to add,

"In developing these lip stains, we took a hard left turn. We did not just want to orchestrate a *bomb ass color* so you could pout *rocking it on the gram*—we wanted lip color stains with purpose to break the weight in more than one way—"

"Oh, I see you. Do tell," Chaka inquired as she held her lip lacquer up to the light.

"Chaka, I feel you—these lip stains have true intention, a declaration of sorts. Dr. T. and I orchestrated them to nourish your lips, but also help with the Weight Taker in you. There are natural botanicals that are infused throughout to also help with appetite suppression—"

"So can I eat the lip stain? Give me a whole box—" Penelope questioned as she opened her color.

"No, not as a meal my sister—girl, you are *a hot mess*! Just like the scent infusion on the lip color, those ingredients are incorporated to help with natural cravings."

"This is so dope. My man likes me as *a thickem's*, however anything I can do to keep my snap back on point after having my two son's is a win in my book," Judge Regi high-fived Dr. Sparrow Mack.

"Well in my Mary J. voice, I'm just going to say *Good Morning Gorgeous!*" Dr. Sparrow Mack gave her sister friend Regi a side hug.

The ladies let out a huge banter that filled the penthouse suite.

"Yes, ladies. Your energy is right on point. Alright, sisters, here is your Weight Breaker Proclamation." Dr. T. handed out a piece of paper for them to write their momentum type down, moreover how they would respond to changing their mindset. The ladies wrote while pondering over the meaning of their lives.

Dr. T. went on to share, "I am going to share a life-changing moment with you, that was the catalyst for me to orchestrate the momentum types—moreover, the idea of the lip lacquer. I did not share the details of this encounter in the *Think Like A Weight Breaker. Not Like A Weight Taker* book. I was on an airplane going to a work-related conference. I was not happy about going to the conference, not because I did not want to go—it was because I was outright exhausted. Can anybody relate to that? I was a new mother, my husband was traveling for work, late nights at the hospital had gotten the best of me. At that time, the only writing I was doing was in a journal from time to time. You understand how it is to burn the candle at both ends?"

The ladies nodded in agreement.

"I was on the airplane, with a cluster of feelings, thinking about how I *juggled* everything, how much both my work life and home life did not have any balance. In addition, how I was trying to fit into *the good ole boys club*, being cautious about how to present my culture, kind of like *The Chameleon*. How I *aspired* to be more and more—that there had to be a way I could *reasonably* enhance who, moreover what God called me to be. Also how, at times, I felt like I was in the *shadows*, appearing to be a *mirage*—making it seem like I had it all under control. All the while, emulating a life that I was not living—being a weight taker."

"That's deep—" Chaka loved the visual.

"Then I felt a little turbulence that shook me out of myself-analysis. I noticed a lady in front of me, her hair immaculate—not a hair out of place. She turned her head, her face was *beat to the gods,* as they say. She looked like she had her own personal makeup artist. I looked into my compact, weary from late nights at the hospital, on post call nights, late nights up with a colicky baby, with her demeanor that put me to shame."

"Girl, I know the feeling. When I see a lady who has it together, it stings my inner core. I think why can't I be as fabulous as her," Penelope reacted.

"Penelope, not so fast—wait for it. Back to the airplane, when the seat belt sign was all clear, I got up to go to the restroom. In passing her, she looked up at me— smiled brilliantly. She was a lady about in her 60s, with a geometric salt-and-pepper short pixie cut. The lady was *Michael Jackson Bad* all the way around. As I left the restroom, walking back to my seat, I looked down at her. She gave a gentle wave with a beautifully manicured hand accented by cherry red nail polish to match her lips. Adorned with beautiful diamond rings, *to die for.* My eyes told it all when I looked her over. She only had one arm—the one finely

330

adorned—no legs. Her beautiful energy radiated. I caught myself from being too taken aback, easing the creases in my mouth, telling the woman her makeup was beautiful, moreover that I loved that lip color. Her bright smile got even bigger, lighting up the plane. She replied, *It's a basic red, but I call this color my Philippians 4:13 Red!"*

Tears welled up in the women's eyes, as they passed napkins around the fire to dab their damp cheeks.

"Are you serious?" Anjali retorted, as she always was the one to covet another's life, not realizing that what she may crave in another's world, they may want to trade with her.

"The grass is not always greener on the other side, always remember that. Everyone is dealing with something, whether you can see it with the naked eye or not. Moreover, on that airplane, with that brief interaction with that lady, I felt totally convicted at that moment. That Bible verse hit my core in my gut. *I can do all things through Christ who strengthens me.* I realized that I did not know that woman's story. However, her momentum, in addition to how she navigated through life was nothing short of a miracle—priceless. I have never seen that woman again in life; however, she was a part of the muse for me writing this book, *Think Like A Weight Breaker. Not Like A Weight Taker.* That brief encounter caused me to realize that, regardless of the weights we are born into, or acquire, we are more than conquerors—capable of handling the proverbial and physical weights of life. So, ladies, I'll tell you this. Whatever your momentum is, you have to proclaim or declare positivity over your life."

With the fire blazoning, the story warmed the women's hearts. Some were tearful—most smiled with endearment.

"Dean Baby, please hand out the lip stains with the ladies' names on them."

"Got it, Dr. T." Dean Baby distributed satin gift bags for the women that aligned with their momentum types.

"Who would like to share their declaration?" Dr. T. requested.

"Okay, I'll participate. I'm Regina—"

"Girl, own your credentials, Judge! Be proud." Penelope was now fired up with encouragement.

"Well, okay—I'm Judge Regina Hinson; my friends call me Regi. All of my life I have been a Juggler. I have been everybody's everything, attempting to keep everyone happy: attempting to be wife and mother of the year. Despite all of my efforts to win the heart of my mother-in-law, she despises that her son chose to marry a woman of color, which is a profound weight. Furthermore—"

Regi's minded whirled back to…

The country fields of Texas—things began to swirl; her little brother was ripped from her hands.

A large tear rolled down her strong cheekbone.

Dr. T. sensed the brilliant woman was forlorn. "Take your time," Dr. T. encouraged as she handed her a Kleenex.

"I can handle the darts of being judged, moreover all that goes with the weights of that title. However, I am terrorized by not being able to let go of the death of my brother when we were children."

The ladies rubbed her back, they attempted to console the pain engrained in her spirit.

She took a deep breath.

"Thank you, ladies. I'm good. I wrote on my proclamation that I will release the overwhelming weight of everybody's life that is weighing me down. The lip stain I got is called *Balance & Winning*. What this means to me is that I will work on the balance in my life—that will cause me to not only win in the courtroom but, moreover, in my family life, including my mother-in-law."

Regi threw her *The Juggler* declaration into the fire; the embers swallowed the wish up, cascading up to the night heavens.

Fawn stood to read her declaration. "Hello, I'm Fawn Paige. I'm a Mirage. On the surface, I want everything to appear as if it is okay, but I'm not okay. I may have breast cancer—I'll get the results soon. Compounding this possible new diagnosis, I carry the weight of being rejected as a child that resulted in excruciating poor self-esteem. I finally felt a little worthy when I lost a significant amount of weight, became a cheerleader—ultimately ending up on an NBA dance squad. I had truly made *squad goals,* but at what cost? The father of my child pretends that she never existed—has moved on, away from us. The one thing that I held onto from the relationship was that tennis bracelet—with my stupid action only moments ago, that was taken away from me. I'm grateful to have my She Declare Sisters right here; I commit to walking in my truth. I'm enough, I don't need anyone's approval to be me!"

Fawn boldly released the declaration into the fire. She put on the lip stain, *Truth & Beauty.*

"I'm going to live my very own beautiful truth!" Fawn stated, the ladies reached over to hold her hand.

"Okay, I can feel the love—you all want me to *kick down some knowledge*." Chaka cleared her throat, taking a sip of her champagne with her pinky finger out—always in comedic mode.

"I am Christina Bu; my stage name is Chaka. In my core, I am a true—*The Aspirational person*. Full transparency, I have not always thought everything out—kind of a fly-by-the-seat-of-my-pants girl. Meeting these women, my She Declare Sisters, has changed that. You ladies are my R.O.D.s"

"Rods?" Dean Baby asked.

"My *ride or die* for life!" The ladies smiled at their sister. Chaka went on, as she threw her momentum type into the fire, she placed the *Dream & Fulfillment* lip stain on her lips.

"Well, it looks like I'm next." Anjali stood. "I'm Anjali Jagruti Nadkarni, to temper the tongues who could never pronounce my name, I decided to change my name to A.J. to make everyone around me feel more comfortable with me being in the room. From elementary school, in which I totally envied my classmates with blonde haired blue eyes with perfect Wonder Bread sandwiches for lunch, as they made fun of me with my cultural lunch of basmati rice with Malai Kofta. I despised my uniqueness because it stood out like a sore thumb. I had succumbed to being a *The Chameleon* because the more of me that I hid, the more I felt accepted. So today, on my declaration, I'm owning my authenticity. I'm going to be bold in embracing my culture."

Anjali placed her declaration into the fire and placed the lip lacquer on her lips—entitled *Authenticity & Boldness*.

"My turn to step to the mic; pardon the pun. I see the irony of what I just said. I trust that what goes on in this penthouse stays here like Vegas, right?"

The ladies nodded their heads.

"Speak your truth, Penelope," Abby urged.

"Well, people see me and they see a smart intelligent lady, but what I see is my weight. I have allowed that physical weight to become psychological weight—it has been so draining. I won't go into detail, but I have been in The *Shadows* all my life. I believe that God has more for me. I have found that this conference has shown me that, in the dark times, what God was really doing—was preparing me to blossom. My She Declare Crew, these ladies right here, have been my fertilizer—"

"So, what you're saying is that we are *full of shit*?" Chaka belted out in her own way to uplift the setting.

The ladies laughed hysterically.

"No, what I'm trying to say is that you ladies, with the *Think Like A Weight Breaker. Not Like Weight Taker* book, are the rays of sun, the loving rain that poured down on me, causing me to grow. So, I surrender the shadow into this fire. I will place a declaration of *illuminating light* on my lips, to step out of the shadows."

The ladies clapped.

"Tabitha, why don't you go next?"

"Well, okay. You all heard my story, transparently I was hesitant to share. I'm a broker, manager, and also a publicist. One of my client's and closest friends, Dr. Sparrow Mack, urged me to walk in my truth about a year ago. That is when I started orchestrating the Savoy Middleton Home Décor Collection from the sketches that I drafted up while living in the trailer with my dying mom. This conference allowed me to free myself from all that had been weighing me down all these years. I'm grateful. I'm Savoy Middleton; I'm The *Emulate*. As Tabitha Blanko, I've learned to embrace both because of the rich history that I had with my mother along with the rich blessings Mr. Blanko, my adoptive grandfather, gave me. I release it all in this flame up to the heavens where both of them are..."

Tabitha placed the paper into the embers—she watched as the smoke dissipated into the starry night sky.

She then placed the lip stain, *I am & I am,* onto her lips.

"Well, I did not play fair," Dr. Clark stated. "Dean Baby told me that he had a lip color that he worked on with Dr. T. for the color series called *The Reasoner*. I just have to make sense of it all—everything. A blessing ladened under a curse. It has taken its toll on me. People think that I have it all together, but I have struggles, too. Newsflash, I'm currently going through a divorce, but I'm going to be okay. The stain that I have on my lips is called *Just Embrace & Flow*—that is what I plan to do."

The ladies high-fived Dr. Clark, in addition thanking her for full transparency.

"Hold on Dr. Clark—" Regi beckoned her counselor.

"What up Regi?" surprise in her dilated pupils.

"I've let the ladies know that you are my therapist. Transparently, I know I've been a total ass, in our sessions I deflected all of my anger on you. I thank you for standing by me to always encourage me. Moreover, I apologize for my behavior, lending to how insensitive I was about making a statement towards you. You know, about you sharing the fibroid journey—"

"Regi, what you did not know is that I let that go as soon as you said that. I could not take on any weight of negativity. It has been forgiven," the women embraced.

"Awe, look at the Golden Girls," Chaka jokes.

"So, Dr. T., what about you?" Chaka asked.

"My momentum type is a mixture of all, depending on the circumstances. I'm grateful for the support from each one of you ladies. The lip stain I have on is called *Be Still & Know*. That is so very crucial for all of us. I will work on doing the work, but it is often hard for me to be still, trusting the process without trying to move too fast through life. Just know that God is working everything out for our good."

The room got a little quiet. Abigail, with her usual snarl, broke through the silenced tranquil scene on the veranda—warm with the heat from the blazoned fire.

"Well, I feel like I can share this with this group. Fawn, I can identify with you all too well. I have been diagnosed with a terminal illness; you may see me slip away from time to time. I have to have medication on hand, embarrassingly enough I must be near the ladies room just in case. I don't have long, however being with you ladies has mustered up my faith. I may have a cold exterior, nonetheless God has the final say. I thank you ladies for lifting me up, surrounding me with kindness along with profound grace."

The newsflash hit all the women in the gut.

"No, Abby, why didn't you tell us?" Fawn asked.

The women came in closer.

"You never know what is going on in my head or my space. I present a stern demeanor, but this is not done by accident. Some may say that I have a sour attitude, but they have not walked a mile in my shoes. Overall, people have no idea what I'm dealing with. Little does anyone know, I'm at the end of my rope, but I present the same exact demeanor—I'm ice cold. I rock labels on my back, slide my manicured toes into the finest shoes, admittedly I snarl when others get too close. All this noise about breaking weight is a crock to me. But, I will say that some of the words I hear on the podcast from *that Weight Breaker chick*, Dr. T., hits me in the proverbial gut."

Her sarcastic shade actually felt good to Dr. T.

"Abby, I knew you would open up eventually," Dr. T. thought as she felt that this was a win—*fruit* that blossomed from the conference.

Abby let out a laughing fist-bumped her friend.

"Girl, I must admit, I'm *The Vault*, I threw the key away long ago. I'm a work in progress. The most meaningful way I have found to do this is to unplug, putting everything on silent mode. The icing on the cake of bad news in my life is that my husband is having an affair with who I thought was my best friend, Margot. So, I will continue to ask for you ladies to pray for me. I suppress all of this down to cast a stern appearance. I know no other way to cope. I fully own that I'm *The Vault*. So, I place this declaration that I will allow myself to be more open, leaning into the loving friendships that God has gifted me. I surrender to God's plan for me," Abigail placed the lip stain *Open & Surrender* on her lips.

All of the Momentum Types gathered around *The Abigail Lancaster,* or who they now affectionately referred to as Abby.

"Abby, just let me know when you want me to beat him down? I'll sell tickets!" Chaka's pupils sincere.

"Girl, come here," they embraced their sister, proclaimed that they would be there for her. In addition, for each other—during their times of need.

Dr. T. left the ladies with a final contemplation as the embers from the fire pit continue to blazon the terrace that moved through the night air,

"Consider that your sacrifices, heroism and excellence are tied together like knots on the rope of your life. Ladies, you've been weight breakers all along…"

33

RECAP OF THE CONFERENCE

"SILENCING THE UNPRODUCTIVE NOISE"

[IT'S OKAY TO PUT YOURSELF ON SILENCE MODE...]

Hi Weight Breakers,

I'm shouting it from the mountaintop—THE CHRONICLES OF THE WEIGHT BREAKERS CONFERENCE was epic!

Weight Breakers, you showed up from around the world, in an effort to enhance your lives. You made connections that can help you grow, evolving into who God called you to be. From the media commentary, it appeared that the conference was one of a kind. I must prompt, that we need to keep the circle of blessings flowing. Furthermore, I want to say a special thank you to each of you for your dedication to your personal growth.

So many of us are busy living hectic lives—we often make requests of God many times, let's just pause, saying thank you to God for all of his blessings. By projecting gratitude, bountiful blessings will come our way. One way to notice the bountiful blessings that we have is by being still—silencing out unproductive noise. Being still, being quiet, in a space where you can be in the midst of the ideas of meaningful change, is imperative. Power strategy comes in those silent moments to identify what you need to take flight; what you will need to put in *the trashcan* of unnecessary distractions. We are going to go from the sidetrack way of thinking, to actually going into silence mode to become prepared, organizing our thoughts. This will cause us to sharpen *our iron* to meet the proverbial/physical weights of life head on. The goals of this challenge are the following: Contemplate, Think, Ponder, Resolve, Deliberate, Meditate, and Engage. Silence Mode: Weight Breaker, let's contemplate! Contemplate on *your why?*

Dr. T. was seated on the veranda of her penthouse suite at the conference host hotel, while she sipped her top shelf grind coffee, premium blend. She exhaled, as she smiled—while watching the opulent sunrise cascading over the hills, feeling the breeze bluster across her face.

337

Weight breakers, why do I want to shed these types of weights? How can I resolve the weights of life better? How can I be deliberate with my motivation towards doing so? You have to press *GO*—move forward, without everything you had in mind. God will make up the difference. How can I meditate on that?

Most of all, how do I, in all practicality, engage within an upward moral space? God wants you to take the first step. He will drop *manna* from heaven to guide you to the next *post*.

Her affirmation of her calling, is resonated by the emoji's that she witnessed—the hearts and prayer hands emojis that populated during her recap podcast.

Let me go a little deeper, as I'm loving the opportunity to share—being transparent with you. Some of my most profound thoughts are when I'm walking; my mind is clear. A couple of weeks ago, I was taking a morning walk, deep into my stride when I stopped as I noticed something intriguing. There was a flower coming through the paved road. It came in full bloom through the cracks. It bloomed as if it was blooming from a field accompanied by the other beautiful flowers of its kind rising to the heavens, showing off its magnificent beauty—that flower was bold. Evidently, there was a seed that planted itself beneath the pavement. That seedling established roots, then found its way to light. The paved hard road was no competition for this powerful flower, as it was obvious that this flower was predestined to be. Weight Breakers learn from this beautiful flower. Poise yourself because you were destined to be great; be bold. In my mind, I could sense in that flower's spirit, that it canceled out all of the unproductive noise that may have whispered all around it: *there is cold darkness around you; there is something above you holding you back; you can't possibly bloom in these conditions.*

Dr. T. adjusted her stance on the veranda to share the sight of beautiful flowers blooming, reaching up to absorb the gentle kiss of the morning sun.

This spot is perfect, look at God. Dr. T. pointed out to a specific flower that she spotted; she zoomed in.

Look right there, what a coincidence—you see that flower, right? What did that flower do? It saw the crack in the pavement, not as a barrier, but an opportunity. Despite the circumstances that attempted to cover that flower's shine, it sprouted anyway, becoming its brilliant magnificent self. In essence, it silenced out every barrier that was in its way. We too must be like that flower, by establishing policies and procedures on how to approach life. That is what I have attempted to do within the workbook, *Think Like A Weight Breaker. Not Like A Weight Taker.* So that you can always breakthrough and shine—despite anything that attempts to hold you back.

The heart emojis penetrated the screen.

Let's take this one step further. When we were all in our mothers' wombs, it was a quiet, dark place with a lot of momentum. Everything around us was productive for the end result—life. When we were developing from a cellular level to an actual being, understand all that it took to make us come into this world. Moreover, all that it takes for us to sustain, evolving into the purpose for our life. Therefore, canceling out unproductive noise is education for our souls. Focus for our spirits, most of all, growth for our mission.

Prayer hands and heart emojis manifested.

I see your smiles regarding this word, which is wonderful. As a part of the Weight Breaker process, with agility, we must know that the world operates in cycles. The sun comes up each day on cue; the moon comes up every night. Our heart beats on cue; there are so many cycles that are good around us. Nonetheless, over time, with life experiences, sometimes we can incur such patterns that are not in our best interest. Breaking the cycle is like trying to learn a new way of life. Cycles can't be limited to a generation; they can be ever-present entities to deal with throughout time. Cycles can be present, including so many different issues—such as dysfunction. Moreover fill in the blank_____ of what you've noticed as an unhealthy cycle in your life. There are cycles of dysfunction that can be self-imposed: negative self-talk, putting yourself down, just plain outright being way too hard on yourself. It is up to you to cancel out the unproductive noise.

Thumbs-up emojis resounded.

Weight Breakers, some takeaways to walk out are: Contemplate; Think; Ponder; Resolve; Deliberate; Meditate, moreover Engage. Weight Breakers, you got this! As each of you are on your way to your respective homes from THE CHRONICLES OF THE WEIGHT BREAKERS CONFERENCE, just know that you are a magnificent existence. Weight Breaker don't you ever forget that: you matter, you can, you will, last and definitely not least—you rock!

Love Y'all,

Dr. T.

Dr. T. signed off the podcast from the suite with a view of the beautiful marina. She looked out of the window, watching the women leaving the hotel—saying a silent prayer for their safe return home.

With bags packed, she embarked the town car to the airport—she looked forward to a much-needed relaxing, uninterrupted family vacation.

34

THE ARRIVAL BACK HOME...

"THE CREW IS FORCED TO BREAK WEIGHT"

[THE WEIGHTS OF A COMMUNITY & THE WORLD WE LIVE IN]

The ladies had their bags in tow—dropped off at the small airport tarmac.

"So, is this what was meant by a surprise, *The Abigail Lancaster?* Damn, girl—I know you said you got two kids, but will you adopt me?" Chaka said as she stepped on board the sixteen-passenger jet with a glass black nose adorned with Seminole red pearl stripes, leather seats, and ingrained wood interior. As they boarded the ladies were handed designer Weight Breaker Mimosas, while being escorted to their seats for chair massages.

Penelope took a sip, "Here I thought this weekend could not get any better. This is so refreshing; I can get used to this—"

"Cassidy rides like this all the time, this is going to be me soon," Penelope sat in her seat, greeted with a shiatsu technique kneading on her tight shoulders.

"Now, hold up. Wait a minute; no talk of *imposters* while we're flossing like this. Girl, you have stepped out of the shadows. You will have a jet like this one day, so silence all of that unproductive noise," Anjali planted into Penelope's spirit.

Regi nodded her head in agreement, she turned towards Abby. "Abby, this is so nice. This weekend has been epic. This conference was the water that my soul needed to grow."

"Let me cut you off right there. I apologize to you for being such a total bitch to you when you attempted to give me Gadsden—*our pup*. The weights of my life have me all twisted up. I've always been on guard; how I behaved was not cool. So not cool!"

"Well, we are The She Declare Sisters; we are *letting bygones be bygones*," Regi extended her glass towards Abby.

The ladies toasted their glasses.

CLINK!

The noise of the fine lead crystal that contained La Grande Dame by Veuve Clicquot caused the other ladies to turn around.

"Oh no, you all are not *toasting* without us—" Anjali stood up, as she attempted to keep steady after the plane reached cruising altitude.

"Okay, ladies, we have momentum now. We are Weight Breakers, no longer Weight Takers. To the Weight Breakers!"

Fawn held up the champagne flute, as the women yelled in unison, "To the Weight Breakers!"

CLINK!

CLINK!

CLINK!

CLINK!

CLINK!

After the short, smooth, relaxing plane ride, topping off the empowering weekend, the ladies were met once again by Mr. Cecil in the luxury black-on-black van at the landing strip. During their ride to their homes, they were still on cloud nine—promising to stay connected. They even committing to *hitting up* Essence Festival or *taking on* Martha's Vineyard real soon. They embraced as they gathered their belongings.

He took each of them to their respective homes. Regi was the last stop, due to her living in *The Hills*…

Regi exited the vehicle, promenading up to her home—smiled, she punched the code on the digital keypad.

CLICK!

Eager to plop her bags down to greet her love's, she billowed into the Hinson entry,

"Hello, I'm home. Boy's, where are you? It's so good to be back—" her words were cut short. A village of flies could have entered her mouth as it dropped open,

Chief Judge Reynolds, at my home?

341

Regi released her bags in utter surprise, her heart sank,

"Judge, what in the world? Is everything okay?"

"Well, it is now," he said as he gave Regi a side shoulder hug, picked up her bags, and brought them into the living room, the home was strangely quiet, absent of rambunctious youthfulness.

"Regi, I'll let you spend time with your family. I will have everything taken care of—"

Judge Reynolds exited the home.

In panic mode, Regi ran through the house, yelling for her boys and her husband.

"Isaiah, Isaac, Zachary—"

There he sat alone in the study, the lights off—quiet. Regi gently walked in, gingerly kneeling in front of him,

"Zachary, are my babies okay?"

"Yes, they're fine," Zachary exuded, wiping his hollow tears.

Regi's near cardiac arrest trended downward from *one thousand to one hundred.*

"Babe, where are they?" she queried, as she scanned their home, longing for the rustling of her little Kings as they would normally be loudly challenging each as they played video games or demonstrating their WWE battle moves.

"They're with my mom—"

That statement made Regi's ears sting—her blood boil.

"Your mom? *That monster* doesn't like me—Zachary why in the hell would you do that?"

"Regi, she's their grandmother. Besides, Judge Reynolds took them over there for me when I got arrested—"

"Arrested? What the hell are you talking about? You're really scaring me—"

Regi bent down as she looked into her husbands' eyes, attempting to unveil the layers of his pain,

"Regi, now I know how it feels…" Zachary sobbed.

"Zachary, how what feels?" Regi's mouth opened, as she awaited discovery.

"How it feels to be black—a man of color, African American."

Regi's pupils told it all.

"Baby, you've been trying to get me to understand racial discrimination—no matter how many marches I participated in for equality; it doesn't compare to being a man of color," crocodile tears funneled down Zachary's face.

"Oh, no, what the hell happened?" Regi clenched her teeth, she recalled all too clearly inequity, discrimination, along with microaggressions that she delt with on a regular basis. Despite all she'd overcome, moreover no matter how adorned her walls were with degrees and accomplishments—she'd resolved that she would always be seen as—black, nothing more at first glance.

Zachary arose from the chair in the study—walked the horrific ordeal out, as if he was living it all over again. The pain embedded in his eyes.

"I was taking the boys to get their haircuts, but before doing so, I stopped for some gas. After getting gas, the boys begged for a slushie, so I pulled out from the pump to the front of the gas station. While parking the car, I saw some young kids hassling a homeless man—those young jerks were clearly out of line. The boys were looking at me like—*Daddy, do something.* So, I went up to the boys, asked them politely to leave the homeless man alone, as he was clearly not bothering anybody. There was a police car parked with an officer sitting in it. I love the police, but this one had a different kind of look about him. I pounded on the hood to get his attention—letting him know about the unfair treatment that the homeless man was getting. He jumped out of the car, ready to attack—"

"What in the world?"

"He insisted, raise your hands up, boy! And I said, no, I haven't done anything wrong. I'm just attempting to get your attention."

Regi envisioned the encounter, all too familiar—due to her melanin.

"I instructed our sons to stay in the car for a minute while I spoke with the taunting boys. Seeing me get confronted by the policeman, for whatever reason, caused the boys to jump out of the car, rushing to me terrified. I held them close. The police officer asked me to raise my hands again, but I wanted to comfort the boys. *I said—NO!* Then he said something I will never forget. *You got you some foster kids, from Africa, huh?* Then I did it. It just came out of the depths of my soul. Hell, no— these are my biological sons. Furthermore, I'm not raising my hands; I have done nothing wrong. I'm going to take my sons to get a slushie, then a haircut!"

Regi's eyes welled with tears.

"I turned to walk away—he grabbed the back of my neck forcing me to the hard pavement. The boys started crying hysterically. I couldn't do anything to protect them. I was helpless. I just kept saying, *Daddy is going to be okay. It's going to be okay.* But clearly it wasn't. Regi, him seeing that I was a white man, did not get me out of that bind. Knowing I was the boys' father, moreover that they were watching me get man-handled for no reason, didn't even phase the cop. He was going to arrest me. He didn't even care to make sure the kids were okay, at all. So, I'm seated in the back of the cop car in handcuffs, at the moment I looked up seeing who I thought was Chief Judge Reynolds in the store. He came over to the car after he recognized our son's, he put two and two together. As the judge approached the car with me in the back seat, the cop jumped back out of the car, threatening to arrest Chief Judge Reynolds until he showed his credentials. It was crazy, Regi. So, from the back of the car I asked Judge Reynolds to take the kids to my mother, because I knew you were on a flight headed back home. I told him her name was in my cell phone that had fallen out of my hands as I was being handcuffed. Judge Reynolds, who you like to call *the asshole*, took the kids to my mother's—then came to the station bailing me out. He said he is going to have that officer's badge."

Regi opened herself up to allow her husband to melt into her arms like butter.

"Oh, baby. This is so unbelievable. I'm going to make sure that jerk rots in jail," Regi said, fuming—her cerebrum going into mama bear mode,

I'm going to have those bastard's badges!

"Can I be honest? I really thought that my skin color could get me out of this. As soon as he saw that I was a man with African American sons, the dynamic of the conversation shifted in intensity, I feared for my life, moreover our son's safety. At that moment, I realized I cannot prepare my son's, how to be black men in this type of world."

Regi laid in her husband's arms of despair. They wept for all of the black lives' that had been lost in situations like he had just experienced.

:Judge, thank you from the bottom of my heart. I really appreciate you. Are you available for coffee in the morning?—Regi H.

:Sure thing. I will personally make sure that justice is served. I grew up in the south, so my family has dealt with injustice all of our natural born days. We have to keep steadfast in confronting injustices in this world for all. Lunch on me soon, none of that salad stuff. A real down-home meal that nurtures the soul.—Chief Judge Reynolds

:Sure thing judge. From the bottom of my heart, thank you again. You will never know how much you helping my family means to me.—Regi H.

Regi drove over to her mother-in-law's, usually, this drive was fueled with angst, however this experience added an overwhelming sadness for what her sons would have to deal with after seeing that the world regarded them not as young, thriving, intelligent boys, but as threats simply because of the diffuse melanocytes inhabiting their skin. Zachary sat in the passenger seat, quiet. She discerned that from this point their life would never be the same, moreover her loving husband was weighted by the new perspective that he'd gained.

Regi arrived at her mother-in-law's home.

"I see smoke, I'm going to go around back—I bet George needs some help with the grill," Zachary kissed his wife.

Regi bit her lip, "I'm going inside to see the boys."

The door opened; her mother-in-law's eyes relayed something different to Regi that she'd never seen before; a welcoming concern.

"Hello Mrs. Hinson, I'm here to see my boys," Regi formalized as if she'd just gone by a stranger's house—not her mother-in-law whose surname she'd had for over a decade.

She'd better not start anything with me today, I'm not in the mood.

Mrs. Hinson's arms opened up as if to embrace her. Regi's surprised eyes told it all; pure shock.

Should I run for the hills? Regi thought, but followed suit, entertaining the deliberate kindness.

"Regina, my dear–come in. The boys are out back swimming. They can stay here for the night. I've got George getting ready to put burgers with bratwursts on the grill. Regi, I even picked up your favorite from the market in the city?"

"My favorite?" Regi took a back with her *m.i.l. 's tenderness.*

345

"I believe you call them Red Hot's? You know those sausage links you like. George put them on the grill first—in a minute you can have one with plenty of fancy diced onions I julienned for you with the hot mustard like you like," she gave a motherly smile.

I can't believe I'm smiling over a Red Hot. Where is all of this love coming from? So it takes Zachary getting man-handled, moreover our son's being scared to death seeing their father being stripped of all of his dignity fighting for his life, for her to have an epiphany?

Regi's expressions fill the room with curiosity.

Her mother-in-law goes on to endear, "You go rest by the pool. Let me have my time with *my babies*—"

Your babies? This term of blandishment startled Regi, as her mother-in-law would not willingly spend time with them in the past, only purely out of obligation—holidays and such.

Her mother-in-law grabbed Reg's hands, bringing her into the family home.

"How are you?" she asked Regi, her eyes riddled with an unfamiliar compassion.

"Well, I was fine until I heard what happened. I knew this day would come, no matter how we had prepared for it, you can never get your head around understanding pure hate."

Her mother-in-law handed her a Kleenex.

"Regi, I'm sorry for how I have always treated you. You are strong, intelligent, most of all you are absolutely beautiful through and through. You are such a gift to my son. I just had a different vision for him, truthfully it has taken me a long time to trust that I have to let my vision go. I prayed for him to have a loving, gorgeous wife and you are just that, and then some—a true gift from God."

Suzanne came in closer, placing her arm around Regi, "I see a lot of what I could have been in you. To be honest, I've always been a little jealous of all you have overcome. You're strong and ambitious. I love you. I want you to know that, I just did not know how to show it."

Regi looked about. Her mother-in-law is curious about Regi's demeanor.

"Girl, I'm bearing my soul to you. Why are you looking around? What are you looking at?"

"I'm looking for the cameras because I'm being *punked, right?*," Regi jokingly snapped back—the women embraced.

"Make me one promise—" Regi pleaded.

"Go on, girl—" Suzanne's willing heart agreed.

"Promise me that you will show up, regardless of your wavering feelings for me, for those little boys out there. Show up for each and every holiday, school play, their basketball games, let's not forget flag football—"

"Shh, girl—I'm already there," the woman embraced her daughter-in-love sincerely for the first time.

Zachary walked in, with Troublemaker—his eyes felt like they were being deceived.

My mom and wife hugging? he thought as he could not wrap his mind around what he was seeing. This was what he'd prayed for ever since they said, *"I Do," almost a decade ago.*

Zachary stepped back for a trice, letting the women envelope in each other's presence.

"Regi, you could not keep me away from my grandbabies," Suzanne said lovingly of the daughter she adopted in her heart, instead of her head.

"Thank you, mom." Regi grabbed her mother-in-law's hand, they walked towards the back yard where their innocent children frolicked in the pool, oblivious of how their worlds from this point on would never be the same, a piece of their innocent childhood stripped from them from the event that occurred on this day.

Zachary slipped out the sliding back door, to help his stepfather manhandle the grill.

"Regi, my beautiful daughter in law, come on by the pool, so we can relax. George will fetch us some lemonade. Hell scratch that, we need a drink. George, open up that bottle of West African Riesling. We shipped a crate back, when we visited Mali last year—"

"You visited Mali?" Regi's heart fluttered.

"Yes, I just had too when my grandson *schooled* me on Mansa Musa from Mali. They'd shared with me about the wealthiest person in history from the books that you bought them. I was moved by their passion to know more about their heritage. So by being the grandmother of these handsome brilliant young dynamic men, I told George to book our flight, so we went."

Regi was astonished, as weights lifted off of her body—her lungs filled her chest cavity for once since she said "I do" to the love of her life; she had no idea that her mother-in-law had any vested interest in the beauty of melanin.

The now endeared ladies clutched endeared hands as they were seated by the pool, attempting to hide themselves from the youthful splashes from their boys.

"Make sure that little stinker doesn't shit on my alpaca rug. Pick him up, Zachary!" his step-father demanded, the pup was retrieved from the sun room.

The pool house was always fixed up for guests. Regi's mother-in-law was insistent that their family stayed over—they obliged.

Regi sent out a high-level text, letting The She Declares Crew know what her family had endured while she was away.

:Are you all okay? Do you need anything? Sean and I are here for you all!—Anjali

:What in the world? This is so crazy. My uncle was a police officer, he served with honor until retirement. He is turning over in his grave about what happened to Zachary and your boys.—Penelope

:You have got to be kidding me. I'm taking my earrings off; got my sneakers on with some Vaseline on my face. Coming over right now, I mean it!—Chaka

:We are at my mother-in-law's. Thank you, ladies. We are fine. Just wanted you to know, to keep our family in your prayers.—Regi

:What? You are at your mother-in-law's? Yep, hell must have frozen over.—Chaka

:Sweetie, let me know if you need anything. I mean anything. I'm her for you!—Dr. Sophia Clark

:Let your voice be heard. I'm your platform anytime you need it! Acts like this have to stop right now!—Abby

In that very instant, hanging under the dark cloud of the injustice that had occurred that day, the Hinson's had truly become a family. In the weeks to come, the news was flooded with the incident and the officer was put on administrative leave. Ultimately, his tainted badge was taken due to that occurrence—a multitude of complaints

348

that had been on that particular officer surfaced. Judge Reynolds, Judge Regi Hinson, and her mother-in-law held news conferences on the subject of diversity, equity, and inclusion. Discrimination was not going to be tolerated in the township. Although the recent tornadic event crippled the community, there was a new declaration pronounced over the population. This would require acts of sacrifice, heroism and excellence for all who lived in that space.

34

THE PODCAST

"TURN UP THE VOLUME!"

[FOCUS ON AMPLIFYING POSITIVITY...]

Hi Weight Breakers,

There has been a lot of talk about race. Let's not just talk about change, let's put our strategies into action. In the studio we have your sister's-in-love and peace; Judge Regina Hinson with Abigail Lancaster. This is a special segment about turning up the volume. Hello, ladies.

"Hello," the panel of women replied.

Ladies, in light of recent unrest that has occurred. We are going to talk about turning up the volume in our lives. We have to be proud of who we are. We are talking about positive things; nothing negative. Turning up the volume will cause you to *leave it all on the court.* Regarding your life—*Go Hard or Go Home*; both are common phrases that are known in the world of athleticism. There are many authors that claim this is their phrase. Yet, it is aligned with the goals of this week. We are going to go from being timid about taking the next step to Turning Up The Volume on our gifts and what is important for our communities.

In this segment, the nuggets that we are going to discuss are—how we are going to: Change the narrative; Amplify positivity; Hold on to all that is good within you; Shadow greatness; Honor your assignment; Walk with gratitude and empathy; and Emulate God's love. Judge Hinson, what's on your mind?

"Well, most of you know what has occurred within my family. My husband, who is Caucasian, was arrested for attempting to assist a homeless man of color, when he was trying to get the attention of the police officer. The police officer found out that our brown sons, who were there with him, were actually his biological children. That is when the arrest occurred."

Wow, that is unbelievable—especially in this day and age. This is so crazy.

"Yes, we are still pretty shaken up about it. Our sons still have night terrors about what took place."

What can we do, Judge Regi Hinson, to make a difference? We can really go deep within this conversation. There are many platforms in which I will choose to do so, so I want you to first check your feelings, realizing that we are all in this together moreover that we have to be kind to one another, loving others as God loves us. And we have to realize that we are all God's creation.

Dr. T. shared; in her eyes you could tell she was disturbed as to what her friend's family had endured.

"I'm encouraging your listeners to turn up the volume on these continued instances in which people are discriminated against because of the color of their skin, or because their culture is different."

"Yes, as soon as I heard, I was so disappointed once again in mankind. God has placed red blood in us that flows throughout our body. We are all one humankind. The sooner that we realize that, the better," Abby reached for the ladies, they locked hands, as the comments began to roll in…

:Kudos to you as you have a lot of diversity and inclusion efforts upcoming for the community partnership with The Chronicles Of The Weight Breakers Podcast as a result of this incident and to follow up on the conference. What happened to your husband has caused a lot of sleepless nights for the public-at-large; we stand right behind you, thank you for shedding light on this issue in our world. It is catastrophic what is going on!—A Loyal Listener

"I see your comment Loyal Listener, we are so grateful for your support. It is always a little easier to remain disciplined in any approach when you are aligned with people that will help encourage you to expand your thinking—to be considerate of others. Surround yourself with those people. Who are they in your lives? Reach out to them, sharing your vision for yourself, along with the role you wish for them to play in that discipline. These are what you call, *Your Accountability Partners!* Then, I encourage you to seek out opportunities in which you can educate as well. Hopefully, we can manifest dreams of a place in which all individuals are judged based on the content of their character, not the color of their skin," Regi blotted her tears.

"Agreed, we can put this in our T.I.P.s practices each day. Caring for others should be placed on our calendars. Make a concerted effort to learn more about different backgrounds, along with the struggles of different cultures," Abigail added.

If you are a Weight Breaker, you are a person who desires to learn about different cultures—and are willing to be kind and generous to those around you. Everybody has their own journey, so we cannot judge anyone. People are going through things that they never reveal, that you may have no idea about, so be quick to listen and slow to speak. And quick to give grace, and slow to judge.

"Shift your gears a little, plan a way to control your forecast—how you are going to walk out how considerate you are going to be in life. Take action because action speaks volumes—talk is cheap. When you see something that needs to be

351

improved, don't wait for another to take the initiative—you be the change in the world that you want to see (author unknown). There are strategies that you have to initiate within your societies in order to work on your forecast—how you perceive the future. As we all know, the standard definition of forecast is the prediction of future or trend. If I was going to allow the weight of life to continue to weigh me down, the forecast would be bitterness; fear of moving forward. There was an epiphany when I realized what I needed to do to make some changes. I knew I had to take action. In analyzing that word these three letters are A.C.T. I needed to act, in order to impact not only our health and wellness, more importantly our streets, neighborhoods, townships, villages, counties, states and our world. We must all do better."

Abby's candor is refreshing, unlike her usual stoic self.

Weight Breakers, The Abigail Lancaster and Judge Regina Hinson will be holding public forums, in addition to news briefings on how to help with the healing of our land—our community. We are to talk about how to turn up the volume in your life is to find greatness, understand it or stand under it. Additionally, you have got to protect yourself; your time. When you are able to do that, you tend to the process of building stronger healthier relationships. By changing your mind about how you approach your life, know that you will have some ups and downs. There will be weeks in which the proverbial/physical weights of life will pound on our mind, body, and spirit. In the midst of it all, know that you can let the situation or issue take you out, or you can look at it as a catalyst for all you are building: your vision muscle, your faith muscle, and don't forget your resilience muscle. Let's Go!

"Weight Breakers, we need to take a risk. Do not get turned all the way up at things that you cannot control; things that really don't matter. Be determined to be nimble and agile throughout life," Abby proclaimed to prompt change.

"May I add, that in this Turn the Volume Up: Episode, we want the listeners to treat your persistence like it is the bull's eye of each of your adventures, dreams, goals, along with your efforts. It is important to journal about how you are going to do this. You can read all of the motivational books on the market, do all of the online courses that are possible, however if persistence is not your target, it is a moot effort. Write all around the target, with the wit, that persistence is the goal (not the task), all of the efforts that you are working on. It could be weight, family enhancement, breaking down social injustice or whatever your heart desires. Persistence is the target! Abigail, you look like you have more to add." Regi passionately shared.

"Yes, indeed. In any given leadership position, in addition to doing your job, if you are seeking a promotion, then you are going to have to illustrate stretching your capability. I'm not inferring that you should work outside of your scope but be able to illustrate that you can expound upon your leadership skills and your talents. Think about how you can stretch your health and wellness. If you have hypertension, set blood pressure goals. If you are diabetic, have personal blood sugar goals—personally, I wish I would have taken my health as seriously as my career. Many times, we hesitate, getting stuck when challenges present themselves to us. We must change our perspective about challenges, diagnosis, or uphill battles. Start viewing challenges as a way to perfect your game—enhancing our wellbeing. The more you stretch yourself, the more opportunities for growth. Even more so—when injustice rears its ugly head—say something. Also, it is so important that you do something!" Abby noticed Regi's emotion with tension in her hands as she made a fist, seated next to her.

BAM!

Regi pounded the table with transparent frustration of what her family had recently gone through.

"Yes, we have got to do something about those inequities. I know we have a broad topic today, so thank you for being patient with me, as I feel that I have a wealth of resources that can assist you in not only equality, but your health as well. Dr. T. and Abigail are absolutely correct, regarding those health examples, first seek the counsel of your healthcare providers to expand on what you shared. We have to walk with empathy! Establish a space at home, where you can take private time and at work. At home, it is my home office or an early morning walk where I can listen to my gospel or gangster rap. Near the courthouse, there is a nice trail and parking lot outside that I use to get away for a moment to collect my thoughts. I've had to use that space to exhale from all that my family is going through now."

Weight Breakers, we have to continue to expound upon those tranquil walks for your self-care—keep it up. When I relax—my mind is sharper. In all transparency, I'm a better version of myself. More capable of walking in gratitude. The more grateful you are, the more capable you are to show empathy to one another. The *stinking ridiculous thinking* has to stop in order to break the cycle. You are so close to your calling, your breakthrough, to your next level—why stop now?

Break the cycle of the "fear of success" or what I like to call, *the almost factor*. Each one of us has a gift, a message, a word of inspiration to share, in which fear has no place. Revelation is a way that your body receives information, and we use revelation as a beacon to help us in our life walk. This innate sense prevents us from going down a path that could be harmful. So trust in the revelation that God gives you. Moreover, as a Weight Breaker, we listen to those revelations, that are revealed—and do not fear.

Dr. T. imparted into Regi's spirit.

"Thank you Dr. T. and The Chronicles of The Weight Breakers listeners. I'm just still shaken up," Regi whispered.

We got you, girl. Please know that your community has your back as well!

Abby leaned into the microphone, "Agreed, Regi, we have your back—no doubt. However, I have to ask, Gospel and Gangster Rap? Regi, interesting combination."

She probed, looking perplexed, then smirked with a side-eye.

"Yes, ma'am, I love them both. Enough about that, we do not want to deflect," Regi shared.

Let's turn up the volume regarding the cost of not being resilient. What outcome can that have? The list is small, yet simple: depression; regret; anger; unfulfillment; deflection; and ongoing pain. Furthermore, wasted time can be a byproduct. We are no longer going to put our resilience on the shelf. It is to be worn with great pride, like a battle scar, that causes us the capability to embark upon the many horizons that await us on the journey of life.

With hate taking up space in your heart, you are not living your best life. Ruminate about one of those experiences in which you felt that the world was not being kind to you. Or when you put in a place that should have broken you down. It could have resulted in a loss or a setback. Let's change our perspective, consider the friction that a diamond experiences to transform into brilliance. Change your mind about the friction ridges, difficulties, and turmoil that come your way. There is an old excerpt, not sure of the author, *that whatever doesn't kill you only makes you stronger.* Share a testimony about your *friction ridges* that you have gone through that will be a lesson of encouragement; even a testimony for others. I know you are listening out there, Dr. Sparrow Mack, please forgive me for *high-jacking* your New York Times acclaimed box office hit, *Friction Ridges*. Nonetheless, that phrase is appropriate to what we are talking about,

:Love you all. Regi, we are here for you and your family. Moreover, justice will be served. Dr. T., thank you for the shout-out!—Dr. Sparrow Mack

Look at Dr. Sparrow Mack the author is listening in, thank you for your support. Furthermore, if you have hatred in your heart, it is hindering all the potential that you have. In addition, for all that you have overcome, know that God has so much more in store for you—and that will not manifest with discriminatory, mean or a hateful heart.

Weight Breaker's approach everything with love, so they can turn up the volume in their life. By this focus, they truly understand that we are all in this together—we were built to love. So what do I mean by that? We were built with two arms to help one another; two feet to walk beside each other; one heart to care for one another; two eyes to see how we can help one another, moreover one mouth to share words of encouragement, that is not a Dr. T. original, however a well-known proclamation.

Dr. T. added with endearment. The Weight Breakers in the studio were pure support for each other.

"Agreed. The best way for us to turn up the volume, Weight Breakers, is to emulate God's love! What is the best way that you can elaborate on the gifts that you have within you? You have cells, you have blood, you have organs, you have nerves, you have muscles, that's a part of your rhythm you need to work in sync. Take a moment, understanding the actual beauty of that gift that is truly priceless. Those all formed to cause you to be born, with robust cells within each component have a sense of rebirth; regeneration to cause you to function. Emulate God's love for you, by using your gift of life to bless one another, not tear one another down," Abigail's usual snarl is softened.

Dr. T. turned towards Regi, she asked her,

Judge Regina Hinson, thank you for being so transparent today. We are going to begin to wrap this podcast up. Do you have any closing comments or additional wisdom to impart?

Regi wiped a tear from her eye, got comfortable in her chair, took off her shoes seated on folded legs—leaned into the microphone.

"I'm going to leave you with one word, that is the foundation of our beliefs as people. As a child, I believe that we all can attest to having the experience with arts and crafts with wooden popsicle sticks. In art, in class, scouts or any youth camps, popsicle sticks were the go-to keep any of us entertained for hours on end. We would see if we could build houses, farms, stores, or even fences to keep our pretend livestock enclosed. Regardless of how much Elmer's Glue we used to mount down our building, if there was not a good crisscross or overlap foundation, all of our hard work was for not because our little masterful building would collapse to smithereens. If our foundation is not love for one another, our souls will collapse. We must work on that as a society. Our foundation is this world must be love," Regi disclosed, having flashbacks of what her family went through.

Abigail sensed Regi's horrific recollection. She uttered to her sister,

"Regi, we got you. You and your family are noble individuals—your community stands beside you. We are your arsenal of support. That is why it is so good to have a good sounding board that you have in your resource of people who can encourage you. There are some that you can talk to about your job and career goals, there are some that you can talk to about your home life, with your children. You will know which person to talk with about which issue, based on that person's background, furthermore how they've shown up for you in the past. That connection can ground you to deal with *the elephants* that intrude upon your life or how you make them more than what they should be."

Abby exuded solidarity.

Weight Breakers, journal on how you plan to Turn up The Volume and Change the Narrative of how you are walking out your life. Write out how you are going to turn up the volume—living out loud, to thinking like a Weight Breaker, Not a Weight Taker. Transform the narrative, amplify positivity, while holding onto all that is good within you. Shadow greatness, honor your assignment, walk with gratitude and empathy, in addition emulate God's love.

Dr. T. attempted to close out the session, when Regi solicited to add one last comment,

"Weight Breakers, once again, walk into your greatness—you are the only you, you've got. Love yourself to the fullest. Please remember that we are our sister's keepers; moreover, we are our brother's keepers, we are our children's keepers, we are each other's keeper—so we must love each other. We are all one kind, that is humankind. As a judge, that is what I attempt to do each day—in full transparency, the injustice imposed upon my husband and our son's—illustrates that there is a huge gap in humankind. We all must do better to turn up the volume, while focusing on amplifying positivity. Dr. T. or Abby, would you like to add any additional commentary? "

Abby rubbed her friend's back—shaking her head, *NO.*

Well, there you have it. Thank you, Judge Regina Hinson and The Abigail Lancaster, for this crucial candid discussion. I encourage the listeners, as with all of my podcasts, please go back and listen to the tactics to impact the positivity in your life. Moreover, remember to love one another as God loves us.

Love, Dr. T.

Dr. T. signed off and the ladies embraced. They established sidebar conversations about orchestrating think takes to discuss strategies to assist the city council to talk about diversity; equity, and inclusion.

:Sending you all hugs. I see you, Regi; Abby. My *She Declares* Sisters!—Anjali N.

:I'm all over it. I'm sending a crew over to the community rally. We love you, girl to the moon and back!—Penelope K.

:Nobody is going to mess with our nephews—I mean that! We got you, girl!—Chaka B.

:We have got to address this head on. Enough is enough. We are all human beings, equally valuable in God's eyes.—A Loyal Listener

36

ANJALI'S SONG

"A.J. LIVE'S HERE NO MORE!"

[WALKING IN HER TRUTH & WEARING HER TRUTH]

"Mom, I'm on my way over. I have an executive meeting in the morning. I need something to wear," Anjali said as she was vowing to walk out of the high-rise office, she turned up her volume on how she could amplify her positivity, along with her uniqueness.

"Yes, my darling. I'm home, Come on by."

"I'm bringing someone very important. Is that okay?"

"Oh, I have to vacuum..."

"No, Mom. Your house is always spotless. This person is more like family."

"I look forward to it, darling. I'll have food. Will your guests like that? How about Malai Kofta?"

How in the world could she have guessed that Sean's favorite is Malia Kofta?

Hand in hand, Anjali walked Sean up to the door of Anjali's family home—she nervously bit her lip. Her palms sweaty, while her gut thundered for the surprise visit to see her mom, introducing the love of her life to the matriarch.

Anjali, you've got this, no throwing up. Just breathe.

The door opened.

"Sean, it is so good to finally meet you officially!" Anjali's mother grabbed him with her full loving arms draped in a sari—she pulled his beautiful melanin-infused skin towards her face. She planted endeared kisses on both of his cheeks.

357

"You remind me of my brother," her mother shared while looking into Sean's soul.

Anjali's eyes were full of astonishment.

Damn, how did Mom know?

She turned towards her mom, whose forehead was adorned with a Bindi,

"Mom, how did you—?"

"A mother always knows," her mother interrupts in a soft tone.

"Here, love." She bent down, removed Sean's shoes. She took his hand, sat him at the head of the table where her father used to sit.

"Give me your hands." She wiped his palms with a warm, mint infused wash towel. The cleansing seemed to remove all of the angst surrounding what the meeting would finally be.

At that moment, Anjali got full permission to become—Anjali.

The trio ate, laughed, the icing on the cake was that Sean was told stories of *the old country*— how her mother grew up. He heard some stories about Anjali's childhood, including some embarrassing ones. It was a most momentous occasion.

Her mother *knew* that Sean liked to watch basketball. After the delicious authentic Indian cuisine, Anjali's mother leaned in to Sean,

"My dear, I have a cold beer ready for you—follow me," Sean smiled. Sean was positioned lovingly in Anjali's late father's recliner. He willingly propped up his feet, while her mother's aged hands placed the remote in his palm.

Anjali left Sean in the living room, hollering at his team to, *Man up on defense*, like her father used to.

The women smiled. "Mom, he sounds like dad—*right?*" her mother agreed, while beckoning her daughter towards the master bedroom. The closet doors opened, Anjali's eyes were that of a little youngster,

I remembered all of these beautiful garments my mother used to wear.

Just beautiful, she thought as if she were that little girl with cold dark ringlets strolling down her back.

"You need something to wear for a big meeting? I have a couple of suits, but not sure if they're your style. They're a little outdated."

"No, Mom, I want to wear this—"

Her mother was baffled. "You want to wear a sari?"

"Yes, Mother, it's time they found out who Anjali really is. A.J. is gone. The purple one—it's perfect."

The women embraced.

"As you say, do you think they're ready for all of that?"

"Well, if they're not, they need to get ready!"

The women chuckled.

"Momma, grab the nose ring, along with henna," Anjali spoke with confidence.

"You've said nothing but a word. Follow me," Anjali fell in formation behind the regal matriarch to the sitting area of the matriarch master suite.

"Anjali, trust me when I tell you that it pained me to see you attempt to hide your true culture like it was a scar that you were ashamed of. I attempted to push our culture on you, especially after your father passed—I was so afraid that our legacy would be lost, buried with him. I did so out of love, for you to understand the brilliance of you, however the reverse happened—you despised yourself. My love, I'm sorry for that. I believe in this culture they say, *When you know better, you do better.*"

Anjali smiled; her eyes wet with joyful tears of finally being seen by her mother.

"Wipe your eyes darling, you've tapped into a power source that is mighty, your uniqueness. In the discomfort that you've gone through, all along know that God was protecting you. Give me your hand, my love—"

Anjali was adorned by her mother as her mother placed Mehndi designs over her hands, draped up to her forearms. Her mother shared more familiar stories that were familiar, endeared to Anjali's heart. Her mother's melodic voice, sang songs of old…

"Remember this one, my darling?" Anjali's mother started to sing to her daughter what she liked to call *Anjali's Song* when she was a little girl. She informed her that she approved of Sean. It was a beautiful encounter.

"Another thing, I have a card for you. One of the ladies down at the library gave it to me. It's Dr. Sophia Clark—I believe that she can help you with what you do in the restroom when you get anxious—"

"But mom, how?" Anjali was baffled by how her mother knew about her bulimia.

"A mother knows—" is all that she said, as she retrieved the garment bag to house the sari in.

The next morning, Anjali's svelte-legged with her red bottoms, skinny slacks draped over by a vibrant purple sari that adorned her shoulders, exposed her henna-tattooed arms. Her tress, that had been highlighted to blend in, showed her thick brunette beautiful ringlets. Her face was accented with a nose ring. Embodied with all the sacrifices she'd made, her heroism draped around her body, along with her acumen of excellence she shamelessly marched into the high-rise office building, her briefcase in tow. In the cold boardroom, she established a new atmosphere—taking her rightful position at the head table. Jaws dropped at the aura that she gave. With her head held high, she looked at her peers, they looked back honoring the Bindi adorning her forehead.

"What does Anjali have on?" were murmurings that she heard when she entered the room—her colleagues were all a little taken aback by her authentic appearance.

She stood when it was her turn—wowed the client. Anjali negotiated a hefty package for the company. More importantly, her consumer was happy.

"We will only secure this deal, if we work directly with Anjali. Winston, make that happen!" The Bollinger C.E.O. demanded.

With Anjali's proposal, Winston Chase looked over at the client, knuckling at the table. A stern look overwhelmed his face. He stood,

CLAP!

CLAP!

CLAP!

CLAP!

CLAP!

"Anjali, now that's what I'm talking about. The contract is yours—Great Work! Bollinger, let's put ink to the deal!" Winston Chase stood at the front of the high-rise boardroom.

Anjali smiled.

Her boss then announced,

"Scott, you will be working as Anjali's assistant on this contract. Take notes, you can learn a thing from her!"

Scott's opulent ego was deflated—he shrank in his chair, fuming.

Anjali's song sealed the deal, she was no longer *the chameleon.*

37

THE PODCAST

"REFRESH YOUR SYSTEMS CHALLENGE"

[YOUR BODY IS WORKING HARD FOR YOU!]

Hi Weight Breakers,

Yes, it is that time of year again. I had my mammogram last week—it was normal, praise God. I will continue to get mammograms each year. I wanted to take a moment to chat with you before my early morning annual general physical examination.

   GROWL!

Pardon my stomach, as you may hear my stomach talking to me, due to me fasting since last night for my annual labs.

Just to recap, regularly you have been posting your: daily decision downloads; working on implementing the T.I.P.s; sharing the intelligences activities; getting your new mindset together; taking inventory and taking action in your life; looking into how you are checking your connectivity; figuring out how to download deep activities; try to find unique ways to upgrade your thought process; and furthermore you have been keeping the *B.S.* out—by implementing your firewalls.

I see you, Weight Breakers. Kudos! I've seen how you have taken time out to put your surroundings in silence mode. I'm loving the pictures of the turn up the volume challenge you all are participating in. You ladies are amazing.

The foundation of THE CHRONICLES OF THE WEIGHT BREAKERS CONFERENCE was about taking care of Y.O.U.—to yield optimal understanding regarding the magnificent existence that you are.

   Dr. T. arrived at the doctor's office for her annual checkup. She pulled into the parking lot, got out of the car, and walked towards the entrance of the medical office.

So, ladies, we cannot forget our body systems that are at work to graciously move us through life. Your care for your systems are like love letters to them. Yes, it is that deep. Poor health habits, excessive self-sabotaging lifestyle, lack of exercise, putting self-care on the back burner, can wreak havoc on our body systems. Both types of weights can take a toll on our mind, body, spirit; most of all our body systems.

Look the scale in the face and speak to it. Imagine yourself telling your physical weight this, "*You* crept up on all of us like a thief in the night, you are no longer welcome! In our minds, you store the mires of life's unfavorable encounters that we have experienced; you stay there weighing us down—clouding our minds. You are driven by the purpose to keep us from progression, causing us to focus on lack, not all the blessings that have been planted deep within our core. You have to find a new address, because a Weight Breaker lives here now!"

Having a disregard for yourself, can lead to: high blood pressure; stroke; diabetes; depression and so many more disease processes.

Dr. T. held up a card,

You see here; I brought my blood pressure log with me to share with my doctor. I always like to jot down my blood pressure and pulse. This will allow the doctor to see how well controlled my hypertension is on the medication that has been prescribed. When I first was diagnosed with high blood pressure, I was on two medications. However, now that I am a weight breaker, I've lost thirty pounds—down to one medication. My goal is to get off all blood pressure medications, ultimately controlling it with a healthy diet with exercise.

My strategy is: Word; Water and Walking—I call it the 3W approach. I did a podcast on this recently, however to recap—my "word" is to read my bible or devotional daily; healthy hydration; and ambulation. Those are the principles I use to get me through my day!

Dr. T. shared a photograph of her "before" implementing those healthy habits and after, to motivate the listeners.

You see my before picture right here; I look totally different. Although, I have a long way to go, at least I'm not where I used to be. Ladies, with small *itty-bitty steps*, you are committed to the practices in my book, *Think Like A Weight Breaker. Not Like A Weight Taker.* I've made the modifications to shift my mindset. My physical weight pounced on me because I made poor choices in self-care.

Imagine this, that you are the healthiest you have ever been. Now ponder there is *an unhealthy you* facing *your healthy you. Your unhealthy you*, is beating you down, not giving *the healthy you* a chance. That is what is happening when we straddle the fence, when we call ourselves working out, then consciously make unhealthy choices. We are counterproductive, undoing all that we have invested. In short, beating ourselves up!

Dr. T. put a poem in the chat that she'd written,

Okay, ladies, let me share this little poem that I wrote about weight, here it goes:
"Weight before I knew it, you enveloped our entire beings—resting heavy on our backs, at times making movement almost impossible. Because of you, we had to buy more clothes because of our expanding waistlines. We have ducked and dodged meaningful moments of life, as you've thrown darts at our self-esteem—we were scared to show up. You caused us to become so creative, so we could camouflage you by wearing all black—sucking it in until we almost passed out. Even though we despise you, you've not always been unwelcomed. In some instances, you've comforted us to keep us warm as we drown our sorrows in the platitudes of life. Ultimately, the highs of life, along with the consumption of delights that you magnetically drew to our senses, caused us to devour them endlessly—that's so not fair. Although you provided us some good by being what we needed to finally carry healthy pregnancies to term, allowing our phenomenal children to be birthed into the world—we are holding you accountable for the collateral damage you've caused. You, both sides of weight, have caused all of us reading these words, distraction, depression, discrimination, heartache, with multiple sleepless nights. I am a weight breaker, no longer a weight taker—therefore the hold that you had on me is no more."

Dr. T. smiled, finally feeling good about going to the doctor's office for once in a long time, pleased with the progress that she had made, and so happy that she was able to share the words of the poem with her listeners. She placed in the chat information on how physical weight can cause diabetes, hypertension, heart disease, as well as so many other health issues. In addition, how both of the types of weights place a tremendous amount of stress on the body.

Ladies, check out the information in the chat that illustrates how powerful your body systems are. Do you understand how much is going on in a fine-tuned concert at once in your body? Your heart is beating. Your lungs are working to bring you oxygen, as well as blowing out CO_2. Your neurons are working, creating synapses, leading to the capability to move. Your muscles are contracting as well as relaxing so you can move, walk, while sitting up straight. Also, while you read eyes to *Think Like A Weight Breaker. Not Like A Weight Taker*, your ocular muscles are hard at work. It is all one magical concert of movement, responses—overall life. You are a force of nature to be reckoned with. This is your time to reflect daily, or however often you deem appropriate, to truly realize the importance of your health systems working on your behalf. When you are able to do that, you will be more mindful as to how you allow the proverbial weight of life to impart in your space; the daily decisions to allow physical weight to put strain on your body. We are going to go from taking our body systems for granted, to cherishing them with The Refresh Systems challenges. The Refresh Systems Challenge is simple: be aware of how hard your systems are working to keep you alive, show them some love, and take some of the weight off of them.

:This is so good—I'm going to start the "3W" approach for sure! I needed to hear this! She Declares Crew, tune in.—Penelope K.

:I'm going to follow up on my biopsy. Pray for me, Sisters.—Fawn P.

Penelope and Fawn, we are with you. Thank you for tuning in. We are praying for you Fawn; we claim full healing for you—God's got you!

Now, we are going to walk through how important your circulatory system is. Not just doing cardiovascular exercise to fit into a bikini or take a *bomb-ass selfie*, but committing to small changes to live our best, healthiest life.

:Let's take care of our hearts.—Regi H.

Okay, ladies, we have a Weight Breaker Refresh Circulatory Challenge: Feel your wrist with about two finger breadths away from the crease that connects your hands to your arm; that is your radial pulse. You have pulses all over your body; all of those pulses come from your beautiful heart. Feel that pulse—give thanks for its wonderful presence.

:I'm taking a deep breath now, feeling my pulse. I'm connecting with myself, celebrating my culture. I'm going to do a better job of getting my cardio in to strike that balance.—Anjali N.

Anjali, I see you in the comments. Not only do you work out your heart with cardio, but you also have two beautiful lungs that take in oxygen. That oxygen penetrates your blood cells to provide oxygen to all of your organs. Your lungs are priceless jewels. Our lungs are invaluable. They expand, inhale to take in the breath of life; as if on cue they're able to exhale CO_2.

:I've got to stop smoking. I was thinking about calling my doctor to help with that. Picking up the phone to make an appointment now.—April C.

That is so great, April. Yes, continued tobacco use can have a huge impact on your lung quality. You are doing the right thing by speaking with your doctor to discuss options to assist with smoking cessation. Now, ladies, take your hand, put it in front of your mouth. Say this phrase: *Be of Service*. You will notice that air will force out onto your hand. We take for granted the importance of our lungs when we speak, saying words. Let's go a little deeper, being mindful of the words that you speak. They're imparted upon from your lips, with the help of your precious lungs. Speaking words of power to yourself, over your life, you are more likely to achieve those goals. If you speak words that are not aligned with positive thinking, you will attract negative energy from negative people. Let the words that your lungs work so hard to manifest be a momentum for wonderous change; a magnificent service to the world.

:Preach, *Sista*!—Chaka B.

:You are so right. I stopped smoking after 20 years. I'm now able to play more with my grandchildren, I feel so much better. I'm not short of breath.—Exodus R.

Weight Breakers, I love your comments; I am so inspired.—Exodus I see you. Now, let's talk about your gut; digestive system. Your mouth, esophagus, stomach, small bowel, your colon—large bowel—are responsible for breaking down the food, causing the nutrients to be absorbed in your body. It is well known that a healthy gut is aligned with your immune system as well. Limiting our indulgent behavior, minimizing junk food, this is to draw positive attention to your gut, and love it to the point of honoring it by what you put into it.

:My stomach is always in knots. I have a lot of stress. I'm going for my physical next month. Thank you for this information.—A Loyal Listener

Yes, please get your annual physicals; go to the doctor as needed. Your body will give you signals when something is not correct. Make adjustments in your diet, based on not only the food's nutritional value, moreover how the food makes you feel.

:Every time I eat dairy, my stomach suffers so much. I'm going to the doctor to get checked out.—Mila D.

Yes, Mila, please get checked out. You may be lactose intolerant, furthermore you may have to adjust your diet. However, be mindful that you must get adequate rest. Adequate sleep causes you to recharge for your day, which has a positive impact on your health, including your digestive system. And please get your colonoscopy as your doctor recommends. Especially, if you have a family history of colon cancer. Any changes in your stool should be discussed with your doctor. You know your body.

:I love to eat. However, sometimes I over indulge, eating the wrong type of food. I will make an effort to do better.—Peggy A.

:Me too. I'm going to get my screening colonoscopy. My cousin died of colon cancer. Thank you for suggesting this!—Indigo M.

That is great news, call and schedule it right now! Also, making healthy eating choices is key!

Okay ladies, next we have the excretory system—it is a part of your body's ability to rid itself of waste. Furthermore, it is well known that this system is necessary to filter out the bodily fluids you have. It deals with water regulation. This *bad-ass system* will remove those products from the body fluids, to help the body.

:I never heard of this system.—Rachel N.

:Yep, this is how we sweat.—Rhonda B.

Many people have not heard of this system. Your excretory system works hard to remove excess, unnecessary materials, toxins from your body. It keeps you in good balance by filtering your blood—removing contaminants. The major players are: two kidneys, along with your bladder. Drinking water and eating healthy foods help this system. The supporting cast for the excretory system are: skin, lungs, gut, nails and hair. Collectively working together to make sure that toxins *hit the highway*—exiting your body. There may be times, from emotional despair, the weights of the world will cause mounting pressures to work against this system.

:I'm going to eat healthy, exercise, drink water, moreover attempt to destress as much as possible.—Amber H.

:I love how you are making our body systems talk to us. This is really resonating with me, the importance of doing a better job of self-care.—Ginger C.

Ladies, I see all the comments. You've got this! Let's talk about your nervous system; known as your central nervous system. It is composed of two big players: your brain and your spinal cord. A multitude of nerves that infiltrate your magnificent body. Nerves permeate your organs to cause them to work. This whole approach to a healthy nervous system is not to dance and party all night long, but to have a healthy lifestyle. In all of my medical books, it has been shown that you have at least seven trillion nerves in your body. Did you get that you're a *trillionaire-of nerves!* So, when someone says, *you're getting on my last nerve*, that is incorrect! Your nervous system causes you to think, move, feel by transmitting from neurons to nerves to your muscles as well as organs. Emotional despair, holding on to the despairs of the weights of the world can cause mounting pressures to work against this system. If there are impairments, lack of blood flow or a blockage, it can cause a stroke. Some signs of stroke are FAST (Facial drooping, Arm weakness, in addition to Speech Difficulties. Time to call 9-1-1 *A.S.A.P!)* This is messaged out by the American Heart Association!

:My mother had a stroke. That is what prompted me to lose weight, get my blood pressure under control, to lose 50 pounds. Now I'm living my best life, eating healthy, exercising, drinking water, as well as distressing, working on my Vision, Faith and Resilient Intelligence!—Raina F.

Raina, you are such a motivation. Kudos, I'm so proud of you. This is what this podcast is all about, to encourage ladies that are *stuck* to release the weights. You have a billion neurons in your body that come together, synapse, to conduct the nerves, which result in you being able to do all of your activities. Google what all your nerves can perform. Make it a point to cherish your neurological system. Your eyes, when they're looking at this book, the light goes into your eye, landing on the retina. The retina absorbs the light into the cell within the retina that are photoreceptors. The light image goes into the optic nerve, traveling up to the brain to process what it is seeing as light or an image. All of this is going on simultaneously while you are doing the activities of daily living, is that not amazing?

:That is deep—pretty astounding. Had no idea all of that was a part of me seeing. I need to get my eyes checked. Scheduling my annual eye exam right now!—Tiffany S.

Great job, Tiffany. I also challenge you to take opportunities to challenge your mind, by reading, doing puzzles, and memorization. Your brain is the epicenter of your neurological center. I absolutely love being creative; writing. My mother loves crossword puzzles. Do something daily to sharpen your mind. Not knocking social media because I believe it is key for staying connected in this virtual world, but go old school. Write someone a letter that you have not seen lately. Pick up the phone and have a conversation instead of texting.

Also, clean air is good for your nervous system. It is so helpful to have a smoke-free environment for your body neurologically. If you are a smoker, speak with your healthcare professional about the impact smoking can have on your body. Deep breathing not only helps your lungs but your neurological system as well. Although there is a little angst about the uncertainty of walking into your purpose, it is as if there is a weight that is lifted when you are aligning with what you are supposed to be doing. Let's get out of our own way, take deep breaths. And get to work!

:Are men allowed to chat?—Dean Baby

Dean Baby, I see you in the chat. We want our men to be healthy and to refresh their systems daily as well!

:Awesome, this is the only body we have. Self-care is key. Proud of you, ladies, know that I am cheering for each of you! Don't forget to pick up The Chronicles of The Weight Breakers Lip stain!—Dean Baby

Thank you, Dean Baby, for your encouragement of the ladies, we will be giving away some gift bags, with *Think Like A Weight Breaker. Not Like A Weight Taker books,* journals and Chronicles of The Weight Breakers Lip Stains as well. I told you all this podcast was going to be *the bomb!*

Next is the Endocrine System, it is composed of several key players: thyroid, parathyroid (you have at least eight of them); hypothalamus, pituitary gland, pineal body, and finally, your adrenal glands. This system works hard to regulate your bodily functions, of metabolism, body temperature, vital signs, reproductive function, and sleep.

:I have Hashimoto's. I follow up with my endocrinologist every six months and my symptoms are controlled.—Natalie D.

That is amazing. Natalie, make sure you continue to get your labs done, and take your medication appropriately. Hashimoto's is an autoimmune thyroid condition. I will do an entire segment on that in the future. Ladies, our endocrine system is the powerhouse to your soul and metabolism. It's needed to get the things done that you need to complete! It is imperative that you are aligned with your energy source. How can you take care of your thyroid today? Diet, exercise, and adequate sleep.

Also, a part of this system are *two little gems*—on the top of your kidneys, that allow you to be able to respond to any given situation. Each of us has heard of *fight or flight*, right? Well, those little glands are called your adrenal glands—they secrete catecholamines that make you have that capability.

:I have heard of fight or flight.—Shirley M.

:I'd like to know about the immune system. I drink water, exercise and vitamin C, Zinc with Vitamin D daily.—Viola D.

You ladies are right on time because next up is the immune system—a very complex web of molecules and cells that battle on your behalf against infection. It is very smart and recognizes things that it has battled before; prepares to combat them again. So, how can you support your immune system? A healthy diet, exercise, stress reduction, and relaxation have a positive effect on your immune system. Remember that when you are stressing over little issues, cardio exercise is a great way to enhance it. You need your immune system to fight off bacterial, viral, and fungal infections. The healthier you are, the more equipped you are for unveiling your gift to the world.

:One of the most cost-efficient strategies to a healthy immune system is sleep, gratitude, hydration, optimism, movement, outdoor time nutrition, antioxidants, fiber and a positive environment.—Yana F.

:I believe that laughter is the best medicine for a healthy Immune System.—Dana Y.

Laugh. Laugh. Laugh—then laugh some more! It really is good medicine. Good for your overall health. Dana, you are so right. Weight Breakers, what makes you laugh? What tickles your funny bone? Is it a comedy, certain types of books, or that funny family member who is downright hilarious? By laughing, you're able to release tension and relax. This is more priceless than you realize. Not a forced or fake laugh, but a genuine laugh. Integrate that into your overall well-being. Laughing can create levity, lighten the atmosphere, making you not so anxious. There are molecules that turn over, dying off, and those that are born to manifest, supporting your body to meet a new day. By the relaxation that comes with laughter, you are creating a less tension filled environment in your body, helping support your immune system.

:Agreed. Laughter is my *secret sauce* on cutting down on stress.—Monica H.

:Rest is key in keeping healthy—Debbie Q.

:Not only rest, but good hygiene. Wash your hands, people! Key for immune health and wellness!—Ryder J.

All of this is so very true. Let's chat about the Integumentary System, better known as your skin. It's the largest organ that you have. It is the shelter and the vehicle that protects all of you. It is built up of layers that encase your priceless organs. So, please protect your skin from damage from the sun by sunscreen and moisturizing your skin.

:Ladies, make sure you have a good cleansing skin regimen. If you need any recommendations, please inbox me.—Dean Baby

Thank you, Dean Baby, for your expertise on skin care. He is right; a great skin regimen and protection are imperative for healthy skin.

:Dr. T., you are cracking me up with these body systems speaking to us. I love it. You know skin is my thing. However, I would like to make sure the ladies moisturize their skin regularly. Please make sure that is a part of your daily regimen.—Dean Baby

Dean Baby, you are preaching. So, the Weight Breaker Refresh Integumentary (skin) Challenge: Moisturize your skin. Dry skin can crack. Your skin is the largest organ of your body. It is the encasement that makes you a human being and it is what allows you to be unique with your culture. Your skin is beautiful. Regardless of race and culture, skin protection is very important. Moisturizing your skin and protection of your skin while in the sun. Use products and body wash that will moisturize your skin. Use sunscreen!

:Sometimes, we forget that our skin is actually an organ. Take care of it.—Janis J.

:I finally love the skin that I am in!—Anjali N.

Next is our beautiful Skeletal System. We are going to walk through how important your skeletal system is, as together we make incremental goals, system downloads in the encouragement pathway. This whole approach is about how to have healthy bones. The major function is to facilitate movement and support. It provides the storage of blood cells.

:I've also been lifting light weights per the recommendation of my doctor at my well woman exam. I told him that my mother had real bad osteoporosis—but I'm too young for a Dexa-Scan. So, she did some blood work, put me on a multivitamin, and told me to exercise along with lifting light weights. I feel great.—Bronwyn W.

Bronwyn, I love how you are being proactive—keep that up. Weight Breaker-Refresh Skeletal Challenge: Your bones are the pillars of your being. You need calcium and vitamin D to make your bones strong and healthy. You can get calcium from dairy (if you are able to tolerate it) as well as certain fruits and vegetables. Love on your bones with nutrition; you need them for this journey. Aerobic exercise and cardio exercise are key to enhancing bone strength. They are the epicenter of your body and its structure. Focus on your posture; your spine is the foundation for your stature. Good posture is key over time and is very good for your body alignment and stability. As we all age, our posture can slump a bit out of habit, and as a result of aging. Take a moment as you are sitting listening to this. Or even when standing, put your shoulders back, straighten up, and feel the life within you. That posture will help you navigate through life.

:My grandmother developed osteoporosis. She's taking medication for thinning of the bones. I'm young, but exercising, making sure I'm getting my calcium and vitamin D in.—Angela C.

Proud of you Angela, calcium and vitamin D are excellent vitamins that can help your bones. Alright, ladies, I wanted to keep muscles separate, so let's talk about them. Just as powerful as your skeletal system is your muscle system. You have, at the minimum, six hundred muscles in your body. We've already talked about one of your most precious, endearing muscles in your body, right? Yep, you guessed it—your heart. You have so many more precious muscles in your body that cause you to navigate through life. We are going to walk through how important your muscular system is.

:Yes, ladies—please don't forget to take care of your heart muscle!—Abby L.

Abby, yes, we must take care of our hearts. In addition, we all have so many types of muscles that help support us: skeletal, smooth, and cardiac muscles. Sit up straight right now, keeping good posture. Moreover, if you do not use your muscles, they will become weak and atrophy. Weight Breaker-Refresh Muscle Challenge: Your muscles are built of muscle fibers. Those fibers work together to contract, relaxing to cause the motions needed to navigate through life. If you don't use those muscles, they will atrophy and shrink.

:I was playing intramural volleyball. One day I forgot to stretch before a volleyball tournament. Guess what? I pulled a muscle. Ever since then I remember to stretch before each game.—Cindy R.

Cindy, I'm so glad you mentioned that. There are times when we have all had a muscle strain or sprain. We extended our muscle and joint beyond what it is supposed to be. When that is done, then it's hard to bear weight on that joint. Appreciate the laxity of your joints, the need to stretch them appropriately. As we age, or rather, I would like to say, *get wiser*, we need to be more mindful of our muscle power and joint health. I learned long ago it does not take long to lose muscle mass, only about a couple of weeks. That is why when you stop an exercise routine, it takes a minute to get back into the swing of things. If you have an adversity or a health setback or even an emotional one or life-changing event, check with your doctor to see when you can resume physical activity. Your body longs for it.

:Muscles are key to your being. My friend teaches a spin class and I have been attending. At first I could only make it through half of the class, barely staying on the bike. Now, I am able to endure through the entire class. Yea, me!—Penelope K.

Way to go, Penelope. All of your Weight Breaker sisters stand with you.

Likewise, often we forget about our Reproductive System, and we shouldn't as it is the main part of human existence. In spite of this, it does not stop there. Make sure you get your check-ups to make sure your reproductive system is healthy. We are all so busy, even as parents, there is a lot on our plate. Whether you have birthed children naturally or adopted or mentored kids, children are a gift, resulting from this system in your body or someone else's, they are the fruits of that. If you are a mother or not, please make sure you have your annual mammograms along with an annual well woman exam.

:I am glad you mentioned this. I need to schedule my mammogram today. I'm so busy working at a jewelry store that I forgot I need to take care of my most precious jewels!—Aster T.

371

Aster, I'm so happy. You scheduling your mammogram is what this podcast is all about—putting your breast health as a priority. Kudos to you for taking care of the Weight Breaker that you are!

Next, we are going to walk through how important your mental health is. This whole approach is towards a healthy mind. If you need help coping with the ups and downs of life, don't be afraid to ask for it. We all need help to balance everything out from time to time. If you neglect the pressure that mounts against your mind, you can break down—crumbling into a thousand pieces. There are things that happen throughout life, and cause all of us to break down. Many people face: trauma, abuse, dismissal, discrimination and so many perils of life can mount on them, along with their mental capability. There is something to be said for protecting your mental space. If you need to seek care of a psychologist or a psychiatrist, seek care. There are professionals that are available to work with you to treat you.

:Mental health is key. Never be ashamed of seeking help.—Dahlia W.

Taking care of our mental health requires a great commitment. Dahlia is so right. Do not be ashamed to seek mental health care.

In addition, your focus on your spiritual health should be a main priority. It will impact how you handle the weights of life. One's personal spiritual system is of relevance. However, you won't find this topic discussed in the anatomy textbooks. Find a way to fellowship together, a prayer or meditation group; establish a place for solace and prayer and meditation—I use my prayer closet to remain connected to my spiritual life. Most of all, show concern for others; this is a great week to walk out your spiritual life.

:My faith is my foundation.—Whitley H.

:God is the cornerstone of everything in my life.—Monica D.

Weight Breakers, I am so honored that you joined this life-changing podcast to listen to how you need to refresh your systems. It's a challenge that we have to be mindful of daily. Upcoming, there will be a podcast on Taking Care of Y.O.U, so stay tuned.

Weight Breaker: Take the Weight off of your Systems, they don't deserve it! Let's rid ourselves of *the weight* to help our systems work to the best of their abilities! We are Thinking Like Weight Breakers, Not Like Weight Takers! Today, journal about how you will monitor your systems and refresh your mindset and read the book, *Think Like A Weight Breaker. Not Like a Weight Taker.* Shock your body systems: show them some love; take the weight off your systems, they're working hard for you; celebrating your body as the God-given machine—like it should be! Imagine all of your body systems speaking to you. They would be telling you something like this,

"I'm so glad that you are committed to giving me the attention that I need, I work hard to nurture your entire body. If I'm neglected, you mount pressure against me. I will be forced to work harder and soon I will give out. I have a huge responsibility; I orchestrate a beautiful concert of rhythm that keeps you alive.

Please do not neglect me; I'm the only body you have. There may be times, from emotional despair, that the weights of the world will cause mounting pressures to work against me. That's not fair, when all I'm trying to do is to remain healthy so you can walk in your purpose.

Please remember me daily. If you don't, there will be a farewell that happens all too soon. Eat healthy, exercise, drink water, destress, work on your Vision, Faith and Resilience Intelligences. Those are all the ways that you can show me love.

Sincerely, Your Body"

Ladies, can you hear your body talking to you?

:Excellent topic. We need to be more mindful of how we treat our bodies.—Angel U.

:Definitely a priority of mine. I need to exercise more. This was the boost that I needed to get started. —Chastity L.

:THE CHRONICLES OF THE WEIGHT BREAKERS CONFERENCE was epic! This podcast on refreshing the body systems was the icing on the cake. I'm considering gastric bypass; however, this gives me a new perspective. I'll keep you posted on my progress. I'm working hard with my diet and spin class that my friend is teaching.—Penelope K.

38

PENELOPE'S TACTICAL WISHES

"HER EFFORT TO DARE & CONQUER"

[LIVE OUT LOUD!]

"Penelope, wow you did great. I can't believe you made it through the whole spin class," Fawn saluted the robust woman who wanted to make a change in her life.

"Girl, I've been watching what I'm eating and getting one mile a day walking in. I'm starting small, but it's really making a difference. I'm officially refreshing my system's challenge, taking care of myself."

"Being a Weight Breaker looks good on you, Penelope!" Fawn wiped her brow with her towel.

"I'm scheduled for my gastric bypass consultation in the morning. With the modifications that I've made in my diet and with your spin class, also with my new found commitment to healthy eating since we left the conference, I'm down—drum roll please, twenty pounds."

Fawn jumped up and down, hugging Penelope's sweaty neck.

"I'm going to cancel the appointment." For once, Penelope wasn't begging for approval from others.

"Girl, I'm so proud of you. You're glowing and that's beautiful that you're taking charge of walking out of *the shadows*," Fawn echoed into the empty dance studio that housed her spin class.

"I know, right! Besides, we only have one life to live; we have to live it to the fullest," Penelope said as she showed Fawn her paperwork for her gastric bypass consultation—then tore it up.

"With The She Declares Crew; the 3W's; Daily Decision Downloads; T.I.P.s and my playbook, *Think Like A Weight Breaker. Not Like A Weight Taker.*—I realize I can do this on my own, however surgery may be helpful for some. Nonetheless, I know that I have the grit to blow up this weight barrier, I'm dynamite! Furthermore, it's as if my diagnosis was before to be a shadow, and the recommended treatment now was to walk into my lip stain—illuminating light."

"BOOM! Sis, you are dynamite illuminating light. Girl, you are doing it—we'll be right here with you!" Fawn hugged her friend's sweaty neck.

As the ladies walked out of the fitness studio, they talked about how they were going to purposefully take care of their body systems, to be the best version of themselves.

"The Chronicles of the Weight Breakers Podcast was wonderful this morning; it connected all the dots for me," Penelope stated.

Fawn challenged her friend. "It sounds like you have the physical weight *on lock*. How are you going to approach your proverbial weights? Being the *shadow* behind Cassidy Gentry? That imposter."

"I have something in *the hopper*; trust and believe!" Penelope spoke confidently.

"Oh, so, we're doing *big things* now?" Fawn inquired.

"Yes, we are," Penelope poised, coming out of the sleuth of despair.

Penelope decided to put down desserts and snacks, cutting back on her food truck regularity—discovering her willingness to be resilient and walk into her purpose with her vision and faith. She honed in on her skills and became all that she desired. Then that day came when the chains of the weights fell off.

There was a story about the upcoming food drive for the area the station served, live with her fellow anchors sharing the news. Cassidy Gentry stormed into the sound booth where Penelope was, while she was behind the scenes watching the B-reel of a community effort piece that was being played during the live news story. Scratching her ditzy head, in her haste to get Penelope checked, she leaned into the sound panel, accidentally hitting the *LIVE* button. Enraged by her less than enthusiastic response to the story, she let loose.

"This piece is so sssssstupid. We cannottttt waste our tttttime on this type of mundane nnnnews. Anotherrrr storyyy about hunnnger? Areeee you ssserious? Where's ttthe damnn piece I had on the cccccome bbback of sssscarves and bbbody wrraps," Cassidy Gentry stated on the air, unwillingly and unbeknownst to herself—on *a hot mic*.

The film crew and producers were *going all ham*, trying to get her to quiet herself; not from her stuttering, but from her inhumane display—as the anchors at their desk were bewildered at the coldhearted comments drowning out their endearing story.

Then in walked Penelope from behind the scenes, out of the sound booth, leaving Cassidy in the dust. She joined the network anchors LIVE, with a svelte, bold confidence, surprising all in the studio. Penelope King took over the camera.

"Hello, I'm Penelope King. We apologize for technical difficulties. However, this food drive is hitting our hearts exactly where it's needed, to take care of our urban core. The food is nutritious, and we are grateful to be able to support this mission. Our hats off to this wonderful organization for their support to the community that we love dearly. Yours truly, in serving and loving our wonderful community, Penelope King," she stood bold in her stance, for once Penelope exemplified sacrifices, heroism and excellence all rolled into one.

"And cut!" Penelope's crew rallied around her, congratulating her on a job well done. A new found self-assurance exuded from every pore of her body.

:Girl, you killed it! Way to go.—Regi H.

:Shadow, stomped in the dust!—Chaka B.

:OMG, I'm so proud of you. Love you, girl.—Fawn P.

:Little Penny, I knew you had it in you.—Abby L.

:Let's Go! On to the next one. We got you, *Boo!*—Anjali N.

39

THE PODCAST

"TAKE CARE OF YOUR VESSEL=Y.O.U."

[WEIGHT BREAKER, YIELD. OPTIMAL. UNDERSTANDING!]

Hi Weight Breakers,

Focus on taking care of you because you are the only one that will! What good is a car or a house if you do not take care of it? In due time it surely will give out way too soon and collapse on you, leaving you stranded—that is so not good. Weight Breakers you have: established the right mindset; evaluated the intelligences that you need to foster your vision, faith, and resilience; looked the proverbial/physical weights of life in the eye; established the momentum types; dug your heels into the strategy of the daily decision clouds; uploaded glory to download greatness; explored a new mindset; took inventory to take action; check your connectivity; evaluated what's in your mental storage; downloaded deep soul activities to upgrade your thought process; built that firewall to keep the B.S. (BAD STUFF) out; gone into silence mode to be still; developed a new strategy on your approach to dealing with the proverbial and physical weights of life; turned up the volume to amplify the positivity of life; refreshed your approach to cherish your body systems; moreover you are taking care of y.o.u. (yielding optimal understanding)—which is the vital ingredient to the recipe of the making of a Weight Breaker!

:We have done a lot. I'm so proud of us.—Anjali N.

Anjali, so glad you were able to join in. This leads to the final thought process, and that is to connect the dots, understanding that all of these things work together, to make sure that you are not a Weight Taker, but a Weight Breaker. It uses The Inspirational Pathway (T.I.P.s) to walk out each day, no matter what weights you are presented with. As a part of this whole person thought process, importance lends to the final Intelligence, and that is Whole Person Intelligence. All of these exercises that we have embarked upon on this journey have led us to this. Whole Person Intelligence: is the capability to understand the necessary importance of addressing your whole person each day. This includes your physical health, mental health, and spiritual health—there is great profit in concentrating on all of these.

:I am finally looking at how I can better take care of myself, thanks to this book. I will keep you posted on my progress.—Fawn P.

Fawn, that is good news. You have been in my prayers. The next daily decisions will give you the appropriate thought process surrounding your health and wellness and going to the doctor. Whole Person Intelligence is embarked upon with ten bonus suggestions of information, to help you when you are going to the doctor's office for your annual examination, follow up appointments after surgery, or on your telemedicine visit call. The Goal of Whole Person Intelligence and Yielding Optimal Understanding: Take a deep breath and we are going to flush out the white coat syndrome; the tactics that you have learned to help you on this journey. Let's be confident about going to the doctor. Become the empowered individual that you are equipped with your vision, faith and resilience!

:Being empowered in every intelligence area is so important, and it takes work. With all that my family has been through, collectively as a unit, we are all working on how we can yield optimal understanding. Ladies, this is so important!—Judge Regi

Judge, you are right on target. These tactics should be not only approached individually, moreover can become a part of how our family operates. Move towards optimal health with Vision, Faith, and Resilience—the vessel that houses our soul is a gift from God.

Our bodies are wonderfully, skillfully made to allow us to push, pull, and balance the forces of life. Ultimately, our health must be a priority. Vision, Faith, and Resilience are the tools required for actualizing optimal health. Daily, our vision must include decisions to be physically, spiritually, and mentally fit.

:I've been meditating to cope with the issues with my father not wanting me to follow my dreams. By doing that I've gained a lot of insight. It has also helped me focus on my stage presence.—Chaka B.

That is so good to hear, Chaka. Also remember this; an exercise of faith is to put your vision into action by managing your medical issues, if you have any. Also, maintaining appropriate lifestyle modifications. Mastering vision and faith does not conclude this journey. The priceless lesson of resilience is practiced when we are forced to reckon with illness and despair. Our health is the dynamic entity that allows us to face challenges and victories. Intertwined in our every thought must be to approach our health with vision, faith, and resilience. Consider this affirmation: I will make decisions that will optimize my health—physically, spiritually, and mentally. Weight Breaker, take a moment and journal on how you realize that being prepared will lead to you having a positive influence on your doctor's visit. This is a moment of crucial investment. We all have some many life requirements that draw us in. However, this time, commitment is necessary to nurture the vehicle that navigates us through life, and as it involves the priceless vessel of your health—your mind, body and soul.

:My body is a vehicle? I like that analogy. I've been working on exercising and moving my vehicle. Keep me accountable, Dr. T.—Dean Baby

Dean Baby, keep moving—Kudos. The objective is for you to get so comfortable with being a Weight Breaker that you should be able to do this and walk this out, *chapter and verse. Drop the mic.* As a Weight Breaker, you will develop an aura that is C.A.S.T. all over you. You will enhance your God-given CHARACTER. You will be able to ASSESS situations to determine if it is a Weight Taker issue, and know how to navigate through it. You will be able to SUSTAIN in any environment, understanding the true value of your magnificent existence and how valuable Y.O.U. are. You will be able to TRUST in the higher power and trust that God will see you through, for God is the *real end* Weight Breaker.

:Amen, I trust that a higher power will get me through this season in my life.—Fawn P.

Fawn, you are right—God will get you through this season in your life. First, know your diagnosis; what are the conditions that you have? Second, know your signs and symptoms that go along with your diagnosis! The signs that you are experiencing is the actual complaint. An illustration, the body changes that you are experiencing, the symptoms are more descriptive of that complaint. For example, the sign is chest pain, and to elaborate, the symptom is chest pain on the left side of my chest that radiates down into my left arm and up into my jaw, along with shortness of breath and sweating, which gives your doctor more of a description of what is going on with you. With this information, your doctor is able to provide you with a more focused physical exam to determine what is going on with you.

In addition, it is important to know what medications you are on!

:You are right. It is so important to know what medications you are on, but also know the dose as well.—A Loyal Listener

Loyal Listener, you are absolutely right. Let's explore the whole thought process of the medications that you are taking. The pronunciation alone, of those medications, can be quite intimidating. It seems as if they just grabbed the alphabet and put all the letters in a bowl and then randomly grabbed a handful of letters and said, *"Hey, let's call this medication, abcdefjhijklmnopqrstivwxyz!"* Literally, that is what it can feel like. It is not good enough to say, *I take a white pill for my blood pressure.* You must know the name, the dose and the frequency—or how often you take the medication. Know the possible side-effects of the medications that you are on! All of us have seen commercials that talk about medications and at the end, there is a fast relay of information about a lot of the side-effects that you may experience while taking the medicine. Still, it is important to have that discussion with your doctor.

:It took me a while. However, I have found a physician that I feel comfortable with, that is so refreshing.—Iris C.

Iris, it is always good to have a great physician-patient relationship. One practice that can continue to enhance that is to take all of your medications to your doctor's appointments! There have been instances in which individuals have been on the brand version of the medication as well as the generic version. So, what does that mean? It means that they had been receiving double doses of the same exact medication, which could have been catastrophic for the individual. Review your medications with your doctor to make sure you are using your medications correctly.

Also, ask your physician what tests you need to follow for your health condition. Understanding your diagnosis is half the battle. It is also very important to be able to clearly understand what ongoing laboratory and tests you need to monitor your health condition. Whether you have hypertension, diabetes, or hypothyroidism, there are tests and labs that you need to have on a regular basis to monitor your diagnosis. It is so very important that you recognize the frequency or how often you need to have those tests.

:Last year, I was diagnosed with diabetes mellitus type 2. My doctor gave me instructions on how often to take my blood sugar; also what range my blood sugars should be in. Also, I was set up with a dietician to make sure I adhere to a healthy diabetic diet. Furthermore, I have to have a hemoglobin A1c blood test every three months to check and see how well controlled my diabetes is. My physician shared with me, based on the great progress that I am making, that I am doing great. I'm taking charge of my health.—Faith A.

Faith, hats off to you for being an empowered patient. You are doing amazing, keep up the great work.

I also want to share with you about having the discussion about what tests you need to have annually. Depending on your age and your gender, there are certain tests that you need to have yearly.

:My doctor told me that I am at the age that I need to start having mammograms yearly. I have no family history of breast cancer. However, I am going to be compliant.—Adrian N.

Yes, Adrian, if you are within the recommended age range or have a family history that advises that you need an annual mammogram—get one. That can be a lifesaver.

Another important factor is to ask your doctor, WHEN SHOULD I CALL 9-1-1? There are certain symptoms of your health condition that will need to be addressed urgently. If you have a heart condition, you should know that you should call 9-1-1 if you start having chest pain.

:Agreed, when my mother started having facial drooping, I recalled that my mother's doctor talked with us about signs and symptoms of stroke. My mom had a mini-stroke years ago, and then last year a big stroke. She is doing well in rehabilitation, hopefully getting out soon. However, if it was not for her doctor giving me that information, she probably would not be here. God is good.—Betty I.

Betty, I'm so glad your mother is doing well. That is why asking those types of questions of your doctor is so important. I will make sure that I keep your mother in my prayers for a full recovery.

:Dr. T. Thank you. Keep bringing this good information.—Betty I.

You are very welcome. Another key question is, what life changes do I need to make for my health condition? If you get a diagnosis, take medications for that condition.

However, if you do not make the life changes needed to help your health, it is not going to yield good results in the long run. Taking your medication and still indulging in high sugar foods, high carbohydrate meals is not good if you have diabetes, or good for you in general. If you get a diagnosis and take medications for that condition, if you do not make the life changes needed to help your health condition, it is not going to yield good results in the long run.

:Due to work stress, coupled with morbid obesity, my doctor told me I was pre-hypertensive. After a lot of soul searching and reading your book, I reconstructed my diet, started a spin class, resulting in me losing weight. I have a long way to go, however I feel great and so encouraged by The Chronicles of The Weight Breakers Podcast's.—Penelope K.

Penelope, I remember you. It is so gratifying to hear about your results. See Weight Breakers, Penelope's testimony is what can happen when you buckle down—doing the work!

Weight Breakers, this brings us to our final nugget is, ALWAYS TAKE WRITTEN QUESTIONS TO YOUR DOCTOR'S APPOINTMENT! It is so important to have all of the questions that you have for your doctor's visit. Stress and anxiety equal life issues, that can cause you to forget what questions you want to ask your physician. Moreover, when you leave the office visit, you will want to kick yourself because you did not get the answers you wanted.

Weight Breaker, Y.O.U are Amazing! Your Whole Person Intelligence allows you to connect the dots regarding your health; your whole well-being. Journal on how you are going to take a deep breath. We are going to flush out the *white coat syndrome* by having these tools prepared when going to the doctor. Let's be confident about going to the doctor; become the empowered patient that you are equipped with by your vision, faith, and resilience. I have spoken on mass media, written about this in my first book *Vision, Faith & Resilience: Affirmations for Life,* spoke about this on prime-time television, and furthermore, written about this in health newsletters and published medical journals—with in each of you, you have the power to become weight breakers.

You can do this; be an empowered patient. Yours truly in whole health and wellness. Walk into your whole self, by taking care of yourself. I salute you for taking this owner's manual of the vehicle that God has blessed you with. This is the only vehicle you got—cherish it.

Love, Your sister and fellow Weight Breaker, Dr. T.

:Thank you Dr. T. for your kind words. Never in a million years did I think that I would be an inspiration to anyone. I'm making strides to come out of the *shadows* of life day by day.—Penelope K.

:Penelope, you are indeed a Weight Breaker!—Dr. T.

:Thank you. I am an empowered patient. I'm in the waiting room right now waiting to find out the medical management plan for my breast cancer. Please pray for me that the cancer is confined!—Fawn P.

:Fawn, we claim divine supernatural healing for you!—Dr. T.

:I know God's got me! And thank you, sincerely.—Fawn P.

40

FAWN'S FAITH FILLED RELEASE

"THE MIRAGE, NO MORE"

[THE STRENGTH IN HER JOURNEY]

"Fawn Paige. Fawn Paige, the doctor is ready for you," Fawn stood up, retreated from the waiting room, following the nurse to the exam room, as she posted on The Chronicles of The Weight Breakers Podcast message feed.

"Miss Fawn, how are you? I love the pixie cut," the nurse stated with a gentle smile.

"I'm fine. Invigorated." Fawn nervously beamed.

"That is good news," the nurse remarked as she measured Fawn's blood pressure. "The doctor will be in shortly."

"Thank you," Fawn said as she began to self-talk,

I'm a Weight Breaker, Not a Weight Taker.

I'm healed.

I'm exploring a new mindset.

My sisters are with me.

I'm not alone, Fawn redundantly thought.

Fawn exhaled, filling the room with her positive affirmations, realizing she would be able to handle whatever the outcome was—the news about her tumor in her breast.

The door opened; the oncologist came in quickly. "Fawn, it is so good to see you. I love your hair—nice cut."

Fawn smiled as she stroked her tress, "Good to see you as well, Dr. Polk. Thank you." Fawn held her cross in her hands that her grandmother had given her.

383

"Well, I have some good news. Your cancer is confined. Your lymph nodes were negative and the surgery and the radiation that we're scheduling should yield a cure for you."

Dr. Polk reached for Fawn; they embraced—both of them exuded tears of pure joy. For once in a long time, Fawn's mind sped forward to seeing her baby grow up and graduate high school and even walking down the aisle when her daughter grew up and found the love of her life. Fawn felt weight lift off her body; she could finally breathe, exhaling the weight that she'd held onto for a while—the weight of impending doom, thinking that she would surely die prematurely.

Dr. Polk got Fawn set up for the radiation treatments. Her She Declares group set up meals for her while going through radiation, providing child care during the evening to help out. Little Alyssa had so many aunties that she did not know what to do.

All of The She Declares group was present for her, even a new friend that she'd met during her treatments—Sally Winters. They bonded quite nicely during their waiting room meet and greets. Sally smiled as she looked over at Fawn in the waiting room when she noticed she was feeling a little down, Fawn gave her the same smile back. They were happy they could support each other through a rough patch in their lives.

Even during the radiation, against the advice of her doctor, Fawn would not abandon her spin class and mostly cheered her students on from the sidelines, participating when she felt up to it, despite battling radiation brain fog.

She received an outpouring of love from everyone, except from where she needed it the most, the support from the father of her baby.

Even though looking at her, she was the epitome of fitness, in the midst of being diagnosed with breast cancer, that was the first time she actually started to make herself a priority.

The rainbow in the storm was that The She Declares group created a schedule and each and every one of them showed up in support of Fawn.

Finally, there was a point in which Fawn was able to experience full healing when she was able to ring the bell at the completion of her radiation treatment, something new that they decided to do at her hospital for the radiation patients as well as the chemotherapy patients. It was an epic event.

"Girl, let's cut this cake," Chaka proclaimed, as all of the ladies gathered around to show a measure of support.

"I have yielded optimal understanding by taking care of my health. When I noticed something was wrong, I was scared however I knew I had to be my very own advocate for my health. Pass me a piece of cake," Fawn exhaled as she was the epitome of sacrifice, heroism, adorned with excellence...

41

THE PODCAST

"YOUR NARRATIVE HAS BEEN CHANGED"

[ONLY FOCUS ON GOD'S NARRATIVE FOR YOU!]

Hi Weight Breakers,

Just because you have made it through this book does not mean that the work is over. I compiled these inspirational, motivational thought-processes from my journal. I'm still adding to it, motivating myself, spending time in prayer, and meditation to make meaningful change. I'm constantly attempting to evolve. One task I have for you is challenging yourself to determine where you are personally from a vision, faith and resilience perspective regarding your intelligence. This should be done quarterly, or bi-annually at a minimum, reevaluate what you are uploading into your space.

:What are some of the questions that we should be addressing during that time?—A Loyal Fan

Great question, Loyal Fan. You would need to tap into: What are you reading? Who are you surrounding yourself with? How are you allowing life's circumstances to impact your mission and goals? Reassess what you are doing regarding The Inspirational Pathway. And how do you need to adjust your calendar, your activities, to make your actions more meaningful?

:Got it!—A Loyal Fan

Dr. T. verbalized further,

Overall, we have gone from taking on the weights of the world in regard to how we view ourselves; accepting the script that others want to put on us. That's not going to happen anymore. We are now changing the narrative: We are Weight Breakers. Not Weight Takers! The goals that we have established need to be looked at on a regular basis.

:I love this, like a *Self-Quarterly Business Review*?—Anjali N.

Hey, Anjali—you hit the nail right on the head. You will ask yourself the following questions during that assessment: How well have I focused on my body systems? How have I worked towards my fitness goals? What benefits have I gained from the modifications that I made? How has what I have gleaned impacted my performance? What new strategies will I implement? How can I challenge myself more? What is my roadmap to continue to move forward?

:I'm putting *"it"*—The Self-Quarterly Business Review on my calendar right now! This will help me to be accountable to myself.—Anjali N.

Anjali, look at you walking The Inspirational Pathway out! You go, girl. Consider the diagram that I posted on social media awhile back. Look at it and realize that this is how we should view what surrounds us. I want you to put your name or m.e.; magnificent existence—in the center of the diagram.

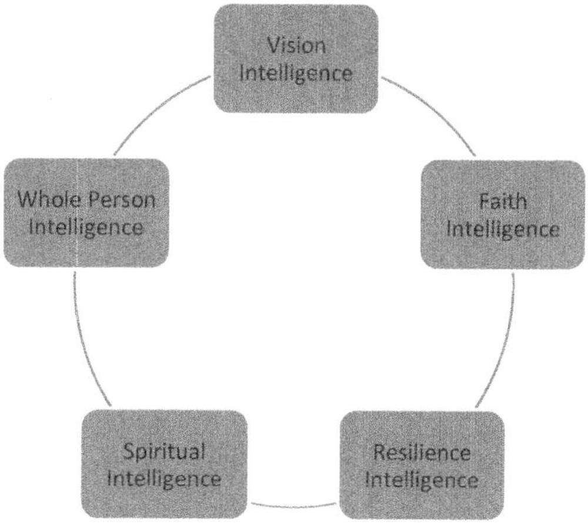

:I remember this diagram; it has given me a new perspective, to deal with all that is going on with my family. This is good stuff.—Regi H.

Regi, thank you for that feedback. I've been asked several times to repost this diagram, because it puts a great perspective on what surrounds everything that we do. Weight Breakers, journal on how you are going to share how these Intelligences are working for you. Be honest with yourself, share how you think these areas have improved, or still need some work. Then map out what you are going to do to make an impact in that area. Now, I want you to get your journals and journaling about how you are going to walk this out.

:I got my journal ready. I just rang the bell the other day for completion of my radiation. God is so good, and I am so grateful.—Fawn P.

:That's amazing! Praying for your continued recovery!—A Loyal Fan

:That's our girl. She's back; bold and beautiful. Go Fawn!—Chaka B.

:We got your back, girl, and loving these intelligences!—Regi H.

:Weight Breakers, we are all in this together!—Penelope K.

:This puts everything in perspective.—Anjali N.

42

THE LAYERS OF THE CREW

"SENTIMENTS OF CHANGE—BIT BY BIT"

[ENJOY THE JOURNEY, IT'S A PROCESS...]

The early morning brisk air hit Chaka's face as she pulled the keys to the Vietnamese restaurant out of her pocket. It was 3:00 a.m.

She flicked on the lights and went right to work, in the family business—prepping the vegetables, then rolled the spring rolls that the restaurant was famous for. No one was in the building as she folded all the napkins over the clean silverware. She did this daily, even though her father kicked her out because, under his roof, the *comedy mess* was not welcome.

In respect to her family, she caught a bus and arrived early before everyone—rolling up her sleeves and getting to work. Before her father arrived at the restaurant in the morning, Chaka was already back at the pool house. She slept after her restaurant shift and then prepped for her long nights doing stand-up—*killing the game*, getting back to Abigail's guest pool house at midnight every night. This illustrated Chaka's true commitment to her family. Meanwhile, she was changing the narrative and walking into her purpose—not just aspiring, moreover having an actual plan.

One day, Chaka's father arrived earlier than usual to the restaurant and noticed that everything was already complete. While he habitually arrived after his staff, his daughter Ashley, and his wife, he came to a realization that everything was already done—the restaurant smelled freshly cleaned.

"What is going on here?" Christina's father belted out, looking around in his stern manner, confused by the tidy prepped area.

"It's Christina," Ashley muttered to the stern patriarch. "She's been doing this every day after her long nights at the comedy club."

389

The staunch man, who often told the story of how he and his brother held steadfast onto inflated basketballs to float through the rough choppy water as a part of the voyage to arrive in this country, put his hands on his hips and stood speechless. He went into his office, closed the door, and sat at his desk. He looked at the picture on his desk of Christina as a child with two ponytails, shaking his head and biting his quivering lip. In that moment, he comprehended that he projected an overwhelming weight, that he felt all of his life, onto his daughter Christina. In that moment, he came to the realization that his actions hampered her dreams, and that was unfair to her.

He wept.

That night, across town, Chaka Bu once again rocked the house with her comedic chops. In no time, she'd advanced from being an opener to a first line opener, which meant that she was able to go right before the headliner. Her goal was to next become the headliner on the circuit of the comedy clubs that were operated by the owner.

"Chaka, you did it again," the owner said as he patted Chaka on the back. "Girl, you are on your way, and don't forget who gave you your first chance!"

"I won't forget you. I aspired to do this all of my life, you gave me my break, man—I owe you a lot!" Chaka exclaimed as she wiped her sweaty neck with a white terry cloth hand towel.

"Okay, next week, let's talk about a headliner cadence. Let's start out small, maybe every other week, and then work our way up, how does that sound?"

"*Amaze-balls*—that's how that sounds."

The owner left the crowded dressing room where all of the comedians sat in between their *beats* on stage. Chaka held a stare into her beautiful, fresh, chestnut eyes, reflecting in the mirror, thinking,

Damn, girl, you did that *shit!*

She smiled at herself, laid her head on her arms as if she were in elementary school when the teacher told her it was *quiet time*. The early mornings setting up the restaurant, the late nights at The Comedy Shop, were catching up with her—she rested.

Suddenly, a gentle touch on her shoulder startled her.

She lifted her head and in the mirror before her was a reflection of her father standing behind her holding a bountiful bouquet of red roses.

"Cha, bố" Chaka sprang out of the chair, grasping her hands around her father's neck for dear life as if he was an I.V. infusing her dehydrated soul with normal saline—the weight of her gift was lifted.

"Chaka, your mother and I are proud of you," her father cried of forgiveness as he held onto his daughter tightly. They were suppurated into each other's souls. In that moment Chaka found the true meaning of her stage name, *Life*. She felt life rush into her with her parents' acceptance of who she was destined to become.

Later the next day, Regi received a text from Anjali…

:Sean, my boyfriend, cuts hair on the weekends in the neighborhood where he grew up. You may know the spot, it's in your old neighborhood—*Crookshank's Cutz*. Have Zachary take the boys over there. I really think they will like it.—Anjali N.

I know where that is; that's my old stomping ground, Regi contemplated to herself.

:Sounds amazing. I'll have Zach get his haircut later as well. Looking at our calendar, we have a date night tonight, so perfect timing.—Regi H.

Regi relayed the message to Zachary. Although he was still a little traumatized by the assault he had recently experienced. However, he was *game* to try once again to get his boy's haircut.

Zachary, alongside his *little kings*, arrived at the barber shop.

"Who is this?" was a silent echo heard as he entered the barber shop as an ivory man that accompanied his two sun kissed sons.

"What up, man?" Sean welcomed them into the legacy neighborhood shop.

A little hesitant, he spoke,

"I'm Zachary—these are my sons."

There was a pregnant pause as Zachary awaited a response when his ivory skin introduced his brown loves of his life—*his little kings*. He stood there, bit his lip as he did not know how the room full of African American men would receive him. You could hear a pin drop.

A man walked towards Zachary.

"What up, Zachary? I'm Sean. My girlfriend Anjali, told me that you would be coming by," Sean gave a cool smile, dressed in his scrubs as he would leave the barbershop later and go straight into his night shift as and E.R. physician.

He gave him some *dap*. The men felt an instant comradery.

This is so cool, I feel right at home, Zachary thought as he released his secure grips of his sons a little so they could go up to the men's hairstyle guide poster to pick out what kind of *cut* they wanted.

Isaiah wanted 13 and Isaac picked out 11.

The boys, even Zachary, loved the vibe of the men talking about sports, food, religion, and politics. Sean called little Isaiah up and started to work on his fade. The group continued their conversation, but when they got to politics and race, Sean hesitated because he knew what could happen.

"Zachary, man are you alright?" he said from across the room.

Zachary looked at his boys and realized that he had a new village of support. He was transparently getting misty eyed.

Sean noticed the angst in Zachary's gut, stopped Isaiah's haircut, and motioned for Zachary to come into the back of the barber shop. "Little man. I'll be right back; me and your dad are going to talk."

Isaiah smiled and played Pac-Man on his phone, with his cape draped around his neck.

Zachary strode to the back of the barbershop that was set up like a lounge with a pool table and everything. There were photographs of Civil Rights leaders and one photo specifically stood out, as if to leap off of the framed picture. Under the portrait in an army uniform was a bronze nameplate that read: Cletus "Crookshank" Gulley.

"Is this the man this shop is named after—*Crookshank's Cutz*?"

"Hell yeah, the man, the myth, the legend," Sean responded with pride.

"Wow, he was in the military? How did he become a barber?"

Zachary asked, inadvertently scratching his head.

"He became a barber because after he served his nation, he couldn't find a job when he returned home after risking his life for his country. Military benefits weren't what they are today. So, he took his own destiny into his hands and built this neighborhood staple in the community from the ground up— *Crookshank's Cutz*. He cut hair for free for the kids' back-to-school program. If you had a job interview, he'd cut your hair for free. He fed many people out of this barbershop."

"I can see why he's considered a legend. Did you know him?" Zachary asked, intrigued.

"Know him? Hell yeah. He was my father," Sean replied as he smiled, wiping the picture off with a rag. "Since his passing, I've kept this barbershop open for the community. I work in the ER during the week, and on the weekend, I cut hair to keep my father's legacy alive. I'm Dr. Sean Cletus Gulley—*Crookshank's* son and proud of it. Which leads me to why I brought you back here. Anjali told me what happened and it's been all over the news. Are you okay?"

"No, I'm not okay," Zachary responded as his pale European skin became flushed, and his eyes welled up with tears.

"Now you understand exactly what your boys are going to face. So, stop all of that *privileged crying; you man the fuck-up*, and get them prepared. I'm going to help you."

Sean reached out his hand to give Zachary a clean handkerchief to wipe his eyes. He told him to get up and give him some dap.

"Now you're going to go back out there and make sure you bring the boys here every two weeks. We have a little youth center around the corner and after I give them a fresh cut, I'll take the boys and you to *my hood* so they can get acquainted. Anjali told me that Regi was from around here, too, and I remember her when we were growing up. Let's make sure they know where they come from. Cool? We're here to help you carry the weight, man. The ladies are not the only ones who can be Weight Breakers, now are they? Here, wipe your face."

They laughed, as Zachary grabbed Sean's handkerchief cleaning his tears off his face.

"Man. Cool! I really appreciate that."

The boys and Zachary both got their hair cut, but more than that, got a lesson about life, the boys' heritage, and a new *Uncle Sean.*

Zachary, now *pulled together*, returned from the back of the barbershop, grinned at how *at-home* he felt in the environment. His sons both looked great and jumped out of the chairs, getting dusted off with Blow Pops in their mouths. Zachary paid the barbers, smiling about *the new world* his sons had an opportunity to experience—which was a blessing. In this encounter, he realized that he needed this village as well to help him raise sons of color.

In walked Cowboy, with his cart. Zachary's eyes were enamored as the attention shifted to what was in Cowboy's hand cart, as the requests rolled in.

"Give me ham and cheese."

"How about some baked chicken, with green beans along with roasted potatoes?"

"You got some chicken and dumplings today? Please say you do."

"I want some collard greens, man."

The crowd gathered around Cowboy, like a popsicle on a sidewalk that was pounced upon by ants—inundated with a swarm of those with a craving.

This was all new to Zachary and his sons as they took notice. The boy's stomachs began to growl from the aroma.

"Hey Dad, can you buy us a plate to take home? It smells like Grandma D's up in here, in the cart that the man with the cowboy hat brought in."

The boy's eyes lit up like Christmas as they gathered around the cart with the delectable aroma that pounded out the scent of rubbing alcohol, witch hazel, and shaving cream. They were now overcome with fumes of Thanksgiving, Christmas, and Easter all rolled up into one. Everyone gathered around, taking their pick at plates and sides.

Sean walked up beside Zachary.

"What's up, Doc?" the man with the food cart rendered.

"I can't call it," Sean spat back with a commonality.

"You saw the Lakers the other night. My man L.J. took it to them. Oh, I forgot you are a Golden State man?"

The men chuckled; giving each other *dap*.

"It's all love; I'm down with either of them making it to the playoffs." Sean turned towards Zachary, who was still smiling from ear-to-ear.

"That's Cowboy; he served in the military with my father. He experienced the same issues my father did when he returned from the war—no employment. So, he and his wife opened up a small store with a diner in the back called *Cowboy's Milk House*. He and his wife cook, they divide and conquer, bringing it to small urban businesses. We are on their Saturday rotation."

"You got some red velvet cake today?" Sean asked, getting his wallet.

"Of course I do, *Lil Crookshank*. I know how you like it, with buttercream icing and caramelized walnuts on top." Cowboy smiled as he was doing business. "What do you want, little men? I got fried chicken, pork chops, oxtails, macaroni and cheese, greens," Cowboy shared, pointing to the labeled Styrofoam containers.

"Cowboy, these are Regi's boys?" Sean added.

"You mean, little Regi from Compton, now Judge Regi? Man, you all are family. Tell your mom you met Cowboy. I remember little *smarty pants Regi*, little badass Rain, and Ryan—that boy sure could play baseball and loved wrestling, it was a shame what happened to him in that twister years ago. But Regi, she's always been a blessing to the community; your plates are on me." He turned towards Zachary.

"Are these your sons?" Cowboy asked, sucking on his cinnamon toothpick.

"Yes, Sir, Mr. Cowboy."

"Get your ass up here and get a plate too. Take one to Regi as well!"

Zachary followed suit.

Sean turned around, his eyes were filled with surprise—of the *Deadman walking,*

"Luke, when did you get in here? I thought you were in a rehabilitation hospital?" Sean asked, concerned.

Luke covered the tracheostomy stoma, replying, "Man, I got a *day pass* to tighten up my fade. Don't tell Sparrow you saw me up in here."

"Man, this is the barber shop. What goes on in here–"

All the men chimed in, "Stays right in here."

The experience of the barbershop filled a hole in Zachary and his boys' spirits, enriching them in the pursuit of putting the pieces together of how to move forward with their lives after the injustice they'd been served. The silver lining in all of it was the comradery that they acquired—a brotherhood that fed their souls and their bellies.

"Okay, little men, see you in two weeks, and don't forget to bring your sneakers. Have them laced up and ready." Sean grabbed his stethoscope, draping it around his neck to get to his emergency room shift.

With plastic bags in tow that housed their delectable soul food dinners, Isaiah turned toward him with a grin. "Okay, Uncle Sean, two weeks; same time!"

"Yes, little man. Make sure you bring your A game on the court." Sean ruffled the boy's hair.

"We are going to be ready, Uncle Sean. I got *handles!*" Isaac hammered back.

Sean smiled. *"Oh snap!* Now, that is what I'm talking about, little man. Zachary, your boys have *swag."*

Across town, Fawn was on the mend—in her healing process. Nonetheless, she was seriously thriving—now back to her regular fitness class schedule. She even had some reconciliation with the father of her child Beckett "B.T." Blaze. He sustained an ACL injury during one of his games right after THE CHRONICLES OF THE WEIGHT BREAKERS CONFERENCE.

It was announced, right when Fawn would start radiation, that his season was over. Shortly after that, his fiancé disappeared into the horizon, along with his career, when his basketball future was questionable—moving on to switching sports, taking her Cartier *encrusted shovel* to do her gold digging from the NBA to the NFL.

Fawn was empathetic, making sure he saw his daughter, which was now the highlight of his day. That's all she allowed, though. She had moved on and found a companion with a kind soul at the studio because she truly believed her truth and beauty.

Furthermore, Anjali decided to cut the crap and started demanding that her nameplate and business cards be changed to her birth name. She even decided to start seeing a psychologist, Dr. Sophia Clark, to help address her eating disorder. Anjali took her place as a Vice President of Marketing and she was overwhelmed by all of the business that was coming her way. She was also seen in public with her beau, Dr. Sean Gulley, as much as possible. Anjali fully walked into her authenticity and boldness.

In midtown, Penelope was being asked to anchor, while Cassidy Gentry was *on leave.* She did not know how to really feel about it, especially being in a space that, all of a sudden, appreciated her. She started to get job offers from other networks and she was really considering new opportunities. In her mind, she realized her talent and was waiting for the right prospect to seize.

Once again, Regi was balancing and winning. She organized her schedule, got her mother-in-law in check, and they worked as a team. Her mother and her become more connected as well. She completed her anger management class and her sons were thriving. They were loving their trips to the inner city and connecting with Regi's roots. Regi finally stopped having nightmares that had haunted her since she had blamed herself all of her life for the death of her younger brother.

To be expected, Abigail was reaching out more and was engaging in group texts. She saw her specialist and her prognosis was not good. Although she began to have some of the signs of ALS, her biggest fear was to be locked in her body, unable to move. She finalized her trust and last will and testament; making sure all of her affairs were in order *on the low*—the area of her life that she remained as the vault. On the contrary, in the vast array of her life, she was open and surrendered to the newfound self-love and friendship that she had been longing for all along. After she signed all of the modified legal paperwork and had a courier take it to her lawyer, she made a phone call that she had been wanting to make, but had to make sure that all of the ink was dry.

RING!

"Hello, this is John," John answered the call from an unknown caller.

"Hey, John. This is Abby," she said curtly.

"Abigail, I'm in midtown in an important meeting..."

"Cut the crap and put me on speaker," Abby demanded and he followed suit.

"You're not at a meeting in midtown. You're at the Four Seasons in midtown in room 1605. I've filed for a divorce, and Margot, bitch, I know you hear me. Both of you are out of the will. John, you'll get a little pathetic stipend monthly; anything to get away from your cheating ass. If you decide to combat it, I have pictures of you and Margot in the Hamptons, in Dubai, in Bora Bora; need I say more? Your SoHo House Membership is revoked. The Yacht in the West Indies—forget about it. Your electronic keys to the villa in Seychelles have been deactivated. Oh, I've also stopped payments to all of the credit cards, yes especially the Black Card. In 5,4,3,2,1—"

KNOCK! KNOCK!

"This is hotel management," came from the other side of the door.

"Yep, that's them. You're going to be asked to vacate the premises. John, all of your belongings are boxed up on the front porch of Margot's rat trap studio apartment. You might want to catch a cab before someone steals them."

Ironically, the only word in that last sentence John heard was *cab.*

"Cab?"

"Yes, cab. Look out the window."

The Lamborghini was being taken away by a tow truck.

"Yep, the Lambo and Maserati are mine. I'm open and I surrender to only good things in my life, no longer *The Vault* that I allowed you to only have the combination to. Good luck—*sucka!*"

Simultaneously, Tabitha continued to be a broker for the elite and continued to walk in her purpose. She realized the benefit of walking in her truth and she was and would always be more than a lip stain. To her surprise, out of nowhere, athletes began to call her, wanting her to represent them. She was honored. In the evenings, over a chilled glass of wine, due to Dr. Mack's prompting and THE CHRONICLES OF THE WEIGHT BREAKERS CONFERENCE, she began to look at her design book, doodling around and drafting up new ideas for the home collection that she always wanted to create—*The Savoy Middleton Home Décor Collection.*

In the meantime, Regi and Zachary got a much-needed date night, and the boys, who were now spending more time with their paternal grandmother, were really forming a bond with her. The darts towards Regi's parenting had calmed down immensely and those who would see Regi and her mother-in-law out, would swear that, despite the clear difference in the melanin in their skin, that they were actually mother and daughter, by their demeanor—just like the lady and her mother-in-law that Regi had helped onto the elevator at the conference. Before they left out, Regi got a text from Abby.

:Hey, girl, what's up?—Abby

:I'm getting ready for date night. What are you doing?—Regi

Regi replied as she put on her Balance & Winning lip stain.
:Nothing, home alone. Where is Troublemaker?—Abby

:He's chomping on a treat.—Regi

:Would you mind if I babysat him? You know I updated his microchip information, adding you as a guardian.—Abby

:Too cute, we have an official four-legged addition to our family. Sure, come by. He can spend the night with you. Like joint custody?—Regi

:Yep, we are co-parenting this little rascal.—Abby

Regi smiled.

Abby came to get Troublemaker—they had a good time in the *Lambo.*

She parked it at the dock at Promise Lake, deciding to take the pup out on a small boat.

She popped some champagne to celebrate her courage to finally free herself from her cheating husband.

She finally opened up, surrendered to her inner truth. She would be "The Vault" no longer.

Her hands wretched the four-carat diamond ring set off of her finger,

Even though I might not have much time left, I deserve better, she thought to herself as she casted the tainted rings of infidelity out into the lake.

"I hope those damn ring plummet to depths of the abyss!"

Abigail looked down at the pup, who jumped up and down on the boat, while her smile cascaded into the dusk.

"I'm free," Abigail belted into the horizon.

43

THE PODCAST

"KEEP THE MOMENTUM GOING"

[ELIMINATE STAGNANCY FOR GOOD!]

The plane touched down; the rain delay from her departing city caused a bumpy ride. Dr. Sophia Clark, fresh from THE CHRONICLES OF THE WEIGHT BREAKERS CONFERENCE, had to give a guest appearance at The Psychologist Summit in Nashville. She pulled into her driveway, eager to get home, settling her stomach, along with her wits from a turbulent *airbus ride,* but lingered in her driveway taking deep breaths.

Tell me why again do I subject myself to all of this travel?

The four-car garage doors opened to her lonely home; this was a far cry from the rural counties within Tennessee in which she was raised. Sophia had come a long way from a broken home, being raised by her relatives *from pillar to post.* Every time she would pull into the driveway of the beautiful custom-built house, a sense of polar opposite emotions came over her, *I made it out versus survivor's remorse.*

Completely spent from the speaking engagement, followed by a meet and greet, followed by a staff to debrief on the commentary about THE CHRONICLES OF THE WEIGHT BREAKERS CONFERENCE that had just taken place, then into the friendly skies she went off to another guest appearance—the story of her reasoner life. She sat in the garage of the classified colonial mansion adjacent to *the who's who of the industry*—hesitant to go into her home, once again alone.

So this is what my life has resorted to—reasonably alone?

BEEP!

The house alarm was already disabled; however, the door chime ignited her senses.

What the hell? Her heart raced.

Today isn't Tuesday— it's late. Why would the cleaning lady still be here?

CLINK!

CLINK!

CLINK!

CLINK!

"Oh shit! Where's my nine?" Dr. Clark whispered to herself, as she tried to remember the combination number that she'd recently changed to her gun safe.

Her eyes zeroed towards here fireplace. She tiptoed over to the fireplace to grab a fire poker. Then a strong hint of a familiar cologne ignited her senses, making her warm all over.

Dr. Clark was perplexed. Then, all at once, she *was* hit with *the song*. The prelude of *Tennessee Whiskey* filled the home of the woman that had declared separation from her husband—the words made her smile. Whiskey glasses with two circle ice cubes placed in them. Her eyes zoomed into her soon-to-be ex-husband's full, luscious lips. Her heart dropped as sensations overcame her. It had been six months since she had seen him, except for in closed-door meetings with lawyers. Her mouth couldn't even get out what she wanted to say: *What in the hell are you doing here?*

However, her real contemplation was that she missed him so much it hurt. His *Idris* presence walked closer towards her, attempting to serenade her—surprisingly on-key.

You better go, boy, she thought, not letting on of her happiness to see him brandished all up in her face. She kept her eyes stern, trying not to let on that she was a witness to his silky button-down Burberry shirt—showing *a kiss* of his chiseled chest.

He handed her a Baccarat Harmonie Double Old Fashion Tumbler—he poured her favorite whiskey. He licked his lips as she swirled the glass—then a sip with his luscious *soup-coolers*.

She looked around her home. She had decided not to change the locks because, deep in her vision, somewhere over the rainbow, hope was in her heart. She wanted him to find his way home, even though she was the one that refused to be healed and loved.

She smiled, and bit her lip as she looked at his notched chocolate goodness. His appearance caused a *proverbial toothache*.

401

Her body singed with passion. *Not too soon, Sophia. You are walking into fire, girl!*

"This is nice," the burn absorbed her throat, she took another sip. He unhanded the glass from the woman he fell in love with long ago, pressing the button on the automated fireplace. The flames burst exactly like her heart was doing. Taking small, methodical breaths, her visions of why she had asked him to leave in the first place was clouded with the desires she held in her pocket that she was inches away from pulling out, throwing down a *Boston on his ass.*

Taking the glass from her, he asked, "Can I bring you closer?"

Her eyes told it all—*Hell Yes!* Within moments, she stepped out of her five-inch stilettos, nestling into his firm chest. He kissed her forehead, while he gently rendered the words of the chorus of *their song.*

You're as smooth as Tennessee whiskey

You're as sweet as strawberry wine…

They paused at the end of the song; he wanted to remain near—she pulled away. He stood there like a kid who had gotten his bicycle stolen on the playground.

Sophia turned off the music box.

"Come on, girl. This is us. I know you miss *our jam—Right?"*

She shrugged her shoulders, now seated on the arm of the cream Italian leather couch.

He kneeled before her. "Baby, let's forget all this divorce shit! What about trying us again? Are you ready yet? I still want those baby girls, but only with you." His eyes misted with regret, resolve, along with remorse.

In all of the arguments I've caused since our magnificent loss, I never cried. I just dove into my work more than ever, attempting to fix the world, Dr. Clark resolved to herself.

However, it was obvious that Mr. Clark wore his emotions on his sleeve.

There was a pregnant pause between the two. That particular request was a little too soon after multiple miscarriages that resulted in the still births of the twins. The cause was her overcrowded womb, with fibroids. That double fold loss catapulted their picturesque world off its axis.

Dr. Clark helped her clients who laid down on her couch in her office in the high-rise building, in addition she traveled around the world adding to her acumen, being an expert in her field. She spoke at conferences, an expert in television appearances and had been quoted in various fields of literature to help the world, moreover to fill her personal void. Yet, her own personal weights had not been addressed—leaving her soul barren.

She was obviously shaken by the thought, with flashbacks that flooded her memory; in a delivery room attempting to give birth to twin girls. The hustle and bustle around her that she felt as if it were yesterday. Her heart's eyes could still see the two pink, hand-crocheted blankets for the twin girls that suffered twin to twin transfusion—one baby taking all the nutrients from the other, along with her nurturing uterus being overcrowded with monstrous fibroids that continuously drained her soul.

The next images that flooded her memory were seeing two small caskets, standing at a graveside, as she held her husband's hand at the cemetery—looking up at him, asking, "Are our babies in heaven?"

Instead of anger, the good psychologist retracted to her reasonable shell like she always did, as she was brought back to the question proposed by her husband, whom she was separated from.

He repeated himself, "Sophia, did you hear me? What about trying us again? Are you ready yet? I still want those baby girls, but only with you…"

She was snapped out of her desolate walk down her horrific memory lane,

"No time for that," her face was less than enthused by the proposition.

The remnants of all that Sophia had gone through with the loss of their babies, were two sets of bronze shoes mounted on marble with the names *Corinthian and Ava* etched into the memorial that was displayed on the mantel above the blazoning fire.

She pulled away, even more as his thoughts were she should be over the loss by now, but no matter how many stages she was on; clients she counseled; book tours she did; podcasts she presented; or bestsellers that she wrote—loss lingered around every corner, ready to remind her of what could have been—motherhood. That was why she wore *the reasoner* momentum to keep busy, so she wouldn't have to remember her pain, leaving all the possibility of hope buried with the two small caskets. Deep down in her barren soul, she felt less of a woman because she could not do what she felt was the God given gift of being a woman, being able to bring life into the world—no matter how hard she tried.

She pulled away.

"Thanks for stopping by, it was good to see you. However, I'm swamped. I've got to listen to this quick podcast before midnight—work stuff. The plane got in late—Dr. T. needs me to approve something—my lawyer will be in touch with you…"

"I get it. Everybody needs you, but me, right?" Neglection resonated in his spirit. "Do what you need to do. At least I tried."

Dr. Clark watched the back of him fade into the cold quiet house.

Tears no longer lived in her spirit, or housed in her tear ducts. She was numb but she would make sense of it all. She was *the reasoner*.

I need to get myself together. She pulled out her compact, fixed her face with self-talk.

"Do not cry. Don't you dare damn cry. You are *Dr. Mother Fucking Superwoman Dr. Sophia Clark*—don't you forget it! You can't be broken, you fix people—you got that!"

With the two pairs of bronze baby shoes on the mantle behind her in the distance, she opened up her laptop—began to work before turning on the LIVE Quiet Storm along with The Chronicles of The Weight Breakers Podcast.

"This is exactly what I need." She took another drink of her Tennessee Whiskey—listened intently, trying to shake off the beautiful man who once again, walked out of her life for her unwillingness to move on after they had suffered a surmountable loss. She wiped tears while working on upcoming client documents, her ears perked up.

Hi Weight Breakers,

Oh my goodness, you would think after jumping out of a plane, that I'd be over my fear of flying—but I just got off one of the worst flights ever. It has been a long day. Sorry for the late podcast. Weight Breakers, let's check in. Would a plane be able to ascend to forty thousand feet without momentum? Would electricity be able to flow through the utility poles without momentum? Would your heart be able to beat without momentum? Everything requires momentum; you are going to keep the momentum going.

This is just what I need tonight. Sophia took another sip of her drink.

Speaking of momentum, let's check in with our momentum types that have journeyed with us throughout this exercise, *Think Like A Weight Breaker. Not Like A Weight Taker: Vision Intelligence, Faith Intelligence, and Resilience Intelligence in The Inspirational Pathway.* You have all the tools to keep the momentum going within you; your support system, this book—the blogs and web series that accompany this book. You are not alone, with handling the Proverbial Weights along with the Physical Weights of Life by utilizing the tactics that are a part of your DNA now. In all honesty, this book was not meant to be a one and done, a read and put down. This book, if it is utilized correctly, should be highlighted until the highlights seep through the pages. It should be dog-eared to the max—the spine should be frayed from redundant use.

Dr. Clark pulled out her book, sure enough—her book looked like it was run over by a bulldozer. She smiled.

More importantly, if you have been blessed by any portion of this book, it would be an honor to have you recommend this book to a relative, friend, or someone that you want to bless with these tactics, to help them break the weights of life, *Think Like a Weight Breaker. Not Like A Weight Taker!* We have shifted to keep the momentum going. Regardless of your momentum type, you decide what's next! You determine that. Conclusion is what you are going to download into yourself. Dedicate the nuggets and pearls that you have downloaded into your own unique maze of life. Write down how you feel about your Vision Intelligence, Faith Intelligence, and Resilience Intelligence; the affirmations that you have downloaded from this book, those you have orchestrated within yourself. Your whole person counts on it. Your systems are so appreciative of you for taking care of them, in The Inspirational Pathway. Live Bold, Big and Amplified on walking into your purpose. As a part of your assignment on earth, regardless of your gifting, ultimate purpose, whether we want to admit it or not, our common purpose is here to serve.

Dr. Clark took a deep breath as she attempted to resolve that, indeed, although she served her clients with their life issues, her efforts at reconciliation may never come to pass in her own life.

We are here to serve others, to be of help to one another—to inspire individuals on how to be the very best versions of themselves. Proverbs 11:25 states, *The generous will prosper; those who refresh others will themselves be refreshed.* We can assess the Intelligences that we are exhibiting; determine how well we are performing in each of those areas. Be real with ourselves, not grading ourselves, just finding out where we need to focus our efforts. Moreover, being an inspiration or a source of refreshment to others.

If your vision is skewed by what life throws at you, then vision is your target for this quarter. If your faith is shaky based on life's circumstances, then faith intelligence is your target. If by chance, when *the rug* is pulled out from under you, and you have a predisposition for wallowing in despair, then resilience intelligence is your opportunity. Pick one, make an adjustment of your focus and do the work. You may circle back, in pursuit of one of the tactics, drilling down to enhance your skillset to make an impact in the area of your life that you feel that you may want to challenge.

You are a Weight Breaker and you have to keep the momentum going. Hashtag it out! Which one of the tactics are you trending now? Survey, self-assess on a regular basis. If you take each of these tactics one by one, you are doing great, you are already winning. Grant yourself some grace, continuing to master each of these tactics one by one. What will be your Hashtag (#) be? You are Thinking Like a Weight Breaker. Not Like a Weight Taker. Goodnight. God bless!

Love, Dr. T.

Dr. Clark rendered a toast to herself, as the podcast affected Dr. Clark like cutting a lemon after you have an open wound on your hand—it stung. She closed her laptop, dashed to the front door, hoping to find her soon-to-be ex-husband still in her midst—she spotted his brake lights release, slowly leaving the driveway. Apparently, he had pondered leaving before he was bold enough to drive off—leaving the woman he obviously loved, yet once again.

"I can't believe he stayed around for me," Dr. Clark spoke out loud—she ran in her bare feet down the circular driveway into the street, the motion detector flipped the flood lights. He didn't look back.

After attempting to heal the broken tormented reasonable woman, once again, he was focused on his windshield; not his rearview mirror.

"Sophia, damn you really messed this up, for good!"

She wallowed in her despair, barefoot in the private luxury subdivision, as she returned to a home of untapped rectification, loneliness.

She grabbed her phone and sent a text,

:Abby, I need to talk—call me. I think he's gone for good?—Sophia C.

:You there? I really need you!—Sophia C.

This is so not like her. Where is Abigail?

With dirt still on the bottom of her finely manicured feet from the pavement of the luxury subdivision streets, she curled up into a ball on her sofa, playing *their song* over and over again, finishing off the Tennessee Whiskey with tears falling down her cheeks. As the quiet bountiful storm began to immerse the night sky, her body lay still. Her tired soul rested, in her sleep she fantasized as to how she could possibly get unstuck, keep positive momentum going, break the cycle of abandonment—possibly ever allowing herself to be worthy of love.

44

THE NEWS

"HOW DID WE GET HERE?"

[AFTERSHOCKS, FOR REAL THIS TIME!]

KNOCK!

KNOCK!

KNOCK!

The pounding penetrated through the strong mahogany door into The Hinson home at midnight the next morning, startling their slumber.

Together, Zachary and Regi arrived at the door, his baby blues peeked through the peephole,

"Baby, it's the police?" his heart pounded due to his recent unfavorable encounter with *the law.*

Zachary stood in front of his wife as her protector, he gingerly opened the door.

There stood two police officers, one with his back to the front door,

What the hell?

At least we have video surveillance, just in case something goes left, Regi thought to herself.

The second officer turned around; he cradled Troublemaker.

The sight of the pup put the couple at ease. Regi outreached her arms towards the dog.

"Did he slip away from Abigail again?" The officer handed him over to her, he nuzzled into Regi's fluffy robe.

407

"So, I take it this is your dog?" the officer sternly asked.

"How may I help you? Where did you find him? He was being dog sat—" Zachary questioned.

"Well, the boat that was rented by Abigail Lancaster was found unaccompanied by the marine staff. They put out a search after it had not returned—"

"What about Abigail? Where is she?" Zachary inquired.

"We don't know. When was the last time you spoke with her?" the officer questioned.

"When she came over last night to get the dog, we were going out for date night," the couple responded, trying to take all of it in.

"Can you tell us if she has been depressed lately? Would she have tried to harm herself, or would anyone try to harm her?"

Regi replied, "No, not that we're aware of. Have you reached her husband?"

"We have people on the ground doing that now. However, it appears that there has been an unfortunate accident—a likely drowning—"

The news frightened Regi, her heart skipped a beat. She began to feel lightheaded; her husband helped her down to a chair, with Troublemaker cupped into her forlorn lap.

Regi, alongside Zachary, was horrified by the news.

Regi sent out a group text to The She Declares Crew to let them know what was going on.

That night turned into a day.

Twenty-four hours turned into forty-eight hours, which turned into seventy-two hours. Candle light vigils were held to summon the angels to Abigail's rescue. However despite all rescue efforts, there was no Abigail. Regardless of the intense recovery efforts, there was still no body—no Abigail.

It was presumed that...

45

URGENT!

"WITH SYMPATHY!"

[CHRONICLES OF THE WEIGHT BREAKERS PODCAST]

Hi, Weight Breakers!

It's your girl, Dr. T. To be completely transparent with you; my heart is very heavy today. I feel weighted to share some unfortunate news. Thank you in advance for bearing with me while I muster up enough courage to get through this podcast. Usually, this space is centered around empowering women. However, today is going to be different.

She couldn't believe that she had to let these next five words flow from her lips.

The Abigail Lancaster is dead.

Tears welled up into her eyes.

Most knew Abigail as a literary critic megastar, but she was one of my dearest friends. She was frequently a guest on this podcast, a *lit* panelist at THE CHRONICLES OF THE WEIGHT BREAKERS CONFERENCE. Our followers are still raving about it, Abigail made it an even more beautiful experience for all in attendance. Furthermore, she supported the launch of my new book: *Think Like a Weight Breaker. Not Like a Weight Taker*.

She took a deep breath to muster up enough courage to carry on.

What we learned at the conference can be summed up in six powerful words: I will be a Weight Breaker. Now come on, ladies, continue walking into your truth—breaking out of that shell like Abigail Lancaster did. It took her some time, but I know that deep down she was a true weight breaker. We can all learn something from her death. Abigail was *The Vault*. You would never know if something was bothering her. Some people judged her on her hard exterior that was embellished with accolades; red carpets, private jets covered with a top-shelf lifestyle. As I got to know her, I called her

Abby, not "The Abigail Lancaster." She went from "*The Vault*" to wide open—surrendered her life, goals, along with her mission. She exuded sacrifices, heroism, and excellence in everything she did.

A tear relished from her eyes.

As tributes are pouring in for Abigail, I ask that you keep her children in your prayers. My Lord, just thinking of those poor kids losing their mother rips my heart to shreds. Please enjoy this presentation of our last interview with Abigail, along with *Wind Beneath My Wings*, the Bette Midler version. Nobody can sing this like Bette. Abby, this one's for you. You will be missed.

Love,

Dr. T.

With tears flowing she played the song. Empathetic sincere messages populated...

:I'm completely devastated. Abigail Lancaster is gone! I'm in tears, but I am also so grateful for her friendship. I recalled recently that we were at The Meadows Country Club where we spent precious time together. Furthermore, she arranged a book signing for me.—Dr. Sparrow Mack

:Abigail, rest in peace. We loved hanging out with you at THE CHRONICLES OF THE WEIGHT BREAKERS CONFERENCE. You stood by my family during the injustice—your support during that time was priceless. I cannot believe this, that you are not with us any longer. As a mom myself, this is heart wrenching. She loved her kids to the end of time. We will take care of your kids—as well Gadsden. Love you, Abby—Judge Regi Hinson

:What are we going to do without her quick wit, snap-back wisdom? I'm so saddened by this. You're the glue to our crew.—Penelope K.

:My sister, you made me realize my true beauty. —Anjali N.

:Tell me this is not true! I refuse to believe this.—Chaka B.

:Not our sister. Words cannot express how much pain I'm feeling right now. She got me through some of my worst days. No, Abigail, no!—Fawn P.

:Prayers for your family. Abigail, you have always constantly told it like it was...—Dr. Sophia Clark

:I just saw this horrific news. This cannot be! Thank you for always brightening my day. Constantly saying things that most of us think, but don't have the *balls* to say. R.I.H.—A Loyal Fan

46

S.H.E. HAS A LAST WILL & TESTAMENT

"ABIGAIL'S DECLARATION"

[FROM BEYOND THE WATER]

Each lady in The She Declares Crew were surprised that they were summoned by The Abigail Lancaster's lawyer to the reading of her will, they arrived arm in arm, ushered to their assigned seats. More importantly, wanting to make sure that her children were taken care of. Furthermore, to show support for them—that was the only expectation.

Her lawyer began to read the will. "This portion of the will pertains to you ladies."

"Pertains to us?" Chaka belted out.

"Shh," Regi warned, motherly.

In walked a couple, they sat at the back. They caught the ladies' attention.

"Is that Abby's ex-husband with that slut backstabbing best friend she had?" Penelope asked Chaka.

"It sure is—" Chaka stood. "Hey low life, get your ass out of here. You don't belong here—"

"Settle down, Chaka. This was Abigail's wishes, written in this document," the presiding lawyer stated. He went on to share,

I, Abigail Gadsden Lancaster, being of sound mind and body, offer each woman in my circle of The She Declares Crew, a part of my *Life End Push* a sum total of $1,000,000.00 per Weight Breaker.

Mouths dropped in pure disbelief.

411

"One million dollars?" You could have knocked Penelope over with a feather.

"*Shh*—be quiet. Let him finish!" Anjali scoffed.

John and Margot smiled, because they knew they would possibly be next in the gifting.

"John Lancaster and Margot Shift—" The lawyer caught the attention of the duo. While the adulterating couple arrived arm in arm, seated straight in their chairs.

> To you John and Margot,
>
> I Abigail Gadsden Lancaster, leave you my unwavering forgiveness for the betrayal that you both exemplified. I had to let all of that hate go, in order to be present with the Lord. Our children will be well taken care of, so you don't have to worry about them. Just make sure you create memories with them, those memories will be priceless…
>
> The Abigail Lancaster

The terrible couple smiled; you could tell in their eyes they wanted to hear more—

> I know you may be wondering if that may be all, I just want you to know that, that's it. You may leave now!

John's eyes bulged out of the sockets knowing that Abigail had taken his name off of all of her life insurance policies, moreover when he received the invitation to come to the reading of the will, he felt that there was some hope that he would be the beneficiary of something…

"John and Margot, you may leave now. Get your trifling asses out of here!" The couple got up fuming—exited the building, Chaka repeated. "Don't let the door hit you where the good Lord split you," Chaka childishly stuck out her tongue at the backstabbers.

The attorney redirected the crowd, "Let's proceed—"

Fawn was given a scholarship fund for her daughter. Surprisingly, along with money for her own aerobics' studio. The Fawn Paige Studio, which was the studio that she'd been working at, but now she had the deed to the building marquee samples so she could pick out orifice signage.

"Fawn, there is something for you under your seat," she reached for a bag, her mouth open. It was as if she was a kid at Christmas fighting through the tissue paper—inside was a familiar box,

"No, this cannot be—" she opened the box, it was the tennis bracelet that was retrieved from her that B.T. had stopped making payments on. Inside, along with a note.

Fawn,

This bracelet is for you and only you. Keep it as a reminder of your worth. One day $40,000.00 will be a drop in the bucket for you, you are priceless. Never cheapen your value, to have the approval of another. You're no longer The Mirage, you better not hock this!

Your Abby

"She is still so bossy, even beyond the grave," Chaka let out a banter.

Fawn realized her truth and her beauty. She didn't have to define herself as the *Bae or a side chick* of a professional athlete. Fawn was no longer *The Mirage,* but she was walking in truth enhanced by her beauty, with an iced-out wrist, that had more meaning than the diamonds that haloed the room.

Anjali sat up in her chair as she heard her name called.

"Anjali, under you seat, please take a look,"

She reached into a large envelope, which housed legal documents. Her spirit awakened,

"You have been willed Abigail's legacy senior seat on the board—making you the President of the Board, owning majority shares of your company," Anjali began to fan herself.

"There's another box, open it." She opened the box, it was a marble desk name plate with her righteous proper name on it, underneath it naming her Chief Operating Officer of her division, with a letter attached to it with her new salary, bonus package, stock options attached to unlimited paid time off. There was a note affixed,

Anjali,

You are so gifted, take this opportunity to make your work environment a place where all are included and feel welcome to allow marketing and branding to keep all cultures in mind. This is your gift, and take time off to

413

spend time with your mom. Go back to your homeland, work
remote to learn more about your culture. Please make sure
you take care of yourself, allowing the man that is in
love with you to love you! Your Abby

Anjali realized that she was leaving being a The Chameleon in the dust, that she would relish in her authenticity along with boldness.

Penelope is handed a robust box by the lawyer's assistant, her expressions revealed pure surprise.

"Thank you, what's this?" Penelope asked intrigued.

"Penelope King, Abigail sent your tapes to the Everyday National Show. They loved your tapes. Penelope King, you have been offered an anchor position, if you ever want to leave your current network. Moreover, all of the Emmy's that you were the voice for, you will get credit—open the box!"

Penelope opened the box—housed within the orifice were the Daytime Emmys that Cassidy won, under the umbrella of the shadow of Penelope's talent.

"This can't be," Penelope's eyes welled up with tears—she hugged the trophies for dear life—seeing her name finally lasered on the awards that she'd earned.

Penelope,

Even though you have been overlooked at your
current television network, this moment in time is to
rectify it all. Penelope, you are a light, you will no
longer be a shadow. By the meaningful stories that you
anchor and have produced, your illuminating light is to
bless the world. You hold the keys now, to The Penelope
King's Morning Show. I know Douglas Gentry personally, and
I have stock in the network that is now gifted to you.
Cassidy is stepping down. Your Abby

"Now look in the box, under your seat." The box was small, she fought the tape on the wrapping paper, it was a B.M.W. key inside, and another key. Penelope shook her head.

"In Abigail's own words, there is a packing company at the apartment, packing only your clothes, and essential paperwork. You have a nice studio apartment in midtown near the television station. And you can retire your bus pass, since your Pinto broke down." Penelope's face is fused with unwavering gratitude.

"Christina 'Chaka' Bu, here is your package," Chaka nodded her head as if listening to music inside her. For once she was speechless, her hands shook. She could not even read the message—it was as if her life sped up 10 years by the words that leaped off the page. She handed the letter to the lawyer to read,

```
                         Chaka,

        Your gift is to make the world laugh; you will be a
   guest host on SNL. Also, you are being offered your own
    HBO special. In addition, Abby paid off your family's
    restaurant debt, so you all can enjoy life together on
   your own terms—creating a bond that does not require your
   father's knuckles to bleed to the bone. You will also be
   meeting with my business manager, Joe. He is the best in
   the business, and kept my career from falling off of the
   rails. Listen to him, I wish I would have listened more,
                not being so stubborn. Your Abby
```

Chaka smiled from ear-to-ear as she was truly living her life fulfillment.

"Dr. Sparrow Mack, Abigail wants to thank you for your sincere friendship. She knows how much you have always loved her *whip*. She is willing to give you the *Lambo*. The Maserati will be locked up for the kids, until they mature. In addition, the endorsement on a guaranteed sold-out book tour."

Dr. Mack cried at the gesture, thinking back to the intimidating encounters at the radio station during their first meeting, to their blossoming sisterhood.

"Tabitha Blanko, Abigail is providing the funding to upgrade the wing to the local hospital cancer unit in honor of your mother. She has laid out the funding for your new home décor line. However, there is a stipulation. You must use your birth name on the collection."

Tabitha was blown away, as her mind wandered back to that trailer, realizing that all of her dreams had actually come true.

"Furthermore, five acres of land that you were bulldozed off of; here is the deed. You are now the owner; no longer living an emulated life."

Then there was a knock at the door.

"Hold on ladies," The lawyer went to the back of the room and welcomed a woman carrying two baby carriers, which seemed a little odd.

"I guess she needs money for her baby? Probably a friend of Abby's?" Chaka chuckled with the undertone of questioning; always the inappropriate comedian in the room.

The lawyer resumed,

"Now, Dr. Sophia Clark, you have sown into me more than you ever know. You try to heal the world. However, you also need some healing. Turn around."

Sophia followed suit. The lady in the back rose to greet her with twin girls.

"Ma'am, are you Dr. Sophia Clark? These two girls are yours, if you deem appropriate. Abigail made sure that your background check was expedited."

Sophia's husband, who she was separated from, entered. He sat alongside his estranged wife.

"If you are willing, these little angels, Corinthian and Ava, would love to be a part of your family."

Sophia,

You've always been a mother; you just did not know it! Also, don't give up on your love, he's a good man.
Your Abby

Sophia let out a wailing of a cry, while she cradled the bundles of joy. The ladies gathered around the couple engulfed in a profound gift of life. The babies had her beautiful green eyes. The love of her life came in to cradle his new daughters, he reached into his suit pocket and ripped up the divorce paperwork.

"Last, but definitely not least Regi, you will be awarded funding for the grant that you did not get that Zachary and you wanted to impact healthcare disparities along with the urban core education enhancement. The check will be directly deposited. In addition, Regi you need to have a trip where you and your mother-in-law can bond."

Tears began to roll down Regi's face; the enormous gesture touched her.

The lawyer then handed Regi a book encased in a leather cover; it was a bible.

416

"Regi, Abigail wanted you to have her bible, this book meant so much to her more than all of the wealth that she had. You see where the bookmark is?"

Regi nodded her head.

"Judge, Abby stated that she wanted you to read this the Passage Matthew 22:37, *Jesus said unto him, Thou shalt love the Lord thy God with all thy heart, and with all thy soul, and with all thy mind.*"

Regi is endeared, looking the book over while holding it to her chest. This was a stark contrast to the Regina of old who long ago, lost her faith in God due the cards of life that were dealt to her. However, during the declare event there was a renewed faith, she opened the front of the bible, where there was an inscription,

Judge Regina Hinson,

You have always been a woman after God's own heart. You have sacrificed, you are a hero, and most of all you are an excellent reflection of God's love for us. You are the real weight breaker—no more juggling. Be an unapologetic Weight Breaker. Pinky Promise. Love, Your Abby

This sentiment touched Regi's spirit beyond measure.

Just then a man walked in from the back of the room, he was chiseled in a suit, this caught Zachary's eye,

"Regi, do you know who that is?"

"No." Regi craned her neck to get a better look while she dabbed her eyes.

"That's El Corazón—"

"Why would I know him?"

Zachary leaned into his wife, "You know the famous WWE wrestler the one the boys are always imitating, causing a ruckus in the house? He's a Christian, he's the one that has Psalms 19:1-2 tattooed on his back. I gave the boy's the figurines last year as stocking stuffers..."

"Oh, yes I remember. You know Abigail knew everyone? Probably one of her celeb friends. You know how she used to roll?"

The attorney noticed the gentleman, "You must be Juan or better known as El Corazón?"

"Yes, sir," he said in his thick Spanish accent.

"Come on up here and stand by me! Ladies and gentlemen this is the world-famous WWE fighter El Corazón," the gentleman's gentle smile, so opposite of his Hulk Hogan appearance.

The ladies nudged each other, glaring at the eye candy.

"Damn, he's fine—" Chaka belted out, "Can I get those digits? Baby I can bring the spring rolls, while you bring the enchilada's."

"Girl, we can't take you anywhere. We are at a will reading, not the after-hours spot," Anjali popped Chaka in the shoulder to get her hormones in check.

El Corazón stood next to the lawyer with a velvet box in his hand, tied with a silk bow. He began to speak, in a soft familiar tone,

"Ladies, it is an honor to be here. A couple of weeks ago I was shocked when I was told that The Abigail Lancaster wanted to talk to me. When I realized why she tracked me down, I felt nothing but gratitude. You see before I was El Corazón, famous and all, I was a little boy raised in the backwoods of Texas—"

Regi's ears perked.

"I was very sick, destined to die—despite all of the doctors and specialists my parents took me to. Until one day—"

The ladies are all looking around at this odd display of walking down memory lane. They attempted to rationalize what this actually had to do with Abigail—her will.

"Judge Regina Hinson, can you please come up here please?" The wrestler asked Regi.

Zachary is taken back by this request of the ginormous man asking for his wife to join him in the front of the room, his cheeks became flushed feeling like he needed to flex to compare. He nudged his wife to go up there.

Hesitantly, Regi walked up to stand in front of the room. She's handed a box by the wrestler. Surprised, she looked around, commencing to unwrap the gift.

"A stethoscope?" Regi is confused.

The man unbuttoned four of his buttons on shirt, his chiseled pectoral muscles blared,

"Don't tell me this fine ass man is going to strip—I have some dollars on deck *to make it rain* up in here—" Chaka reached into her purse to get her wallet.

"Chaka, be quiet!" Penelope grabbed her arm to restrain her antics.

On this man's sternum, there was a scar. The man placed the stethoscope on Regi's ears, then the bell on his chest,

"You are listening to Ryan's heart—"

Regi's eyes told it all, the story of regret, unforgiveness of herself, all these years she'd sacrificed her peace for her little hands not being able to hold onto her baby brother Ryan during the tornado.

Regi's mind quantum leap backwards to the outskirts of Texas, a rural county. Sirens blazoned echoing into the county sky. The clouds rolled in aggressively when all of the clothes that Aunt Edna hung on the clothes line were swept away.

"Regina, get Ryan, we've gotta go to the storm shelter," Aunt Edna demanded of Regina.

Little Regi's feet ran through the house, to find her brother—they'd just completed an innocent round of hide-and-seek, in which Ryan was the obvious winner again—he flexed in his notorious WWE pose.

"Regina, I won again," he taunted his older sister.

"Come on, Aunt Edna said we have to go to the shelter."

On each hand, Aunt Edna held her sister's children, because they were entrusted to her for the summer to escape the big city life. Uncle Clarence had gone to town to get some feed for the cows.

Regi's eyes were amazed by her mother's older sister, who was able to get the big slat wood doors open of the shelter with such ease, "Go on down there, I know it's dark. There's a lantern that I will turn on once we are in there. Regina hurry now, the winds are picking up."

Regi walked gingerly down the plank wood stairs, trusting her aunt's voice. Once inside, Aunt Edna's robust arms yanked the aged storm shelter doors, placing a makeshift lock on the rusted lock.

Although beneath the ground, more so on the side of the house, the earth shook—that caused Regi to bring her younger brother closer to her.

419

"Regina, hold on to him tight! I'm going to start the lantern, to get us some light," her aunt disappeared into the back of the shelter.

All at once, it got eerie, so quiet you could hear the mice in the backdrop squeaking. This silence, ironically made Regi loosen her grip a little on her brother, she smiled thinking that everything was all over.

FLICK!

The light came on, Aunt Edna was finally successful in getting the lantern to work. She looked at Regina, scolding,

"I told you to hold your broth—"

BAM!

WHOOSH!

Ryan, who was closer to the door of the small shelter, was ripped from Regi's arms—her tiny hand shook as her small hands tittered to reach for her brother's small fingers. His eyes widened with a fear that she'd never seen before, as his body flew upward into the swirling dark clouds. The sound of the freight train drowned out any wailing that came from Little Regi's lungs. Aunt Edna's robust arms were able to crane Regi into her full thick waist—then it was all over…

Long ago, Regi forfeited any type of joy in life, because this was the one area in her life where she was not the hero. Furthermore, despite all of the degrees, honors along with awards of what she'd accomplished in her excellence—the thorn in her crown was the guilt of her brother's death, however the daily reminder was the scar was permanently affixed to her hand as a reminder of her failure.

My mom used to tell me that it will all make sense one day.

I just can't believe that she never told me that they gave the gift of life from Ryan's passing, through organ donation.

I guess my parents thought I could not handle it—at that time, I couldn't.

Regi jumped up and down with unspeakable joy, Zachary listened in as well, life exuded from their faces.

"I can't believe it's really him. It's Ryan," Regi took the stethoscope earpiece from her ears—she reached, her hand planted on his chest. The scar on Regi's guilt-ridden hand was planted on the scar of the man's chest, divinely the scars connected forming a cross. Regi's hand pulsed from the beating of Ryan's heart. The man that was a famous stranger only moments ago, all at once felt like family.

With each beat of Ryan's heart she closed her eyes, as she recalled endeared moments with her baby brother: racing down the street barefoot; eating fried bologna sandwiches while watching Good Times; reading the back cereal boxes together before school; going to the Juneteenth celebrations eating snow cones in the sweltering heat as their tongues turned blue and red; playing kick ball biting the dust when they slide into the bases, watching WWE wrestling while eating snicker bars—she'd laugh when her brother attempted to flex his bird-like chest. And most of all his loud boisterous laugh as they ran through the fire hydrant on hot summer days. She envisioned Ryan telling her,

"Regi, big sis—it was not your fault. I'm doing well, I'm watching over you and the family every day."

In that moment she opened her eyes, those were the words that she'd longed to hear all of her life. She turned to her husband and crew, they encircled the weight breaker that was finally free leaving juggling behind—she finally could walk in balance and winning, with a peace that surpassed all understanding.

"Okay, everyone take your seats!" The judge beckoned to the enamored crowd.

Zachary escorted his wife back to her chair, along with *her brother*—who received a second chance at life going on to becoming one of the all-time WWE wrestlers, which was his ministry. El Corazón was the truth.

The attorney continued to read Abby's words.

Ladies,

You may have thought that I was always dipping out on you, however I was dealing with a terminal illness. In addition, I needed to prepare all of what had taken place within the reading of the will. So I apologize for the absence that you felt in me not physically being there for every happy hour, book club, spa day, or spin class. Being able to do each of these things for you, has served me well in this life and my final days, it eased the glimpse of the pain that I was going through.

Although I always cheated on myself depriving myself of happiness, after my first husband died, connecting with you all makes me grateful for all experiences—the good and the bad. And that being The Vault as well as a weight taker, would no longer hold me hostage. And I learned that I don't need to apologize for the new weight breaker that I became. There are a couple

of stipulations with the funds—no stipulations with the
children, however. Each of you have been given stock in
Gadsden's Grocery Store—you have to make sure to stay
connected. You must make sure that it stays local, to help
the community, as well as assuring that all of the repairs
to the store are fully up to The Abigail Lancaster's
standards. Moreover, you all are surrogate aunties to my
beautiful daughter as well as my little boy. Lastly, you
ladies have to promise to stick by each other, remaining
the best of friends through thick, most of all thin times.
You ladies have been the gift that I've prayed for all of
my life, never in my wildest dream did I ever think that I
would have sisters. God is so good, moreover each of you
are angels that he used to guide me into enhancing my
vision, faith and resilience intelligence. Unbeknownst to
myself, when I met you all, I would understand that the
sacrifices, heroism and excellence that I'd experienced,
was not in vain. Thank you from the bottom of my heart!

The ladies held hands tight, their bond enriched even more by
this endearment of Abby from beyond the grave.

The attorney gave the ladies a moment before concluding, he
cleared his throat, reading the final words,

Furthermore, you ladies have allowed this *Vault* to
open up and surrender. The hard work you have put into
your life, your families, your communities has weighed you
down, causing you to have a lot of delayed gratification.
Know that I am just a vessel—God loves you for your
sacrifices, heroism, and excellence. More so, I love you
too, you're the sister's I never had—Weight Breakers you
rock! Furthermore, declare over your lives what you will
do, and God will make it come to pass. I trust that you
will keep the momentum going and you will change your
trajectory. Your Abby…

Weight Breaker You Will!

SHE declares

"Ask and it will be given to you; seek and you will find; knock and the door will be opened to you."

Matthew 7:7

47

THE UNION

"YOU WILL KEEP THE MOMENTUM GOING!"

[TULLE & TUXEDOS, MIXED WITH TRIUMPH!]

There was tulle everywhere, adorned with flowers galore. Chairs were being set up. A red carpet was being rolled out.

Dark, beautiful thick ringlets were being curled. Nose-to-ear piercing was in place. Fresh henna adorned svelte arms and gentle hands as they laid against an ivory satin dress.

"Isn't she beautiful?" Chaka said of her friend.

"She sure is," Penelope chimed, adjusting her lace veil.

"I wish Abby were here," Fawn said as she helped Anjali put on her four-inch white satin, red bottom stilettos.

"She's here in spirit," Regi eagerly popped the champagne bottle—suds flowed as she jumped back, so she would not dampen the wedding gown.

"Abigail would have really gotten a kick out of this day. She was integral as to how The She Declares Crew was born," Chaka chimed in as she lifted her champagne glass.

"To Abigail."

The bridesmaids echoed, "To Abigail!"

Music started, there was a knock at the door,

"Ladies, it's time."

Anjali bid a wave to her four beautiful bridesmaids that were dressed in form-fitting hues aligned with their *lip stain color*.

"Anjali, we're ready for you, my dear," her mother beckoned, taking her daughter's hand. Anjali paused

"Mom, you know what? After wading through all of the chronicles of life, I final see my break—"

Her mother kissed her cheek, "Yes, my dear. You are a weight breaker—everything you ever went through were just the chronicles that got you to this point—which you can sum up to pure bliss! This day is a true reflection of the bible verse, Matthew 7:7, *Ask and it will be given to you; seek and you will find; knock and the door will be opened to you.* Your father, rest his soul, and I asked the Lord to send our daughter a wonderful man to love our daughter sincerely from the day you were born, and he did just that. You, Anjali, *knocked* on the *door of life* and God has opened up bountiful blessings for you."

"That's so beautiful mom, thank you," they were joyfully teary eyed, they embraced.

"My love, you are glowing."

"Mom, I think it's my *turmeric glow*," Anjali smiled.

Her mother brushed her cheek with adore love.

PING!

"It's Sean," pleasantry exuded her enamored face, with the thought of her love.

:Anjali, always remember I love you exactly as who you are—don't ever change.—Sean G.

Smiling, her mother kissed her cheek,

"Love birds. I'll leave you two alone," she exited the room with a twinkle in her eye, wanting to respect the privacy between her daughter and *the approved love* of her life, via text.

"Gadsden's shoppers, please stay in the outer aisles," was the overhead announcement.

Troublemaker was adorned in a pup tuxedo—wagging his cute little tail down the aisle, with the adorable ring bearers—Regi's sons.

Sean stood awaiting his queen, along with his best friend, Zachary Hinson, whom he'd become quite the pair with. They were always hanging out in the man cave, taking the boys to the inner-city community center to shoot hoops.

The presiding minister was none other than El Corazón, adorned in a robe with a bible in hand ready to pronounce the nuptials for the beautiful couple.

425

Dr. Sophia Clark along with her reunited husband cradled their beautiful twin daughters dressed in white lace, with binkies in their mouths. The couple bypassed divorce court. Now smiling hand-in-hand, their love emanated.

Anjali was ready to meet the love of her life at the end of the aisle.

"Mom, it's time," she was escorted down the aisle by her mother as she walked in elegantly— The She Declares Crew cried tears of pure joy.

Surprisingly, arriving a little late, was Beckett "B.T." Blaze bearing roses. He sat, smiling towards the mother of his daughter, who he obviously was attempting to regain favor with—it appeared that *the script was flipped.*

Regi, while carrying her phone with her next to her bouquet, received a text.

:Regi, you won't believe this, but Chief Judge Reynolds just announced his retirement. You *are up to bat for* sure, you are *shoo-in.* Seems you have redeemed yourself with Chief Judge Reynolds, he appointed you as his successor. All you have to do is accept the request.—Patrick L.

Regi was overwhelmed by the news that she finally had earned this promotion.

How in the world am I going to manage all of that responsibility?

Penelope noticed her contemplation, "Girl, you okay?"

"I'll tell you afterwards—work stuff."

The music faded; the minister began to officiate. The ceremony flowed beautifully. There was not a dry eye in the grocery store chapel, as Anjali recited her heartfelt vows to the love of her life, Sean. He placed the complete five carat canary diamond wedding ring set from her vision board on henna adorned ring finger.

Halfway through professing their commitment enfolded with a ring ceremony, their nuptials were interrupted by murmurings from behind.

The bridal party looked up.

Anjali paused as a voice echoed from the back.

All of the guests turned around—gasping at the *haunting vision.*

426

"I wouldn't have missed this for the world," declared The Abigail Lancaster, or better known as Abby...

Weight Breaker
Let's Go!

declares

And we know that for those who love God all things work together for good, for those who are called according to his purpose

Romans 8:28

48

THE PODCAST

"SHE ALWAYS MATTERED; DID'NT SHE?"

[LET'S GO!]

My Beloved Weight Breakers,

Hello, clawing out from the back of our cerebrum, all we want is to be bold, *bad-ass chicks* that are fulfilling our purpose, while burning midnight oil, kicking self-care to the curb, adding arches in our back, stiffening our jawlines, while standing calm to secure our places in this world.

Immense pressure can weigh us down like cement bricks on our feet, all while *talking shop*, maintaining our femininity, attempting to remain true to who we are.

It's common knowledge that pressure creates diamonds. Consider those diamonds that are crushed to smithereens during the process—rendered invaluable dust. Although in a million little pieces, they are still fragments, pieces of a diamond are still valuable. Regardless of what we have been through that leaves us tattered and torn, broken into a million little tiny pieces—we have that same value as those diamond rhombus fragments.

Each of us has so many weights that we carry on our backs. Coming together to shed *proverbial weights* and *physical weights* of life would create more love, sisterly kindness—changes in our vantage points, while yielding unity and resulting in a *Weight Breaker Sisterhood*. This kinship encourages us—cultivating accountability while we collectively sweep out cobwebs of our mind attics. It sparks an alliance that helps to banish negative connotations that we hold about ourselves, purge insecurities, self-doubts, along with unnecessary comparisons.

What generally makes us question ourselves are unique things that make us stand out—I generalize that as our momentum type. Simply put, momentum can be defined as the speed or rhythm that you navigate through something. In a bigger scope, how one can move through life.

A woman has the momentum to unleash her power when she declares her life's trajectory. *SHE*, through her sacrifices, honor, and excellence will become a Weight

Breaker. This book is dedicated to you. You are destined to be a WEIGHT BREAKER, not a weight taker!

I proclaim bountiful blessings over each reader along with their own personal weight breaking chronicles that they're living towards while being Weight Breakers in their own lives. You've established by being a weight breaker that you hold fast to Romans 8:28, *"And we know that for those who love God, all things work together for good, for those who are called according to his purpose."*

When you realize who you are, *whose you are*—that you are one of God's gifts to the world, you will fully understand deep down in your soul that:

You Can!

You Matter!

You Rock!

You Will!

Let's Go! You Go into your assignment!

Think Like A Weight Breaker. Not Like A Weight Taker.

Or better yet, let the world see that,

She Can!

She Matters!

She Rock's!

She Will!

& She's Got This!

She Goes into her assignment, when she declares!

Regardless, of everything that she was going to accomplish, from this point forward, if she failed—she'd declare to cause herself to *fall forward* into being a weight breaker, leaving weight taking in the dust.

Fully acknowledge that weight-taking stops when *SHE* declares it so.

Most of all, a woman can unleash her power when *SHE* declares her life's trajectory.

Let's Go!

Love, Dr. T.—The Weight Breaker.

The End.

WEIGHT BREAKER, WRITE THE VISION AND MAKE IT PLAIN!

"Therefore, seeing we also are compassed about by a great cloud of witnesses, let us lay aside every weight, and the sin which doth easily beset us, and let us run with patience the race that is set before us."—Hebrews 12:1

Consider this poem I wrote about weight:

Weights of Life, we have some unfortunate news for *you*, our dysfunctional relationship is over. The weight of exclusion, discrimination, perils, narrow-minded thinking has no room in our space.

We know that we are blessed beyond measure, an absolute gift to this world. So, negative, proverbial weight, you are no longer welcome. See your way out via the nearest exit because this is the last dance.

Goodbye!

We will reach the healthy weight that was specifically designed for us, enjoy life in the way that it was meant to be lived—to the fullest. We value our health and wellness!

Therefore, each pound that we lose will no longer be stored in the cloud, waiting to pounce back into our lives. Weight, you will not plant yourself, eternally hugging our waists, grasping around our thighs, or encroaching upon our hips. You will not cause our arms to flail in the wind. Dear pounds of physical weight, you are welcome only in a healthy realm. Beyond that, this excessive undaunting relationship is over! This is our last dance for good. So, go ahead; jiggle *your* way out the door. *You* are not welcome here anymore.

Because from this day forward, we will Think Like a Weight Breaker, Not a Weight Taker.

The next time you walk by a mirror, take a few extra minutes to appreciate the miracle of God—you! Understand that beyond the shadow of a doubt, God did not make any junk.

Most importantly, you are the only you, you get—so cherish yourself. Although there are various nuances along with the polarities that are the make-up of you, fret not—God made no mistake when he put you together.

One of the most direct ways to cherish yourself is to take charge of your health—physically and mentally, that is the essence of what a Weight Breaker is.

Weight Breaker, journal on this page—how you are going to exemplify sacrifices, heroism and excellence to Think Like a Weight Breaker, not like a Weight Taker.

_____
_____
_____
_____
_____
_____
_____
_____
_____
_____
_____
_____
_____
_____
_____
_____
_____
_____
_____
_____
_____
_____
_____
_____
_____
_____
_____
_____
_____
_____
_____
_____
_____
_____

GRATITUDE & ACKNOWLEDGEMENTS

My highest thankful praise cannot be compared to all blessings that You have bestowed upon us, God. God you are the Chief Executive Officer of my life, I am honored to be your humble servant, you paid it all on the cross for us. For my loving, supportive husband, brilliant son, and loving parents—I am eternally grateful. I pray that our later days will be even more phenomenal than our former days. Please take heart in this masterpiece of a poem.

"Our deepest fear is not that we are inadequate. Our deepest fear is that we are powerful beyond measure. It is our light, not our darkness, that most frightens us. We ask ourselves: Who am I to be brilliant, gorgeous, talented, and fabulous? Actually, who are you not to be? You are a child of God. Your playing small does not serve the world. There is nothing enlightened about shrinking so that other people won't feel insecure around you. We are all meant to shine, as children do. We were born to manifest the glory of God that is within us. It's not just in some of us; it's in everyone. As we let our own light shine, we unconsciously give other people permission to do the same. As we are liberated from our own fear, our presence automatically liberates others."—Marianne Williamson-Poet, Author

To all life lessons, you did not break me—you made me stronger. Last and definitely not least, to my mother who instills my creativity, my in-laws whose love is unwavering, I appreciate you and cherish you. To the most bountiful blessings, my husband and my son, you are my prayer warriors and my ultimate loves of my life.

This book is dedicated to all weight breakers who have sewn into my life. My parent's and in-laws who broke down the weights of racial disparities. My grandparents who broke the weights in education, domestic servitude, and manual labor. And to our son, who was built to be a weight breaker—I am so honored that God chose us to be your parents, to guide you towards your purpose with a circle of dynamic legacy, moreover with the hands of God to guide you.

The messages in this book are dedicated to every vision surrounding your purpose, to your faith that you must nurture daily, and to the resilience in us that we cling to. I'm so grateful to God for revealing knowledge and for allowing us to see the work of His hand reflected in our lives and all around us. I'm truly grateful for the blessings that He has bestowed on my family and me. Read, clinging to the words below as you crack this book open.

A woman can unleash her power when SHE declares her life's trajectory...

433

SHE

/SHē/

pronoun

1.　　used to refer to a woman, girl, or female.

noun

2.　　a female; a woman.

Sacrifices. Heroism. Excellence.

DECLARE

/diˈkler/

verb

1.　　say something in a solemn emphatic manner.

2.　　acknowledge possession of (taxable income or dutiable goods).

Imagine if *SHE* DECLARED happiness, peace, wellness, and joy over *HER* life; how much brighter will *HER* light shine?

How much more vision, faith and resilience will *SHE* exude when *SHE* faces obstacles that present themselves as weight in *HER* life?

SHE scratches *HER* surface!

SHE is a "Weight Breaker"—if only *SHE Declares.*

WHY T.T. MCGIL'S LATEST BOOK

CHRONICLES OF THE WEIGHT BREAKERS,

IS THE EMPOWERED CHICK LIT BOOK YOU NEED TO READ?

Midwest-based author T.T. McGil tells us about her latest book, *Chronicles of The Weight Breakers*—which is a fascinating take on when smart women from different backgrounds world's go awry, until a chance encounter brings them together to face lift the weights of life! If you love chick lit woven throughout women's truth and beauty, you should check it out!

When you come across the term chick lit, one's mind tends to gravitate fun filled book full of shopping, spa days, with relationship trouble, however this book deviates from cheesy duplicative settings with fairytale endings, as the new age fire age of chick lit is here through the eyes of acclaimed author T.T. McGil, in *Chronicles of The Weight Breakers*.

A new age type author, T.T. McGil has been penned with highly sought-after mystery suspense thriller novels with the arrival of *Sparrow: The Water's Edge (2018); Sparrow: The Night Ends (2020)*; now Chronicles of the Weight Breakers. *The Declare Chick Lit Genre* is finally here to stay, thanks to new-age writers like T.T. McGil.

The Midwest based author resonates with Dr. Sparrow Mack, one of the novel's supporting characters who is described as a *literary gangster*. This author uses *Sparrowism's* to encourage, inspire a higher level of thinking. An incurable optimist who has taken up the task of bringing *Weight Breaking* to life for the characters in her head, is enamored by writing story lines based on women's fiction that includes sub-genres such as chick lit thrillers. She writes contemporary women that explore complex human feelings in all their loving intensity, cumbersome, and resilient beautiful harrowing experiences—*Chronicles of The Weight Breakers (2022/2023),* is aligned with the epic *declared chick lit* experience.

Q &A WITH THE AUTHOR:

What does the book *Chronicles of The Weight Breakers* essentially revolve around?

All of my story lines are relatable and capture the essence of real-life experiences. In this book, I focused on the incomparable vigor of strong dynamic women, who are family-oriented however inhabit their own quirks, unique plights which illustrate circumstantial ebbs and flows of life, accompanied with added spice of hot topics.

Chronicles of The Weight Breakers have several superb chick-lit protagonist's like: Judge Regina "Regi" Hinson; Fawn Paige, Christina "Chaka" Bu; Penelope King; Anjali "A.J." Nadkarni; The Abigail Lancaster; Dr. Sparrow Mack; Dr. Sophia Clark; and last but definitely not least—*The Weight Breaker*–"Dr. T."

Having said that, these women have had the natural serious obstacles of life— issues. However, a rare unique supernatural incident, *The She Declares Natural Disaster* brings them together—yielding a tight knit bond, which is the crux of the story.

Tell us one unique aspect of the narrative? Something that connects with you?

Chronicles of The Weight Breakers is composed in an inimitable chick lit style—using chronicles of each of the women with keenness accompanied with infinite humor, which adds levity to life's circumstances.

Tell us about a few writers who inspire you?

I'm so glad you asked that question. I deem I yield from the experiences of life. More importantly, I glean infinite wisdom from those who are overcomer's. Those who see their life for what it is—choosing to make the absolute best of it. That in itself, is amazingly inspiring—is it not?

Could you explain your writing process?

Each story is a seed, moreover stories come to me because so many of them are curing in my mind at any given point. Henceforth, I simply compose the narrative when I am reasonably poised to develop the outline of the plot—that is the story trajectory.

Do you have any other literary projects in the pipeline?

Yes! The Sparrow Mystery Suspense Thriller Series, along with the spin off storylines are ever evolving. I am excited about the fan base that these plots have garnered. More importantly, I listen to the *T.T. McGil Hive*, thus taking their feedback as to what they want to hear about next. I'm extremely honored that God chose me to birth these stories of inspiration through me. I am a vessel.

What is WEIGHT BREAKER-OLOGY? What should it mean to the reader of Chronicles of The Weight Breakers?

In any standard dictionary "ol-o-gy" is a noun—meaning the subject of study; a branch of knowledge. Within the book Chronicles of the Weight Breakers, you see the women as they navigate through their lives, utilizing a tool, Think Like A Weight Breaker. Not Like A Weight Taker, that provides T.I.P.s for approaching what life throws at these dynamic female protagonists, against the antagonist—which is the weights of life. It lends to look not dwelling in the valley, however speaking mountain top proclamation's over the cumbersome situations. For example,

"I'm overweight, I will never be healthy and well," which is the Weight Taker perspective.

The Weight Breaker-ology perspective is to take out the negative connotations is the verbiage surrounding situations, like the word—never. A Weight Breaker perspective approach utilizing that same factual data is,

"Yes, I realize I am overweight. In order to be healthy and well, I will make small changes in my diet to accomplish my health and wellness goals, to be the best person God has called me to be."

You see the difference in the tone, perspective. You have to speak, write positive affirmations over your life, in order to walk into the promises of God.

Your AUTHOR, T.T. MCGIL

Chronicles of The Weight Breakers

T.T. McGil is a physician, administrative clinician, wife, and mother of one based in the Midwest. Since early childhood, along with the goal of helping people, she dreamed of writing stories that would resonate with the readers, allowing them the opportunity to step inside the book—stories that would cause the readers to sit on the edges of their seats with eager anticipation. She finally decided to take a leap—orchestrating notes that she had about complex storylines, debuting her first novel, *Sparrow: The Water's Edge*. She is also the author of the novels *Sparrow: The Night Ends* and *Chronicles of the Weight Breakers*.

For more information, scan the QR code below.

Stay connected by visiting:

Website: www.TTMcGil.com

Facebook: TT McGil Book Club

Twitter: @TTMcGil1

Instagram: TT McGil

Author of Sparrow: The Night Ends & Chronicles of The Weight Breakers

T.T. MCGIL

RETRIBUTION.
ANGST.
SUPPLICATION.

Entangled with regret, cause you to question all you thought you knew...

SPARROW
THE
A PREQUEL
WATER'S EDGE

"Sparrow: The Water's Edge is a mixture of family secrets, family love, and best of all-family drama. That's the perfect recipe for gripping suspense!"

- Tonya Holloway-Film Director

Dr. Sparrow Mack's storybook life explodes when the echoes of Luke, her childhood best friend comes to kill, steal and destroy everything connected with him. Forged into one of the darkest periods in her life, she is thrust into being a self-proclaimed detective as dire circumstances catapult her to be hot on the trail of the unforeseen while dodging bullets, and blood-infested waters while keeping her storybook life afloat.

The question that will keep your heart pounding is, can she survive the blood-infested waters of her tormented soul?

"T.T. McGil is a mystery and suspense author that is grabbing the attention of readers leaving them wanting more. *Sparrow: The Water's Edge* is the first in the Sparrow Mystery Suspense Thriller Series and it's sure to capture the hearts and minds of all who grace its pages."

--- Kym Whitley-Actress, Comedian & Author

"T.T. McGil has served up a fresh novel with an ambitious and witty protagonist whom readers will love keeping up with!"

--- Camika Spencer-Best Selling Author & Award-Winning Playwright

T.T. MCGIL is the dynamic Mystery Suspense Thriller Chick Lit Author of *Sparrow: The Water's Edge; Sparrow: The Night Ends* and *Chronicles of The Weight Breakers. Sparrow: The Water's Edge* has been a featured novel at Essence Festival; performed as a screenplay on stage and screenwriting, ready for screen production. T.T. McGil answered the call of The Sparrow Hive of followers, with the sequel *Sparrow: The Night Ends* and the spin-off novel *Chronicles of The Weight Breakers.* Buckle up for an unpredictable ride with this writer who, with every page, you turn, will cause you to question your reality!

T.T.McGil calls home in the great Midwest, surrounded by devoted family and friends. Her goal is to interact with your followers, and listen to them while attempting to impart some form of inspiration with the worlds that she crafts embedded in her unique storylines. She is honored to be...

Your Author T.T.

www.TTMCGIL.com

T.T. MCGIL

CAPTIVATED.
SHOCKED.
HORRIFIED.

THIS IS A RIVING SAGA THAT WILL LEAVE YOU BREATHLESS...

SPARROW
THE   A SEQUEL
NIGHT ENDS

"In *Sparrow: The Night Ends*, T.T. McGil expands upon the mystery that begins
with Sparrow: The Water's Edge. It's a story with a lot of twists and turns."

George L. Tarrant, Jr.–Screenwriter

New age fiction is on fire! The storyline pulls you in and holds you captive leaving you shocked, horrified, and wanting more. *Sparrow: The Night Ends*, is a riveting saga of the mires of the invisible yet tangible forces that bind the human spirit through the beauty of life—all the while seemingly casting a web of infinite uncertainty, strife, long-suffering layered with guilt that entangles the characters in this book. *Sparrow: The Night ends*, has been classified as a masterpiece tale that illustrates the full boldness of regret and retribution. Each devoted reader gets a front-row seat to view what happens next, since the cliffhanger in, *Sparrow: The Water's Edge*.

"We got ourselves the second coming of Steven King all wrapped up in Black Girl Magic! T.T. McGil, mad props and big ups to you for this great book!"

—Buddy Lewis, Actor, Comedian & Writer

"Intense. Nail-biting...yet satisfying. This story is a perfect mix of what you'll need for a good evening of fiction. This is my first book by the author, and I cannot wait to get my hands on her prequel, and hopefully any sequel(s). Dr. Sparrow Mack cannot end here..."

—Dr. Harini P. Murali, Physician, Artist & Blogger.

T.T. MCGIL is the dynamic Mystery Suspense Thriller Chick Lit Author of multiple books that have generated a robust following of T.T. McGil Hive of followers. Her books include *Sparrow: The Water's Edge; Sparrow: The Night Ends* and *Chronicles of The Weight Breakers. Sparrow: The Water's Edge*, the prequel has been a featured novel at Essence Festival; performed as a screenplay on stage and screen written, ready for screen production. T.T. McGil answered the call of T.T. McGil Hive of followers, with the sequel *Sparrow: The Night Ends*, as well as the chick-lit spin-off novel *Chronicles of The Weight Breakers*. Buckle up for an unpredictable ride with this writer who, with every page, you turn, will cause you to question your own reality!

T.T.McGil calls home in the great Midwest, surrounded by devoted family and friends. Her goal is to interact with her followers, and listen to them while attempting to impart some form of inspiration to the worlds that she embeds in her unique storylines. She is honored to be.....

Your Author T.T *McGil*

www.TTMCGIL.com

Made in the USA
Monee, IL
03 March 2023

28684457R00252